The Cailiffs of Baghdad, Georgia

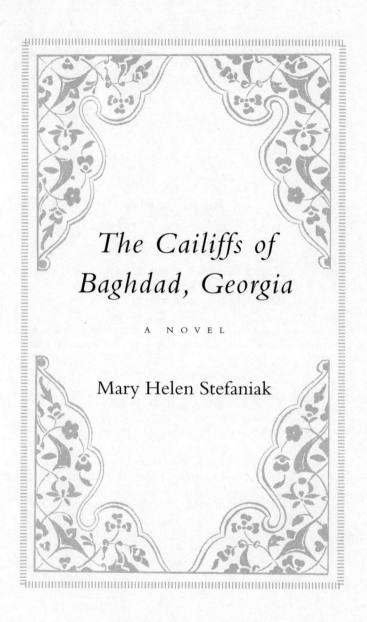

The Cailiffs of Baghdad, Georgia

A NOVEL

Mary Helen Stefaniak

W. W. NORTON & COMPANY

NEW YORK   LONDON

For information about permission to reproduce selections from this book,
write to Permissions, W. W. Norton & Company, Inc.,
500 Fifth Avenue, New York, NY 10110

For information about special discounts for bulk purchases, please contact
W. W. Norton Special Sales at specialsales@wwnorton.com or 800-233-4830

Manufacturing by Courier Westford
Book design by Ellen Cipriano
Production manager: Julia Druskin

Library of Congress Cataloging-in-Publication Data

Stefaniak, Mary Helen.
The Cailiffs of Baghdad, Georgia : a novel / Mary Helen Stefaniak. — 1st ed.
p. cm.
ISBN 978-0-393-06310-3 (hardcover)
1. Teachers and community—Fiction. 2. City and town life—Fiction.
3. Depressions—1929—Georgia—Fiction. 4. Georgia—Fiction. I. Title.
PS3569.T3389C35 2010
813'.54—dc22

2010019098

W. W. Norton & Company, Inc.
500 Fifth Avenue, New York, N.Y. 10110
www.wwnorton.com

W. W. Norton & Company Ltd.
Castle House, 75/76 Wells Street, London W1T 3QT

1 2 3 4 5 6 7 8 9 0

For my mother
Mary McCullough Elleseg

In memory of her mother
Mattie Califf McCullough

Throughout history, the powers of single black men flash here and there like falling stars, and die sometimes before the world has rightly gauged their brightness.

W. E. B. DU BOIS
The Souls of Black Folk
1904

Baghdad, the city whose name has a power of evocation that neither far distances nor other-world civilizations can destroy. The Baghdad of old is only slumbering beneath the Baghdad of today, and is awakened to life by almost every incident and sight and sound that we encounter.

JANET MILLER
Camel-Bells of Baghdad
1934

The Cailiffs of Baghdad, Georgia

1

Miss Spivey, For and Against

MISS GRACE SPIVEY arrived in Threestep, Georgia, in August of 1938. She stepped off the train wearing a pair of thick-soled boots suitable for hiking, a navy blue dress, and a little white tam that rode the waves of her red hair at a gravity-defying angle. August was a hellish month to step off the train in Georgia, although it was nothing, she said, compared to the 119 degrees that greeted her when she got off the boat one time in the place she called Al-Basrah. I believe her remark irritated some of the people gathered to welcome her on the burned grass alongside the tracks. When folks are sweating through their shorts, they don't like to hear that this is *nothing* compared to someplace else. Irritated or not, the majority of those present were inclined to see the arrival of the new schoolteacher in a positive light. Hard times were still upon us in 1938, but, like my momma said, "We weren't no poorer than we'd ever been," and the citizens of Threestep were in the mood for a little excitement.

Miss Spivey looked like just the right person to give it to them. She was, by almost anyone's standards, a woman of the world. She'd gone to boarding schools since she was six years old; she'd studied French in Paris and drama in London; and during what she called a "fruitful intermission" in her formal education, she had traveled extensively in the Near

East and Africa with a friend of her grandmother's, one Janet Miller, who was a medical doctor from Nashville, Tennessee. After her travels with Dr. Miller, Miss Spivey continued her education by attending Barnard College in New York City. She told us all that at school the first day. When my little brother Ralphord asked what did she study at Barnyard College, Miss Spivey explained that *Barnard*, which she wrote on the blackboard, was the sister school of Columbia University, of which, she expected, we all had heard.

It was there, she told us, in the midst of trying to find her true mission in life, that she wandered one afternoon into a lecture by the famous John Dewey, who was talking about his famous book, *Democracy and Education*. Professor Dewey was in his seventies by then, Miss Spivey said, but he still liked to chat with students after a lecture—especially female students, she added—sometimes over coffee, and see in their eyes the fire his words could kindle. It was after this lecture and subsequent coffee that Miss Spivey had marched to the Teacher's College and signed up, all aflame. Two years later, she told a cheery blue-suited woman from the WPA that she wanted to bring democracy and education to the poorest, darkest, most remote and forgotten corner of America.

They sent her to Threestep, Georgia.

Miss Spivey paused there for questions, avoiding my brother Ralphord's eye.

What we really wanted to know about—all twenty-six of us across seven grade levels in the one room—was the pearly white button hanging on a string in front of the blackboard behind the teacher's desk up front. That button on a string was something new. When Mavis Davis (the only bona fide seventh-grader, at age thirteen) asked what it was for, Miss Spivey gave the string a tug, and to our astonishment, the whole world—or at least a wrinkled map of it—unfolded before our eyes. Her predecessor, Miss Chandler, had never once made use of that map, which was older than our fathers, and until that moment, not a one of us knew it was there.

Miss Spivey showed us on the map how she and Dr. Janet Miller had sailed across the Atlantic Ocean and past the Rock of Gibraltar into the Mediterranean Sea. Using the end of a ruler, she gently tapped such places as Morocco and Tunis and Algiers to mark their route along the top of Africa. In Egypt, she said, they stopped long enough to climb a pyramid, a sketch of which she drew for us on the board, next to the map. "I wish I could convey to you children its true size and grandeur," she said. From there, they went on through the Gulf of Suez and down around Arabia and right up the Persian Gulf, which Miss Spivey said was the most beautiful body of water in the world. They spent twenty hours on the train to Baghdad, she said, swathed in veils against the sand that crept in every crack and crevice.

I pictured them with scarves pulled across their faces, like a pair of lady bandits.

"And can you guess what we saw from the train?" Miss Spivey asked. We could not. "Camels!" she said. "We saw a whole caravan of *camels.*" She looked around the room, waiting for us to be amazed and delighted at the thought.

We all hung there for a minute, thinking hard—you could see the anticipation on Miss Spivey's face fading as the seconds passed—until Mavis Davis spoke up.

"She means like the three kings rode to Bethlehem," Mavis said, and she folded her hands smugly on her seventh-grade desk in the back of the room.

Miss Spivey made a mistake right then. Instead of beaming upon Mavis the kind of congratulatory smile that old Miss Chandler would have bestowed on her for having enlightened the rest of us, Miss Spivey simply said, "That's right." I think maybe she was so flabbergasted that we didn't all of us know what a camel was that she wasn't sure what to do next, and what she *did* do only made Mavis feel all the more underappreciated. Miss Spivey turned from the map—actually, she *whirled* around with all the flowery layers of a dress the Superintendent of Schools would later call "inappropriate" fluttering around her legs— and she pointed with her piece of chalk straight at *me.* My heart was making such a ruckus in my ears as I stood up that I hardly heard her ask my name. I thought she already knew it, based on the name cards she'd stuck on our desks.

"Ma'am, it's Gladys," I said.

"Your last name, please, Gladys."

"Cailiff?" I said.

"You're not sure?"

"Ma'am, it's Cailiff!"

"Can you spell that for us, please?"

Of course I could spell my own name. I was the number one pupil in the fifth-grade row that particular year. Miss Spivey wrote my name on the board, letter by letter, as I called them out. The chalk squeaked a good one when she crossed the double *ff*, and when she revealed that the ruler of far-off Baghdad was *also* a Cailiff, nobody was more surprised than I was. Mavis snorted loud enough for half the room to hear, but Miss Spivey only smiled. Then she wrote *Caliph* on the board, and the way she lined up the letters under my last name, everybody in the room could see what she was getting at, even my brother Ralphord and the ones who couldn't read.

Only Mavis looked annoyed. "Them's two different words," she said.

"Yes, *they* are," said Miss Spivey, "and yet they sound the same." She asked us if we could think of other words in English that looked different but sounded the same. One of the Veal boys offered up *whale* and *well*. Miss Spivey hesitated, chalk in hand, until he explained, "One of them's like a big fish. The other you dig."

At lunchtime, out in the schoolyard, Mavis Davis complained about everything from Miss Spivey's plaid tam to the way she asked us for "other words *in English*." "Like we'd be prone to answer in Eye-talian! Besides, *whale* and *well* don't sound the same at all." (She might have said *well* and *whale*.) "And *Cailiff* don't sound like nothing"—Mavis sneered at me—"but *Cailiff*."

Except for her lunch, which she carried to school in the canvas knapsack she used for a pocketbook, Miss Spivey took her meals Monday through Friday with Mr. and Mrs. Bibben, who also provided a room for her in their home above the store. Weekends were a different story. The Bibbens were too busy fishing on Saturday and praying on Sunday to feed a schoolteacher, so the ladies of Threestep set up a rotation whereby they handed Miss Spivey off to one another, everybody taking their turn at least one Saturday or Sunday per month. One measure of the increasing trouble Miss Spivey got herself into as the school year progressed was the rate at which folks dropped out of the rotation, until, toward the end, she was taking all her meals with the Bibbens or with us Cailiffs. Mavis's mother—Mavis Davis, Sr., as we thought of her—had the foresight to decline participation from the start.

Miss Spivey had her first supper at our place early in October, as I recall, an occasion for which Momma killed three chickens. (Daddy looked up from his newspaper on the front porch when he heard the third squawk and said, "Sounds like Christmas.") My oldest sister May had asked my brother Force well in advance if he would carry her and her children to Threestep that Saturday from where she lived out near McIntyre. Force, who was seventeen, was happy to oblige. He loved to drive anybody anywhere. May's husband Ed was out on the road at the time with our brother Ebenezer, fixing stoves for a living.

Momma kept finding chores for me to do while we were waiting for Miss Spivey to arrive that afternoon, but every chance I got, I ran down to the road to see if she was here yet. Finally, my ninth or tenth time down the lane, there she stood at the end of it, having come along on foot like she said she would. I skidded to a stop. Miss Spivey was looking across the road at a weevil-wasted cotton field, her back to me, and she was smoking a cigarette. My momma puffed on a tobacco pipe now and again, but I'd never seen a woman smoke a cigarette before. It was pretty the way she held it between her fingers, like a pencil, her hand floating up to her face and back down again, little clouds of white smoke blooming around her head. I coughed to let her know I was behind her. She spun around.

"Well, hello!" she said. Her cigarette hand took a dive and came back up again, as if it didn't know what to do with itself. She smiled.

I said, "How'do, Miss Spivey."

She dropped the cigarette, or what was left of it, and pressed it into the red dirt with a delicate twist of her hiking boot as she looked up the lane toward our house, which was maybe a hundred yards away, a corner of the Boykins' place peeking out behind it. The Boykins' thirty acres were mostly pine and pecan trees, with a lopsided peach orchard near the house. Their land sidled up to our land in such a way that to get from the road to their house, you had to go down a short lane past ours. Giant pine trees shaded the lane. On the far side of our house, the yard rose up to meet the first of our daddy's watermelon fields, the fenced one, where the hogs could go and eat any ruined melons Daddy left for them. Their pen was as far from both houses as Daddy could make it, and downwind, most of the time.

Both our house and the Boykins' were gray unpainted clapboard, a single story. Ours had a red brick chimney at either end and a front porch notched into the middle. It was not a big house, but it wasn't tiny, either. Our daddy surmised that at one time the front porch led into an open-air hallway that ran the length of the house, right down the middle, but someone had closed it off years ago by putting a door at either end of the hall. Tucked in the angle between the back of the house and the added-on kitchen there was a big back porch where we ate supper as long as the weather held. When it rained just right, a curtain of water ran off the porch roof and surrounded us on two sides. It was like eating supper under a waterfall.

"The home of the Cailiffs!" Miss Spivey announced, and as if her words had conjured him, my little brother Ralphord appeared on the front porch.

"She's here!" he hollered into the house. Momma came down the porch steps, smiling and wiping her hands on her apron, her cheeks extra rosy from the kitchen heat. Before Momma reached us, Miss Spivey turned around for a second, facing me. She tapped two fingers to her lips, then one. I understood immediately that her cigarette, signified by the two fingers, was supposed to be our secret, signified by the one. My heart swelled a little at the thought of Miss Spivey having a secret with me alone. (What would Mavis Davis think about *that*? I wondered.) I didn't have a chance to say a word anyway, because Momma took charge of Miss Spivey and sent me on back to the Boykins' house to fetch the dessert. I took off across the yard in hopes of getting back before I missed anything, but by the time I came out the Boykins' door with two pecan pies warming the palms of my hands and a tin cup of thick cream balanced on top of each one, our T-Model Ford was cooling off in the lane. There on the back porch, where Momma had the table all laid out, I saw Miss Spivey holding out her hand to my sister May, newly arrived from McIntyre. At first I thought she was giving something to May. We weren't so accustomed to women shaking hands back then. I inched toward them the best I could, balancing my pies.

They looked to be the same height, which pleased me. Miss Spivey was wearing a light blue blouse (and matching tam) over a blue pleated skirt that looked like she had never sat down in it in her life, the pleats were so sharp. May had on a red and yellow calico dress I had always thought of as pretty, although it was wrinkled, no doubt from riding in the car with sweaty little Ed, her youngest, in her lap. May favored Daddy, like Force did. She had the same deep, deep blue eyes and wavy black hair. Hers already had some strands of gray in it. May and Miss Spivey were almost exactly the same age, I found out—they both turned twenty-nine in 1938—but having babies like clockwork every one or two years had taken a toll on my sister, anybody could see that. May's oldest was eight, and the rest ranged on down, five of them now, to her only boy, who was still in diapers. Her husband Ed hadn't wanted to waste any time getting a family started, on account of his age—he was eleven years older than May—and she had dropped out of her last year of high school to oblige him. Neither Momma nor Daddy could convince her to do otherwise. "She wasn't but seventeen," I heard my mother say one time to Mrs. Boykin. "I should have put her across my knee."

There wasn't room for all of us to be at the table together with Miss Spivey, so Momma fed the smaller children first (which included Ralphord) along with my brother Force, since May's girls had ahold of him and wouldn't let him go. Like most everybody else in Piedmont County, they were in love with their uncle Force. It wasn't just his looks, either. What Force liked best in the world was passing the time of day with people who liked him, and since that was just about everybody, he was pretty much always doing what he liked to do best, and that put him in a kind of permanent ready-for-fun good mood, which made everybody like him even more.

Being eleven, I was deeply grateful to Momma for letting me sit down with Miss Spivey and Daddy and May and my sister Ildred. Momma herself never did sit down. She took part in the conversation as she went back and forth, keeping bowls and platters full, asking Miss Spivey questions such as what kind of meals she had eaten so far in other people's houses and what it was like to live above Bibbens' store. Did she get enough breeze upstairs? When the talk turned to a recent field trip to Milledgeville, I was asked for a report. I said I found it very educational. Miss Spivey had taken us to the Georgia State College for Women, where we had our picnic lunch; to the Old State Capitol and Military Academy, which looked like a castle but was really a high school for boys (Force waved at us from a classroom window); and also to St. Stephen's Episcopal Church, inside which General Sherman had stabled his horses on his way to Savannah and the sea. (I omitted from my report how Arnie Lumpkin kept muttering, "Yankee son of a bitch," the whole time we were there.)

While we were on the subject of Milledgeville, Ildred mentioned that she had graduated from Peabody High School, which was on the college grounds. Miss Spivey asked May, who'd hardly said a word so far, whether she had gone to school there, too. May looked up from her plate and said, "Yes." For a second there, from the way she lifted her chin, I thought May was going to plunge ahead and make *sure* that we didn't think she was trying to give Miss Spivey the false impression that she, too, had *graduated* from Peabody—May could be a stickler about things like that—but just then we heard the high, sweet ring of metal striking metal, and May's little girls came tearing around the side of the house to the porch steps hollering, "Horseshoes! Horseshoes!" Force was right behind them. He had set up the stakes out front.

Miss Spivey had never pitched a game of horseshoes in her life, she said. Force volunteered immediately to help her out. When it was her turn, he stood right behind her and took her hand, the one holding the horseshoe, and swung her arm along with his to make the toss. With his help, she got two ringers in five throws. Little exclamations and applause arose from everyone with each satisfying *ting!*

It was on account of me and Ralphord that Miss Spivey got to know my brother Force as well as she did. Force walked me and Ralphord to school every morning on his way to where the bus picked him up and carried him eighteen miles to Milledgeville. After school, Ralphord and I did chores for Miss Spivey—closing the shutters and sweeping the floor—while we waited for Force to come by, so we could walk home the three of us together. Sometimes Miss Spivey had a job for Force, too, when he got there. Not long after her first supper at our place, she asked him and Ralphord to go back and fix the door of the outhouse. "A couple of the boys were swinging on it like a gate," she said, "and they ended up pulling a board off." After Force and Ralphord went out-side, Miss Spivey said to me, "Your brother has an unusual name." We were watching them from the window next to her desk as they walked across the schoolyard, Force with the hammer resting on his shoulder and Ralphord swinging the bucket of nails and kicking up a cloud of reddish dust on purpose.

I told Miss Spivey how Ralphord was named after a man my father knew in the Great War. "Ralph Ford saved my daddy's life in France," I said. Daddy wanted Ralphord to have both names—Ralph and then Ford for a middle name—but Momma had almost married a man named Ford at one time and she didn't want folks getting any wrong ideas. "So she's the one come up with putting the two names together," I said.

Miss Spivey was still looking out the window at that point. Force and Ralphord were visible now and then, their shirts flashing through the laurel branches between the school and the outhouse area. She said, "I was thinking of your brother Force. He has a *very* unusual name."

I didn't say anything right away. I waited, in fact, until Miss Spivey turned from the window and looked at me.

Of all my brothers and sisters, Force was the only one to be born in a hospital. What I knew about it I had pieced together from things I'd overheard, and most of it was information that I was *not* likely to share with Miss Spivey. I knew there was something wrong about the way Force was situated, that somehow his foot had moved down before it was time for him to be born. For weeks, Momma had to stay in bed at her sister's house in Savannah, where she was visiting at the time, to keep from losing him. Then, having put his foot out to test the waters, so to speak, he seemed to decide against coming out at all. They had to grab his tiny hips and pull him into the world. In regard to his name, Momma had made some kind of vow—if she and the baby came through this alive and all—which she may have regretted but was scared not to keep. I believed that "Forceps" was the name of the hospital in Savannah where he was born. So that's what I told Miss Spivey, while Force and Ralphord were out there fixing the outhouse door.

"Force is short for *forceps*?" she said. She struggled to contain some strong emotion, so much so that her face went pink. My face was pink, too, and hot, I could feel it. I was at an age where having seen the births of piglets and puppies and kittens and a foal only made me that much more embarrassed to picture my mother in such a fix. It was to draw Miss Spivey's attention away from any such imaginings that I set out to explain all of our names to her. There were six of us Cailiffs, everybody but me and Ralphord with a good four or more years in between because Momma was a woman who knew how to put her foot down. (That was another thing I'd overheard.) I told Miss Spivey that my sister May was named for the most beautiful month, when everything's green and nothing's started to get eaten up by weevils and the like. Also, May is the month she was born in. After May came Ebenezer. He was a little bitty wrinkled old man of a baby, born in December, and when they put a white cap on his head, Momma said he looked just like that fellow in the Christmas play they put on in Milledgeville every year, which Daddy took her to see one time.

Ildred came next. She was going to be *Mildred*, I told Miss Spivey, but the sight of her shook Momma some, so the *M* she wrote on the paper was nothing but a big old blob of ink. Later, when she saw what she'd put down for Ildred's name, Momma said she knew it was meant to be, on account she was ill and filled with dread the whole time she carried that child, and after Ildred was finally born, they had to worry about her short arm, and did that mean there were things wrong inside her little body, too. (Ildred was three years old before Momma could go in and look at her in the morning without holding her breath that the Lord might have taken her from us during the night.) After Ildred came my brother Force and then came me. Momma didn't know what to expect after those two, but I didn't give her any trouble at all. I told Miss Spivey that I was *Gladys* because, in my momma's own words, which I had committed to memory: "I was so *glad* to see you, sugar!"

When I finished telling all of that—having also mentioned that Ralphord, the youngest, had snuck up on Momma just two years after I was born—Miss Spivey was gazing out the window again, looking lost in thought. At last she said, "Force is quite tall for—how old did you say he was?"

I told her he was seventeen and due to get a sight bigger, since our daddy was upwards of six feet four.

2

Halloween

IT WAS LATE IN OCTOBER—you could tell by the stains on everybody's fingers from picking walnuts and pecans up off the ground—
when Force and Ralphord and I came to school one morning and
found Miss Spivey wrestling something big out the back of Mr. Bibben's
delivery truck, which was parked under the walnut trees out front. Back
in old Miss Chandler's day, this was the time of year when we could walk
to school in our shoes and take them off at the door, or vice versa, as
long as we did not bring our walnut-stained soles inside to leave black
footprints on the rubbed pine floors. Miss Spivey, being young and red-
haired and several inches *over* five feet tall, did not in the least resemble
her predecessor. Still, I was surprised to see that she had changed out
of her hiking boots into the ballet-type slippers she sometimes wore, and
here she was outside, risking their ruin.

When she saw us coming, Miss Spivey cried, "It's the Cailiffs! Can
you give us a hand?"

We all three broke into a run. Teetering at the edge of the truck bed
was a steamer trunk, dark blue stamped metal, it appeared to be, leather
straps and handles and a humped lid. Ralphord and I could both of us
have fit inside. Force and Miss Spivey had just tipped it off the truck into

the air when Mr. Bibben appeared on the steps of the schoolhouse with
what looked like a red beehive on his head. My first thought was that
he'd had some kind of accident, but Miss Spivey said that Mr. Bibben
was wearing a turban. Ralphord and I watched him walk to his truck,
holding his head very straight and still.

"It's right cool under this thing," Mr. Bibben remarked, as he stepped
up on the running board. "Beats a cap for comfort, once you get used
to it."

He didn't mention why he was wearing a turban, and we didn't ask,
although we wondered, naturally.

Inside the schoolhouse, Miss Spivey told me and Ralphord to scoot
ahead to the teacher's desk—which sat on a little stage that ran across
the front of the room, one step up from the rest of us—to sweep her
books and papers aside. "Watch your step," she said to Force at the edge
of the platform, and together they hoisted the trunk up onto her desk. I
thought Force would leave then and catch his bus to the Military Academy, but before you knew it, Miss Spivey had talked him into sitting
down on her teacher's chair to get his head done up in a turban, too.

Force took off the uniform jacket for which our daddy had paid
half a melon crop and sat very still, his feet flat on the floor. Looking for
all the world like a magician pulling scarves out of a hat, Miss Spivey
drew a length of silky white cloth up and up out of the trunk. She had
Force hold one end of it to the top of his head while she walked around
and around his chair with the rest of it gathered in her arms, taking
small whispery steps in her ballet-type slippers. (They did not appear to
be stained at all.) She swept the silk cloth down over his right ear and
across the back of his suntanned neck, then up over his other ear so it
skimmed the edge of his forehead. Gradually, the white silk covered all
of his wavy black hair. It made a frame around his face, which he kept
as still and solemn as he could. Miss Spivey smoothed the folds with her
fingertips. She tested the shape with the flat of her hands. Force sat up
straighter whenever she touched his neck or brushed his ear. One time
she said, "Excuse me."

In the meantime, other children had started showing up at school.
I heard one little girl ask in a whisper if that was a coffin up there on

Miss Spivey's desk. Ralphord, who was nine years old, whispered back, "Might could be."

When Miss Spivey turned to write *turban* on the blackboard, in preparation for a subsequent lesson regarding the geographical distribution and significance of this particular kind of headgear, my brother Force stood up to take his leave. Except in color, his turban was identical to Mr. Bibben's, although Mr. Bibben did not look like an Arabian prince in his. Force strolled regally down the center aisle between the desks, among his people, and paused in the doorway for Mavis Davis, who happened to be coming in. We could see him through the windows as he made his conspicuous way down the road toward Bibbens' store, where the bus stopped.

Temporarily dumbstruck by her encounter with Force in a turban, Mavis Davis took a while to find first her desk and then her tongue. She saw the trunk and asked what the rest of us were waiting patiently to find out, namely, "What's this all about, Miss Spivey?"

Costumes! Miss Spivey said. It was about *costumes*. The trunk on her desk was chock-full of turbans and veils and other articles of clothing, most of which came straight from the bazaars of Baghdad. She said she aimed to put everybody's name into a hat and conduct a drawing in order to select the lucky individuals who would get to *wear* these genuine articles!

After a brief silence, Mavis Davis asked, without any *particular* rancor in her voice, although I think you can imagine how Miss Spivey might have heard it otherwise, "Why would we want to do that?"

Miss Spivey stiffened a little. Even after she said the words "Halloween Costume Ball," it took a few more minutes before we understood that she was talking about throwing us a party in the schoolhouse on Halloween night with everybody in town invited.

My brother Ralphord asked, "What kind of ball are you fixin' to throw?"

"A *costume* ball, Ralphord," Miss Spivey said.

She put us to work at once making invitations for the folks at home on pieces of orange paper cut out to look like pumpkins. With varying degrees of speed and skill, we copied from the blackboard the place and time of the party (from dusk till midnight, which was thrilling right there) as well as words like *candy apples* and *haunts* (as in House of Haunts), which everybody but Miss Spivey pronounced "haints." She strolled back and forth amongst our desks, offering encouragement and additional suggestions for spelling and punctuation.

Most of us had already written the date on our pumpkin-shaped invitations when Mavis piped up to say, "You can't have no party on October thirty-first, Miss Spivey. It's the last Monday of the month."

Miss Spivey replied, in a particularly pleasant voice, "October thirty-first also happens to be Halloween, Mavis."

"Then I reckon you can't have no party on Halloween," Mavis said.

"Yes, you can!" Ralphord cried. He'd already drawn a picture of a pirate costume on the back of his invitation.

"Well, I sure wouldn't," Mavis said, "if I was y'all." She looked around the room significantly.

By now everybody's heart was sinking, except for Mavis's. She was thoroughly enjoying herself, I could tell. She just loved the fact that all the rest of us had been too excited, with the turban and the pumpkin-shaped invitations and all, to notice that October 31 was the last Monday of the month.

In Threestep, Georgia, the last Monday of the month was Klan night.

My momma said you couldn't blame Mavis for being the way she was, based on what that girl had seen of the world thus far. One thing she had seen was her father swinging from the end of a rope tied at its other end to a beam in what had been his barn before the bank repossessed it, along with the rest of his farm, in 1933, when Mavis was eight years old. Nobody blamed B. Bob Davis for hanging himself, everybody could understand that. What folks couldn't understand was why he'd done it while his wife was off in Irwinton looking after her mother, which left his little girl to find him. Once I heard my daddy say, "I don't reckon

Bob was pondering his wife's whereabouts when he got to standing at the edge of that hayloft." I asked, "What *was* he pondering, do you think?" and Daddy looked down at me, surprised, like he'd just heard from someone he never met before.

Mavis Davis didn't blame her father for what he did or when he did it. She didn't blame her father for anything. She blamed the bank, which she heard a lot about, of course, imagining from what she heard that behind the heavy iron door of the vault was a great big dark mouth that sucked up houses and farms and livestock. Later she blamed FDR, whose New Deal payments to farmers arrived a little too late to save her daddy. She also blamed the man from Claytonville who bought the farm and the colored family who worked it for him. Years later, when the kaolin company leased the farm for mineral rights and knocked down the barn so they could put a road through for their trucks and such, Mavis blamed the kaolin company, too. But she never did blame her daddy. I have always thought that showed there was some quality to Mavis Davis, even at her worst. She was a worthy opponent for Miss Spivey, and thus, a real danger.

Piedmont County Klan nights were presided over in those days by Mr. John B. Gordon, who happened to be Threestep's only lawyer. Mr. Gordon claimed to be the great-grandson of General John B. Gordon of the ex-Confederate armies, the first Grand Dragon of the Ku Klux Klan in Georgia. When I asked my daddy one time if that was true, he said, "I reckon Mr. Gordon must have to be *somebody's* great-grandson."

As the great-grandson of the Grand Dragon, Mr. Gordon considered himself bound in kinship and duty to keep the spirit of the Klan alive, even though there wasn't another member in good standing, which is to say, one who could or would pay the three-dollar annual dues, in all of Piedmont County in 1938. There was no denying that the times had been hard on the Klan. Mr. Gordon could hardly bring himself to talk about the recent sale of the Imperial Palace on Peachtree Street in

Atlanta—formerly the main lodge statewide—to a group of *Catholics.* They were fixing to use it for a church, he said.

It was not much like the good old days, Mr. Gordon said, back in the 1920s, when he was a young man, and all the best people were Klansmen, and they all got together on Stone Mountain every year to pay their respects to the Imperial Wizard and welcome new Ghouls (which is what you call your rank-and-file), offering them special deals on life insurance and discounts on the pointy white hoods. Back then, in the 1920s, there were so many Ku Klucks going around whipping folks for everything from loafing and not going to church, to working *too* hard and getting ahead of their place in the world, that the City of Macon Police Department in nearby Bibb County was obliged to put on a special anti-flogging detail.

Mr. Gordon was not just a Ghoul but a Grand Goblin. On the last Monday of every month, men would park their vehicles in the woods behind his law office and go in by the back door. Dues-paying or not, the members were forbidden to reveal what transpired at these meetings. Daddy said he was pretty sure they played pinochle most of the time. Once or twice a year, when Mr. Gordon and his Ghouls were in the mood for "something big," they'd go out and burn a cross made from the trunks of two pine trees, or, if they had too much trouble attaching one trunk to the other, they'd burn two pillars instead. On these occasions, Mr. Gordon himself provided regulation robes and hoods for those who could not afford to "dress up." One time they burned a pair of pillars up the road, close enough to our neighbors' pecan grove that my daddy had our whole family filling barrels and buckets with water, just in case. The deputy sheriff showed up and gave the Ghouls their choice of either peacefully dispersing (after putting out the fire) or removing their hoods right then and there, in compliance with the state of Georgia's mask law, which was passed back in the 1870s and which prohibited grown-up persons from wearing masks while carrying on in public. Except on certain special occasions. Like Halloween.

Shortly after that incident with the Boykins' pecan grove, there appeared in the window of Mr. Gordon's law office on Main Street a printed sign that said TWK. The sign was only a tad larger than a postcard, but in a little town like ours, things like that get noticed. Mr. Gordon saw me and Ralphord stopped on the sidewalk one day, looking at his sign. He came right outside and told us that when times were good, every business in Threestep had one of those in the window. I said, "What does it stand for?" He said, "Ask your daddy." So I did. Daddy folded up his newspaper and rocked back and forth a few times, making the porch boards squeak, before he told me that it meant "Trade With a Klansman."

"But Mr. Gordon said it used to be every store had a sign like that," I said. "Does that mean they all were Ku Klucks?"

Daddy looked like I was asking him about something he hadn't given thought to in a long while. He also looked like he would have preferred to keep it that way. He said, "I don't rightly know, Gladys."

"I thought the Ku Klucks was a secret," I said. I didn't know yet that the darkest, most dangerous secrets are the ones that everybody knows.

After Mavis made her point about Klan night, Miss Spivey collected our pumpkin-shaped invitations and put them in a pile on her desk. From time to time that day, while we were doing arithmetic or copying spelling words off the blackboard, Miss Spivey would pick one up and look at it a while, maybe give it a slash or a poke with her pencil before she put it back on the pile. After school, when it was just me and Ralphord left, Miss Spivey made an exit through the half-room, which led out into the schoolyard, "to get a breath of air." Ralphord went for the invitations immediately, looking for the one he'd made. When he found it, he cried, "She messed up my invite—Gladys, look!"

He held it up. For a second I thought he was complaining about the eye patch on the jack-o'-lantern's face. Then I saw the black line through *October 31.*

"I reckon she's fixing to change the date, Ralphord, that's all. On account of what Mavis said." I didn't say so, but I couldn't understand why Miss Spivey felt obliged to listen to Mavis Davis. It didn't make a bit of difference if Monday was Klan night, it seemed to me, because Mr. Gordon wasn't likely to come to the party anyhow. Of course, Miss Spivey might have been thinking about schoolteachers getting tarred and feathered. I imagine Georgia history was part of her WPA training.

"Miss Spivey didn't put no other day on it, Gladys," Ralphord said. He sniffed. "Somebody's smokin'. Do you smell smoke?"

A little wisp of it was floating past the window. Miss Spivey followed shortly thereafter. She appeared to be on her way around to the front door, but instead of coming inside, we heard her stop on the steps and say, "Hello!" to somebody. It was the deputy sheriff's voice in reply. A few minutes later, I was glad I never moved in closer to hear, because I'd have gotten walloped when one side of the double door flew inward and Miss Spivey came marching in. Ralphord stuck his invitation back in the pile.

Miss Spivey went straight to the big steamer trunk—it was resting now on two chairs in the front corner of the room—and started tossing things out. Ralphord and I made it our business to catch as much as we could and spread it out on nearby desks and benches. Ralphord caught a red felt cap that flew out in the wake of something long and filmy. He put it on his head like a deep dish upside down. I draped the filmy stuff, which turned out to be a harem outfit, languidly over the back of Miss Spivey's chair. She said, "Ralphord, remove that hat!" He placed it delicately on an empty desktop. Soon the air was thick with the camphortype smell of whatever had been put in the trunk to discourage eaters of cloth. When the trunk was about empty, Miss Spivey straightened up and gazed around. It looked like a colorful clothing bomb had gone off in the schoolroom, robes and veils and you couldn't tell what all. At the sight of it, Miss Spivey appeared to run out of steam entirely. She sank down onto her teacher's chair, heedless of the harem costume, closed her eyes, and threw her head back. With her face aimed at the ceiling, speaking in a strained voice, Miss Spivey demanded to know if either of us had ever heard of the state of Georgia's anti-mask law. She didn't wait for an answer. "The deputy sheriff knows *all* about it," she said. "Apparently, it makes Halloween an extra-special evening for Mr. Gordon and his friends."

"I don't need no mask to be a pirate," Ralphord offered, in case that would help. "Just a eye patch."

In the same strained voice, Miss Spivey said, "If I'm not willing to change the date, the deputy sheriff expects me to cancel the Halloween Costume *Ball*."

"Oh, don't do that, Miss Spivey!" Ralphord cried.

Miss Spivey opened one eye and seemed to consider certain ceiling cracks. "I thought Mavis was making it up," she said.

Ralphord shot me a desperate look. I said firmly, "You don't have to cancel no party, Miss Spivey."

She made no reply.

Gloom hung over the schoolroom while we waited for Force to arrive to walk me and Ralphord home. The light outside turned from golden afternoon to mostly dusk.

When the schoolhouse door swung open again, it had somehow aligned itself with the last, nearly horizontal beams of the setting sun. Those beams shot past my brother Force in the doorway, framing him with blazing orange light and casting his shadow before him, sharp and black and bigger than life, across the schoolroom floor. The white turban, tinted gold, was still on his head. It appeared a little the worse for wear, one end hanging like a tail to his shoulder, but this only gave him the look of one who had passed tests of courage, which, in fact, he had, wearing that turban all day long. Ralphord rushed at him, waving the invitation. I looked at Miss Spivey, who was looking at Force, and from the little smile on *her* face—even *before* he read the invitation and said, "You want to scare the pants off everybody comes in, you'd best get Theo Boykin to see about your House of Haints, Miss Spivey!"—I knew that we were back in business.

3

A Bedouin at the Window

THEO BOYKIN WAS the smartest person in Piedmont County, and
everybody knew it. Whether folks liked it or not was another matter.
Theo, who was about the same age as Force, could do sums in his head
better than Mrs. Bibben's adding machine at the store, and he could
read you anything he laid his hands on, even if he never saw it before in
his life, without ever stumbling over a single word. One Fourth of July,
when the parade marshal of Piedmont County waited till the last minute
to line up his post-parade program, he couldn't find but one person in
Claytonville, Brennan, and Threestep combined who knew all the words
to the Declaration of Independence. Theo was ten or eleven at the time.
You'd better believe a murmur went through the audience when he
stepped up to the podium on the courthouse lawn in Claytonville that
day, but by the time he got to "life, liberty, and the pursuit of happiness," he had the whole audience in the palm of his hand. I'm told they
applauded louder and longer for Theophilus Boykin than they had for
the tap dancers or the Land of Liberty tableau.

He could draw, too. Miss Templeton, his teacher at the colored school
out in the country, said one time that Theo was a Renaissance man, by
which she meant he could do anything he put his mind to. This led to

Miss Spivey calling him "Signor da Vinci" later on, when he was drawing up plans for the Baghdad Bazaar, beautiful sketches with numbers and arrows to show what went where. None of us knew who Signor da Vinci was until we had a lesson at school on him and Michelangelo that included the opportunity to lie on your back and paint whatever you wanted on the underside of your desk for as long as your arm could stand it.

When Theo came to Threestep School to see about Miss Spivey's haunted house, Force and Ralphord and I came with him, as did his brother Eugene, a quiet boy who was a little younger than Theo but bigger and taller than all of us. Eugene waited outside, leaning against the trunk of the walnut tree. Miss Spivey invited him to come in, but he declined.

Theo hesitated at the back of the schoolroom himself, which caused me to remember something from a long time before. When I was in the first grade, my brother Force brought Theo to school with us one time, I don't recollect why. Our teacher Miss Chandler met us at the door and explained that even though Theo Boykin was "smart as a whip," the law prohibited her from allowing him inside Threestep School. She might have said that she could not permit him "to get a foot in the door," but what I heard was "to put his foot on the floor," which made me wonder. If somebody would pick him up and carry him, could Theo come inside? Or what if we put a carpet down for him to step on? I had some idea that his feet were the problem—like ours in walnut time—and I know I thought about pointing out to Miss Chandler, in my first-grade wisdom, that the bottoms of Theo's feet were the lightest part of him and no threat at all to her floor. I had noticed this paleness on the hands and feet of colored people only recently. In fact, it was Theo Boykin who pointed it out to me. We were all cleaning white clay off ourselves after digging some out of a hole in the Boykins' yard, when Theo rubbed his palms together and said, "Well, look at here, Gladys. That white dirt bleached the color right off my hands and feet!" This seemed plausible to me, especially in Piedmont County, where white dirt is abundant. His momma set me straight on the matter. She scolded him for teasing.

In the doorway of Threestep School, Theo Boykin took off his work

shoes and carried them, one in each hand, across the threshold. He set his
two bare feet flat on the pine floor, under which crickets were singing
their swan song, it being late in October. You could see him take a quick
inventory of the place: the neat rows of desks in three graduated sizes,
the map that pulled down like a window shade, and the blackboard as
big as the whole front wall of the room, except where the door to the
half-room broke into it. The long tall windows, four on each side of the
room, had glass in every pane but one, due to a ball game last winter.

Miss Spivey, who was waiting for us, acted like it was the most
natural thing in the world for Theo Boykin to step inside Threestep
School—"Come in!" she said, and "Please take a seat"—but she did
seem a little shy about telling him what she had in mind for the haunted
house. "Well, I thought we'd hang some sheets and wet string in the
half-room," Miss Spivey said, "and make people walk through it in the
dark?"

Theo paced the length of the glorified closet that constituted the
"half" in our one-and-a-half-room schoolhouse. It had no windows and
no electric light and was almost completely dark. When he stood in the
doorway, his white shirt and expertly patched gray pants were easier to
see than the expression on his face.

Miss Spivey said, "What do you think?"

"Ma'am," he said, "a white sheet never fooled anybody. What you
need is something *moving*. We can fix it so if you open the door, things
drop down and slide around—ghosts swooping like they're coming to
get you, like that. Spiders are good, too, and easy to fix up. And I *might*
have time to make a skeleton, if I could get some help with that. I've
got a skull we could use." We all held our breath for a second when he
said that. "A *deer* skull," he said. "They're about the right size. Skeleton's
the best, Miss Spivey. Nothing's scarier than a skeleton rattling its bones.
D'y'all know why?"

We knew just to wait, but Miss Spivey said, "Why?"

"Because everybody knows they've got one of those alive inside of
them," Theo said solemnly. "They've got to carry it into bed at night."

The next morning, Miss Spivey set all twenty-six pupils of Threestep School loose in the woods around the schoolhouse to hunt up sticks and branches in specified sizes. By afternoon, all the fifth- through seventh-grade boys in possession of pocketknives were busy whittling the bark off the sticks and branches, turning them into skeleton bones. The rest of us used Miss Spivey's stock of school scissors to cut large and small gray spiders out of a pile of old felt blankets she brought in. I, Gladys Cailiff, was part of a select group handpicked by Miss Spivey to thread and tie the whittled sticks together with scraps of fine copper wire, following a kind of bones-by-number system Theo had devised to enable us to construct what he called "a respectable fac-simile" of a skeleton. It took us three days to assemble the skeleton, and in the end it was not precisely like the ones we carry into bed with us at night, but close enough.

When Miss Spivey changed the date of the Halloween Costume Ball from Monday to Sunday, she lost Mr. Bibben, who had agreed to judge the pumpkin-carving contest in his turban, and also Mrs. Bibben, of course, and a few other folks who prayed on Sunday to the exclusion of everything else, but nobody held it against her, not even the Bibbens. Some people expected Reverend and Mrs. Stokes from Threestep Methodist Church to bow out, too, but they did not. The Reverend's original position on the party was that it would keep the young folks out of mischief on Halloween night. Now that it was changed to the night before Halloween, Reverend Stokes claimed that his presence was needed more than ever to ensure a certain level of decorum and maintain the moral caliber of the event, seeing as it would take place on the Lord's Day.

The Baptist Reverend Whitlock was heard to say that this was the most highly original interpretation of the Third Commandment he had ever heard.

Every evening that week, pounding and sawing and clattering could be heard coming from the schoolhouse. Theo and Force and my sister Ildred were working on a system of ropes and wires and pulleys to hang the ghosts and the skeleton. Ildred, who was three years older than Force, was mechanically inclined, even though she was a girl and born with one arm. (She used to say there was only one thing she couldn't do, having only one arm, and that was to clap her hands.) They kept the side door out to the schoolyard locked, except for deliveries of supplies, which included biscuits from Momma and Mrs. Boykin, and odd boards and hoary objects scrounged by Ildred during the day. Miss Spivey spent every one of those evenings keeping watch over the half-room while they worked, often propping her teacher's chair in the doorway to shed light on the project. Some nights, Eugene Boykin lent a hand, or one of the Veal boys. Usually they worked until almost eleven, stopping minutes before Mr. Wicker turned off his generator behind the barbershop, and the electric lights in Threestep, such as they were at that time, went out all at once, like a door slammed shut.

On the Friday before Halloween, it looked like everybody in town had come to see the costumes "straight from the bazaars of Baghdad" that Miss Spivey had hanging in the back of the schoolroom on a clothesline cleverly arranged by Theo Boykin to look like a giant spider web. Miss Spivey was worried that the men would balk at wearing the long brown robes that Force called "them dresses." (Our momma muttered, "Don't see why. They got no problem with *white* ones.") To overcome any such resistance, Miss Spivey prevailed upon Force to dress up like a Bedouin, which is a man of the desert, in a long brown robe with a white-and-black scarf thing on his head and a pair of red leather boots that were killing his feet. Fifteen minutes before the drawing was set to commence, Miss Spivey sent him striding down through the middle of town as best he could in those boots, with the robe flying behind him and that scarf fluttering away from his square jaw, and before he reached the end of Main Street she had the deputy sheriff and a half dozen other men, including Reverend Stokes—along with most of the bigger boys in our school—lining up to drop their names into the hat in hopes of getting themselves fitted out like a man of the desert.

For three lucky female partygoers, Miss Spivey had hung on the wall three long gowns that she called "*abayas*"—one in blue, one in plain black, and one in black silk that was embroidered with gold thread. Each *abaya* gown came with a matching veil. You could see from the way they were hung on the line that, worn together, they would pretty much cover a body from head to toe. I put my sister May's name in for the blue *abaya,* mainly because it was way too long for me to wear and blue was May's color and maybe if she won she would come to Threestep for the party instead of waiting on pins and needles at home in McIntyre for her husband Ed to show up. Ed and our oldest brother Ebenezer traveled all across the state and clear up to Tennessee with their stove repair business, going into people's homes and dismantling their stoves, replacing oven door hinges and cleaning stovepipes and the like. Their busiest time was from August until mid-October—after canning season but before winter—when folks could best afford to have their stove laid out in pieces in the yard. Neither Ed nor Ebenezer had any training in how to fix a stove, whether wood-burning or bottle-gas. They just went in and did it. They were already one week past due on their return from the stove repair circuit, so May was a wreck with worrying.

Miss Spivey waited until the last minute to pin up the harem lady costume, which consisted of long full trousers made of filmy sheer fabric, like voile or chiffon, to be worn over the smallest of short pants, with a little satin blouse that left most of Mamie Eskew's middle showing when she tried it on after the drawing. It was the only costume in Miss Spivey's trunk that did *not* come from Baghdad, she said, having been sent to her by a friend who lived in Hollywood, California. When Pinkie Lou Griffith saw it, she swore that it was identical to the outfit worn by the actress who stole the heart of Douglas Fairbanks, Sr., in *The Thief of Baghdad,* for which she, Pinkie Lou, had played the organ at the Dixie Way years ago. This Miss Spivey could not confirm or deny, so we were left with the *possibility* that Douglas Fairbanks, Sr., had touched the very costume that was pinned to the schoolroom wall. *Where* he might have put his hands was a question you couldn't think about for long without straying into forbidden territory.

Mrs. Reverend Stokes and the Baptist minister's wife Mrs. Whitlock, both of whom were present at the costume drawing, tried to enlist Reverend Stokes in a campaign to ban Mamie's harem costume—the Reverend being famous for his annual "whores of Babylon" sermon about the dangers of going to the movies—but somehow he couldn't see the harm in it. He was too busy sliding his knobby toes into the red leather boots to see if he could wear them with the Bedouin outfit for which Miss Spivey had already drawn his name. To the Reverend's delight, the boots were a near-perfect fit.

Waiting for the doors to open on the night of the Halloween Costume Ball, my sister May, Florence Hodges, and Miss Pinkie Lou Griffith all looked like fancy ghosts floating around the schoolyard in the genuine Baghdad *abayas* and veils they'd won the chance to wear. May's little girls were made up like Three Blind Mice in shirts and rolled-up pants from Ralphord, cardboard mouse ears, and dark glasses Ildred had made for them out of wire, with "lenses" cut from a cheesecloth bag stained black by walnuts. My own daddy joined my brother Force and Reverend Stokes as men of the desert—the Reverend's red leather boots polished to a shine—while Mr. Hall looked more than fit to judge the pumpkin-carving contest in a green turban and a long blue "robe of honor," Miss Spivey said it was. Cyrus Wood's daddy and two other men wore their turbans with long white robes we knew they would be wearing again very soon with a change of headgear, Monday being Klan night. Roy Kemp and Ollie Harvey—sixth-graders both—were required by Miss Spivey to wash their hair in kerosene before she would consent to touch their heads, much less do either of them up in a turban. They went around all night smelling like torches.

In between wrapping turbans, Miss Spivey showed all the girls who'd come up with their own *abayas* and veils made of croker sacks or window curtains—which group included me—how to "tattoo" a ring of little blue crosses, such as Arab girls wore, around their ankles. We drained the inkwell on her desk bone-dry. Mavis Davis declined the blue crosses, insisting that she was a witch, not an Arab lady, although I noticed that she watched everybody else get theirs.

Miss Spivey herself wore a long, straight dress with a square neckline that seemed to be woven of different-colored threads in such a way that you couldn't exactly say what color it was overall. This, she said, was the sort of dress that married ladies wore at home in Baghdad.

"How does *she* know what married ladies wear at home?" Mavis Davis said to the rest of us in the schoolyard while we held our makeshift gowns up off our ankles and waited for the ink to dry. "She ain't married to anybody."

I couldn't help myself. I said, "How do *you* know what Miss Spivey is or ain't?"

Mavis gave me a pitying look. "Gladys," she said, "her name is MISS Spivey. Don't you know what *Miss* means?"

"I reckon it means she's *missed* her chance," Florence Hodges said, and that set them all to giggling.

I was saved from pinching Florence Hodges, or otherwise getting myself in trouble, by a long and undulating shriek that could only mean Miss Spivey had unlocked the door to the House of Haunts and Terrors, thus allowing the first of the partygoers to find herself face-to-face with the ghost that dropped down from the ceiling when you opened the door. It was Pinkie Lou Griffith who went in first, we could tell by the melodious quality of her scream.

Except for the Gordons and Arnie Lumpkin's folks, along with the most fervent of the Baptists and Mavis Davis's mother, it looked like every white person in Threestep and the surrounding district was present at the costume ball, most of them in costume. Miss Spivey collected almost five dollars in three-cent admissions to the haunted house in the first hour alone. Everybody wanted to go through at least twice. The whole party would have gone off without a hitch if Mavis Davis hadn't set out to find a little dance music on the radio. It was well before the ten o'clock time frame that Miss Spivey had designated for dancing (following the pumpkin-carving contest), but Mavis was tired of bobbing for apples and she had no intention of sticking her hands in any pumpkin guts, she said.

The radio was a tabletop model in a green Bakelite case bequeathed to the school by our old teacher Miss Chandler's last will and testament. Enthroned on a table between two windows, the radio was surrounded on this occasion by a little army of caramel-coated apples and bowls of roasted pecans and the like. Mavis twirled the tuner knob until she found an orchestra playing in a hotel ballroom in New York City, at which point she turned it up as loud as she could without losing the music in a cloud of static. Everybody looked at Miss Spivey, who was helping the little kids carve pumpkins in the corner, to see what she thought of Mavis turning on the radio. Before Miss Spivey could say a word one way or the other, my sister Ildred—who'd bucked the Arabian tide to come as a turtle with half a cracker barrel for a shell—dragged our brother Force out into the open space between the apple bobbers and the pumpkin carvers for a foxtrot. Off they went, turtle shell, Bedouin robes, and all. Two more couples joined them—first Momma and my sister May (with her veil off but still looking lovely in the blue gown), and then Miss Spivey herself, with none other than the deputy sheriff in striped prison garb he'd borrowed from his cousin. Mavis—who was, I'm sure, expecting to annoy Miss Spivey—ignored the invitational gesticulations of Florence Hodges and sulked on the sidelines, though not for long. The dancers didn't get once around the room before the radio announcer cut into the music and took us to New Jersey for a news report from a late-breaking story. Some kind of meteor-type object had fallen from the sky and made a big hole in a farm field out that way. The couples dancing bumped to a stop and everybody stood looking at the radio and listening to the reporter on the scene.

In 1938, a lot of folks in Piedmont County were still pretty much in awe of the miracle of the airwaves. The radio at Threestep School was one of only three in town, the others being in Bibbens' store and at the home of Mr. Wicker, whose generator provided electricity for *some* folks in Threestep. The Gordons had a radio, too, but they lived closer to Claytonville, which was a bigger town and already electrified by then. We listened, entranced, in the schoolroom as the reporter described the object, which was shiny and smooth and didn't look like a meteor at all, he said. Then he got even more excited because there was a door opening up on the object and out came somebody carrying something that sent out a brilliant ray of green light! Before long, you could hear a lot of screaming in the background, which was pretty disturbing, until all of a sudden, in the middle of a sentence about the green ray getting closer and closer, the report went dead. There was a moment of shocked silence while we looked at each other in our robes and gowns and turbans and veils and stripes and turtle shell, and then, just as the announcer came back with something about technical difficulties and a return to the ballroom and the music of Ramone Somebody, the double doors at the back of the schoolroom flew open, both at once. Arnie Lumpkin's daddy came stumbling in, drunk as a skunk and smelling about as bad.

Over by the punch bowl, dressed as a ghost (he claimed) with a pillowcase over his head, Arnie looked like he was trying to hide himself in the crowd. His daddy was a trial to the whole Lumpkin family, but Arnie bore the brunt of it, seeing as Mr. Lumpkin always commenced beating on his firstborn and passed out, as often as not, before he got to anybody else. Arnie edged toward the half-room door while his father bellowed, "Zmah boy here?"

"Hold on there," the deputy sheriff began, stepping toward Mr. Lumpkin, but he was drowned out by a chorus of "Ssshhhhh!" The radio announcer had broken into the music again to say that similar reports about smooth and shiny metal objects were coming in from all over the world. I don't know what all else he had to say, because Ildred, who was standing right next to me, suddenly spun around toward the window and hissed, "Whoever is knockin' on my shell better knock it off di-*rectly*!"

There was a Bedouin standing outside the window behind us with his headscarf drawn across his face. In Theo Boykin's voice he said, "This is that *Mercury* show on the radio! *Mercury Theatre*."

"Where'd you get that outfit?" I said. On the radio it was something about spaceships.

"Listen to me," said Theo. "It's *Mercury Theatre* on that radio. They do a different story every week. What he said about Martians? It's not for real. It's just a story. D'y'all understand what I'm saying?"

In a flash, Ildred understood. "Go git Force over here," she told me, and then she plunged under the table, in search of the electrical plug.

In the meantime, all ears were tuned to the radio. Even Arnie's daddy looked like he was listening. Another reporter was talking now, more excited than the last one. He was broadcasting from a hotel in New York City, he said. Martians were coming across the Hudson River there. A thick black fog was rolling in with them, he said. They were a hundred yards from the hotel where he was. He promised to stay on the air as long as he could, but he was coughing already. The Martians looked like giant insects, he said, talking fast. They had tentacles.

Somebody whispered, "*What they got?*"

The fog was rolling toward the hotel. It was fifty yards away. Thirty, the man said, coughing and coughing.

"What is it?" Arnie Lumpkin's daddy was swaying on his feet and looking around at everybody like he wondered who we all were. "What the hell is goin' on?"

Mr. Hall said, "It's Martians, for God's sake. They're fixin' to take over!" He sounded about equal parts annoyed with Mr. Lumpkin and plain scared to death.

Twenty yards, said the reporter. He could barely get the words out. Ten. There was a sound like something heavy hitting the floor. And then the radio went dead.

Ildred had unplugged it. Her intentions were good but her timing was bad. By the time she could get herself out from under the table and up on her feet, Arnie Lumpkin's daddy had figured out the sense of what Mr. Hall had said about the Martians. Mr. Lumpkin dropped, sobbing, to his knees and cried, "Oh, my Jesus Lord, save us!" whereupon Mrs. Reverend Stokes fainted dead away, her fortune-teller's bells and beads jingling down into a heap on the floor. Efforts to find another station on the unplugged radio were to no avail, which only seemed to prove that there was nobody left on the air, and I swear there was some genuine wailing and gnashing of teeth going on when my brother Force—him and Ildred and Theo having put their heads together over by the window—got himself up on a chair. He lifted his magnificently robed arms.

"Hey!" he cried. "Hey! Y'all listen up!"

The sight of my brother on that chair with his arms open wide and

his handsome face framed by desert headgear caught everybody's attention. The wailing and gnashing petered out until only Mr. Lumpkin's
sloppy sobs could still be heard. Force called to Theo over his shoulder,
"Now tell 'em what you told me."

All eyes turned to the Bedouin outside the window. With his scarf
pulled across his face, the way a man of the desert might do in a sandstorm, there was no way to tell by looking that it was Theo under there.
Even when he began to speak in his calm and reasonable Theo voice,
folks still didn't seem to recognize him. I heard murmurings around me
of, *Who is that?* and so forth as he told them that there was no cause for
alarm, they were listening to *Mercury Theatre on the Air*, which program
Theo had listened to one week ago on the Bibbens' radio. They had
announced last week that tonight's show, special for Halloween, would
be "The War of the Worlds," based on a book by H. G. Wells. That's what
we all heard on the radio, he said, and if we could just cut it back on, he
was pretty sure everything would turn out all right. The Martians get
wiped out by earth germs in the end. "Anyhow," Theo said, the cloth
poofing away from his mouth with every syllable, "that's what happens
in the book."

"Who the hell is that under there?" Arnie Lumpkin asked
menacingly.

"It's Theo Boykin!" somebody said.

Arnie followed that with a snarl. "Y'all got *Negroes* at this party?"

Negroes is not the word Arnie used.

Miss Spivey told Arnie sharply that it was time for him to take his
blubbering father on home. She didn't actually say *blubbering*, but then
she didn't have to, because he still was. Arnie did not utter another word,
but if looks could kill, like they say, Theo would have been dead right
then. Miss Spivey, too, I expect.

I caught sight of Mavis Davis over by the radio, sinking her teeth
into a caramel-coated apple with obvious satisfaction. If she thought
she'd succeeded in ruining the party, however, she was wrong. Miss
Spivey clapped her hands the way she did at school to restore order. She
pointed at two boys to help Arnie pick his daddy up off the floor, and

we got the radio back on in time to hear Mr. Orson Welles (no relation to H. G. and spelled with an extra *e*, Theo explained later) inviting us to tune in next week for the chilling story of "Brian's Brain." He wished us all a happy Halloween.

After the fact, most folks who were at Miss Spivey's Halloween Costume Ball remembered the whole Martian episode—even the part where Mrs. Reverend Stokes had to be revived with a splash of cider—as if it were all part of the entertainment, which, in a manner of speaking, it was. People like to be scared, as long as it comes out all right, although Momma and my sister May were both up half the night comforting May's little girls, who kept waking up and needing a story or a song to chase away the pictures in their minds—not of Martians, but of all those grown-up people bent over the radio in their peculiar outfits, their usually calm and knowledgeable faces distorted by bewilderment and fear. It was some consolation for me to recall waking up during the night to hear May's voice in the next room, singing or telling the girls a story.

The question of Theo's costume came up. Miss Spivey said she had given it to him as a reward for all the hard work he'd put into the decorations for the party. Theo Boykin had remained outside the schoolhouse while the party was in progress, after all, and it was a measure of the success of Miss Spivey's Night-Before-Halloween Costume Ball that everybody agreed—and Mr. Gordon himself later confirmed—that there was no rule of law, written or unwritten, that a colored boy could not wear a costume on occasion. If anything, Miss Spivey said at one point, a trifle bitterly, didn't the state of Georgia's "mask law" give every citizen express permission to cover his face and dress up like *any* kind of fool, on Halloween?

Nobody cared to remind her that the party did not take place on Halloween.

The deputy sheriff cost us a moment's breath at school on Monday, after the party, by showing up like he was on official business. He hadn't come for anything but to tell Miss Spivey that, for all the excitement, no complaints had been filed. "You don't have a thing to worry about," he told her.

"Well, that *is* a piece of good news, isn't it?" Miss Spivey said, leaving poor Deputy Sheriff Linwood Perkins baffled as to why she looked so put out over a piece of good news.

On the evening of that same day, October 31, 1938, the last Monday of the month, men in hoods and robes did gather at Mr. Gordon's law office, but the big doings they had planned—to take full advantage of the holiday exception to the state mask law—did not occur, even though Mr. Gordon had spent Saturday and Sunday helping his yardman hack the branches off two twelve-foot pine trees and then supervising some of his best Ghouls as they erected a great big cross on a ridge outside of town. They claimed it would be visible, lit, from as far as Milledgeville. At home on Sunday night, however, Mr. Gordon had rested from his labors by listening to the radio, and even though he knew by the end of the broadcast that it was just a made-up story, the night sky looked different to him afterward. All of a sudden, he couldn't work up any enthusiasm for burning a great big cross out in the open on a hill you could see from Milledgeville. It felt too much like lighting up a signal fire to catch the eye of someone watching from the heavens. Months would pass before Mr. Gordon's enthusiasm for such doings returned in full.

4

Tootering

IN THE FIRST WEEK or two after the Halloween Costume Ball, Miss
Spivey couldn't turn around without hearing about the Threestep Fall
Fair, last held in 1931 when I was only four years old. Her predecessor
Miss Chandler had founded the original Fall Fair as a fund- (and fun!)
raising kick-off for the school year back in 1904. Miss Spivey listened
politely to numerous hints but remained noncommittal in regard to the
Threestep Fall Fair (which used to put Toomsboro Days to shame every
September). She had other things on her mind. After all the work Theo
Boykin had done for Halloween, Miss Spivey felt we owed him more
than just the chance to look like a Bedouin for a day. One morning she
said to Ralphord and me, "What can we *do* for your friend Theo?"

That was the first time I ever heard anyone call Theo Boykin our
friend. I could tell that it struck my brother Ralphord, too, and was
amazed he had the sense not to say a word about it.

There was no denying that we Cailiffs spent a lot of time with our
neighbors, the Boykins. Eugene could almost always be persuaded to
thrill and entertain us with feats of strength like lifting Ralphord up off
the ground with one hand, and Daddy liked to say that Momma and
Mrs. Boykin were thick as thieves. But it was Theo and Force and Ildred

who really had a bond. If they weren't inventing labor-saving devices, a few of which—like the chicken feeder that didn't have to be filled but once a week—actually saved folks some labor, they were conducting experiments or repairing automobiles, sometimes both at once. Last spring, for example, when the circus was in Oconee and our T-Model Ford was sitting half on and half off the lane with a hole in its fuel tank, Theo Boykin had an idea how they could "fix" it with a piece of copper tubing and a No. 2½ tin can. Force and Theo and Ildred worked all day long on that car. (Daddy was gone to Macon at the time.) We had just sat down for supper, Force and Ildred still smelling like gasoline, when we heard a popping sound from the yard out front, and here came our T-Model Ford, chugging up the lane with Theo Boykin at the wheel, his eyes fixed in deepest concentration on the tin can they'd set in front of the windshield with a tail of copper tubing that snaked on down to disappear under the hood. Force had to drive almost as slow as walking, but that tin-can fuel tank got us to Oconee in time for half the circus that night, including the part where the littlest Flying Marengo twirled three times in midair, sparkling in her spangly outfit like a flame.

All I could think of to tell Miss Spivey in response to her question about our friend Theo was that the teacher at the colored school, which was located in the country outside Threestep, was bound and determined to get him to college. "Miss Templeton says there's a college he can go to where they can teach him to be a lawyer or a doctor," I said.

In case Miss Spivey had any trouble believing that, Ralphord added, "They got colored doctors at the Negro hospital in Macon." Momma had told us.

"Have y'all ever heard of a college like that, Miss Spivey," I asked her, "where Theo could go?"

"Of course Theo can go to college!" Miss Spivey said. "He could go to Morehouse in Atlanta, for example." She paused. "Or Howard University, back East." Those were two she could think of offhand, she said.

I told her Ballard Normal School in Macon was the one Miss Templeton had in mind for him, at least to start. (His momma said Atlanta was too far.) One hitch was that he had to go to high school first. Now, Ballard had a high school, too, but there was another hitch. Theo's father was dead and gone, passed away some years earlier in the middle of chopping wood to stoke the kilns over at the pottery during a week of record heat. The way Mrs. Boykin told it, "My man just laid down and he was so hot and so tired that he never did get up. Boss came and shook him, said, 'Get up, now. There's work to do,' but he was dead." That meant Theo was the man of the house and had been for a while. When he turned sixteen last year, Mr. Veal over at the pottery offered him a job doing the same work his daddy had done, and Theo took it. It tore Miss Templeton up, but as Mrs. Boykin said, "A boy's got to eat, no matter how smart he is." You'd see him walking along the road on his way to work, his nose in a book, leaning forward into the pages like a person walking into a stiff wind.

That's when Miss Templeton came up with the idea of teaching Theo his high school subjects by tutoring him herself. They had been meeting early in the morning for over a year now. Theo was always coming along telling us something he learned about the properties of electricity or the Peloponnesian Wars, or quoting his favorite lines from Shakespeare, such as, "Prick us and do we not bleed?" or "To thine own self be true." ("That sounds pretty," he told us one time, "but the man who said it was a jackass." He meant Polonius, not Shakespeare.) Theo had to set off walking at about five to get to the country schoolhouse before Miss Templeton's regular day began. They'd tried meeting in the evening, but he couldn't stay awake once he sat down after work. (His momma found him sound asleep at the table one time, his head on his plate.) Miss Templeton rode almost five miles to the little country school herself, on horseback, from the opposite direction. She lived with a minister and his family near Brennan. "They're the ones loan her the horse," I told Miss Spivey.

She looked thoughtful. "I don't want to step on anybody's toes," she said, whereupon Ralphord glanced at her hiking boots, "but doesn't it make more sense for Theo to get his lessons here, in Threestep? He could study an extra hour in the time he would save walking."

I was *this* close to pointing out that there was no colored teacher in Threestep to give him his lessons when I realized that Miss Spivey meant that *she* was fixing to do it. I must have had a look on my face, because she asked me did I think Miss Templeton would object to the idea. Would Theo? I didn't know what to say. I told her I reckoned he *would* save time, just like she said.

She had a chance to put her questions to Theo himself after school that day when he came with my brother Force to pick up the deer skull we'd used for our skeleton. Force was still in his school uniform. Theo had on overalls that were dusty with dried clay from the pottery. Miss Spivey told Theo that she had been thinking of ways she could help Miss Templeton help *him* with his high school studies.

Theo glanced at Ralphord and me. Then he shrugged. "Fact is, I haven't been going out there since school started again, ma'am."

"Why not?" said Miss Spivey.

"We ran out of books."

"How's that?" said Force.

"I studied all she had."

Force whistled.

"We're saving up to buy the rest from a fellow in Milledgeville that Miss Templeton knows. She's teaching somebody else meanwhile," Theo said. "A girl," he admitted.

"Goodness," said Miss Spivey. "Can't Miss Templeton get a set of books from the high school in Claytonville?"

That's where the colored high school for Piedmont County was.

Theo looked wary now, as if this might be a test, as if there might be some particular thing Miss Spivey did or did not want to hear. He took his wire cutters out of his pocket, turned them over in his hand, and put them back. Then, having come to a decision, he said, "Ma'am, we don't want their schoolbooks."

Miss Spivey said, "I beg your pardon?"

Miss Templeton wanted him to study from white high school books, Theo told Miss Spivey. "Miss Templeton says they're better. More up-to-date."

"I got high school books," said Force.

"You *have* high school books," Miss Spivey said.

"Sure do," Force agreed. "I reckon they're the white kind. I get to bring 'em home if I care to."

Miss Spivey gave him a thoughtful look. Then she folded her arms and said, "I believe it's high time I met my colleague down the road."

Miss Leona Templeton was a sweet-faced, soft-spoken woman who might have been about the same age as Miss Spivey, or even a year or two younger, I couldn't tell. Her salary was also paid by the WPA, but Miss Templeton started teaching in Piedmont County before Miss Spivey came to Threestep, back when we still had old Miss Chandler at our school. I had met Miss Templeton once and I'd seen her several times more, when she came to visit the Boykins. She had marcelled hair that might have looked old-fashioned on somebody else. It had the opposite effect on Miss Templeton, adding, like her Chicago accent, to her romantically mysterious air. Some of the mystery I assigned to Miss Templeton may have been due to her resemblance (at least in terms of her pale skin color and overall good looks) to an oval-framed portrait that Mrs. Faith Boykin had hanging on the wall in her parlor. The portrait was a photograph of Mrs. Boykin's sister, I'd been told, the one who decided that she could go up North and pass for a Greek or an Italian, for what that was worth. I had the impression that the sister's story was not a happy one, but Mrs. Boykin never did give me any tragic details. All I knew was that the sister lived on an island now, off the coast of Georgia. I might have thought the island part was a story Theo and Eugene made up, except the Boykins used to visit her sometimes when Mr. Boykin was still alive. They would take a train to the coast below Savannah and someone would pick them up in a boat. I used to be crazy with jealousy over Theo and Eugene getting a boat ride, which I hadn't ever had in my life.

My brother Force offered to carry Miss Spivey to Miss Templeton's school on Saturday. Momma sent me along to sit in the backseat of the Ford and look out the window, so that anyone could see it wasn't just Force and Miss Spivey going for a ride in the country.

I had never seen Miss Templeton's school before. As the crow flies— and as Theo walked—it was only three miles from Threestep, but to drive there, you had to go five miles straight on through Claytonville and take an old logging road that switched back to the right in a south- westerly direction. This about tripled the distance. Even when you got there, it was set back far enough from the road that you were likely to miss it if you didn't know where to look. The building was made out of unpainted pine, the kind that turns dark brown with time and weather. There were no windows, properly speaking, just some openings covered in oil paper. Most of the light came from the doors at either end and from a pair of kerosene lamps on the teacher's desk, which was set in the middle of the room for maximum illumination. Coming in from broad daylight, we never even saw the skinny girl sitting on a bench in the back of the schoolroom until Miss Templeton told her to stand up. It was that dark inside.

The girl was Etta George, the other student in the high school course. Etta George did not look big enough to be in high school. She had smoldering eyes and not a word to say while she shook hands with "Miss Spivey, Mr. Force, and Miss Cailiff," which was how Miss Temple- ton introduced us to her. I think Etta George would have preferred to skip the handshake, but Miss Spivey never gave anybody a choice in such matters. She stuck her arm out like a pump handle and left it there until you got the idea. Etta's hand was cool but damp, I noticed in the second or two that our palms touched. She appeared greatly relieved when Miss Templeton called her over to the teacher's desk to look at the box full of high school books that we had brought along to show we meant business.

Force had brought these books home from school in Milledgeville during the past week, a few each day so as not to arouse suspicion, since he was not a boy known for his studiousness. Etta George pulled a small book bound in black from the box and used her sleeve to dust the spine. I could say her face lit up, but that would understate the case considerably. "Look at this, Miss Templeton!" she said. "It's Virgil!" After that, the two of them tore through that box like it was Christmas. They kept exclaiming to each other over what they found. Did we really have Millikan–Gale's *Practical Physics*? Miss Templeton said there weren't five high schools in the state of Georgia so advanced as to be using that book. And look here! Seymour's *Solid Geometry*. The whole fourth year of high school was in that box. Miss Templeton straightened up and asked, "When can we begin?"

On the way home, Force and Miss Spivey were silent. This was unnatural, especially for Force. He could not abide a long silence between people. In the passenger's seat, Miss Spivey gripped the door with one hand and her hat—a teal-blue tam that matched her short wool jacket—with the other. We were bouncing along some of the worst roadbed in the county, and Force could hardly afford to turn his head, but he was working up to something, I could tell. Finally, he said, "So they'll be three of them coming."

Earlier, in the schoolhouse, when they were talking over the details—which days they'd meet, what time they'd start, where Miss Templeton could tie the horse, how it would be better to approach the schoolhouse from the woods behind it than from the road out front—during all that talk, I could tell that Miss Spivey was hiding her surprise that Miss Templeton intended to ride all the way to Threestep twice a week instead of getting a little extra sleep while Miss Spivey took over Theo's lessons.

"Three of whom?" she said, almost shouting over the road noise and the engine.

"Theo and Miss Templeton and this Etta. Etta George."

"Oh," Miss Spivey said. "Three of *them*." She sounded almost cheerful when she said it, or maybe the bumps in the road put the lilt in her voice.

"I didn't mean anything by it," Force said.

"Of course not."

"Just, some folks won't like it, that's all."

Miss Spivey looked over at my brother. It was hard for me to read her expression from the backseat, where I was hanging on to the box of books to keep myself in place. He tried again, more directly this time, to make his point.

"Like that Superintendent," Force yelled. "He won't take kindly to you teaching them at Threestep School, Miss Spivey, no matter how early in the morning. It ain't done."

"It is now," she yelled back, sounding too pleased even to correct his grammar.

Miss Templeton showed up at Threestep School on horseback the following Tuesday, as agreed, wearing a black velvet riding jacket and hat and those very funny riding pants that look like you're carrying two loads sideways. The horse had a bit, halter and reins but no saddle. Miss Templeton had been selling things to buy books and supplies. Behind her on the horse, hanging on to her for dear life and probably for warmth, too, sat Etta George. She had on a yellow dress with the skirt hiked up for riding and brown shoes that looked big as footballs at the ends of her long skinny legs. Theo came outside with a lantern and held the horse for them while they dismounted, politely averting his eyes when Etta George's skirt hitched up even higher as she slid down to the ground, and then he tied the horse up behind the schoolhouse, away from the road.

Since Ralphord and I were there, too—Force having decided grimly that a little extra studying wouldn't hurt him, either—Miss Spivey gave each of us a secret mission. My mission was to make sure that anything written on the blackboard in the early morning session was erased "to the point of utter invisibility." I fetched an extra bucket of water for cleaning the blackboard to Miss Spivey's satisfaction. Ralphord was assigned to be the official lookout. He could have performed his duties by watching the road from the schoolhouse door or even through a window, but where was the glory in that?

On the very top of Threestep School, where the four triangles of roof over the schoolhouse came together, there was a little wooden

belfry. It had a weather-vane lightning rod on top and louvered openings on the four sides that were probably meant to let the school bell
clang out in every direction, except that there was no bell, and never
had been. A narrow ladder led up from a door in the half-room ceiling
to a tiny room just big enough for a theoretical bell to swing back and
forth in it. The belfry was murderous in the summer and freezing in the
dead of winter, but in November, with the walnut trees out front being
mostly leafless, Ralphord prevailed upon Miss Spivey to let him keep
watch from up there. "I can see the road a mile in both directions, Miss
Spivey. Won't nobody get past me." She made Ralphord repeat ten times
"Nobody *will* get past me," and then she used a skeleton key to open
the door in the ceiling. Force did a quick sweep with a straw broom for
bats and cobwebs before he boosted Ralphord up through the door. We
heard a little scrambling overhead, and then Miss Spivey called, "Are you
all right up there? Ralphord?"

"I can see Bibbens' store from here, Miss Spivey," he replied.

If anybody came down the road, Ralphord was supposed to do
his magpie call to sound the alarm so that Theo and Etta George and
Miss Templeton could slip out the door and into the woods behind the
schoolhouse, where the horse was tied up and waiting. After the first
half hour's worth of magpie calls—including some from a real magpie, for Ralphord was good enough to fool the birds themselves—Miss
Spivey amended her instructions, calling for an alarm if somebody *suspicious* approached the schoolhouse. Ralphord complained later, "I won't
never get to make a peep if I got to wait for somebody *suspicious* to come
along." I asked him if he knew what "suspicious" meant, and he said,
"Leave me alone, Gladys."

The tutoring—which I know Ralphord pictured as "tootering" in
his mind—worked out better than my brother Force thought it would.
Miss Templeton's horse came and went, swift and relatively silent, in the
early morning darkness, and Theo looked a lot less tired than he used to
in the old days of walking back and forth to the colored school. About
three weeks out, in response to a request from Daddy for a demonstration of something he'd learned thus far, Force conjugated two and a
half Latin verbs right at the supper table. With the third one, he only

got as far as *amat*, which meant, he said, "*you* love," at which point he switched to telling us about Etta George being almost as smart as Theo. "That girl don't say much in English, but in Latin she's quick!" The fact is Etta George wasn't as good as Theo in solid geometry, but she definitely had the edge in third-year Latin, and she kept him on his toes in everything. Although Force trailed behind the both of them, his grades at school began to improve almost instantly—"I passed a Latin test!" he reported—and he was good for everyone's morale. Ralphord kept himself entertained by learning to do catbirds and cardinals and jays—he'd get them making such a racket in the woods behind the schoolhouse that folks began to wonder what had gotten into the birds lately—but he was saving the magpie for when a suspicious character appeared, assuming (correctly) that one day, one would.

5

One of Us

FIELD TRIPS WERE ANOTHER BEE in Mavis Davis's bonnet—both Mavises' bonnets, in fact. Her mother called them "days off."

Miss Spivey believed in field trips. The first time she proposed one, a number of us thought, naturally enough, that she was fixing to take the whole class out to do something like picking cotton. That, of course, is not what she meant at all. "Experiential learning," she kept saying, "is the cornerstone of education for democracy." I doubt the Superintendent of Schools in Claytonville knew what she was talking about any more than we did, but he must have thought it best to play along, at least at first. The WPA was paying Miss Spivey's salary, and the Superintendent did not want to jeopardize that—not to mention, taking any kind of action in regard to Miss Spivey would have required writing a report to the Piedmont County Board of Education. It was widely known that the Superintendent was deeply reluctant to take any step that required the writing of a report. This worked in our favor for a while.

The farthest Miss Spivey ever took us on a field trip—almost a hundred miles each way—was to Andersonville Prison Park, where twelve thousand Union soldiers had died of gangrene and scurvy and thirst. Miss Spivey said she wanted us to see both sides of the coin. Nobody knew what she meant by that. When we arrived, there was nothing much to see: just graves, graves, and more graves—mostly plain white crosses—and a line of white cement posts that showed the outline of where the prison used to be. Miss Spivey did not look one bit disappointed. She marched us to a stone pavilion that marked the spot where a thunderstorm had washed away some dirt on the prison grounds in 1864 and uncovered a freshwater spring that saved the whole town—including some of the prisoners, which fact disappointed both Arnie Lumpkin and Mavis Davis, you could tell—from perishing due to drought.

The trip to Andersonville was the last time the Superintendent let us use the county school bus, a converted Ford truck with wooden sides and benches and a canvas roof. It was open-air, no glass in the windows. Only the fourth- through seventh-graders had gone to Andersonville, which lightened the load some, and we like to flew along that asphalt on Highway 49, but we still didn't get back home before dark. (Mavis's mother had the county sheriff out looking for us, which only made matters worse.) Miss Spivey said we didn't need a bus anyway. From then on, she just begged us a ride off somebody who didn't have much to do on a weekday afternoon. Often, it was Deputy Sheriff Linwood Perkins, although there were some places he refused to drive us, such as the pottery where Theo Boykin worked, on account of the rough language we were likely to hear out there. Our own daddy carried a dozen of us to Hardwick with a truckload of cotton one time to see the textile mill and the Hardwick Asylum. We were glad to have that cloud of cotton bolls to cushion the ride, even if it was a little prickly.

It was Mr. Bibben who delivered us to the public library in Claytonville, after Miss Spivey discovered that not a one of us had ever read a book by H. G. Wells or by any other author she happened to mention. In Claytonville, Miss Spivey made everyone in third grade or above obtain a library card. (The only exceptions were Mavis Davis, who was absent that day, and Florence Hodges, who already had one.) When the librarian, Miss Eunice Spears, pointed out that it was highly irregular to issue library cards to children without their parents' signed consent, Miss Spivey said, with what I thought was a certain dramatic flair, "I'll take full responsibility." Miss Eunice Spears did her best not to look concerned as she watched dozens of her library books, most of them tucked under skinny arms clad in raggedy sleeves and holey sweaters, disappearing into the back of Mr. Bibben's delivery truck.

Tucked under Miss Spivey's arm was a book about camels. She'd found it while helping the librarian demonstrate the card catalogue. At school the next day, she used it to teach us our first camel fact: the difference between a *dromedary* and a *Bactrian* camel—one hump vs. two—a fact she said we could remember by comparing the letter *D* (for dromedary) with a *B*. She also told us that she and Dr. Janet Miller had been the guests of a camel merchant in Baghdad, which is where she learned how to ride one, but she had seen her first camel long before that, at the Museum of Natural History, when she was a girl at boarding school in Paris, France. That camel had belonged to Napoleon Bonaparte, who brought it home from a campaign in Egypt, she said, and donated it to the Paris Zoo. This was back in 17-something-or-other.

Ralphord whistled. "That ol' boy must've been a hunnerd years old when you saw him, Miss Spivey. At least."

Miss Spivey looked at Ralphord as if he were a kind of specimen himself. "It was stuffed, Ralphord," she said. "Napoleon gave it to the zoo, and when it died, the zoo gave it to the museum, and they stuffed it."

"What'd they stuff it with?" Ralphord wanted to know.

"Cornbread," said Miss Spivey.

Ralphord looked like that made pretty good sense to him, but I believe that Miss Spivey felt guilty about misleading him. Before the week was out, she had half the school packed into the back of Mr. Bibben's delivery truck once again, this time for a trip to Toomsboro, where the mortician, Mr. Peeler, had a taxidermy business on the side.

Miss Spivey sat up front with Mr. Bibben, which left Mavis Davis free to make up stories about her in the back of the truck, the most outrageous being that Miss Spivey had been kicked out of school when she was in the fifth grade in none other than Toomsboro, Georgia. "Her mother had to come all the way from Nashville to get her," Mavis said. She had to yell at the top of her lungs, as Mr. Bibben's delivery truck was filled with the noise of the road.

"Those are foul lies," I yelled back from the other side of the truck, trying not to get elbowed while Ralphord and Dalton Veal arm-wrestled at my feet. "What would Miss Spivey be doing at school in *Toomsboro?*"

Mavis stretched her neck over the heads of Florence Hodges and Harriet Eskew. "Her *people* are from Toomsboro," Mavis shouted. "Didn't you *know* that?"

I informed Florence and Harriet that there was no sense in listening to a crazy person.

Mr. Peeler the mortician was a stringy old bachelor of sixty or so. Luckily, he did his taxidermy out in the carriage house behind the funeral home so we didn't have to walk past any dead bodies of the human variety. The first words out of his mouth were about Miss Spivey's grandmother, whom he claimed to have buried out of Toomsboro some years earlier. He did not recall having met Miss Spivey at the funeral, he said, although quite a lot of the family and various friends had come down for it from Tennessee. Instead of telling Mr. Peeler that he must have her mixed up with somebody else, Miss Spivey said, "I was out of the country at the time."

You could have knocked me over with a feather when she said it.

"She was in Baghdad," Ralphord put in, incorrectly. She was at school in France is what she told Mr. Peeler.

I couldn't get over it. If Miss Spivey's people were from Toomsboro, Georgia, didn't that make her one of *us*? Force just laughed when I asked him after school. "And not a Martian, you mean?"

I didn't say so, but in a manner of speaking, that was exactly what I meant.

On our next trip to the Claytonville Public Library, Ralphord's friend Dalton Veal presented Miss Spivey with a book he had located by flipping through the "A" drawer of the card catalogue. (Dalton wasn't the only one who liked to flick his fingernail along the tops of the cards that fit so nicely in those long narrow drawers.) "It was the title caught my eye," he said, "and look here, Miss Spivey." He showed her a full-page illustration of a fellow in a long robe and turban leading a camel on which a veiled lady rode up top in a fancy box. Miss Spivey proceeded immediately to the "A" drawer herself to look for another edition of *The Arabian Nights*, but there was only the one. "A children's picture book!" she said then, sounding so put out that Miss Eunice Spears hurried over to assure her that, despite the turbans and all, there was nothing offensive or inappropriate for children in the book. She had made certain of that.

Not long after that field trip to the library, which proved for a variety of reasons to be our last, the Central of Georgia whistled to a stop in Threestep and left on the cinders beside the tracks another trunk addressed to Miss Spivey. Although it was smaller in its dimensions than the one filled with costumes, this one had almost thrown Mr. Bibben's back out when he presumed to lift it all by himself into his truck. We enjoyed two or three delicious days of speculation regarding what kind of weighty cargo might be inside, after which the mystery was solved when Miss Spivey brought to school Volume I of *The Arabian Nights' Entertainments*, also known, she said, as *The Book of the Thousand Nights and a Night*. There were ten volumes all together. It was a privately printed limited edition translated from the Arabic by Sir Richard F. Burton, Miss Spivey said. They were thick books with hand-cut pages and pale green covers, the titles pressed in gold letters on their spines. Together with a black and gold Underwood typewriting machine, as Mrs. Bibben called it, they made the second trunk that arrived for Miss Spivey, possibly from the bazaars of Baghdad but definitely by way of Nashville, Tennessee, considerably heavier than the first.

In the interest of broadening our minds through exposure to other civilizations, Miss Spivey made room in her already crowded curriculum for regular—in fact, daily—readings from Sir Richard Burton's *Arabian Nights*. Miss Spivey was an excellent reader. She had the way of reading that made beautiful harem girls and handsome youths and shining cities underground come rising up off the pages like *jinni* rising up out of those lamps that look like gravy boats. (*Jinn*, you may know, is the proper word for *genie*. *Jinni* means more than one.) Volume I introduced us to the beautiful, virtuous, and resourceful Shahrazad, wife of the Sultan, who told her husband stories every night and always stopped at the most interesting part, to keep him from cutting off her head in the morning.

"Why would he want to do that?" Mavis Davis asked.

Miss Spivey thought for a minute before she said, "The Sultan did not trust women."

Mavis frowned. "What didn't he trust 'em about?"

"He didn't trust them to behave properly." Miss Spivey put a delicate hint of emphasis on *behave* and paused to let that sink in where it would. In the fifth-grade row, I felt my face flame up. I have always been a blusher.

"I reckon *that* sure enough kept 'em from misbehavin'," said Arnie Lumpkin. He leaned toward Mavis and used his finger as a knife to cut his throat.

"It don't make sense to cut your wife's head off just to make her behave," Mavis grumbled.

Nobody could argue with that.

Some of the stories Miss Spivey read to us all at once. Others took more than a week, in which case it was hard waiting all Saturday and Sunday to find out what would happen next. We soon found that Miss Spivey especially enjoyed reading the descriptions of handsome young princes who were "like the moon on the night of his fullness," and so forth, the more detailed the better. We preferred stories like the one where the handsome prince gets turned into an ape right off the bat when a giant evil *jinn* catches him dallying with a beautiful damsel who was previously kidnapped by the *jinn* and imprisoned in an underground chamber. That's the kind of story we liked.

Miss Spivey always skipped over the dallying parts.

One gray December day when Miss Spivey was reading us "The Tale of the Lame Young Man and the Barber of Baghdad," Mavis Davis raised her hand to ask, "Miss Spivey, what *is* a harem?"

This was not a real question. Mavis already knew what a harem was. I heard her telling Florence Hodges that her mother had looked it up in Claytonville.

Miss Spivey gave herself a minute to think, I expect, by writing *harem* on the blackboard. Then, brushing the chalk dust briskly from her hands, she said, "A harem is a kind of family." That was a good answer, and she could have stopped there, but she didn't. When it came to making trouble for each other, Miss Spivey and Mavis were two of a kind. "It's a family of wives who are married to the same husband," Miss Spivey specified.

"At the same time?" Mavis said, and when Miss Spivey said, "Yes," Mavis said, "The Bible don't allow that. It's not Christian."

"They're not Christians, Mavis, the people in the story."

"They're heathens, you mean."

"No, that's not what I mean. They had a different religion." Miss Spivey looked inspired all of a sudden. She said, "*Their* bible allows it."

"Ain't but one Bible," Mavis said immediately.

I was *extremely* glad Miss Spivey didn't argue with that.

The fact is, there was one thing about *The Thousand Nights and a Night* that came to trouble all of us at least a little—even me—and that was the way the tales always ended. No matter if the girl married the prince, or Alaeddin won the princess, or the fisherman outwitted the *jinn* and threw him back into the sea—at the end of the story, everybody who would have lived happily ever after in another kind of fairy tale wound up "abiding in all cheer and pleasures . . . *till* there came to them the Destroyer of delights and the Sunderer of Societies and the Shatterer of palaces and the Caterer for Cemeteries, to wit, the Cup of Death." That happens to be from the end of "The Seventh Voyage of Sinbad," but all the tales are about the same in this regard. It's the Cup of Death for *everyone* except "the Living One who dieth not!" which, Miss Spivey explained, was Arabian terminology for God.

"How come them stories always end up with everybody *dead*?" Mavis asked in the schoolyard on the day Miss Spivey finished reading "Sinbad."

After a moment of the careful silence with which we all greeted Mavis Davis's questions and complaints, I said, "Do you reckon it's because everybody always does?"

"Does what?" Mavis demanded.

"End up dead."

"Exceptin' Jesus!" Dovie O'Quinn exclaimed, in case He was listening.

Mavis just about turned her face inside out with scowling at me. She said, "That ain't what you read a story for! You want folks to get married and live happily ever after. That's what you want. Ain't it?" She looked around. People nodded vigorously.

She had a point, although I was not about to allow her that in the schoolyard in front of everybody. It did seem kind of dismal to keep reminding folks that everybody winds up six feet under, no matter how happy this particular story turns out. Mavis Davis's mother made it known to the Superintendent of Schools that she did not believe children should be subjected to these dismal reminders. She had already complained about a number of things, as a matter of fact, from the Andersonville field trip to the week we spent on the study of camels, all of which had gone, as her daughter liked to report, "into Miss Spivey's file."

It was shortly after Mavis Davis raised the "harem" question that we came to school and found, neatly printed on the blackboard, a list of tales we had read thus far from *The Thousand Nights and a Night*. We had almost reached the middle of the school year, Miss Spivey said, and it was time to start thinking about the festivities that traditionally marked the last day of school in the spring. (I looked out the window at leafless trees, but who was I to point out that spring was a long way off?) Usually we put on a pageant with Miss Pinkie Lou Griffith accompanying a variety of songs, dances, and recitations by the students. What Miss Spivey had in mind *this* year, she said, was a dramatic production based upon *The Thousand Nights and a Night*.

"A tab blow, you mean?" asked Ralphord. We were familiar with tableaus.

"No, Ralphord," said Miss Spivey, "not a tableau. I mean a dramatic production, full-fledged. A play."

Florence Hodges raised her hand. "Like the plays at the college?"

"Yes!" said Miss Spivey.

"Where they learn the whole thing by heart?"

"Exactly!"

The schoolroom fell silent.

We would vote by secret ballot, Miss Spivey said, to choose one of the tales on the board, but first she wanted to open the floor for discussion. The silence held for another moment—Ralphord's weren't the only eyes that skimmed the wooden floorboards for the opening she mentioned—and then everyone started talking at once.

The little kids wanted "The Tale of the Birds and the Beasts and the Carpenter," not knowing that Miss Spivey had skipped certain unpleasant parts of that story. There were votes for "How Abu Hasan Brake Wind," of course, and Arnie Lumpkin wanted "The Porter and the Three Ladies of Baghdad" because it had the word *bitches* in it so many times. "The Second Kalandar's Tale" was a general favorite, but to stage that one, we'd have to come up with an ape costume for starters, and then there was the battle scene where the sorceress and the huge powerful Ifrit kept turning into lions and bats and a dozen different things, one after the other—a great thing to imagine, Miss Spivey pointed out, but pretty near impossible to perform onstage.

Another tale that most everybody liked was "Alaeddin: Or, the Wonderful Lamp," which was in Volume III. Alaeddin (which is not how most folks spell it, I know, but Miss Spivey went by the book) had several points in his favor. He wasn't so handsome that we would have to listen to her describing his every last mole and eyelash until we were ready to pull our hair out, and he wasn't a prince, either. He was "a scapegrace and a ne'er do well." We liked that. His poor daddy tried to teach him the tailor trade, but Alaeddin "would not sit in the shop for a single day," the story said. And yet, thanks to good luck and sharp wits and a magic lamp, he made it good. We liked that even more. Alaeddin had at his command the most talented and agreeable *jinn*, when it came to producing treasure or sumptuous meals and erecting palaces in the blink of an eye. The erection of palaces, Miss Spivey noted, was incidental to the plot and thus could happen offstage, without significant loss to the action.

Cries of "I hear and obey!" were going up on behalf of Alaeddin when Miss Spivey put a stop to all wild behavior by calling the question, which meant, she explained, that it was time to vote. She told us to tear a corner off a page out of our notebooks—this, I might add, was very difficult for me to do to my one and only notebook—and copy down from the blackboard the title of our choice for the *Arabian Nights* entertainment. She went up and down the aisles, collecting all the bits of paper in a feed sack, and then she had Dovie O'Quinn and myself stand up at her desk and tally them. This was our first real experience with democracy in education. "The Second Kalandar's Tale" had the most votes, despite its technical difficulties, with "How Abu Hasan Brake Wind" a close second. "The Tale of Alaeddin: Or, the Wonderful Lamp" came in third. We handed the results to Miss Spivey. She looked them over, pursing her lips and drawing her lovely eyebrows together, and then her face relaxed into the same kind of little smile she'd smiled that time when my brother Force showed up at the schoolhouse door in the white turban he'd worn all day, glowing with the sunset and looking as regal as any Arabian prince.

Alaeddin it was, she announced.

6

Touzling

IF THE HALLOWEEN COSTUME BALL had folks expecting something big at Threestep School for Christmas or Thanksgiving, they were bound for disappointment. Miss Spivey had little use for holidays overall. She especially disdained what she called *prescribed* holidays, the ones whose observation was required or encouraged by the *Piedmont County Handbook for Teachers*. On Friday, November 11, for example, Miss Spivey had flagrantly ignored the required Armistice Day exercises, which included the teacher's choice of flag ceremonies, patriotic songs, and a pageant or parade where appropriate and practical. Instead, she marched the whole school the half mile to Bibbens' store to pull taffy and drink lemonade. "We went to Andersonville," she told us. "That's enough about war for one school year."

"But we lost *that* one, Miss Spivey," Florence Hodges pointed out. Florence was a sixth-grader. Her mother wrapped her hair in rags every night so she could have locks like Shirley Temple. "Armistice Day is to celebrate for beating the Germans and all."

"Beating the Germans, you say? Hmmm." Miss Spivey licked her buttery, taffy-sweet fingers one by one. Between licks, she asked us who had been reading the paper lately. "Well," she said, digging into her knapsack for a rolled-up *Macon Telegraph*. "Let's see what the Führer is up to today." She unrolled the *Telegraph* and gave it a shake to straighten out the front page. "Look at this photograph where he's inspecting his troops in Austria. Don't look terribly beaten, do they?"

Miss Spivey was always trying to keep us informed about the world situation, but when we heard "Czechs," we pictured tablecloths.

Thanksgiving didn't fare any better than Armistice Day. Where old Miss Chandler liked to deck us out in white paper collars and Pilgrim hats and arrange us into a Plymouth Rock tableau, Miss Spivey let Thanksgiving come and go at school without so much as a turkey feather. She appeared equally content to ignore the whole Yuletide season, although she did loan her supply of robes and turbans and veils to both White Springs Baptist Church and Threestep Methodist, the eventual result being the most authentic-looking shepherds and Wise Men ever seen in middle Georgia.

In the final weeks before Christmas, when our former teacher Miss Chandler would have had us setting up her twelve-panel folding cardboard Nativity scene, Miss Spivey undertook decorating the back wall of the schoolroom (where she had formerly displayed her Baghdad costumes) with scenes from the *Arabian Nights*. Most of the scenes were pictures she called "colored plates." They had arrived with her books, packaged in a beautiful leather envelope that Miss Spivey called a portfolio. Other scenes were done in pencil and colored with crayon on the kind of unruled paper she gave us once a week to do Art. Only Ralphord and I knew that Theo Boykin had drawn these early in the morning while we waited to hear Miss Templeton's horse snort and whinny in the woods behind Threestep School. Theo had made a picture of Alaeddin in the cave of treasure, and another picture in which he knelt, cowering, before a huge-shouldered and somehow familiar-looking *jinn* whose lower end tapered off into the mouth of a brass lamp. A third scene showed a fellow who somewhat favored Mr. Bibben pulling his net from the sea with a great sealed jar tangled in it. That one was depicting THE FISHERMAN AND THE JINN. Above all the pictures, Miss Spivey had stuck black felt letters to the wall, arranged in an arch, to spell out THE ARABIAN NIGHTS.

On the very last day of school before Christmas, as was customary, we all brought presents for the teacher—a pair of pine cones from the Brookins twins, Florida grapefruit from me and Ralphord, little jars of orange and coconut ambrosia (Miss Chandler's favorite) from half a dozen different kids, and so forth. Much to our amazement, Miss Spivey made us give them to each other instead. I got a candy cane from Dovie O'Quinn that lasted me, a lick a day, until March. While we enjoyed our unanticipated treats that day, Florence Hodges noticed a new "colored plate" on the back wall and promptly raised her hand to ask Miss Spivey if she was fixing to read us "a reg'lar fairy tale." The picture, in which a handsome youth in princely clothing gazed with adoration upon a girl sleeping in a fancy bed, had made Florence think of "Sleeping Beauty."

Miss Spivey looked highly interested in the question. "What do you mean by a 'regular fairy tale'?" she asked Florence.

Mavis Davis answered for her. "She means a real fairy tale, where the girl marries the prince and they live happily ever after."

The sleeping beauty picture was from the "Tale of Kamar al-Zaman," which happened to be Miss Spivey's own personal favorite story from The Thousand Nights and a Night, she said. It also happened to be a story in which a princess does marry a prince and they do live happily ever after—up to a point. This being the last day of school before Christmas, Miss Spivey broke with her anti-holiday tradition and proposed to read us her favorite story as a kind of treat, instead of doing arithmetic— which was, she often reminded us, another gift from the Arabs. Miss Spivey got no arguments against trading arithmetic for Arabian Nights, not even from Mavis Davis, who had insisted earlier that we should be reading about Baby Jesus and no room at the inn, this time of year.

The "Tale of Kamar al-Zaman" was definitely the kind of story you would expect to be Miss Spivey's favorite. It featured a Prince and a Princess who were "as like as peas in a pod" and so good-looking "they were a seduction to the pious." Most of the story concerned two Ifrit-type jinni (the most powerful kind) shazaming back and forth between the distant palaces of the Prince and the Princess, trying to decide which one was more beautiful than the other. Miss Spivey's money was on the Prince. No surprise there. He had the usual rosy cheeks and eyebrows arched like bows and eyelids half lowered "like those of the gazelle." His face "shimmered and shone like the rising sun," she read, and his "breath exhaled a scent of musk." When Miss Spivey looked up from the book after reading that part, her face was shining with pleasure.

You would think people could feign interest in the breath and eyelids of a handsome prince out of pure gratitude for the break from arithmetic, but no. Arnie Lumpkin had already put his head down. He was either sleeping or fake-snoring like a jackass. Miss Spivey refrained from comment about his rudeness. Instead, she walked back and forth between the rows, calm as you please, reading the whole time, until she got to Arnie's desk and kicked the chair with her hiking boot. Arnie sat up, blinking, just as the Ifrits snatched the sleeping Princess from her bed and carried her off in the middle of the night.

Now, this, at least, was a promising development. Everybody liked to see Ifrits carrying somebody off. They made the trip to the distant palace of the Prince in a matter of seconds and laid that Princess right next to the Prince (who was also asleep) for purposes of comparison.

"You mean they just put her back to bed?" Ralphord asked. You could hear his disappointment that they hadn't locked the Princess in a casket or turned her into something else, as Ifrits were wont to do.

Miss Spivey looked at Ralphord. She had stopped next to the desk I was sharing with Dovie O'Quinn, and now she put the big book down in front of me. Miss Spivey's finger tapped the page. "Start right here, Gladys," she said. She did that sometimes—handing over the book and having one of us read for a while. She called it participatory learning. Depending on *whom* she gave the book to, it could be a very painful experience for all participants, reader and listeners alike.

I did all right, though. I read how the Ifrits still couldn't agree on who was better-looking, so they smote the ground with their feet to summon up another of their kind to serve as tie-breaker. This one "had nails as the claws of a lion, and feet as the hoofs of the wild ass," which word caused a little titter to cross the room like leaves rustling before a breeze. I blushed, nevertheless enjoying the audience response.

The third Ifrit suggested waking up the Prince and the Princess, one at a time, to test their virtue, the idea being that handsome is as handsome does, so the female Ifritah turned herself into a flea and bit the Prince, never mind where. He woke up, and in the very scene pictured on the schoolroom wall, he took a gander at the Princess and went head over heels. How could he help himself? "Her lips were as coral," and "the water of her mouth"—here I could see another cuss word coming up, but I decided to go on ahead anyway, there being an official reason to say the word, like a preacher would have to say it sometimes whether he wanted to or not. "And the water of her mouth," I read as solemnly as I could, "would quench Hell's fiery pain."

"Are they talkin' about her *spit*?" said Mavis with disgust.

Arnie, who was sitting up straight now, said, "Hush up, Mavis, and let folks read."

But Miss Spivey had taken the book back, and I knew from looking ahead down the page that she would skip the parts that were coming up next, which were the parts of the Princess that Arnie would have liked best to hear about.

"No need to read *all* the descriptions," Miss Spivey said. She glanced up at the clock—it was a quarter after two—and then, as if she'd suddenly made up her mind, she surprised everybody by wishing us a merry Christmas and added, "Class dismissed."

That schoolhouse emptied as fast as if the Sunderer of Societies had paid us a call. Benches and chairs squealed back and clattered onto the desktops, where everybody knew to put them at the end of the week, and a heartfelt chorus of "Merry Christmas, Miss Spivey!" floated above the deeper thunder of footsteps pounding right on out the door. Ralphord ran off to O'Quinn's with Dalton Veal. By eighteen minutes past two on the schoolroom clock, Miss Spivey and I were alone.

I set to work washing the blackboards and cleaning the erasers, as usual. Miss Spivey sat down at her desk. When I was finished inside, I went outside to close the shutters, except for the ones on the window right next to her, which she liked to have open a few inches even in the winter. Then I lowered the flag and folded it up the way Daddy showed us to do, which he had learned in the Army. I took my time about it, and when I came back in, Miss Spivey was writing in a notebook, with the light from the window shining on one side of her face and setting her red hair on fire. The rest of the schoolroom was in that grayish dark you get when you close up a room in the daytime, stripes of light leaking through the shutters. I stood just inside the door with the triangle of American flag in my arms and watched her for a while. When I shifted my weight on the squeaky wooden floor, Miss Spivey looked up.

"Gladys," she said. "You're still here?"

"Yes, ma'am." I stepped up to offer her the flag. She took it from me with both hands and set it on the desk. Then I said, "Miss Spivey?"

She folded her hands on top of the flag. "Yes, Gladys?" she said.

Right then I wished I had gone ahead and bought her a package of cigarettes for Christmas, like I'd had a mind to do. They had a box at Bibbens' store with a *camel* right on the front, but Mr. Bibben wouldn't sell them to me unless I told him who they were for. So here I was, empty-handed, and here was Miss Spivey, waiting to hear what I supposedly had to say. I could have taken this opportunity to ask about her Toomsboro days, if any, but the time didn't seem right. That's when my eye lit on *The Thousand Nights and a Night* on her desk, lying open to the page where we'd left off.

"Miss Spivey," I said, "d'y'all reckon it's *possible* to fall in love with somebody, when they don't even know you're there?"

That wasn't what she was expecting me to ask—I could tell by the way she moved her shoulders—but she didn't miss a beat. She turned my question around on me, the way teachers do. "What do *you* think, Gladys?" she said.

"Don't seem likely to me. I mean, what can you tell about a person just by looking at 'em? 'Specially if they're asleep."

"Asleep?" she said. Her face changed again. "Oh—you mean in the story!" She sat back a little. Then she pushed the flag off to the side and pulled the heavy book into the light. "Well," she said briskly, "let's just see."

She started reading to me at about the place where I left off. I was so caught up with worrying over whether I'd made a fool of myself by asking such a question that I wasn't really listening at first. It took me a while to realize that Miss Spivey had gone right on reading, even when she got to the Prince admiring such parts of the sleeping Princess as her "breasts like two globes of ivory, from whose brightness the moon borrows light," and her "thighs smooth and round," and her "calf like a column of pearl," and her "back parts"—her back parts, mind you—"like a hillock of blown sand." (Later, I did think to wonder how the Prince could admire her breasts *and* her back parts at the same time. She must have rolled over.) Pretty soon Prince Kamar's "reason was confounded" by the beauty of the sleeping Princess and "natural heat began to stir in him," but Miss Spivey still did not stop reading, not even when he "loosed the collar of her chemise," at which point the Ifrits did us all a favor and put him back to sleep.

Whew, I thought.

My relief was premature. Those Ifrits woke up the Princess next, and things got worse. She went and "opened the bosom" of Prince Kamar's shirt, and her hand "slipped down to his waist," and "her heart ached and her vitals quivered." Miss Spivey was breathing light and quick, like somebody walking uphill, but she still kept on reading, right up to where the Princess, who admitted to being "ashamed of her own shamelessness" (and rightly so, I thought), went all out and begged that Prince to wake up, saying, "'My life on thee, hearken to me, awake and up from thy sleep and look on the narcissus and the tender down thereon, and enjoy the sight of naked waist and navel, and tumble me and touzle me from this moment till break of day!'"

There, finally, Miss Spivey stopped reading. She straightened up and looked around, as if she had just remembered where she was, which was how she wound up staring directly into the blue, blue eyes of my brother Force, who was standing *outside* the window next to her desk, where I, for one, hadn't seen him until just this very minute.

How long had he been standing out there listening? It seemed like an important question after the fact, but at the moment I was too busy asking myself if I understood what I thought I did from what Miss Spivey had just read. Of course I knew what *naked* meant—it was a word that focused the attention—and I also knew *navel*, and I happened to know that *narcissus* was a flower because it was one of my mother's favorites in the spring.

Tumble, I thought, could mean a lot of different things.

All the while I was thinking, Miss Spivey and my brother Force were looking straight at each other, my brother's eyes gone deep as midnight the way they do, and his cheeks all rosy and his eyebrows arched like bows, and Miss Spivey gazing back at him as if she had been turned to stone. Then Force said, "Mind if I have a look at that there?" at which point Miss Spivey jumped to life and dropped the book into her lap like a hot potato. If that hurt, she gave no sign. She picked the book up, real slow, and handed it through the window. She didn't even have to get up to do it, the window was that close and so was he. Force said, "Thank you, ma'am."

He hunched over that book for a long time, resting his elbows on the outside windowsill, turning the page back and forth, before he asked her, "What does this word *touzle* mean?" He said it to rhyme with *bamboozle*.

For a moment, it looked like Miss Spivey either didn't know or couldn't bring herself to say. She cleared her throat, delicately at first, and then in a businesslike fashion. After one more glance at Force, she twisted in her chair so as to give him her back and explained to me that in some contexts the word *touzle* was a synonym—I knew *contexts* and *synonym* from previous explanatory situations—for *twiddle*. "As in 'twiddling one's thumbs,'" she added quickly, and she lifted her hands from the desk to demonstrate.

7

Ohio

THE YEAR 1939 BEGAN with a cold snap. On the Monday we returned
to school, Ralphord and I scraped frost off the schoolhouse windows
while Force hauled in more wood. Miss Spivey was worried about
attendance, she said, but children started to arrive before long, puffing
like dragons in the doorway, the smoke pouring out of the schoolhouse
chimney drawing them in. I couldn't remember Arnie Lumpkin ever
returning to school after the holidays, but here he was, wrapped in a
blanket like a cigar-store Indian. Other children were similarly swaddled
in blankets and oil cloth, some with jackets and coats underneath, some
without. I recognized a pair of velvet drapes from their daddy's funeral
parlor on the Brookins twins.

The cold kept Miss Templeton and Etta George home on Tuesday
morning, which proved to be a lucky thing. Momma had declared that
it was too cold to walk a mile, so Daddy carried us to school—Force and
me and Ralphord and Theo Boykin—under a layer of hay in his wagon.
Neither his Model A truck nor the T-Model Ford would start. Ralphord
looked grateful when Miss Spivey said it was too cold to climb up to
his lookout post. He was dozing in a cocoon of blankets later when we
heard a loud grunt and a scraping sound, followed by the sudden rattle

of one of the shutters, as if someone had fallen against it. Force leaped up and ran outside, just in time to see someone plunge into the laurel bushes behind the outhouse and take off crashing through the woods, so bundled up Force couldn't tell who or what it was. Miss Spivey called him back. She said we'd find out soon enough who it was and added, to my delight, that we might as well light the stove. Smoke hadn't been curling up out of the chimney five minutes—Force and Theo both having vacated the premises—before children started showing up at the door. The velvet-clad Brookins twins were the first to arrive. Mavis Davis was the second or third, depending on how you counted the twins.

On Wednesday, Mavis couldn't say just *how* the Superintendent of Schools in Piedmont County had found out that Miss Spivey was teaching lessons to a colored boy and a white boy together at Threestep School. "Why can't she just say Theo Boykin and Force Cailiff, for heaven's sake?" my sister Ildred exclaimed. "Everybody knows what boys she's talking about!" Mavis *was* able to report, however, thanks to her mother's habit of keeping her ear to the ground in her capacity as secretary to the Superintendent, that this information did not sit well with him. Miss Spivey had to close school at noon on Thursday and hitch herself a ride to Claytonville for a scolding.

The Superintendent started by taking the reasonable approach, Miss Spivey said later. He pointed out that there was a high school for Theo to attend in Claytonville, and that the Piedmont County Board of Education, at whose pleasure he himself served, was responsible for determining the curriculum best suited to the needs of students in that school and every other school in the county. Could she imagine what it would be like if *every* teacher was at liberty to choose whatever she saw fit to teach to each individual student? (She *could* imagine that, but she didn't say so.) He even allowed that Miss Spivey's impulse to assist the colored boy was no doubt a selfless and commendable one.

However.

In the country schools, of which Threestep was one, teachers were required to focus their energies on the elementary grades, where basic skills were learned and where the great majority of the population was likely to be served. Regrettably, Miss Spivey had shown an unfortunate disregard for her youngest students, as she preferred to lavish her attention—she knew he was getting warmed up when he said *lavish*, Miss Spivey said—on two adolescent boys. When it came to that, he was not even going to mention the impropriety of meeting, in secrecy, with two boys who were nearly old enough to be considered young men. One of them colored. And the other—well, the Superintendent was not at liberty to reveal details, but he did not mind telling her that Force Cailiff had a history.

"Everyone has a history," Miss Spivey had said, even though she must have known a smart mouth wouldn't get her anywhere.

There would be no more tutoring, the Superintendent declared, pausing, Miss Spivey said, after each word. For. Emphasis.

"I thought he was finished then," Miss Spivey reported. "But he was not."

The Superintendent had many more things to object to, now that he'd gotten started. Field trips, for example. When Miss Spivey called them an "indispensable pedagogical tool," the Superintendent informed her that Miss Chandler, who taught school in Threestep for more than forty years, had never taken anybody anywhere. He was getting so many complaints—mostly from the parents of the smaller children Miss Spivey often sent home on field trip days—that he felt obliged to inform her that parents expected their children to spend the school day in *school* (especially children who were too small to be useful at home, although he didn't put it that way). He said it went without saying, although he was taking great pains to say it at considerable length, that the children were supposed to be learning their lessons, and not gallivanting all over the county.

There would be no. More. Field trips.

For that matter, there could be a lot less of these "Arabian Nights" in the schoolroom, from what he'd heard. Children, especially the younger ones, were highly impressionable and some of them had a hard time distinguishing fairy tales from reality, a fact of which he would have expected her to be aware, given her advanced training in the field of education and her fancy degree. (He didn't say "fancy degree," but he was thinking it, Miss Spivey said.) Children were coming home and spilling kerosene out of lamps to look for genies. They were digging up front yards and pastures in search of secret trapdoors into the earth.

"I had no idea," Miss Spivey said, sounding pleased.

The Superintendent informed her that she had given him no choice but to write a report to the county Board of Education (really, to have Mrs. Mavis Davis write a report which he would then edit heavily, lest the board think that *scandalous* and *hussy* were *his* favorite words). If it weren't for the reluctance of the board to jeopardize future WPA appointments in Piedmont County, the Superintendent said, he would feel compelled to take more serious disciplinary action at this time.

We were waiting for her at Bibbens' store when Deputy Sheriff Linwood Perkins brought her back from Claytonville that afternoon—me and Ildred and Momma, and Force and Ralphord and Mrs. Bibben, who was minding the store. The deputy sheriff didn't say howdy or even wave at the crowd who came out on the porch when he dropped her off, which we immediately took as a bad sign. In fact, from what I could see of him through the windshield while Miss Spivey got out of the car, he looked mad. Miss Spivey had a scarf pulled up over her face against the cloud of dust the deputy sheriff's tires raised as he pulled away faster than he needed to, but when she let the scarf fall, she looked as cheerful as ever. Her foot had not yet landed on the first porch step—she wore the hiking boots to go see the Superintendent! we saw with dismay—before I burst out, "Are y'all fired?"

Miss Spivey laughed. "Gladys," she said, hustling us back inside the store, "that is the very same question Mr. Perkins asked me after my little chat with the Superintendent."

Linwood Perkins had, in fact, waited for her on a bench in the hall outside the Superintendent's office with his hat in his hands.

Miss Spivey sat down on an overturned barrel next to the Bibbens' woodstove. She plucked her felt tam off her head and dropped it in her lap. "No, I am not fired," she said at last.

I let out the breath I'd been holding.

"I'm on probation."

"What's that mean?" Force asked her.

"He'd like to send me packing, is what it means," Miss Spivey said. "But he can't afford to do it."

She untied the white scarf around her neck and gave us her report. "I don't know what makes him think we limited our gallivanting to the county," she said when she came to the field trip part.

"I hope you didn't say that to him, Miss Spivey!" Momma said.

"No, Mrs. Cailiff, I did not say a word. I bowed my head and beat my breast and vowed to amend my ways. No more field trips, no more tutoring adolescent boys of any kind or color, and no more *Arabian Nights*." Miss Spivey looked around Bibbens' store at our long faces and added, "I lied, of course!" We brightened up immediately. Then she turned thoughtful. "We'll have to find some other place to meet, however. For the tutoring, I mean. We can go to Miss Templeton's school, if we have to. How far is that from here—Force?"

"Five miles to Claytonville and another, say, four on the switchback. Nine miles driving, Miss Spivey." Force knew how far it was to everywhere. He got around.

"That's a long piece to drive before daybreak." Momma sounded doubtful. "In the dark. On that old road."

"And you'd have to go through Claytonville to get there," Ildred pointed out. She was sitting on the inside ledge of the storefront window display, leaning against some bags of chicken feed. Ildred hadn't said much to me about the high school lessons, or tutoring, or "whatever they call it." I think she found it worrisome, just like Force did, but she could see how important it was to Theo, and she didn't want to be the one to talk it down. "I reckon you'd have to hide folks"—she meant Theo, Miss Templeton, and Etta George—"when you were driving through town."

"That doesn't sound very convenient," Miss Spivey said.

"Or y'all could go to May's in McIntyre."

Everybody looked at me. Momma frowned. "That's just as far, Gladys. Farther, I expect."

"But going the opposite way," I said. Nowhere near Claytonville.

"It would be just as dark."

"Not if we went on Saturday!" That was Force, proving that there was a brain inside that handsome head of his. "On Saturday, we wouldn't have to go so early. We could wait till it was light."

"But Theo works on Saturdays, don't he?" asked Mrs. Bibben, who had learned of the tutoring only recently and didn't outright disapprove. Also, to her credit, she did not mention that Miss Spivey was in the habit of minding the store on Saturday morning, so the Bibbens could go fishing.

Ildred said, after a tiny pause, "Theo only works at the pottery till noon on Saturday."

"Then y'all could do your schooling business on Saturday *afternoon*," Mrs. Bibben pointed out happily.

Miss Spivey, meanwhile, was giving me just the kind of thoughtful look I was hoping for. She said, "Your sister May might not appreciate having us underfoot."

"I expect she'd enjoy the company," I said. "Don't you think so, Momma?"

Momma frowned. "Might be *too* much company for Ed."

"He'll go along with it," Force said. "Ed always goes along."

Momma looked like she was not so sure that Ed would go along, but she did allow that McIntyre was in the next county. Wilkinson.

"And this *here's* Piedmont County," Force said, just in case anybody had forgotten. "Piedmont County Superintendent don't hold no sway in Wilkinson, does he?'

"No, he *does not*," Miss Spivey said.

Force carried us to McIntyre the very next Saturday in Daddy's truck. Ralphord and I both went along as usual. Ralphord got out near O'Quinn's mill to go fishing, at which point Theo Boykin climbed into the back of the truck and ducked under the tarp to stay out of sight. Luckily, the weather had warmed up considerably. We picked Miss Templeton up behind the second little white church east of Threestep. Miss

Spivey said it was a real crime, to make a grown lady hide out in the back of the truck like that, but Miss Templeton said there was no sense asking for trouble. "Any more than we already have," she added, tying a scarf around her head, hat and all, in preparation for the ride. She punched up the cushion she'd brought to sit on and let Force and Theo each take a hand to help her up into the truck.

I am sorry to say that Etta George did not go with us out to May and Ed's place. She was afraid to get any more mixed up in it, Miss Templeton admitted. Etta continued to study Latin with Miss Templeton in the early mornings at their country school, using my brother's third-year Latin book, which he had to pay for out of his own pocket when he told his teacher it was lost.

May was waiting for us on the porch that ran across the front of their tin-roofed house, little Ed in her arms. She was wearing the same calico dress she wore on most special occasions, with a man's canvas jacket over it. Her hands were lost in the sleeves. She had her Sunday shoes on and her hair pulled back with the mother-of-pearl combs she got for a wedding present years ago. Little May was leaning up against her momma, one arm hooked around May's knee, and the three bigger girls stood in a clump next to her, all in calico dresses and sweaters, looking like smaller versions of May.

As soon as Force cut off the engine, May handed little Ed to the girls and hurried down the two wooden steps and across the yard to open the car door for Miss Spivey.

"Y'all mind if I join in?" she said before Miss Spivey's foot touched ground. "Ed says it's all right."

I followed May's glance back over her shoulder and saw Ed in his overalls, standing in the doorway to the barn. He waved and yelled, "Howdy," before he retreated into the darkness behind him. Ed was a quiet man overall, compared to his business partner Ebenezer, but it wasn't like him to miss a chance to talk to folks. I expect he wanted us in the house and out of sight, in case somebody else happened by the place while Theo and Miss Templeton were on the premises. Ed spent the three hours out in the barn, banging and clanging things—he didn't have any livestock inside, just old hay and stove parts and an automobile carcass—so we wouldn't forget he was there. After a while, May sent me out to make sure the girls weren't climbing up in the hayloft, their daddy not being accustomed to keeping an eye out for danger the way May was.

Out in the barn, Ed asked me, "What're they doin' in there?"

I said, "Algerbra." May wasn't ready for solid geometry, Miss Spivey said. I asked Ed if he happened to know that *algebra* was named after an Arab called Al-Jabr. I also pointed out that the Arabs invented numbers as we know them.

He shook his head. "What's she wanna learn algerbra? What's it good for?"

I had no idea, but thinking of Theo, I said, "For going to college, I reckon."

While Ed and I were talking, the girls were busy pulling out handfuls of hay and throwing it all over the place under the hayloft, squealing and sneezing. Little May got to her feet on top of a bale and when Ed snatched her up with one arm around her middle, she said, "Daddy, I'm hungry! I want some pie." They knew there was pecan pie in the house. They'd seen Theo carry it in. That set them all off.

"Kin we have pie?"

"Daddy! I want me some pie!"

"I'm *hungry*, Daddy!"

Ed blew out a breath and swung little May to the barn floor while they kept up pouncing on him. "I sure don't see no college 'round here."

"I know," I said, but I was thinking that I wished he'd go inside and see for himself how May bowed her head over the algebra book and marked the place with her finger while she copied numbers and letters into the notebook Miss Spivey had given her. I'd never seen numbers and letters put such a blissful expression on anyone's face before. "I reckon she's just—interested—in it, Ed."

"Beats me why." Ed looked mournful, like he couldn't see how his wife's interest in algebra was going to bring any good in his direction or hers.

"Beats me, too," I said, mostly to be agreeable, and I thought Ed looked like he felt a little better.

The Superintendent of Schools may not have been at liberty to reveal the details of Force Cailiff's "history" to Miss Spivey, but either he went ahead and revealed them anyway, or somebody else must have told her about my brother and the college girl from Ohio who started asking him for rides in the country back when Force first learned to drive the T-Model Ford. He was studying how to park in Milledgeville one day and pulled right up to where that girl was standing on the curb waiting to cross Columbia Street. That was how it got started. It ended with her having to leave school, and Force crying and carrying on because she was gone back up to Ohio, which was where she was from, and how was he ever going to see her again? He was set to marry her, he said, no matter if she was four years older than he was, but Momma said he wasn't marrying nobody at the age of fifteen. He even climbed out a window one night and walked all the way to Claytonville, intending to hop a Southern Railway freight when it slowed down at the siding. He was fixing to follow her all the way to Toledo. The deputy sheriff, who went with our daddy to bring him home, asked Force if he wanted to get that girl in more trouble than she was already in by forcing the law to go after her for corrupting a minor. "A who?" Force said. "You mean me? She didn't corrupt me none. She just—"

"Stop right there, son," the deputy sheriff warned, "before you say something incriminatin'."

We were two years past that particular disaster, and Force had long since stopped sending letters that the girl's parents probably tore up before she ever got a chance to see them, but it had been news to Miss Spivey, whatever her sources, and it had a certain effect on her. We all noticed it at school. For days after her chat with the Superintendent, Miss Spivey kept talking about Ohio. Geography lessons, history lessons— they were all about Ohio. "What fortification important in the French and Indian War was located where the Allegheny and the Monongahela rivers come together to form the mighty *Ohio*?" Miss Spivey would ask, her skirt flaring when she said *Ohio*.

The answer, in case you're wondering, is Fort Ticonderoga.

At about that same time, all my agitation over how to ask Miss Spivey about her Toomsboro connections without her taking offense proved to be for naught. When I finally asked her after school one day if what I'd heard about her being from around these parts was true, Miss Spivey freely admitted that her daddy's people came from Toomsboro.

I was standing beside her teacher's desk. Through the window I could see Ralphord in the schoolyard, moving toward the outhouse. He was hopping on one foot. I said, "You don't talk like you're from 'round here."

"I never lived in Toomsboro," said Miss Spivey. She straightened up the notebooks she'd been correcting. "But I did spend one summer with my grandmother there. I thought we were going to a place she had on the sea islands, but it was Toomsboro for the duration. I didn't take it well, as I recall. It was too bad, really. A chance to get to know Grandmother Spivey—they kept me away from her most of the time, she was a *do-gooder*, you see—and all I did was sulk. I was about your age, Gladys, but obviously not as mature." Miss Spivey looked regretful, and then she told me the amazing fact that she *had* attended the one-room school in Toomsboro for three days while she waited for her mother to come get her at the end of that summer. "My grandmother thought I might enjoy the experience, and she *knew* my mother wouldn't like it, so off I went."

I wasn't sure what to say to that. I asked, "*Did* you enjoy it?"

"It was very different from what I was used to," Miss Spivey said, and she added, in that slightly sad voice people use when they can't believe how long ago something that seems like yesterday really was, "That was back in 1921."

She looked out the window then, as if the past might be spread out there for her to view. Instead, there was my brother Force, loping up into the schoolyard from the road. He saw us through the glass when he got closer and waved, handsome as usual in his uniform jacket and gray pants, and then he kept on going around the back of the school, out of view. I said, "My brother Force was born in 1921."

Miss Spivey sat up a little straighter behind that big desk of hers. "Oh, yes," she said. "I know."

Her eyes had gotten bright, watching Force cross the schoolyard. I could tell she wasn't thinking about her grandmother in Toomsboro anymore when she peered around the room, as if to make sure there was no one else in earshot. The only thing resembling a person other than the two of us was the skeleton we made for Halloween, which was still hanging in the corner as if he'd misbehaved, sporting a big old gourd for a head in place of the deer skull. Miss Spivey leaned toward me. Both of her lightly penciled eyebrows, which were high and round like little crescent moons most of the time, went straight and dark. I was sorely afraid she was about to tell me that she *did* get thrown out of that one-room school, just like Mavis said, but Miss Spivey hunkered down over her desk and divulged to me instead that my brother Force, the only one of us to be born in a hospital as you'll recall, had been switched at birth with the son of an Arabian princess who was in exile at the time, having fled certain death back home in Baghdad. (It seemed the usual way to remove a person from office there was to remove his head and the heads of all his relations.) Switching the babies was an extra precaution, Miss Spivey said, in case the new Caliph's henchmen ever caught up with the princess and her entourage, which, sad to say, they eventually did. In Ohio, as a matter of fact. My real brother, Miss Spivey said, had perished with the rest in Ohio.

I said, "Are you sure about that, ma'am?"

She was sure.

"Y'all're saying that Force is no kin to us at all?"

"You must never tell a soul," Miss Spivey said.

"Force never said nothing about it."

"He wouldn't know, would he?" Miss Spivey said.

"But what about Momma?"

"She doesn't know, either." Miss Spivey's eyebrows were one dark line now. She said, lowering her voice further, "I shouldn't have told you this."

But seeing as she had, she also told me where to look for proof. Inside the crook of my brother's right arm was a scar about the size of a quarter. I'd always heard that it was from some hot wax that dripped on him when he was little, but Miss Spivey said no. She said that's where his birthmark shaped like an eagle used to be. She even showed me, in a book she had, where it said that the caliphs of Baghdad were descended from the kings of Georgia, and how heirs to the throne were born with the mark of an eagle on their right arm. "I never heard of them having kings in Georgia," I said, but Miss Spivey explained that there was another Georgia someplace way over on the other side of the world. I didn't believe that at first, but it was true! She showed me on the map.

"And this here other Georgia is where Force's people come from?"

"That's right," she said. "In the distant mists of time, before they moved south to Baghdad."

Miss Spivey and I turned as one to look (south) out the window. We saw Force and Ralphord, the both of them side by side, swinging on the outhouse door.

"We were testing it," Force explained when they came in to get me. "To see how it was holdin' up."

On the way home, I kept stealing glances at Force. He was wearing his jacket, so I couldn't see the pale skin on the inside of his arm, right in the crook of his elbow, where a patch that was pinker and shinier than the rest of him had always put me in mind of a pink butterfly. When Force caught me looking, I knew before he said a word that she had told him, too. He stopped in the road, letting Ralphord go on without us, and said, "That's just a story she told you, Gladys."

I was so surprised that I forgot to pretend not to know what he was talking about. I said, "You don't believe Miss Spivey? You reckon she *lied*?"

"I *reckon* she made up a story. There's a difference, Gladys, between lying and making up a story."

I waited, but he didn't say what the difference was.

8

White Dirt

IT MAY SEEM OBVIOUS to you that my brother Force was *not* an Arabian prince switched at birth, and that Miss Spivey had indeed made up a story, possibly one that she did not expect me to believe any more or less than I believed in Alaeddin and his lamp. I was eleven, after all, old enough to know better. However, the more I thought about the story she told me, the more it seemed to explain—if it happened to be true.

Folks were always asking Momma, in a dreamy voice, as if they were ruminating on one of the mysteries of the universe, "Miz Cailiff, where *did* that boy of yours come from?" I heard Mrs. Faith Boykin use those very words one time when she and Momma were watching my brother Force chop up a tree that fell between our house and theirs. Force was making two piles of firewood, one for us and one for the Boykins. He had his shirt off, and they could see him gleaming from the porch. Momma said something like, "He come in from Milledgeville on that three o'clock bus, Miz Boykin. It's likely he left school early again." But Mrs. Faith Boykin shook her head. Watching her woodpile grow, she said, "I believe that boy come straight from heaven."

At school, Miss Spivey would read a tale about some "youth cast in beauty's mould, all elegance and perfect grace; so fair that his comeliness deserved to be proverbial," and all I could think about, once I made sense of the vocabulary, was how that described my brother Force at age seventeen to a T. Who would deny that he, too, was capable of "ravishing every heart with his loveliness," and so forth? If I tried to point that out to Force, he'd just ruffle my hair and say, "Looks like you'd *want* me for your brother, Gladys, if I'm good as all that."

I did want him for a brother, but the way I was starting to look at it, if Miss Spivey's story *was* true, then I would not be losing a brother so much as gaining a prince. I daydreamed of harem ladies hiding in wagons pulled by magnficent horses, rolling up through Georgia on their way to Ohio and their doom. I pictured men of the desert in red leather boots chasing after them with swords drawn and robes flying, and on another, quieter road, I imagined an Arabian princess on a solitary camel, hoping in vain to elude those rival horsemen, with the baby who should have grown up to be my brother Force hidden under her long veil. If you picture Mary fleeing Bethlehem on a donkey with the baby Jesus, you'll know roughly what I had in mind. Except on a camel. And meanwhile, miles away at the hospital in Savannah, my own mother would be singing a lullaby (in a voice just like my sister May's) to the tender young prince who would grow up to ravish pretty near every available heart in our humble town of Threestep, Georgia, and the surrounding area. I ask you, who could resist a story like that? Not me.

And don't forget the way he looked in that turban.

On Saturdays out in McIntyre, May and Miss Spivey hit it off right from the start. All the shyness that my sister had shown when she first met Miss Spivey quickly turned into a kind of easy friendliness that I had never seen in May outside of her relations with family. May told Miss Spivey where to sit, just like that, and asked her personal things, such as how she got her hair to curl up so nice on the ends. Miss Spivey told May that with a voice like hers she ought to run away to New York City and make herself a fortune on the radio. (I was glad Ed didn't hear that.) When Miss Spivey told May to call her by her first name, Grace,

May said, "Mmmm, I don't think that's a good idea, Miss Spivey. You're the teacher."

Miss Spivey said, "You know, you're absolutely right, Mrs. Peacock," that being May's married name, and they both laughed like girls.

May admired Miss Spivey's teal-blue tam with so much enthusiam one Saturday that Miss Spivey showed up the next week with a pink one to give May. (Miss Spivey had a whole wardrobe of those tams, which she called *berets*.) I thought this would be a problem, seeing as how my sister was well known for her refusal to take anything from anybody for fear she might be accepting charity. Once, when Ed was on the road and she was down to one potato in the house, May spent a whole day walking eight miles to Threestep with her girls in a line behind her and little Ed a tiny baby in her arms, rather than "borrow" something from one of her neighbors. After that, Momma used to get Mr. Bibben to stop at May's while Ed was gone to make sure she didn't run out of food again. May wouldn't take a single can of condensed milk even from Mr. Bibben unless he swore up and down that Momma and Daddy had paid for it in advance. Mr. Bibben told Momma that if he never got to heaven, it would be on account of all the fibs he'd had to tell May. And yet, when Miss Spivey placed that pink tam on my sister's head at a jaunty angle, May did not utter a single word of protest. "With your black hair?" Miss Spivey said, stepping back to get a better look. "May, it is *stunning.*" My sister not only consented to keeping that tam-o'-shanter, she wore it every time she stepped out of the house for the rest of the winter (and sometimes inside as well).

Of all of them, the person who was most serious about the tutoring—the one who made sure that a full hour was spent on mathematics, one on Latin, and one on literature every Saturday, with only the briefest of breaks in between—was Miss Templeton. Miss Templeton gave the impression, from the moment they sat down, that time was running out, which, in more ways than we knew, was quite true. Miss Templeton taught solid geometry to Theo and Force, and did third-year Latin lessons with Theo alone, now that Etta George was out of the picture. Her absence was like a shadow over the table. It was hardest on Miss Templeton, but I think we all missed the sound of Etta's voice going back and forth with Theo's when nouns were being declined or Cicero recited, sentence by sentence. Miss Spivey covered beginning Latin for both May and Force. He had learned so little at school that he needed to start all over again.

I loved to watch May and Force study Latin together. To me, it was worth going to McIntyre every Saturday just for that. If he was an Arabian prince, then May had to be a princess, they favored each other that much. Their eyes were the same changeable blue, and they both had the same unruly curl, stubborn as a cowlick, falling onto their foreheads, even if May pulled her hair back tight with her mother-of-pearl combs. May's face was a thinner, paler version of his, her chin a little sharper, the lines etched a little deeper at the corners of her eyes and lovely mouth. She was twelve years older than Force, after all. They would sit side by side at the table, May in a pink sweater set that someone had sent to Miss Spivey ("Do I *look* like a person who could wear pink?" Miss Spivey had said) and Force in a threadbare uniform shirt demoted to Saturday use, each of them writing out answers in Latin to questions in the book they shared. Force would wait until Miss Spivey wasn't looking, and then he'd lean closer and closer to May until his chin was resting sweetly on her pink cardigan shoulder, their faces almost cheek to cheek, so he could copy what she had written down.

Literature they all studied together, both English and American. They had a whole pile of plays by William Shakespeare that everybody in high school had to learn. I didn't know what half the words meant, if that, but somehow the sense of it usually came through. You knew Iago didn't mean Othello any good just by the sound of what Force and Theo were reading off the page. They were all good readers—including Force, who could sound words out and utter them with conviction even when he didn't know what he was saying—but May was the best. When May said, "The quality of mercy is not strained," you had to believe it. You could *hear* it "droppeth as the gentle rain upon the earth below." You could feel it falling on your shoulders.

We hadn't been going out to May's on Saturday for all that long when Ralphord and I came to school one Monday and found that the black felt letters on the back wall, right above where all the pictures were, no longer spelled out THE ARABIAN NIGHTS. Now they said, THE B IN NI TS. Miss Spivey was standing on a chair, so intent on making two new words up there underneath THE B IN NI TS that Ralphord and I did not say good morning for fear she might fall off the chair. We stood quietly behind her instead, far enough back so as not to look up her skirt (a tartan plaid that she wore with a white blouse trimmed in velvet). We watched while she combined the original letters, which Theo Boykin had made for her, with new ones, clearly the work of a lesser talent, to spell out: BAGHDAD BAZ R.

Miss Spivey stepped down from the chair. She did not appear surprised to see us when she turned around. "I need *two* more A's," she said.

She had taken up a scissors and set to work cutting out another A, when she looked up suddenly and asked us, "Where's Force?"

I told her Daddy had dropped us off. A shadow of disappointment flitted across Miss Spivey's face. She cut a few more snips and held up a new A, which was completely different in size and shape from the ones that were already up there.

Ralphord said, "That's real nice, Miss Spivey."

Sometimes that boy surprised me.

Everybody noticed the new sign. The first word was no problem for anybody. After all *The Arabian Nights* we'd been through, even the first-graders knew *Baghdad*. We could say it, we could spell it, we could make Sir Richard Burton's version of it rise up in our minds: narrow streets, onion domes, magic lamps, and all. The other word was new. Hands went up.

"Not *bizarre*," Miss Spivey said. "*Bazaar.*" It meant a kind of Fall Fun Fair, she told us, except ours would be held in the spring. Late May or very early June, she was thinking. She seemed unconcerned about when the school year was officially over. "That should give us enough time," she said.

"What about Alaeddin?" asked Dovie O'Quinn.

Alaeddin was still on, Miss Spivey said, but it would be part of something *bigger*. "Something *lucrative*," she said, and pointed to the blackboard. *Lucrative*, which we'd encountered in "The Ruined Man Who Became Rich Again Through a Dream," was up there, connected by an arrow to a row of dollar signs.

Mavis Davis spoke up from the seventh-grade row. "You mean a Fall Fun Fair like Miss Chandler used to have?"

Mavis was old enough to remember the 1931 Fall Fun Fair better than anyone in the room except for Arnie Lumpkin. Her tone of voice unmistakably suggested that she was glad Miss Spivey had finally developed sense enough to do like Miss Chandler did.

"Yes, but with Arabian costumes!" Miss Spivey said, putting extra *isn't-that-a-marvelous-idea* verve in her voice. While some of us tried to picture doing the Cake Walk in Bedouin robes or a veil, Miss Spivey's gaze remained on Mavis. Holding Mavis eye to eye, she added, "And camels, too, of course."

That set all of us back in our chairs. Camels, did she say? "Stuffed or 'live, Miss Spivey?" Ralphord asked.

"Alive," she said.

"We ain't got any camels, Miss Spivey," said Cyrus Wood, a boy whose role in life, or at least in school, was to state the obvious. "Where're you fixin' to get camels from?"

"First things first," Miss Spivey said, and she wrote the word AUDITIONS on the blackboard in all capital letters. She underlined the AUDI that it shared with *audience* and *auditorium*, both of which she printed underneath it, lowercase. She seemed to consider the pictures on the wall behind us, squinting over the tops of our heads, before she announced that we would begin today by choosing someone to be our *muezzin*. "Moo-ezz-in," she pronounced as she wrote on the blackboard a word that looked, I thought, like a cross between *music* and *magazine*. She made us repeat it after her until we got it right. The *muezzin*'s job would be to sing out announcements at the Baghdad Bazaar from up in a thing called the *minaret*, which was a kind of tower, she said, and she drew something on the blackboard that resembled the silo next to

O'Quinn's barn. Cyrus Wood stirred on his bench, ready to point out the obvious, but Miss Spivey beat him to the punch.

We were going to *build* a minaret, she said, sounding only a little surprised to hear herself saying it.

You had to wonder how much of the Baghdad Bazaar Miss Spivey had planned in advance and how much she made up on the spot.

Our *muezzin* would climb up into the minaret we built, she continued, and sing out news from there about events and special attractions and the like. In between announcements, he (or *she*, Miss Spivey said) would add to the authentic atmosphere of our Baghdad Bazaar by singing little songs that were meant to sound like a real *muezzin* calling the faithful to prayer, although our *muezzin* would be encouraging folks to try the Dunk Tank, and so forth. Obviously, Miss Spivey said, whoever played the part had to have a strong and melodious singing voice.

"What kind of *prayer*?" Mavis Davis asked with narrowed eyes.

Now, I would not have been surprised to learn that Mavis Davis secretly wanted to be the *muezzin* at the Baghdad Bazaar. She liked to sing, and she certainly would have enjoyed looking down on everybody from up there in the minaret and telling folks what to do. Sometimes I wonder if asking a snippy question like "What kind of prayer?" was the only way Mavis Davis could bring herself to show interest in what Miss Spivey was up to.

"Oh, just a simple prayer," Miss Spivey said. "Like this." And she sang in a high, wobbly voice some words that sounded like "Ooo la, la la! Ah! Ooo sha la, la la!"

"What does it mean?" asked Ralphord.

"Don't sound Christian," Mavis kind of growled.

"Oh, it isn't *Christian*," Miss Spivey said, ignoring Ralphord's question, and I knew right then that what she'd sung didn't mean anything at all. Miss Spivey was egging Mavis on. She was saying to Mavis, for all intents and purposes, *Why don't you tell your mother to put this in the Superintendent's pipe and smoke it?*

Mavis fell for it. "I don't think we should be singing it, then," she said, "if it ain't Christian."

"Is that a fact?" Miss Spivey said, and she looked kind of thoughtful for a while, as if she were considering Mavis's objection. "You don't *think* we should be singing it."

"I sure don't," said Mavis, but there was a doubtful note in her voice now, a tang of suspicion, as if she understood something that she hadn't noticed before. Mavis kept a sharp and narrowed eye on Miss Spivey, who continued to look thoughtful as she sauntered down between the desks to the back of the room until she was standing right next to Mavis, at which point she leaned down and whispered something in Mavis's ear that made that girl's face turn red as a beet. Miss Spivey straightened up again. The expression on *her* face was a cross between pure righteousness and the cat who swallowed the canary. On her way back to her desk she called the Avant boy, a skinny ten-year-old, up to the front to sing "What Child Is This?" Everybody knew the words to that one. Both the Methodists and the Baptists sang it.

Miss Spivey spent the rest of the morning auditioning everybody in alphabetical order, even though it was obvious, once she got to Ralphord Cailiff, who was going to be the *muezzin*. Not a one of us could make the hair stand up on your arms the way my brother Ralphord did, especially when he got to the part that goes, "This, this is Christ the King, whom angels guard and shepherds sing." He got the words switched around there like that every time—with the angels guarding and the shepherds singing—but you didn't care, listening to him. At the age of not quite ten, my brother Ralphord could hit any high note as easy as sighing.

Mavis Davis did not go up to audition when Miss Spivey called her name. Mavis sat stiffly on her bench with her fists clenched in her lap and steam just about coming out of her ears until lunchtime, when she went home for the rest of the day. Arnie Lumpkin, who sometimes sat in the seventh-grade row with Mavis, swore that he heard what Miss Spivey whispered to her. He went around telling everybody, of course, and you can bet nobody ever asked Mavis for confirmation one way or the other. According to Arnie, Miss Spivey had whispered: "Mavis, I don't believe you *think* at all."

Miss Spivey was wrong about Mavis Davis, if she said that. Mavis was always thinking. And when *I* think of all the trouble Mavis was yet to cause, I can't help but wish that Miss Spivey had never said any such thing to Mavis Davis, in spite of how satisfying it was to imagine her saying it at the time. It just goes to show that it's true, what my momma always said. Sometimes your mouth can ruin you.

The weeks that followed her chat with the Superintendent proved to be a time of fateful utterances on Miss Spivey's part. After revealing the "secret" of my brother's birth, announcing the Baghdad Bazaar, and whispering whatever fateful thing she had whispered in Mavis Davis's ear, Miss Spivey turned to my brother Force on the way out to McIntyre on Saturday and asked him, out of the blue, "May I drive?"

It was easy for Force to pretend he hadn't heard her in Daddy's rattletrap of a truck, but I saw the muscle twitch in his jaw and so did Miss Spivey. She asked again. Force gripped the wheel.

"This ole truck, she's kind of a tricky lady," he said.

"This old truck is a truck," said Miss Spivey.

She had been looking out the window at the pine trees flicking past like big green brushes, but now she looked at him again. I was entirely invisible on the front seat between them.

"The clutch sticks some," he said.

"I once drove from New York City to Denver, Colorado," Miss Spivey said. "On the Lincoln Highway."

Now Force took his foot off the gas, pushed in the clutch, and turned to look at her—to see if he'd heard her right, I expect. She gave him a big smile, and instead of going around the next sharp curve in the road, he drove Daddy's Model A truck straight into a ditch. He yelled, "Damn!" and Miss Spivey said, "Oh!" and there we were, each of us with our arms out straight and hands on the dash to keep from pitching forward into the windshield. We had a fine view of the ditch the truck was aimed down into, along with the underside of a huge sweetgum tree that was already uprooted at the edge of the ditch. Around the roots of the sweetgum, the exposed dirt was white as snow, and bluish white water that looked like dirty milk filled the crater the roots had left when the tree fell over.

"What is that?" Miss Spivey bent her elbows to get closer to the windshield. "Is it snow?" she asked, causing me to think that her brain was addled by the accident—temporarily, I hoped.

"No, it ain't snow!" said Force. He didn't sound addled at all. He craned his head around, trying to see out the back window. "Are they all right back there?" He meant Theo and Miss Templeton in the back of the truck.

Miss Spivey opened the passenger-side door. "It looks like snow," she was saying as she stepped down. Her hiking boots looked newly cleaned, the brown leather gleaming, so I said, "Best not step in that white dirt, Miss Spivey." She stopped and turned to look at me.

"White dirt?" she said.

I slid out across the seat, leaving Force with both hands and his forehead on the wheel, and got out after Miss Spivey. Theo and Miss Templeton had already picked themselves up and climbed down from the bed of the truck. Miss Templeton was pushing her little felt hat back into shape. She asked what happened.

"It's white dirt, Leona!" Miss Spivey said, as if we had driven off the road on purpose to have a look.

As soon as we all were clear of the vehicle, Force dropped her into reverse. The truck made plenty of noise and it bucked once or twice, but it stayed in the ditch. Force tried it again, and then again, sending a pink fountain of red clay mixed with white dirt up from under one hind wheel. Off to the side, hoping to avoid getting run over or suffocated or both, Miss Templeton and I watched Theo and Miss Spivey poke long branches into the bottom of the ditch. "What makes it white?" we heard her shout.

"Aluminum," he shouted back. "There's aluminum in it and silica— that's like sand, Miss Spivey, but finer pieces. Folks call it white dirt, or chalk, but it's not really chalk. Over to the mine they call it kaolin."

"Kay-OH-lin," Miss Spivey said. She had been stirring her stick in the ditch like she was mixing up a bowl of cake batter, but now she pulled it out.

"Yes'm. They got it all over here, Miss Spivey. I'm surprised you've never seen it before."

"I never have," said Miss Spivey. She looked at the stick, coated white, and I thought she was about to say something more, but she didn't.

Behind us, the truck's engine finally coughed and fell silent. Force had given up. Or run out of gas. In the sudden silence, Theo said loudly, "Some folks like to eat it."

"They *eat* it?" Miss Spivey said. She brought the white end of the branch closer to her face as if she might try a lick.

"They take it for indigestion," Miss Templeton explained. "Like milk of magnesia."

I expect that Miss Templeton knew as well as Theo and I did that it was mostly women who were in a family way that felt a craving to eat white dirt, but none of us said a word about that. My sister May ate so much of it before little Ed was born that she gave herself cramps and constipation.

"Do they scoop it out of ditches like this?" Miss Spivey plunged her stick back in a little deeper and brought it up a little whiter.

"Sometimes they do," said Theo. "They've got whole mines and pits full of it, too." He pointed up the red dirt road, which climbed to a rise that had nothing but blue sky above it and pine trees on either side. "Right there on up the road," he said.

"Are y'all fixin' supper in that ditch, or what?"

Force was standing on the road above us with his hat in his hand and his hands on his hips. His noble white forehead was as red as the rest of his face, except for a streak where he'd wiped the sweat off and left a smear of white dirt behind. "We better get walking," he said. "See if we can borrow a mule and some rope."

Miss Spivey handed the white stick to me—I carried it all the way back home with me and kept it, thinking she wanted it for something—and she brushed her palms together, all the while giving the truck an appraising look. "I don't think a mule will be necessary," she said. She

held out her hand for the key. Force handed it over. What else could
he do?

She made us all climb into the back of the truck, including Force,
and told us where to stand, crowded up as close as we could over the
right rear wheel. (She said the left at first, but changed her mind.) Then
she went around and started her up. Daddy had affixed wooden sides
to that truck, and we were all hanging on to the top board, waiting for
the lurch, when Miss Spivey backed that truck out smooth as you please
onto the road. Theo and Force looked at me and Miss Templeton—all of
us struck dumb with astonishment—and then Force said, "Goddamn!"
and slapped his hat on his pants, releasing a cloud of pink dust. "Beggin'
your pardon, Miz Templeton," he added.

"Force said that was some mighty nice driving, Miss Spivey," I
reported when I climbed back into the front seat. Miss Spivey patted
my knee.

Force rode in the back with Theo the rest of the way and Miss
Templeton rode up front with us, never mind asking for trouble. I don't
know about Miss Templeton, but I had never ridden in a motor vehicle
driven by a woman before, and I think it made me feel a little giddy. I
was fascinated by the sight of Miss Spivey's hiking boot pushing in the
clutch as she threw Daddy's Model A truck into first gear, then straightened her out. There was enough white dirt on the road for us to feel
the tires slide, first to the left side and then, when Miss Spivey tried to
compensate, to the right. Miss Spivey didn't cuss or make impatient
noises like some people I knew. She just slowed way down. We inched
along for a while, until my brother Force knocked on the back window.
He waved his hand as if to say, *Move along! Pick it up!* A cloud of dust
was coming up the road behind us. "All right, all right," Miss Spivey said,
not that he could hear, but every time she tried to put on a little more
speed, the wheels started slipping again.

The cloud of dust wound up having Linwood Perkins's official
county vehicle in the middle of it, with him and Mr. Gordon the lawyer
inside. Miss Spivey, with both hands on the wheel and her hair sticking
to her face from all the excitement, gave the deputy sheriff a cheerful

nod when he pulled alongside Daddy's Model A and stayed there. She slowed to a stop and so did he. Still smiling, she said quietly out the side of her mouth, "Gladys, what county do you think we're in?" I said, "Wilkinson," and hoped it was true. Next to me, Miss Templeton slid down as far out of sight as she could. She pulled her felt hat like a helmet over her hair.

"Afternoon, Miss Spivey," Linwood Perkins said, ducking down so he could talk past Mr. Gordon in the passenger seat. Mr. Gordon looked like he was going to break his neck, the way he was craning it to see who all was in the truck. "What brings y'all way out this-a-way?" the deputy sheriff said. You could tell, Miss Spivey said later, that what he really meant was, *What in blazes are you doing behind the wheel of that truck?*

Miss Spivey took a quick look at the rearview mirror—Daddy's truck had just one, on the driver's side—and she straightened her shoulders. Mr. Gordon's eyes kept flicking back toward the truck bed. I still don't know what it was made me come out of my shell at this particular moment—maybe the triumph of Miss Spivey's driving skill—but in a burst of inspiration, I leaned forward and said, "We're taking these boys to do some shoveling yonder." I was pretty sure Mr. Gordon had seen them back there, and I knew, as Miss Spivey did not, that there was a pit mine over the next rise in the road.

"They got work at the mine?" the deputy sheriff said, looking interested.

It wouldn't take much for him to drive up to the office in McIntyre on Monday and find out, so I backpedaled as fast as I could.

"I don't know about that, Sheriff," I said. (Saying *sheriff* instead of *deputy* was, Miss Spivey said later, a clever *stratagem*.) "But my sister May? She lives over to McIntyre. We're collecting some white dirt to ease her digestion." I paused, waiting for the deputy sheriff to point out there was white dirt all over the county. He didn't, but just in case that's what he was thinking, I said that my sister had it in her head that the mines had the *purest, whitest* kind of white dirt. "You know how it is," I said. By that I meant to imply that she had notions due to being in a family way. I felt ready for anything he might throw at me. I had my fingers crossed and my ducks in a row. Unless he asked why we needed two big boys to collect enough white dirt for one ailing woman. If he'd asked me that, I'd have been stumped.

"Collecting it? Stealing it, you mean," Mr. Gordon said.

Linwood Perkins raised a hand as if to cut off whatever else the other man had to say. The hand kept on going until he was tipping his hat to Miss Spivey. "Y'all be careful driving 'round here, Miss Spivey. It gets pretty slick."

"I see that it does," said Miss Spivey, in an uncharacteristically humble tone of voice. "I'll be very careful." Miss Spivey was playing her I'm-just-a-woman card. This was another stratagem, she told me later, to counteract the fact that she was at the wheel. It was an age-old stratagem, she said.

Linwood Perkins tipped his hat again. Grinding the gears, he backed up, turned around, and took his cloud of clay dust on down the road the same way it had come, which is to say, back into the heart of Piedmont County.

Miss Templeton sat up a little straighter. "Were they *following* us, do you think?"

Miss Spivey laughed. "If I'd thought so, I would have given them a run for their money," she said, "white dirt or no." She let out the clutch and we rolled forward toward the next rise in the road.

Later that day, after we'd finished our tutoring out at May's, Miss Spivey drove Daddy's Model A truck all the way back to Threestep. She navigated down our lane past the towering pine trees toward the front porch, where Daddy was in the rocking chair reading a newspaper—out loud, it looked like—while Momma shelled beans on the steps. They looked up when they heard the truck, and as it drew close enough for them to see, through the windshield, that Miss Spivey was at the wheel, they both rose slowly to their feet, as if somebody were pulling them up on the same string.

When we stopped, Miss Spivey gave them a cheerful little wave from the running board before she hopped down to the ground.

9

Chief Engineer

THE FIRST THING we actually built, after a period of scrounging up lumber and wheels and retrieving old nails and hinges and the like, was the minaret. When Theo carried the preliminary drawings over to our house to see what Force and Ildred thought before he showed them to Miss Spivey, my brother Ralphord took one look and said with delight, "That there's a crow's nest! Are we making a crow's nest?" (Prior to the arrival of Miss Spivey and *The Arabian Nights*, Ralphord's favorite story was *Treasure Island*.) To most of us at Threestep School, Theo's idea of a minaret looked like a balcony with a hidden ladder up the back and nowhere to go from there. Mavis Davis saw a nine-foot-tall version of the baptismal font in the back of Threestep Methodist Church—a resemblance that she found blasphemous and which she conveyed to us via Florence Hodges, Mavis herself having nothing to do with the Baghdad Bazaar, on principle. Later, when we got it painted white, everyone could see that Mavis had a point.

The lumber and nails came from an abandoned springhouse in the woods behind Threestep School and the unburned half of our old chicken coop, which my brother Ebenezer helped us take apart board by board.

Miss Spivey supervised the construction according to Theo's specifications, with a certain amount of well-meaning interference from Mr. Bibben, who was sworn to secrecy about the whole thing. To start with, she lined up a dozen volunteers after school, each of us with a hammer in hand and a pile of springhouse or chicken coop boards stretched out on the dirt at our feet, nails sticking up everywhere. Our job was to bang the nails out backwards just far enough to flip the board over and use the claw end of the hammer to pull them out the rest of the way, so the boards could be used again. Each person also had a little sack to save the nails in. It took a while to get a feel for the work, but I can tell you there's a real sense of satisfaction when you catch hold of a nail head just right and pull that whole nail up out of the wood smooth and straight as drawing a knife up through butter, even though the wood is squealing about having to let it go. Miss Spivey said it was no coincidence that big strong fellows like Arnie Lumpkin couldn't get the hang of it, whereas girls like me and Harriet Eskew got really good at easing those nails out of the wood. She said that applying the right kind of pressure in exactly the right place was superior to the application of brute force, at which point my brother Force stood up and pounded his chest like Tarzan in the movies.

Miss Spivey also set us to experimenting with white dirt, both in school and out. We were looking for an unlimited quantity of free white paint and plasterlike material, she said, and everybody whose yard was full of the stuff was required to bring in a bucket or two. We painted boards with every kind of combination she could think of: white dirt and water (cracked when it dried); white dirt, cornstarch, and water (cracked less); white dirt and corn oil (slipped off); white dirt and kerosene (stank). With all that experimenting, we were still no closer to what Miss Spivey was after, until Ildred stopped by Threestep School very early one morning on her way home from O'Quinn's pond with a foot-long string of bluegills that she planned to cook up for breakfast. Nobody was at school yet, but the door was open, so she slapped those fish down on Arnie Lumpkin's desk in the back row—we all could smell the evidence of *that* for the rest of the day—and she proceeded to examine the results of our experiments thus far, which were laid out on the floor by the windows:

When she determined that we were not going about our research in a sufficiently systematic manner, she took over for us. She set out like a regular scientist in the remaining half of the scorched-black chicken coop adjacent to Daddy's melon fields, where she lined up her tin cans half full of white dirt (ground and pounded to varying degrees of fineness) on the rough wooden shelves where the chickens used to roost. She added different things to the white dirt in each can, carefully wrapping a label around it so she'd remember what was what. The labels were tied on the cans with bits of string and strips of cloth, which gave them a festive look. (Ildred could tie any knot with one hand, don't ask me how.) Leaning against the shelves behind each can was a piece of wood the size of an individual blackboard slate. Some of the boards were solid white but cracked all over, most had dark spots where chunks of white coating had fallen off, and some were barely gray, as if the whiteness had been absorbed by the wood. About a week into her experiments, Ildred showed Miss Spivey a board completely coated in white that was solid and dry and only slightly flaky at the edges.

"This here's what you get if'n you mix white dirt with butter beans."

Miss Spivey took the board and tilted it to the light. She tried to pick a bit off with her fingernail and looked pleased. "Butter beans," she said.

"It sticks pretty good to wood. Must be something in the beans works as a bonding agent."

"What kind of agent?" I said.

Ildred shot me a look. "Theo was over here, him and Force, with the chemistry book. He said that's what we're looking for. A bonding agent. To make it stick."

❦

Theo Boykin knew white dirt from experience as well as books. At least half the Boykins' little farm was nothing but a thin layer of red dirt over untapped depths of white. When a tree fell over in their yard, a white cave was exposed underneath it. Ants brought up little balls of white along with the red clay, which made their anthills pink. Once, in a serious dry spell, the Boykins' old well turned milky, but Theo's father dug them a new one before he died. The white dirt beneath the surface of their scrubby acres did not matter much to the Boykins, except insofar as it limited what they could plant, until Mr. Gordon started trying to get them to sell him the rights to mine it.

In addition to being keeper of Klan night and Threestep's only lawyer, Mr. Gordon went around the county regularly, trying to talk people into leasing him the mineral rights to their farmland. The way Mr. Gordon explained it, if the owner of the farmland signed a lease, he (or she, as in Mrs. Boykin) would get a certain amount of rent money per acre per year just to keep anybody else from having the right to dig up any white dirt underneath that farm. Once a company started actually mining, they would pay the farmer even more for the white dirt taken from the land, Mr. Gordon said, as much as ten cents per ton, on top of the annual rent. Theo Boykin's daddy died in 1934, I believe, which was about the time the kaolin companies were getting very interested in the surrounding farmland, enough so they sent fellows like Mr. Gordon around to see what they could buy up. Mr. Boykin used to say he'd be happy if they could suck all the white dirt right out from under his feet, but he sure wasn't fool enough to sign control of his land over to anybody in the meantime.

Mr. Gordon sent a heap of flowers for Mr. Boykin's funeral and he waited a decent interval before he started coming by the Boykins' place again with his papers, encouraging Theo's momma to sign. He came to our place, too, not because it was loaded with kaolin, but he thought if we signed and started getting our annual rent, for doing nothing whatsoever, we might help talk "the widow" into signing, too. With Mr. Boykin gone, Mr. Gordon thought it was only a matter of time before he got his lease, but Mr. Gordon hadn't reckoned on Theo. Theo had already thought to take a bucket of white dirt from his yard over to the pottery, where Mr. Veal the foreman was pretty nice to him on account of his daddy dying on the job there. According to what Mr. Veal told Theo, Mr. Gordon was going to turn around and sell those leases to a kaolin company in an arrangement that would mean a lot more money for him and the company than for the farmer who signed the lease. "The better your dirt, the bigger the gyp," Mr. Veal said. In a shed heaped with broken bricks and cracked clay tiles, he helped Theo mix vials of his white dirt with various liquids and all, to determine the quality of it. Theo said Mr. Veal glanced around the shed and lowered his voice to say, "Don't sign nothin' yet. That's my advice, boy, but don't tell nobody I said so. Don't sign a thing."

Planning for the Baghdad Bazaar gradually took up more and more of our time out at May's on Saturdays, much to Miss Templeton's mostly unspoken dismay. When we were finished with lessons, we would sit around the table talking and eating biscuits with maypop jelly. A lot of the time, it was Miss Spivey telling us about Baghdad, the real Baghdad, while Theo Boykin took notes—not in words but in pictures. With a few pencil lines and shadings in his notebook or on a sheet of art paper, Theo could make you see tunnellike streets with buildings crowding over them, as if the arched windows and stone balconies on one side had secrets to whisper to the houses on the other. He could make you see a boy leading a laden donkey to the stone bank of the Tigris River just below Miss Spivey's hotel window, or the cool white and black stone tiles on the floor of her rooms there, or the arched and domed house next door, where "little married ladies," as she called them, would gather on the flat part of the roof in their long dresses and veils. In Baghdad, Miss Spivey said, people used their roofs like we used our porches, for a cool place to sit in the evening or to sleep on a hot night. (Except in Baghdad, there were *no mosquitoes*!) The roof had a wall along the edge, waist- or shoulder-high, for privacy and safety, she said. The little married ladies on the roof next door liked to show Miss Spivey things: an arrangement of flowers, a fancy box, the fabric of their dresses, or a new pair of shoes. "They'd climb up on a chair or a stool so I could see them better," Miss Spivey said. Once, one of them held up a baby for her to see, wrapped, like Jesus, in swaddling clothes. All the while Miss Spivey was talking about these things, Theo would be hunched over his notebook, and when she was finished, he'd slide it across the table and show us what he'd drawn: three little figures in long gowns and veils that left only their eyes showing, one holding a baby up over her head, another one waving a bunch of flowers, the third one standing on top of the wall, her arms out for balance. He'd even drawn her toes curled over the edge.

The pottery where Theo worked made mostly bricks and hollow tile in rows of kilns that looked like Eskimo igloos, except that they were built of blackened firebrick, instead of blocks of ice. Theo spent most of his days either swinging an ax and stacking wood, or standing and sweating at the back of the kilns, keeping a sharp eye on the vents, waiting for the diminishing smoke and a signal from the foreman to tell him it was time to open the iron door in the back and push in more wood. Previously, Theo might have passed the time while he waited for the foreman's signal by counting the bricks in the great chimneys that rose from the back of each kiln. He might have rearranged the bricks in his mind to make a tower or a bridge or a great wall that went three-fifths of the way around the pottery. (There were only enough bricks in all the chimneys put together for three-fifths of the way around. Theo's imagination was mathematically precise.) Now, instead, he conjured up Baghdad as Miss Spivey had described it to us. He watched it shimmer in the waves of heat rising up from the kilns.

"You won't get to college drawing pictures for Miss Spivey," I heard Miss Templeton warn him once—not, of course, in Miss Spivey's hearing—but that didn't stop him. In time, he would draw up all the plans for the Baghdad Bazaar—not just the minaret but the balconies and gates and arches and everything else, each one detailed as a blueprint, showing every board and cut and nail.

I expect Miss Templeton knew it wasn't Miss Spivey he was doing it for.

The deputy sheriff was the first official person Miss Spivey approached with her plans for the Baghdad Bazaar. Linwood Perkins was a valuable ally, she said. He would be useful later, Miss Spivey felt, in negotiations with the Reverends Stokes and Whitlock. They would be tougher nuts to crack. After school one day—it must have been in March—Miss Spivey lent me her umbrella and sent me through a steady rain to the deputy sheriff's office to deliver a sheaf of rolled-up papers that included drawings, lists, and the like. She called these papers "specks" for the Baghdad Bazaar. Attached to the specks was an envelope with a note inside. Threestep had two blocks of wooden sidewalk on both sides of Main Street in those days, with a slough of red mud in between when it rained. I took my shoes off to cross the street and held them in one hand, the umbrella in the other, the roll of specks under my arm like a baton. Deputy Sheriff Perkins paid no mind whatsoever to the muddy tracks my bare feet made leading up to his desk. He recognized Miss Spivey's handwriting on the envelope I gave him and sat down to read the note. "Go on now, Gladys," he said, waving me and my clean shoes on our way. I forgot the umbrella behind the door, as instructed.

Miss Spivey took me with her when she dropped by to pick up her umbrella the very next day. "We don't want to give him too much time to think," she said.

The afternoon was sunny and warm, more like June than March, but the street was still muddy in patches from yesterday's rain. Miss Spivey stopped to scrape the mud off the bottom of her hiking boots on the edge of the wooden sidewalk, first the left one, then the right. She was wearing a green-checked dress with sheer white puffy sleeves and a pair of silk stockings. She usually wore cotton ones to school. I wasn't used to seeing her legs looking bare from midcalf to the tops of her ankle-high hiking boots. Neither was the deputy sheriff.

Linwood Perkins stood up when we came in. He was not a bad-looking man, a little too skinny to be completely convincing as an officer of the law, and mysteriously unmarried. In one flurry of movement, he patted his shirt pocket flap as if to check the position of his badge, hitched up his belt to make sure that his trousers hadn't dropped too low, and combed the fingers of one hand through his sandy hair without undoing one iota of the damage his hat had all day to inflict upon it. "Good afternoon, Miss Spivey," he said, nodding his head smartly in what amounted to a kind of bow in her direction. He looked a little surprised to see me trailing after her, but he sounded friendly enough when he said, "Hey, Gladys." There was a little business about the umbrella. "Are you sure?" "Gladys left it?" "Ah, here it is!" That put the deputy sheriff at ease by giving him a chance to "come to my rescue," just as Miss Spivey said it would.

I sat, meanwhile, on a bench against the window under the word JAIL, which I could read backwards in shadows on the floor at my feet. Linwood Perkins pulled a creaky leather chair out from behind his desk for Miss Spivey and squinted at the papers in his hands. Miss Spivey had typed them up in a neat and professional manner on the gleaming black Underwood she had in her room: a map of "Baghdad, Georgia," as well as detailed specifications for the booths, games, stage, and audience areas of the Baghdad Bazaar, all of which centered around Main Street. Several scenes from *The Arabian Nights* that Miss Spivey had taken from the back wall of the schoolroom were soon spread across his desk. In addition, Miss Spivey had brought with her today, rolled up and tied with a blue ribbon, Theo's latest drawing of Main Street, which was done on a long piece of pale brown wrapping paper from Mr. Bibben's store. Unrolled, it showed every arch and all the balconies (both working and purely decorative), along with a minaret somewhat grander than the one we'd been working on, an onion-domed ticket booth, benches lined up in the street for the audience, and the wooden part of the sidewalk turned into a stage with footlights aflame. In the center of the stage, a scowling *jinn* in a turban floated over a lamp, his massive arms folded across his chest.

The deputy sheriff held one end of this drawing down on the desk while Miss Spivey held the other. Anyone could see that Miss Spivey was aiming high.

"Y'all want benches set up in the street?" he asked, as if that were the most astonishing aspect of the scene.

"That's right. For the audience. See, here? They'll be facing the stage."

"Beggin' your pardon, Miss Spivey, but ain't nobody fool enough to sit out there in the sun."

He paused, but Miss Spivey didn't say anything. So he continued.

"And it ain't only the audience, Miss Spivey. All these here booths and tables—ain't a spot of shade for them, either. Unless you're plannin' to have a tent, and I can't guess where you'd get enough tent for all of this here."

Miss Spivey sat back in the deputy sheriff's chair. Whether she had her next statement planned all along, or if she made it up on the spot, we'll never know. She said, "They won't be sitting in the *sun*. They'll be sitting in the dark."

"Come again?" said Linwood.

"It will be dark. It will be night. This is the Arabian *Nights* we're performing."

"You mean y'all're fixing to put on this . . . show . . . after dark?"

This was news to me, too. There were a lot of lit torches in the drawings, but I thought that was for atmosphere. I wondered if Theo knew Miss Spivey pictured the Baghdad Bazaar going on in the dark.

"It don't get dark till pretty near nine o'clock that time of year," Linwood added.

"Curtain time is twelve o'clock," Miss Spivey said decisively.

"*What* time?"

"The show starts at midnight!"

"Now, a wait a minute, Miss Spivey. D'y'all expect folks to stay up half the night?" He shot a glance at me, like he was looking for help here, but I kept my face still as stone.

"Not half—the *whole* night. Because before they see Alaeddin, they'll be hungry. They'll be looking for a little barbecue and a piece of pie. And afterward, they'll want another try at the Turkey Shoot and the Dunk Tank!"

I have to say that, coming from Miss Spivey's mouth, *Turkey Shoot* and *Dunk Tank* sounded about as foreign as *Ifrit* and *vizier* coming from anybody else's.

"But it'll be dark!" he said. "How they gonna shoot turkeys in the dark?"

"There are ways," said Miss Spivey.

Linwood Perkins leaned over the drawing spread out on his desk, searching for clues, I expect, as to what in the world she might be thinking. In the meantime, Miss Spivey gave *him* a look like she was sizing him up as Dunk Tank material. He was just the right height and heft, it turned out—brought in more money than anybody except for Reverend Stokes.

Linwood straightened up, as if something had just occurred to him. "I don't know what plans you've got for lighting up your bizarre, Miss Spivey, but I hope you're not countin' on Horace Wicker kickin' in, not for free. He'd as soon part with his skin as a nickel's worth of electricity for free. If I was you, I wouldn't even ask the man, Miss Spivey."

That's when Miss Spivey looked the deputy sheriff straight in the eye and said, "You can call me Grace." This was another surprise both to me and to Linwood Perkins, and it caused him to flush pink clear up to the roots of his sandy hair. It also put an end to their conversation, since there was no way for him to get the word *Grace* out of his mouth in reference to Miss Spivey—not, at least, on such short notice.

When we were back outside on the wooden sidewalk, I asked her, "How *will* they shoot turkeys in the dark, Miss Spivey?"

Whatever she had in mind—and I also hoped it wasn't Mr. Wicker—Miss Spivey was feeling pleased with our visit to the deputy sheriff, I could tell. She plunged both hands deep into the pockets of her green-checked dress, bouncing a little on her toes as she walked, and set herself to whistling in a tuneless, breathy way I recognized. My brother Force whistled like that when he was thinking about something good. We stepped from island to island of dry ground crossing the street and when we reached the other side, she finally answered my question. "I don't know, Gladys. Any ideas?"

I had one idea—really, it was the only idea in town, apart from Mr. Wicker—but I was not supposed to mention it.

Mr. Horace Wicker owned and operated the only functioning electrical generator in Threestep, Georgia. He used to turn on the lights from dusk until eleven every night for those who could afford to wire their place up and pay him $2.50 a month for electricity. Not many people could do that in 1938 or '39, although more than could afford it in 1936 or '37. Mr. Wicker's list of customers kept growing until the 1940s, when the REA came into Piedmont County and set out to electrify the countryside. In the meantime, the Bibbens paid Mr. Wicker extra for twenty-four-hour electricity so they could buy an electric icebox, as we all called it, and Mr. Wicker had wired up the schoolhouse out of public duty, but much of Threestep and all of the outlying country were still pretty dark at night.

It was Horace Wicker's son Cecil who came home from electrician school in Atlanta in 1933 and built that electrical generator for his daddy. Theo Boykin wasn't twelve years old at the time, but he was over there every day, watching Cecil bolt and screw and solder and weld that thing together in his daddy's junkyard. Theo had made Cecil a little nervous at first, standing in a block of shade alongside the clapboard cottage that served as the junkyard office, silent and watching. Not that Cecil thought Theo was up to no good necessarily. It was just that look of concentration Theo always got when he was thinking hard, which was most of the time, as if he might be seeing right through whatever he was looking at, seeing straight to the innards, the gears and whistles of the thing. (Miss Spivey said that's why Theo was good at drawing: he knew how to look at something.) If he was looking at you and thinking hard, sometimes you felt like he could see your bones and blood cells and all, maybe your heart and soul, too. I believe that look was what made Cecil Wicker and his daddy Horace sweat a little.

Theo spent three or four years collecting parts and working in the shed out back of the Boykins' place on a contraption that looked like it was cooking something, my momma said the first time he took us around back to see it. I don't pretend to know how it worked. There was a thing like a giant spool of thread, as big as two one-pound cans of peaches put end to end. The spool was all wrapped up in shiny copper wire and sitting in the middle of an axle that went out through a hole in the wall. The axle hooked up to the big rear wheel of a steam-driven tractor outside the shed. When Theo fired up the tractor, the wheel turned and the axle turned and so did the spool. This was somehow supposed to make electricity and send it through two copper wires wrapped in long spirals of rubber cut from old tires. These thick black wires ran from the spool out through a hole in the roof of the shed to the Boykins' house, where they disappeared into another hole Theo cut for them, just under the eaves. Although the generator hadn't made any electricity as yet, except for a few sparks, Theo was prepared for long-term operation. He had a sizable woodpile stacked up very neatly next to the steam-driven tractor, complete with a wooden-handled ax buried in a stump for splitting more. Theo had painted signs on the side of the shed that said: DANGER! DO NOT TOUCH WIRES! YOU WILL BE DEAD! In case you couldn't read, he had drawn a picture of a very unhappy fellow in overalls holding on to a wire with his hair standing up on end and his eyes popping out and smoke coming out of his ears. My sister Ildred thought it looked like Arnie Lumpkin. "On a good day," she said.

It wasn't too long after Theo completed his electrical generator and explained to us how it (theoretically) worked that I was looking out our kitchen window after supper one night and saw all the front windows of the Boykins' house—formerly lit by the flickering yellow glow of kerosene lamps—suddenly filled with what was, comparatively speaking, a blaze of light.

All of us Cailiffs were outside in a heartbeat, along with some O'Quinns from down the road and a half a dozen other neighbors from the woods beyond the Boykins' house, everyone standing in and about the neat yellow squares cast on the ground from the Boykins' windows. At the front of the crowd, her face bathed in light, Mrs. Faith Boykin kept saying, with as much fear as wonder, "Lord, Lord, Lord. Lord, Lord, Lord. He made it light." Adding to our numbers was a steady trickle of folks who must have been passing by on the road and stopped, attracted like moths, leaving their wagons and one automobile in the lane.

Theo was just about to take a group of us around the back to show us the generator in action—"But y'all don't touch the wires, don't touch *anything*, you hear?"—when we heard another automobile rumbling down the lane toward us, its horn honking like a goose. Soon its head-lamps appeared, adding their feeble glow to the general illumination, and then it rolled to a stop alongside our house. Mr. Horace Wicker, his son Cecil, and three other men came stomping into the light. Before they said a word, my daddy stepped right in and said, "Evenin', Horace, Cecil," as if they'd just come to call. There wasn't a thing they could say in return but "Evenin', Jefferson," that being my daddy's name. Daddy greeted the rest, too, real friendly. Of course, he knew what had brought Mr. Wicker grumbling down to the Boykins', so my daddy went ahead and nipped him in the bud, saying, "Horace, I hear tell it's your boy Cecil taught Theo here how to light up the place."

"Cecil never told that boy he could hook his house on up to our generator," Mr. Wicker said in a rush. "Y'all know for a fact we can't make no 'lectricity for free."

That was kind of a low blow, seeing as how we Cailiffs couldn't afford Mr. Wicker's electricity, either.

"I sure know that, Horace, and that's why Theo here just built himself an electrical generator all his own. Ain't it so, Theo?"

Theo looked at Mr. Wicker, as much as at my daddy, and said, "Yes, sir." It was amazing to me how much *So there!* Theo was able to pack into that "Yes, sir."

"We were just going around back to have a look," Daddy said. "Care to join us?"

Mr. Wicker declined. Cecil left, too, with his daddy, but he came back the next day to admire Theo's setup and also to suggest, quietly, that Theo might want to cover the holes in the walls of that old shed and put a padlock on the door.

And that's how Theo Boykin made his momma's house the first and, as far as I ever heard of, the only colored family's house in the county to have electricity before the Second World War. He was going to connect us up to his generator, too, along with another family named Turpin, but there was a windstorm that December—this was in 1936, I believe, two years before Miss Spivey's arrival—and it knocked a big old pine tree down right on top of the shed. Theo was suspicious enough to check the trunk and see if it was cut at all, but no, it was just uprooted by the wind, the usual crater of white dirt opened underneath it. He wanted to move the tree and fix the generator, but Mrs. Boykin was against doing any such thing. She believed the tree falling was a sign, a warning. Theo was outraged.

"From Mr. Wicker, you mean? I told you, Momma, the *wind* blew it."

"Not from Mr. Wicker," his mother said. All along, Mrs. Boykin had been more afraid of fire from the wiring than of anything Mr. Wicker might do. It seemed like every other week some house or barn was burning down after being electrified, according to the newspapers Mr. Bibben passed along to our daddy. They'd had a fire once, the Boykins did, before I was born, and Mrs. Boykin had been extra-fearful ever since. "I'm talkin' about a sign from the Lord."

"Well, Momma!" Theo said, throwing his hands in the air. "Let's go on back to the Dark Ages, then."

He never did tell his mother or mine how, in the weeks between the lights going on and the tree coming down, he used to find his wood-cutting ax in a different place almost every time he went out back. The first time, when he found it stuck in a log on the ground, he thought he must have forgotten to put it back in the stump. The second time, he knew better. The ax would be buried in one tree trunk or another, or it would be stuck in the door of the shed, or, one time, when he *might* have left the padlock off by mistake, he told Force, he found the ax cleaving the dirt *inside* the shed, right next to the big spool of copper wire that was the heart of the generator. He took the ax inside the house with him after that.

Theo didn't try to fix his electrical generator after the tree fell on it—not because of the roving ax or Mr. Wicker, but because his mother asked him not to. One year after the tree mashed its roof in, that shed was so overrun with vines and voracious groundcover that a person would be hard put to find it at the edge of the woods behind the house, the generator tending toward rust inside of it, like a dead man in a tomb.

I never said a word to Miss Spivey about that generator, but with the Baghdad Bazaar on the horizon, I suspected that its resurrection was at hand.

The minaret turned out better than any of us dreamed it would. Except for the variously colored lumber making it obvious that it wasn't made of stone—this was before we got it painted up with white dirt and butter beans—it looked almost exactly like Theo Boykin's drawings. Miss Spivey left off calling Theo "Signor da Vinci," and started calling him our Chief Engineer. When Florence Hodges pointed out that colored engineers were not allowed by the railroad—this was something she knew for a fact from her uncle, a conductor on the Central of Georgia—Miss Spivey said simply, "Not that kind of engineer." Not a one of us was familiar with any other kind, and so Theo Boykin became our model and definition of a term that seemed to be another word for *inventor*, *artist*, and *magician*, all rolled into one.

Linwood Perkins continued to blush when Miss Spivey called him Linwood and he broke into a fit of coughing every time he said "Grace," but he did prove to be a valuable ally, exactly as Miss Spivey predicted. When she asked him to round up the businesspeople of Threestep, he came through for her without so much as a *Say who?* or a *What for?*

Not that there were many businesspeople to round up. In 1939 some parts of the country had already turned the corner around which prosperity was said to be waiting, but in Threestep, like most of the South, we were a few steps behind. Dot's Café had been the first to go under. Lumpkin Feed & Grain (which had belonged to Arnie's more prosperous uncle) was another fading memory, three years gone. At the lumberyard, Mr. Hall said he could count on the fingers of his two hands—the left one of which had lost its pinkie in a sawmill accident long ago—the number of cash-paying customers he'd had since 1932. Mr. Tuttle of Piedmont Paints & Hardware fared a little better, O'Quinn's mill and cotton gin hung on from year to year, or at least it had so far, and Bibbens' store did a balancing act whereby a trickle of cash sales carried along a raft of folks who bought on hope and credit. Apart from scouting for the kaolin company and planning Klan nights, no one knew what Mr. John B. Gordon, Attorney-at-Law, did all day, but his wife's bang-banging on the typewriter (the only one in town other than Miss Spivey's) continued even though the bell over the door never rang.

Not a one of the businesspeople of Threestep, Georgia, had anything better to do on a weekday afternoon than come to the deputy sheriff's office, where Miss Spivey was fixing to unveil her picture of Main Street transformed for the Baghdad Bazaar, which Theo had colored in and mounted on a piece of wood since the deputy sheriff saw it last. She set the picture up by the window, using the deputy's chair for an easel, and covered it with a sheet so she had something to whisk off when she said, "Ladies and gentlemen"—Mrs. Bibben and the Reverend wives being the ladies—"Baghdad, Georgia!"

They all leaned in, squinting at Theo's picture. Truth is, when Miss Spivey first showed us that picture at Threestep School, we all felt a little bad for her. Not a one of us believed that our Baghdad could look like the one she and Theo had in mind.

"Well!" said Mr. Hall, when he straightened up again. "That's real nice, Miss Spivey." Mrs. Bibben, who was in the know, said it looked like something from a storybook, didn't it, though? Mr. Tuttle remarked that he had heard of Cairo, Georgia, and also Arabi, but never any Baghdad. He asked, "Where's it at, Miss Spivey?"

Her plan was to direct their attention to the window and say, with a wave of her hand, *You're looking at it,* or something to that effect. She hadn't counted on the late afternoon sun hitting the dust on the glass, turning the window into an opaque curtain with JAIL printed on it, backwards. Miss Spivey skipped the window and looked at the doorway instead, where I stood with Force and Ildred and a handful of compatriots (which was what Miss Spivey called us when we volunteered) that included Dovie O'Quinn and the Veal boys. Miss Spivey raised her eyebrows. That was our cue.

We disappeared like a passle of *jinni,* swift and silent, out the door.

Ralphord was waiting for us around the corner, sweating it out in the long narrow bar of shade the minaret cast on the street next to the hardware store.

"Damned if y'all don't look just like a A-rab," somebody said. We turned around. It was our brother Ebenezer coming up the street to the hardware store. He helped us roll our masterpiece out into the middle of Main Street and then up over the ruts to a spot right in front of the deputy sheriff's office. When a nine-foot-tall tower of white stone-looking stuff stopped outside the open door, they were all looking right at it. By the time Ralphord had sung his first "Oooooo la la, ooooo ahhhhh la," the businesspeople of Threestep, along with Mrs. Reverend Stokes and Mrs. Whitlock, were spilling out the doorway onto the sidewalk to hear the weird little melody, the notes bubbling up from the top of the minaret like a clear stream singing over stones. You could hardly believe that voice was coming out of Ralphord, because he sure didn't look much like any kind of angel, although the long robe helped. Add in his checkered headgear fluttering and flying in front of his face, making the sound waver in the sweetest, most delicate way, and there wasn't a one of us standing there in the street who wasn't covered in goose bumps before he finished. Mrs. Reverend Stokes asked Miss Spivey, "What's that he's singing?" and Mrs. Whitlock jumped in to say that she'd heard it was a prayer of some kind and not anything Christian.

"A prayer?" Miss Spivey said. "Oh, goodness, no. I made the song up myself. It doesn't mean anything, Mrs. Whitlock, I assure you."

"Then it's not some kind of incantation?" Mrs. Whitlock asked warily.

"And he's not supposed to be a high priest up there or something in that line?" asked Mrs. Reverend Stokes.

"Not at all," Miss Spivey said. Our *muezzin* would be more like a town crier, she told the Reverend wives.

They looked at her blankly. Linwood Perkins said, "You mean like Paul Revere?"

Miss Spivey said, "Yes, Mr. Perkins!" as warmly as she could. She couldn't call the deputy sheriff "Linwood" in front of everybody. "Like Paul Revere."

Listening to Miss Spivey explaining the role of the *muezzin* to the businesspeople and Reverend wives of Threestep, I couldn't help but feel a little sorry for Mavis Davis, who'd gotten herself riled up for no good reason, it looked like. She would have had no objection to Paul Revere.

Mr. Gordon meanwhile stood in the long skinny shadow of the minaret, showing Mr. Tuttle some white stuff he'd scraped off the wood with the blade of his pocketknife. "Curious about your white paint," Mr. Gordon said to Miss Spivey. Really it was more like plaster than paint, we'd spread it on so thick. Mr. Gordon made no apology for the inch-wide stripe of bare wood his knife had left behind. "Ralphord here tells me it's white dirt and—what did you say it's mixed with, young fella?"

"Our secret bounty agent," Ralphord said from the minaret.

Mr. Gordon turned his amiable smile from Ralphord to Miss Spivey. "You've got a lot to paint up in that picture of Main Street. I reckon you'll be making another trip out McIntyre way in Jeff Cailiff's truck before long."

Jeff—short for Jefferson—Cailiff was my daddy.

"I don't think that's likely, Mr. Gordon," Miss Spivey said, also smiling amiably. "We have quite a supply right here."

"Well, now, I know *that* for a fact, don't I?" said Mr. Gordon. He wiped his pocketknife clean on his handkerchief, first one side of the blade, then the other, before he snapped it shut. "I just thought you might be needing the *purest, whitest* kind." He looked straight at me when he said that, and I felt cold to think that I had said something that he remembered, something for which I might be held to account.

10

Auditions

THE UNVEILING OF the minaret—and the typed "specks" passed around afterward with the peach cobbler—had exactly the effect Miss Spivey was aiming for. Not only did Mr. Hall contribute a stack of lumber and Mr. Tuttle provide kerosene for us to kill the termites in it, but the next time Miss Spivey attended a Sunday service at United Methodist Church in Claytonville (as she did from time to time, mostly for the stained-glass windows), the wife of the Superintendent of Schools introduced herself on the way out of church and said she wanted to help make costumes for the Baghdad Bazaar. The name of the Superintendent's wife was Lucretia Louise Blount—which meant the Superintendent must have been Mr. Blount—but everybody called her Lulu, she said.

"Pleased to meet you, Mrs.—Lulu," Miss Spivey said.

Mrs. Blount wanted Miss Spivey to know, by the way, that her daughter Louise was an extremely talented actress, having distinguished herself in several dramatic productions at Sidney Lanier High School, from which she would be graduating next spring. Louise was a lovely girl, Mrs. Blount told Miss Spivey. She had violet-blue eyes and raven curls.

Back in Threestep, Miss Spivey was warned by Mrs. Reverend Stokes of Threestep Methodist Church (which had no stained-glass windows) that Mrs. Blount was not a talented seamstress. Mrs. Stokes based this opinion on various items of clothing that Mrs. Blount had donated to the Methodist Mission from time to time. "I wouldn't dress my dog in anything made by that woman," Mrs. Stokes said, none too reverently. She did not, in fact, have a dog. Miss Spivey was too tactful to suggest to Mrs. Reverend Stokes that perhaps the items Mrs. Blount chose to donate were ones that hadn't turned out as well as she might have hoped.

In McIntyre on Saturday, when Miss Spivey pointed out that Mrs. Lulu Blount owned a genuine Eldredge sewing machine—the only electric-powered sewing machine in the county, it was claimed—May and I exchanged glances. I said, "She might tell that Superintendent about every last thing we're doing, Miss Spivey, being his wife and all."

Miss Spivey didn't think she would cause us any trouble, not if we gave "the daughter" a good part in our production of *Alaeddin*.

"There's only one good part in *Alaeddin* for a girl," May pointed out, meaning, of course, the Princess. "Unless you count Shahrazad." She paused. "I can't really picture Louise Blount being Shahrazad."

Miss Spivey said she hadn't met the daughter yet.

"She's more the harem-girl type," I explained.

Miss Spivey wouldn't hear objections from anybody. "We *want* to get people involved," she said. "This is a community effort." Besides, the Superintendent's wife's brother owned a down-and-out cotton mill in Brennan. "She said he's got bolts of muslin and calico feeding the mice in that warehouse of his," Miss Spivey said. "That's another man who needs to get involved, wouldn't you say?"

Well, he did get involved, to the tune of one hundred bolts, twenty-five yards each, of plain white muslin only partly riddled with holes. Daddy and Force carried Miss Spivey to Brennan to pick up the cloth. In addition to her sewing machine and her daughter Louise, Mrs. Lulu Blount also volunteered the use of her genuine silver gravy boat, which looked more like the lamp Alaeddin found in the underground chamber (according to the colored plates and illustrations in Miss Spivey's book of *Arabian Nights*) than any of the oil lamps and kerosene lanterns kids had been rubbing and spilling all over town for months.

Miss Spivey took charge of the gravy boat, but the muslin wound up in our barn due to the fact that our own mother, Daisy Cailiff, also got involved. All that spring we had our big iron washing pot full of blue or red or green or brown or yellow dye bubbling over a wood fire in the yard. Momma would be out there stirring the pot with a big stick, or lifting out wet lengths of cloth to see what color they had got to. The green looked for all the world like giant collards cooking. We all had to help wring out what Theo figured to be over a mile of cloth (100 bolts times 25 yards per bolt equals 1.42 miles of muslin, to be pretty exact) and hang pieces of it on the clothesline and the fences and what was left of the old chicken coop—everywhere but near the pigs. Pigs liked that dyed cloth *better* than collard greens, as we had the misfortune to find out. We lost two whole bolts one Saturday when we hung a batch on bushes that were just close enough to the pen for a few enterprising snouts to poke through the fence and grab ahold of it. Ildred, who looked after our vegetable garden, wound up with a week's supply of green and blue manure.

At Threestep School, Miss Spivey had the boys move her desk way back into the corner of the schoolroom to make the stagelike platform up front available for auditions and rehearsing. There she sat in the corner, tapping away at our increasingly unwieldy story, she and her Underwood typewriter surrounded by open volumes of *The Thousand Nights and a Night,* from which she stole freely. We kept ourselves busy, teaching each other arithmetic, checking each other's spelling and handwriting, the older children reading to the littler ones, or vice versa, while Miss Spivey stitched together the script.

She held auditions in the schoolhouse, starting on a Friday evening, while the script was still a work-in-progress. There was no shortage of roles to play. She had customized "Alaeddin: Or, the Wonderful Lamp" until it was crowded with subplots, so in addition to him and his mother and the evil magician who set out to steal the lamp in the first place, Miss Spivey needed emirs and nabobs almost by the dozen. She needed a gullible Sultan and a Chief Eunuch and a Grand Vizier. She needed merchants named Ali and Ahmed, Mustafa and Ma'aruf. She had a harem to fill. She needed a beautiful Princess and the tireless Shahrazad. She was ready to offer a part to anyone brave enough to get up on the platform at the front of the room and repeat, with feeling, the lines she whispered to them from her prompting position, a seat in the first-grade row. Miss Spivey prompted everybody in this fashion. She said it was so they wouldn't get her one copy of the script all messed up, but it was really to keep folks with limited reading experience from being too embarrassed to try out. A lot of the parts didn't require any talking anyway. The harem girls—of which I was one eventually—just sat around onstage between dance numbers, and the eunuchs would spend most of the play standing like statues with their arms folded across their chests.

Miss Spivey had already handpicked her Alaeddin, of course, although she made my brother get up there anyway and play two scenes over and over again, one with Alaeddin's mother and one with the Princess, as different girls tried out for each part. This was a clever stratagem. When word spread that a girl could audition for a part in the dramatic production at the forthcoming Baghdad Bazaar by playing a scene with Force Cailiff—and that anybody could come and watch—the schoolhouse audience and the number of auditioning hopefuls doubled. Fourteen girls, including five or six from the college up in Milledgeville, tried out for the part of Alaeddin's mother, and all of the above plus another ten or more tried out for the role of the Princess, even though pretty much everybody suspected that Miss Spivey had already cut a deal with Louise Blount's mother (which she had).

Mavis Davis wasn't having a thing to do with the Baghdad Bazaar, at least not publicly. Secretly, she was coaching Florence Hodges to try out for another highly coveted role, that of the storyteller, Shahrazad. I think Mavis may have had some ideas about sabotage, but we'll never know, since Florence didn't get the part. Plenty of girls tried out for that one, too, knowing from the pictures Theo drew that Shahrazad would get to wear a costume of midnight-blue "silk" adorned with golden moons and stars. Plus, she got to read her lines instead of having to memorize them. The Shahrazad hopefuls included the college girls and some high school students, plus three girls from our school and my sister May.

To try out for Shahrazad, each girl had to sit in a chair in the middle of the platform up front and read any two pages picked at random from a fat green volume of *The Thousand Nights and a Night*. Before they got started, Miss Spivey reminded them that everybody who tried out was automatically guaranteed a place in the harem, if they didn't get the part. I saw Florence Hodges exchange a quick look with Mavis Davis, who was standing in the back and who had already announced to all and sundry that her friend Florence would not stoop to wearing a harem-girl outfit in public. Mavis was wrong about that.

Miss Spivey sat in the front row, as usual, so she could prompt people when they stumbled over *auspicious* or *withal* or any of the long and unfamiliar words that Shahrazad was so fond of. She let each girl read the whole two pages, no matter how many times she stumbled. There was a certain amount of suspense in the process. That's what kept it interesting, at least to me, in spite of the stop-and-go delivery. The most impressive tryouts before May got up there were two of the college girls from Milledgeville, with nine and ten stumbles apiece, and Florence Hodges with only seven. I was keeping score, unofficially.

May went last.

I might have been the only person there, other than May and Miss Spivey, who was aware that Miss Spivey had been coaching May for weeks in advance of the auditions. They did it on Saturday while Force and Theo were working on Shakespeare's major tragedies in the kitchen with Miss Templeton, and May and Miss Spivey were supposed to be studying *The Merchant of Venice*, a second-year high school requirement that my brother had actually studied in his second year. May would open up the little blue *Yale Shakespeare* book that Miss Spivey loaned to her and then she would send me out to check on the girls. "You know they never do watch little May the way they should," she'd say. Or else she might ask me to see if little Ed looked like he'd be waking up from his nap anytime soon. "Can you just wait on him to wake up, Gladys, and bring him out here when he does? I'm scared to death he'll get out the bed and wander off."

They were getting rid of me, I could tell that easy enough. It hurt me some, until I spotted the first volume of *The Thousand Nights and a Night* in Miss Spivey's knapsack one Saturday. I knew what they were up to then, although I never let on that I did.

Fair or unfair, when it was May's turn to audition, she didn't stumble at all, not once. She sat up straight in the chair—with the dark blue veil Miss Spivey provided to each girl draped over her hair and shoulders—and she read the first two pages of the prologue in a voice as rich and smooth as sweet-potato pie. When May said, "It hath reached me, O King of the Age, that there dwelt in the city a tailor, withal a pauper, and he had one son, Alaeddin hight," you didn't have to know what *hight* meant, or even *pauper*, to appreciate the spell that the voice of Shahrazad cast over the Sultan for a thousand nights and a night. May looked the part, too. Maybe it was the veil, or maybe the late afternoon sunlight reflecting up from the pages of the book, erasing the tired lines around her mouth and rearranging the shadows under her eyes and cheekbones. Her face looked years younger, it looked lit up from within. I heard Billy Bonner's mother, who used to rent to Ed and May before they moved to McIntyre, whisper to Ildred behind me, "Who is that girl up there, Ildred, honey, with the sweet voice?"

"Why, that's my sister May, Mrs. Bonner," Ildred said, sounding a little surprised herself.

There was only one student from Threestep School who came in secret to ask Miss Spivey for a part in our *Arabian Nights* entertainment, and that was Arnie Lumpkin. In public, Arnie insisted, like Mavis Davis, that he didn't want anything to do with something as sissy and fake as any *Arabian Nights*. He wouldn't be caught dead in those bloomers and little vests that Mrs. Blount was already sewing up for *jinni* and slaves and harem girls alike.

Arnie Lumpkin was a case, no matter how you looked at him. A big boy with squinty eyes—round in the belly, thick in the arms and legs, and as tall as a man—he was the very image of his father, Rufus Lumpkin, a sharecropper who raised cotton and corn on a farm that belonged to Mr. Gordon. Arnie should have been in high school or maybe graduated by now. The problem was he could not read. He came to school every September, his poor mother always hoping that something had happened to his brain over the summer that might make all the difference. What really might have made the difference was a pair of eyeglasses, but Arnie's daddy wasn't likely to pay good money to have his lamebrained son's eyes examined on the advice of a loopy schoolteacher.

Arnie came looking for Miss Spivey early on a Saturday morning, which was when Miss Spivey minded the store so Mr. and Mrs. Bibben could take their one morning off per week to go fishing. The Bibbens were two hours gone by the time Arnie arrived, at about half-past seven. Miss Spivey was in the yard out back, keeping an eye on the store through what she alone called the service entrance and tending the fire under a big iron pot in which she was cooking up a twenty-five-yard bolt or two of sand-colored cloth. She looked up when Arnie came around the corner of the store.

"Well, Arnie Lumpkin!" she said, as if he were the last person she expected to see. "What I can do for you?"

He hemmed and hawed for such a long time that Miss Spivey began to entertain the notion that he might be here to confess and apologize for something—maybe for the latest desecration of that tomb in the cemetery that somebody was always breaking into, searching for a trapdoor to hidden treasure. But Arnie had no such thought in his head. There were things that Arnie knew, like how to be a bully, and there were things he didn't know, like how to tell Miss Spivey why he'd come. What he really wanted was out of his reach, and he knew it. He wanted to be Alaeddin. He wanted to marry the princess. He wanted to rub the lamp and make the *jinn* do his bidding and deliver his heart's desire. Gathering all of his courage and swallowing what he had of pride, Arnie asked Miss Spivey if he could be in that show of hers.

"Of course you can," she said, hiding her surprise. She looked him up and down, and up again, and offered the opinion that he might be *just* right for the role of Chief Eunuch.

Naturally, Arnie Lumpkin asked, "What's that?"

Miss Spivey explained. "He's the one who keeps watch over the women of the harem." This piece of information made Arnie's eyebrows twitch. Miss Spivey lowered her voice as she continued. "The Chief Eunuch is the only man, other than the Sultan himself, who is permitted to look upon the Sultan's wives unveiled."

Arnie rubbed his palms on the seat of his baggy overalls. "What's he got to wear, this yoonick? In the show, I mean."

Miss Spivey had just begun to describe billowing purple pants gathered at the ankle when Arnie, who had a view of the lane leading up to the store, interrupted her with an urgent, "Somebody's coming!"

Miss Spivey looked over her shoulder. "It's probably Force and Ebenezer Cailiff. They're supposed to help me wring out all this cloth when it cools."

"I got to hide!" Arnie cried.

"What for?" said Miss Spivey.

"They'll know I come and ast you." Arnie was already backing toward the Bibbens' new outhouse.

"Well, Arnie, everyone will know if you're in the play, won't they?"

"I thought they was veils over your face and things," he said, whispering now and backing away faster.

They could hear Force and Ebenezer talking, out around the front of the store. Arnie turned to run for the outhouse.

"Not in there!" Miss Spivey said in a loud stage whisper, and Arnie stopped dead, his shoulders hunched in alarm. He turned toward the second outhouse, the old one, but she said, "No! The springhouse, Arnie—not the woodshed, no, no, no—the springhouse. Go!" Poor Arnie stopped and started and stopped himself from seeking refuge in one place after another until finally she let him run for the cool darkness of the shed farthest from the store, where the cold spring that bubbled up out of the ground used to keep the Bibbens' milk and butter from going bad before they got their electric icebox. Miss Spivey went back to stirring her sand-colored cloth.

Hiding in the springhouse, afraid that Force and Ebenezer had seen him before he got all the way inside the door, Arnie was too busy worrying about himself to wonder why Miss Spivey wouldn't let him hide in the old outhouse or the new one or the woodshed or the chicken coop. What Arnie didn't even know he didn't know was this: He was not the first to come see Miss Spivey that morning, shyly and in secret, to seek a part in the pageantry. The deputy sheriff had arrived so early the sky was still pink, and it cast such a flattering light on Miss Spivey that Linwood Perkins almost forgot what sort of role he was after. When she asked him to come to the schoolhouse to audition, Linwood mistook her intentions momentarily and said, "It's a date!" He was in the woodshed now, feeling foolish enough to hide from Mr. Hall, the lumberman, who was second to arrive. Mr. Hall was in the Bibbens' new outhouse with his hand over his nose, Reverend Stokes was in the old one being very careful of the rotted wood over the hole, and none other than Rufus Lumpkin, Arnie's father, had hidden himself in the Bibbens' abandoned chicken coop only moments before his son came up the lane. With the exception of Reverend Stokes, each man had listened as intently as Arnie had to Miss Spivey's description of the Chief Eunuch's place in the harem of the Sultan. To Reverend Stokes, whose thorough knowledge of the Bible no doubt made him familiar with the concept of eunuchs, she had suggested he audition for the role of the Sultan himself. Reverend Stokes had looked pleased. He replied that he would pray and think on it—and also ask his wife.

She would say no.

In the midst of the auditioning, Miss Spivey took it into her head and couldn't get it out that Eugene Boykin—Theo's six-foot-tall little brother—ought to play the Ifrit (which is a kind of *jinn*, you may remember) in *Alaeddin: Or, the Wonderful Lamp*. The Ifrit's job was to do Alaeddin's bidding whenever he rubbed the lamp, which meant he had to carry off the Princess from time to time. It wasn't only Eugene's overall size that made him right for the part, Miss Spivey said, or his big dark shoulders, or the way his arms looked when he folded them over his chest. It was the scowl he could put on his face when he chose to. Ifrits like to scowl, and Eugene Boykin was a champion scowler—a scary prospect, given his size. Folks from out of town didn't mess with him. Miss Spivey said we could not have found a more perfect Ifrit if we'd sent off to ninth-century Baghdad for one.

The key word in Miss Spivey's campaign to swing public opinion over to the cause of Eugene playing the Ifrit in our *Arabian Nights* entertainment was *verisimilitude.* At fourteen letters, *verisimilitude* may have been the longest vocabulary word ever written on the blackboard at Threestep School. It certainly was the one with the most occurrences of the letter *i.* As Miss Spivey explained it, the word meant "resemblance to the truth, apparent likeness to reality." She said that Eugene Boykin's *resemblance* to a "real" Ifrit was so perfect and complete, so *verisimilitudinous,* that it would cast an aura of reality over the whole production. (*Aura* went up on the board, too.) People would be so astonished by the sight of the Jinn of the Lamp that they would forget they were sitting in the middle of an unpaved street in Georgia. They would be transported—we would all be transported—to Baghdad, just like that! All we needed was that one utterly convincing detail: an Ifrit who looked the part.

"Miss Spivey *really* wants Eugene to be in that play," I said to Ralphord.

"I do, too!" said Ralphord. "Don't you, Gladys?"

I suppose I did, although it gave me a fluttery feeling in my stomach sometimes to picture Eugene Boykin in close proximity to Arnie Lumpkin and Florence Hodges and Dalton Veal and all. It made me want to warn Eugene to watch his step.

Miss Spivey's idea led to some heated discussions around town. Among the white folks, the question was: Could a colored boy play a part in *The Arabian Nights*? To help them picture it, Miss Spivey invited everybody to stop by anytime to see Theo's drawings of scenes and characters on the back wall of the schoolroom. Various individuals did so, often enough that we came to ignore the creak of the door and the rustle of whispers coming and going all day long. In my own personal favorite among the pictures on the wall, Theo had drawn the mighty Ifrit as a swirl of smoke rising from the lamp and growing into a towering figure that bore a considerable resemblance to his brother Eugene, with his bare black arms folded over his chest, and a glimpse of spangly red vest above the smoky bloom of what Mrs. Lulu Blount persisted in calling pantaloons. The Ifrit's scowling face was aimed at a small, pale, astonished-looking figure of Alaeddin way down there on his knees beside the lamp. Once people saw the pictures, you could hear the same argument a hundred times, all over town:

"But he'll be a Ifrit. I believe they're supposed to be colored."

"Well, we could rub coal on somebody."

"But ain't nobody near as *big* as Eugene Boykin. Ifrit's supposed to be big."

"How about Arnie Lumpkin? He's big—"

"In the belly, sure, but Eugene's got them shoulders. Didn't you see the pictures?"

To get the Superintendent of School's permission for Eugene to take part in our production, Miss Spivey played her trump card, or cards: the Superindent's wife and their daughter Louise. All Mrs. Lulu Blount needed was Miss Spivey's guarantee that Louise would play the role of Princess Badr al-Budur, Alaeddin's heart's desire, and she, Mrs. Lulu Blount, promised to bring her husband into line on the Eugene question. The only additional stipulation laid down by Mrs. Blount—one upon which she felt sure that the Superintendent would also insist—was that Eugene was not to touch any of the white children (particularly Louise) while playing his part.

It was no problem for Miss Spivey to give Louise Blount the part of the Princess, thereby dashing the hopes of dozens of other girls, but the second stipulaton (which should have gone without saying, some people thought) threw a wrench into the plot, which called for the Ifrit to carry

Princess Badr al-Budur to Alaeddin's castle not once but three times.
Miss Spivey went ahead and swore to Mrs. Blount that Eugene would
not touch any other person in the play, but when she sat down to change
the script accordingly, she kept running into trouble. At school one day,
when we were practicing our penmanship by the Palmer Method and
she was tapping away, trying to figure how to get the sleeping Princess to
Alaeddin's castle in front of the whole audience without the Ifrit to carry
her there (a technical problem that Theo would solve later, as he did so
many others), Miss Spivey pushed herself away from the typewriter. Out
of patience as well as ideas, she announced that she was sorely tempted
to forget about Louise Blount and cast a colored girl as Princess Badr
al-Budur. Miss Spivey mentioned Etta George (who would have eaten
rocks before she'd get up on a stage surrounded by white folks) and also
the family who lived behind the Boykins. They had a girl about Theo's
age, didn't they? Maybe *she*'d like to be a princess. "That would serve
everybody right!" Miss Spivey said.

When Louise Blount somehow caught wind of this remark, probably via the Mavis Davises, she hit the ceiling over in Claytonville. Louise didn't care if Eugene toted her all over town as long as she got to
kiss my brother Force at the end. She was broad-minded that way. She
came driving down to Bibbens' store in her daddy's car, a 1932 Hudson
convertible that left her raven curls in serious disarray, and pitched a fit.

"That colored girl can't be no princess, Miss Spivey! The princess
has got to kiss For—I mean, the princess and Alaeddin they got to kiss
in the end, don't they?"

"Yes, Louise," Miss Spivey said wearily, "I suppose they do."

Louise Blount figured she had Miss Spivey over a barrel then. I never
liked Louise Blount. She was always asking me things about Force or
making comments about how bad this or that girl looked in a harem
outfit. (It was true that no one else filled out her costume as well as
Louise did.) One time, during an afternoon dress rehearsal, while Miss
Spivey was showing my sister May how to situate herself in Shahrazad's
balcony, Louise Blount whispered to me, "I wonder why Miss Spivey
ended up an old maid. She ain't bad-looking."

"You better be glad she never did get married," I snapped back at

Louise. We were awaiting her cue, sitting in the shade of the Piedmont Paints & Hardware awning. I was already annoyed with her for her inability to pronounce *Alaeddin* the same way two times in a row. "You better be real glad, 'cause if she did, we wouldn't never have heard of *Alaeddin* or Shahrazad, now, would we? We wouldn't none of us know a damn thing about Baghdad!"

"Watch your language, Gladys Cailiff," Louise said, with a bigger sniff of moral superiority than she had any right to.

"What's so great about getting married, anyway?" I asked her, suddenly feeling sad and sullen, I didn't know why.

"Oh, Gladys!" Louise sighed, her bosom rising and falling. "Only a dumb little girl would ask a question like that."

At May's for tutoring that following Saturday, Miss Spivey wanted us to be the first to know that *both* Reverends and their wives were now in favor of Eugene playing the Ifrit in the *Arabian Nights* entertainment at the Baghdad Bazaar. (She was largely correct in her belief that once she got the go-ahead from the Reverends, everybody else in Threestep would fall into line.) She did not mention, although it became widely known, that Reverend Whitlock had been persuaded to change his position upon learning that the Ifrit was also known as "the Slave of the Lamp," and could not but do the bidding of his master, the possessor of the lamp, who was, for most of the show, my brother Force as Alaeddin.

Miss Spivey looked around the table, beaming, at Force and May and Theo and Miss Templeton and me, as if she expected us to burst into applause. "Who knows?" she said. "Eugene may be the first Negro actor ever to share the stage with white people in the state of Georgia!"

"What about Fourth of July when Theo recited the Declaration of Independence?" Force said. "There was white people on the stage with *him*."

"There *were*," Miss Spivey said.

"Yes, ma'am. A pile of 'em. Important folks."

"Well, I stand corrected!" Miss Spivey declared, as cheerful as ever, and she moved right on into describing the special touches she had in mind for Eugene's costume, such as a golden fez for him to wear on his head and a big curving sword and all, as befitted the all-powerful Ifrit, the greatest of all the *jinni*, the mighty Slave of the Lamp. She expected Theo to be drawing these things as she described them, but I could see that he was doodling swirls of smoke in the margins of his notebook instead. Finally Miss Spivey slowed down a bit and peered across the table to see how Eugene's costume was progressing. When she saw only smoky doodles in Theo's notebook, she asked him if he knew what she meant by a "fez."

At that, Theo, so to speak, erupted. "I don't see why Eugene has got to be the Slave of the Lamp!" he burst out. "I don't see why he has got to be the *slave* of anything."

This surprised Miss Spivey, we could tell. She tried to exchange looks with Miss Templeton, but Miss Templeton kept her eyes on the book in front of her on the table. Miss Spivey turned to Theo. "The Ifrit *is* a very powerful *jinn*, you know. No task is beyond him. He can travel the globe in an instant. He can build a palace in the wink of an eye. With the snap of his fingers"—and she snapped hers—"he can level a mountain or dry up the sea!"

"Long as somebody lets him out of the lamp first," my sister May said.

We all looked at her. Miss Spivey lowered her finger-snapping hand to the table.

"And *commands* him to do it," Theo added. "What I wish I knew, Miss Spivey, is where does a *jinn* go when he's *not* doing somebody's bidding? That's what I've been thinking about. Where does he *go*? Does he get time off? Does he get to conjure things up for his own enjoyment? Or is he just stuck inside that little old lamp, all cramped up and small and . . . *incapacitated*?"

Incapacitated was a vocabulary word from weeks ago. Suddenly I was picturing Eugene Boykin curled up inside a silver gravy boat with his head between his knees. What *did* happen to a *jinn* when he wasn't doing somebody's bidding? I'd never thought to wonder until now.

Miss Spivey said she'd look into it.

Later that week, I was helping Ildred wash the supper dishes when a heavy knock at the back door made both of us jump. As we turned around, the door flew open and Ildred dropped the pot she was drying. Over the clatter she cried, "My Lord amighty!"

Eugene Boykin filled the doorway from bottom to top—billowing pantaloons, glittering vest, folded arms, scowling face, and golden fez. He had some kind of pointy shoes on his feet, and stuck in a wide scarf tied like a belt around his middle was a curved and gleaming sword. Momma and Daddy and Ralphord had all come running to see, and while we stood there, all of us, speechless, Eugene took a deep breath and announced in ringing tones, while scowling for all he was worth, "Behold the mighty Jinn of the Lamp. Your wish is my command!"

Then he broke into a grin, and we saw Theo behind him on the steps. They both came in. Before long, Ralphord was wearing the fez and swinging the sword, the curved wooden blade narrowly missing the kerosene lamp on the table. Daddy snatched the sword away from Ralphord and held it up in the light. "Wherever did Miss Spivey get a thing like this?" he asked Eugene.

"Theo made it," Eugene said proudly. "With Mr. Hall's jigsaw."

Theo was slouching around next to the back door with his hands in the pockets of his overalls. I could just see how Miss Spivey had reeled him in. He was not the kind of boy who could resist a chance to use that jigsaw.

"Where'd y'all get the paint?" Ildred asked him. She meant on the sword.

"It's really tar," Theo said. "I sprinkled white dirt on it while it was sticky."

When you looked at it closer, you could see that's what it was— black speckled with white—but from a distance, it gleamed.

"Well, son of a gun," Daddy said, turning it back and forth.

Momma said, "It shines so nice."

"That's the egg whites," Theo said. "I shellacked it with egg whites to shine it up." Theo took the sword when Daddy held it out. He touched the pointed tip of it with his thumb, like he was testing how sharp it was (not very). "You, know," Theo said, "Miss Spivey told the Reverends that Eugene was playing a slave. That's why they said he could do it." Theo ran his thumb along the whole curve of the sword's wooden blade. "Slaves don't carry swords," he said. "I guess the Reverends didn't know that."

11

April

IN APRIL, WHEN the dogwoods bloomed, Miss Spivey abandoned reading, writing, and arithmetic as we had previously known them, and threw the whole school into full-time preparations for the Baghdad Bazaar. When we weren't painting gold stars and moons on miles of blue and red and purple cloth, or mixing up enough white dirt, corn oil, kerosene, and butterbeans to paint the whole county white twice over, we were coming up with harem-girl dance routines and doing something Miss Spivey called blocking scenes for Alaeddin. Full-fledged rehearsals took place on Sunday afternoons, when the various college girls and other out-of-towners, including my sister May, could be present. Both Reverends turned a blind eye.

It had come to light toward the end of March that May was expecting again. (Momma pressed her lips together when she heard, and then she sighed, but when she saw May, she hugged and kissed her and said, "Maybe it'll be a brother for little Ed.") By April, May was more than five months along and showing already, skinny as she was. Miss Spivey declared that May being in a family way (Miss Spivey said "with child") didn't matter one bit. Shahrazad was a storyteller and could spend the whole time sitting in a balcony at the Sultan's feet, all covered up in fancy robes that would hide her condition anyway, no matter how much she was showing by showtime.

That really got Mavis's goat. She went around trying to drum up some righteous indignation on the part of folks like Florence's mother and the Reverend wives, by asking: Who ever heard of a pregnant lady in a play on a stage anyway? Miss Spivey knew exactly what Mavis was up to, so she asked us in school one day if we happened to be aware that Shahrazad gave birth to not one but three babies in the course of *The Thousand Nights and a Night*.

This piece of news shut everybody up, except for Ralphord, who said, "I thought she was tellin' stories every night of the week."

Miss Spivey took the last green volume—number IX—from the shelf behind her desk. (She never brought in Volume X, which was mostly notes by Sir Richard Burton about his sources of information and things he left out for reasons of decency.) Miss Spivey paged through the book until she found the place, almost at the end, where Shahrazad has the nurses and eunuchs bring in her three sons—"one walking, one crawling, and one suckling," the last two being twins—to show them to their father the Sultan. For the sake of their sons, Shahrazad asks the Sultan to spare her life, whereupon he announces that he had already made up his mind *not* to cut off her head anyway, because she was "chaste, pure, and pious," to use his exact words, which were not words I would have used to describe her, given the stories she liked to tell. Then everybody puts on robes of honor and gets ready to abide in all pleasure and solace until, of course, as usual, "there took them the Destroyer of delights and the Severer of societies, the Desolator of dwelling-places," and so forth.

Miss Spivey closed the book on her desk and folded her hands on top of it. By now I realized that if Shahrazad had three babies in the space of 1,001 days, or nights, she must have been expecting most of the time she was telling those stories. No wonder Miss Spivey didn't think my sister May's condition was a problem, dramatically speaking.

I thought my sister would be as surprised as I was—and maybe a little disappointed—when she heard about Shahrazad having three sons. When I first told May, months ago now, how Shahrazad's stories held off the will of the Sultan for 1,001 nights, May said, and I remember it shocked me considerably, "I wonder if that would work on Ed."

I said, "May! Ed don't want to cut your head off, does he?"

She said, "No, Gladys, honey, he sure don't."

But May already knew about the babies. Miss Spivey had shown her those pages a while ago to convince her that she could still try out for the role of the storyteller, even if she was in a family way herself. May said she did wonder how Shahrazad managed it, though. "What d'you think, Gladys? Did the Sultan give her nights off? Or did she just keep on talkin' straight through?"

She did take some time off for the twins. It says so right in the book.

May was having a lot of trouble with her condition this time around, more than she'd had before. Sometimes she'd get a pain in her lower back so fierce it like to crippled her. The truth was, even Momma didn't know how much trouble May was having, although she worried about her being miles away from us in McIntyre as her time got closer. Ed stayed home more than usual that spring, and when he did go out with Ebenezer on short trips, Momma had Force carry me and Ralphord to May's to help her out. One time, I went in and found May curled up on the floor in the bedroom, sound asleep, with the door shut and her two youngest sleeping on the floor up against her like puppies or kittens or something. Not till they all woke up did I see that she had little Ed and little May each tied around the waist with a rope that was tied at the other end to May's arm, just in case they woke up and she couldn't go after them. May didn't want Momma to know about the rope, and she sure didn't want Miss Spivey to think that Shahrazad was *incapacitated*, so she made me swear not to tell how I found her on the floor.

It was, without a doubt, the dumbest promise I ever kept.

Something went seriously wrong with Mavis Davis, too, about this time. From a naturally bossy and perhaps understandably mistrustful person, she'd turned into a pillar of hatred. I thought it was on account of what Miss Spivey whispered to her, but Momma said that what happened to Mavis was what happens to a potentially good person when they are behaving in a way they know is wrong. They have to harden themselves. There was only one way for Mavis to keep on doing like she was—and we didn't even know the half of what she was doing at the time—and that was to hate Miss Spivey more than she hated herself.

We Cailiffs came in for a share of it, too. Although Mavis herself would not have a thing to do with the Baghdad Bazaar, she started asking everybody if they had noticed that all the best parts in the *Arabian Nights* entertainment had gone to the Cailiffs. When Harriet Eskew said wistfully, "But the Princess is Louise Blount," Mavis told her to shut up.

I didn't know what to make of the charge of favoritism, which was not exactly without due cause. I should have known it wouldn't do any good to point out that some of us Cailiffs had small parts in the play— like me and Ildred, we were anonymous harem girls—and that there was nobody in town who would have picked anybody but my brother Force to be Alaeddin. (It would have been like telling Tyrone Power or Clark Gable, "Don't call us, we'll call you.") As for Ralphord and May, they had their voices going for them. Sometimes that kind of thing runs in a family. When Ralphord and I tried to make our case to the O'Quinn girls after school one day, Mavis shouldered her way into the group. Arnie Lumpkin was right behind her. I think he was beginning to fancy Mavis Davis, which was just too bad for him.

"It's because y'all're Cailiffs," she accused.

"It is not."

"And nigger lovers," Arnie added.

"We are not," Ralphord said. I poked him. Sometimes I probably expected too much of Ralphord. He was still only nine years old.

Mavis got a smug look on her face. "I bet they don't even know why their momma and daddy love *Negroes* so much." The O'Quinns turned to Mavis, their faces full of expectation. Mavis sneered at Ralphord first, then she told the O'Quinns, "It's all on account of Ralph Ford."

"I didn't do nothing!" Ralphord said. Between me poking him and Mavis's meanness, he looked about to cry.

"No, stupid, not you. *Ralph*." She paused. "*Ford*. That soldier saved your daddy's life, which story, I might add, we are mighty sick and tired of hearing about."

I'd told Mavis about Ralph Ford once or twice at the most. (That was before my mother reminded me that once might be too many times to tell that story to someone whose own daddy was dead and gone.) I said, "I don't know what you're talking about, Mavis Davis."

"I am talking about Ralph"—she paused longer, for emphasis, this time—"Ford."

"What about him?"

"He was a colored man."

"I still don't know what you are talking about."

"I'm *talkin'* about Ralph Ford was colored," she said.

All I could think of was how would she know. I said, "How would you know?"

She didn't answer that. She spun around to Ralphord instead. "You're named for a colored man!"

Everybody looked at my little brother with interest now. I expected him to say, *Am not*, but to his credit, he recovered quickly. He said, "Ralph Ford saved my daddy's life. He won him a medal for bravery."

"He was a nigger!" Arnie Lumpkin said.

"You're a jackass!" said Ralphord.

Arnie Lumpkin stuck his face in Ralphord's face. He had to bend down to do it. Ralphord drew back, which was wise, I thought, until I saw that my little brother was making a fist. Arnie saw it, too. He laughed and straightened up again.

Then Ralphord said, "I don't care!" and he turned and ran down the dusty slope of the schoolyard to the red curve of the road, and I think he would have kept on running all the way to Bibbens' store if he hadn't collided with Force, who was coming the opposite way to pick us up at school. Mavis and the rest of them scattered. They left me standing alone in the schoolyard while my brothers came slowly up the road, Force with his hand on Ralphord's shoulder. When they got closer, Force said to me and Ralphord, "Y'all know better than to believe them two."

Still, Force had no facts to offer us about Ralph Ford one way or the other. About halfway home, we came around the bend and there was Theo Boykin up ahead, walking the same way we were, toward home, and moving slow, which meant that he was dead tired or thinking hard or, most likely, some of both. When he saw us, he stopped and we caught up, except for Ralphord, who'd fallen behind us to watch his own feet shuffling through the dust. We walked in silence for a while. Then Ralphord scooted up closer and said, "Theo? I got a funny question to ask you." He paused, then continued in a rush, "How would you feel if you found out that you were named after a white person?"

It *was* a funny question—one that I was surprised Ralphord would even think to ask—but Theo didn't laugh. He said, "I'll tell you what's funny, Ralphord. Practically every Negro in Georgia is named for one white person or another. Didn't you know that?"

Ralphord shook his head.

"Boykin was the name of the man who owned my great-granddaddy," Theo said. "On my daddy's side."

Ralphord shuffled along. "And that don't bother you none?"

Theo did laugh then. There was something so sharp in his laughter that for a moment he didn't sound like Theo. "Hell, no, Ralphord," he said. "Black folks just love being named for old white massas. How come you're asking?"

Ralphord told him.

Theo shook his head. "Two of my daddy's brothers were in that war. They had a separate regiment for Negro soldiers. There is no chance your daddy would've been fighting alongside a Negro. Mavis Davis was lying to you, that's all."

We were already well into rehearsals—far enough that I knew Louise Blount's Princess part by heart from feeding her lines every evening—when Mrs. Lulu Blount confessed to Miss Spivey that she had been unable to talk her husband, as Piedmont County Superintendent of Schools, into allowing a colored boy to play a part in our *Arabian Nights* entertainment. "I thought that was settled a long time ago!" Miss Spivey cried, while Lulu wrung her hands.

Eugene Boykin was even more disappointed than Miss Spivey. "I lost my big debut," he said, *debut* being a word Miss Spivey applied to everyone's performance except for the dramatically experienced Louise. Eugene pronounced the word *day-bue*, like Miss Spivey did. Arnie Lumpkin said that was just because Eugene didn't know how to read.

"He sure as hell does," I said, taking a quick glance around to see if anybody else heard me cussing. "He's been to school more than you have."

"Well, he ain't never seen Miss Spivey write it on the blackboard," Arnie said. Not that Arnie could read it one way or the other, but on the board it did look like *dee-butt*, which was how most of the boys at Threestep School said it every chance they got, usually with a little snicker.

Unlike the rest of us, Theo was not particularly disappointed on his brother's behalf. Theo said maybe it was for the best if someone else played the part. "Like Arnie Lumpkin or that Wallace Turnipseed." Wallace was another boy very large in girth, if not height. "I'd like to hear one of *them* say 'Your wish is my command!'"

But Miss Spivey said, "Don't give up just yet, Eugene."

And then, as if we didn't have enough to set us back on our heels, we lost Miss Templeton. If you wanted to know why she up and left town in the dead of night during that last week of April, all you had to do was ask the CME minister and his wife, who provided room and board for her over in Brennan, or Mrs. Faith Boykin, who was her friend. Any one of them could have told you that Miss Templeton received a telegram from Chicago, which came to Bibbens' store and had to be delivered to her miles away at the minister's house in the country, so there's another person, Mr. Bibben, who could have told you the truth about Miss

Templeton's sudden "disappearance." After reading in the telegram that her mother had taken sick up in Chicago and wasn't expected to last the week, Miss Templeton had tearfully accepted Mr. Bibben's offer of a ride to Macon right then and there to catch the next train.

One person it *wouldn't* do you any good to ask what happened was Etta George, even though she had been staying with the minister's family, too, and had, in fact, picked up the telegram when Miss Templeton's trembling fingers let it fall to the floor. Trouble was, ever since Miss Templeton boarded the one-thirty a.m. Central of Georgia for Atlanta and points north, Etta George couldn't finish a sentence without starting to cry.

Given all that, it's hard to imagine how some folks came up with the story that Miss Templeton left town because she was suddenly with child. By noontime the day after she left, it was just as if the telegram, which Mr. Bibben actually had a copy of for his Western Union records, never existed. It didn't help that Miss Templeton was good-looking and soft-spoken and so graceful in her ways that the Superintendent himself was heard (by Mavis Davis's mother) to say that Miss Spivey could have learned a thing or two from the teacher at the colored school—a remark that made even *his* name come up when people took to whispering. It was enough to make a person's skin crawl, once you understood what they were talking about. Theo got whispered about, too, in that regard, which made him blush so hard you could see his very dark skin go pinkish, and of course my own brother's name was mentioned by some. You couldn't look like my brother Force without people suspecting you of all possible crimes of the heart.

My momma blamed all such talk on meanness and jealousy in the heart of the talker. "There's some people can't stand to see a person as sweet and smart as Miss Templeton, without they have to bring that person down by talking ugly about her."

Theo Boykin did not have much to say about Miss Templeton's departure. "She left me a pile of books," he was willing to admit out at May's the next Saturday morning. He'd brought three of them along and started passing them around to show us: two small cloth-bound books— one by Frederick Douglass and the other by W. E. B. Du Bois—and a new-looking one with a title that made you want to pick it up and start reading without delay. It was called *Their Eyes Were Watching God*.

Theo dug his thumbnail into a groove in the pine tabletop. "Miss Templeton was saving these books to give me when I went to college. She said she wanted me to know what kind of company I was in." He looked up at us. "She said someday *everybody* would be reading them—in high school and college and all."

"Instead of Shakespeare?" Force said.

"I think in addition to," said Theo.

Etta George came to live at the Boykins' after Miss Templeton left town. This was Miss Templeton's idea, Etta told me later. She was worried that Etta might end up just cleaning house and taking care of the children if she stayed on with the minister and his wife in Brennan. At the Boykins' she would be closer to those up-to-date schoolbooks.

Moving in with the Boykins was a great trial to Etta George—not because she had anything against them, but because there were only two ways to get to the Boykins' house from anyplace else: you could cut through the woods or go down the lane past our house. Either route required Etta to face one or the other of her two greatest fears.

The woods were full of snakes. Our house was full of white people.

I once heard Mrs. Boykin tell my momma that, prior to the lessons with Miss Spivey, Etta's only experiences with white people had been something to do with a landlord in Brennan to whom Etta's mother owed considerable amounts of back rent. By mutual agreement, Momma and Mrs. Boykin set about trying to help that girl get over her extreme fear. Mrs. Boykin would send Etta George to borrow something from Momma every chance she got, or else to deliver a pie or a bag of pecans, and Momma would ask Etta to come on in and wait just a minute, set herself down, help herself to a biscuit. I didn't see that their efforts had much effect on Etta. If she came on over to our house with Theo or Eugene, everything was fine, but if she was alone, well, you could look out the kitchen window and watch her trying to bring her fist up to knock on our back door, taking deep breaths and closing her eyes, for a full minute, or two, or three, until her face was glistening and you wanted to open the door but you were afraid she'd faint dead away if you did.

It was equally hard to watch her come down the lane past our house from the road. Sometimes she'd go along on the far side of the pine trees, worrying the grass ahead of her with a long stick. Other times she'd stay on the lane but stick to the shadows, gliding from tree to tree like a ghost. Or she might just pick up and run past our house to the Boykins' as fast as she could. One time, she was halfway there when an automobile turned off the road behind her. I figured she'd bolt straight ahead for safety, but instead she froze in the middle of the lane right next to a big old pine tree, my favorite one to climb. I believe that Mr. Gordon, who was busy looking for white dirt in the ditch instead of watching where he was driving, might have knocked her over if I hadn't been halfway up in my tree. I called down, "Up here! Etta, up here!" just in time for her to spring out of Mr. Gordon's way and into the green cave of branches below me. She started climbing as fast as she could, and to get out of her way, so did I. Pretty soon, we were as high as you could get in that tree, with a view of the Boykins' place laid out in front of us, Mr. Gordon's car pulling up to a stop a few yards away from the house.

We watched Mr. Gordon get out of his car, a sheet of paper in his hand. He wore a white shirt and a tie and shiny black shoes and the kind of hat most men only wore on Sundays. A fedora, I believe it is called. He didn't go up to the house. Instead, he stood in the yard under a pecan tree and waited until Eugene stepped out on the porch. Mr. Gordon sent him back inside to get his mother. When Mrs. Faith Boykin came out, Mr. Gordon might have lifted his hat or he might have just pushed it down farther, you couldn't quite tell.

"You cain't lose!" was the first thing we heard him say. He had a way of making his speech thicker when he was talking to country people. When Theo came outside with his notebook under his arm, Mr. Gordon ignored him completely and spoke straight on to Mrs. Boykin, raising his voice a little in case she couldn't hear every word. "You get one dollar per acre every year, before they even start mining. How many acres y'all got? Ninety-four? All right, that's ninety-four dollars a year just for settin' on y'all's porch, doin' nothin'."

I had never seen Mrs. Faith Boykin doing *nothing* ever in my life. Her hands were always busy, pulling cotton bolls off the stems, or sewing patches on pants or buttons on cuffs, or slicing up tomatoes, or shelling pecans, or rolling out crust for a pie.

"And when they do start mining," Mr. Gordon said, "they'll pay y'all even more for what they take out the ground." He said all this as if it might be news to her, as if he hadn't come by and said it a dozen times before.

"And my pecan trees?" Mrs. Boykin said. Theo was right alongside her now.

"What about 'em?" said Mr. Gordon. I noticed that he had himself situated at the edge of a piece of shade in such a way as to leave Theo and Mrs. Boykin squinting in the sun.

"Kin they dig out that white dirt without messin' up my trees?"

The Boykins had the most beautiful pecan grove you could possibly imagine: nineteen acres of mature trees planted in rows that ran as straight in both directions as a checkered tablecloth. In the 1870s, Mr. Boykin's grandfather bought twenty acres of fallow fields and four bushels of pecans from the man whose property he used to be. The Boykins had pecans falling like rain every October.

"I'm sure y'all could tell 'em to leave them trees standing," Mr. Gordon said.

"No, sir, you can't."

That was Theo. As he spoke, he sidestepped into the shade and took his mother by the arm with him. It was a sweet little move he made. Up in the pine tree, I whispered to Etta George, "Mr. Gordon will be sweatin' soon—you just watch." She stared up at me in surprise for so long, instead of looking back down at the yard, that I had to point and say again, "Watch!"

Theo kept talking. "Sir, I read one of them leases." In fact, Mr. Veal down at the pottery had helped him with it—and so had Miss Templeton—but Theo knew better than to mention either of those persons to Mr. Gordon. "It says the company can dig up whatever part of the leased land they want. And it doesn't even have to be for digging out the clay, either. If we sign that paper, they could come and cut them a road right through our grove, just like that."

"Now, why would they do that?" Mr. Gordon took a step toward

Theo and sure enough, the sun hit him full in the face. Mr. Gordon squinted but he didn't back off. "Why would they cut a road through your grove when they got a road right out front to drive their trucks on?"

"I don't know why, Mr. Gordon, but they could do it if they cared to. It says so right on that paper you've got there, sir."

Mr. Gordon turned to Theo's mother. He pushed his hat back from his forehead and gave the paper a little shake and said, "What I have here is the opportunity of a lifetime. The good Lord gave you that white dirt as a gift, and I'm askin' you to put that gift to good use. It's the chance of a lifetime. It's something for nothing."

Mrs. Faith Boykin stood her ground. "I reckon the Lord give me them pecans for a gift, just as much as any white dirt underneath," she said, "and the peach trees, too, what's left of 'em. My children have never gone hungry."

Mr. Gordon was sweating something fierce now. We could tell by the action of his handkerchief.

"Miz Boykin," he said then, and that was a little shock to our ears. It was rare to hear a person like Mr. Gordon call a colored person Mrs. or Mr. or Miss, for that matter. Mr. Gordon was going a very long way in his mind, I am sure. He was bending over backwards. "Miz Boykin, I'm not talkin' about *not* going hungry. I am talkin' about y'all gettin' *rich*. You got a fortune wasting under them trees. Don't y'all want to be rich?"

Theo made a move as if to say something, but his mother put a hand on his arm and said, "I reckon I'm rich as I care to be for right now, Mr. Gordon."

"Well, then, good for you!" Mr. Gordon said, and when he turned on his heel to go back to his automobile, we could see that his shirt was stuck to his back with sweat.

After he was gone, Mrs. Boykin sagged a little. "Oh, baby," she said to Theo. "Do you reckon we should sign that paper? Ninety-four dollars!"

"No, Momma," Theo said, flipping his notebook shut in a decisive manner. "I *don't* think we should."

In case she still had doubts, Etta George and I both stuck our heads out of the upper branches of that tree, like a couple of giant pine cones, and said, "Don't sign nothing, Miz Boykin!" which made her laugh. It was hard climbing down from as high as we were, enough so Etta grabbed my ankle once to keep from falling. We were all of us too busy to notice what Momma saw from our house and remembered later: Mr. Gordon up on the road at the end of the lane, watching us from his car.

12

Camels

FROM THE OUTSIDE, Theo Boykin's notebook was an ordinary school notebook with a marbly black cardboard binding, the same as the ones Miss Spivey gave to all the rest of us. I'm not sure when she gave him one—after Halloween or maybe when we started the tutoring—but once she did, it seemed like he was never without it under his arm or stuffed into the pocket on the front of his overalls. Ildred teased him one time about carrying that notebook like other folks carried a rabbit's foot. Theo told her, "You carry a rabbit's foot, nobody knows if you can read or write."

She said, "Theo, everybody knows you can read and write."

"Maybe they know I *can*, but I carry this, and they know I *do*."

He had everything in there: sketches and plans—including alternate and final versions—for everything we built, measurements, favorite lines from *Alaeddin* and other literature, lists of materials and of names and of places he wanted to go someday. Baghdad was on his list, of course, the one in Iraq, and also Atlanta and Stratford-on-Avon (the original one, in England), and Nashville and Chicago and Washington, D.C., and other places I can't remember. There were figures and faces, doodles and curlicues in all the margins, "to do" lists that covered every aspect of the Baghdad Bazaar, and several pages devoted to a complete hand-printed calendar for 1938–39, with dates of special significance colorfully decorated in the manner of those man..scripts from the Middle Ages. Theo's birthday was marked and Eugene's and his momma's, the Halloween party, the day we went to the circus in Oconee, every day of tutoring both at Threestep School and out at May's place, the date of Miss Templeton's departure, three or four different dates for the Baghdad Bazaar (Miss Spivey kept moving it back to give us more time), and a day marked "BNW," which is a day I've yet to tell about, when he and Miss Spivey put their heads together to cause some real trouble. We'll be getting to that soon enough.

By May the ninth we had most everything built: the minaret, of course, and the onion-domed ticket booth, the arched entrance to the food and sales area which Miss Spivey said constituted the *bazaar* proper, the big gates for the end of Main Street, and most impressive of all, two sections of false front—"flats," Miss Spivey called them—that Theo had designed to roll right up to the real buildings on Main Street, one on either side of the sidewalk stage. Each flat was one and a half stories high and a storefront wide, with a "functional" balcony upstairs and arched doorways on ground level. Theo decided that it would be easier and safer to build the balconies this way, rather than try to attach them to the real fronts of buildings in town. ("And we can use 'em again," he said, as if he already knew that the Baghdad Bazaar was destined for posterity.) Like the smaller pieces, which we built inside Bibbens' barn, the flats had wheels so we could move them out to their designated places when the time came, but they were much too large to fit through any barn door. They had to be built out back of the barn, lying flat on the ground— this was, I thought, why Miss Spivey called them *flats*—with various big boys and men and my sister Ildred hammering and sawing on them at all hours of the day.

When the first flat was ready for painting, Miss Spivey had us start in the middle of the whole thing and work outward to the top, bottom, and side edges. We didn't have to worry about drips, since the flat was laid out on the ground, so we were able to lay the white dirt mixture on pretty thick, with plenty of little peaks and swirls, like meringue on a pie. We let it dry flat for two days, keeping a nervous eye on the weather. Then Force and Theo and a bunch of other boys used Theo's system of ropes and blocks-and-tackles to hoist it upright, and let me tell you, we were all astonished at how it turned out, with that white stuff on the window arches and the balcony and all. I don't recall who discovered that adding a little kerosene—which we used originally for the purpose of killing termites—also made the white dirt mix crack a lot less when it dried. I won't say that it looked exactly like stone, but it didn't look like wood anymore, either. It was like a building covered in stucco, with a lot of fine lines and little cracks that gave it, Miss Spivey said, "the appearance of antiquity."

Once they had the whole thing upright, they leaned it against the barn, wrong side out, to protect it from the weather—just in time, as it turned out. According to Theo's calendar, on May the tenth a hailstorm struck in patches throughout our three-county area, pelting seven hundred chickens to death on a poultry farm north of Claytonville, all of which had to be dressed and sold as fryers in the space of one day. Miss Spivey said we weren't taking any more chances with the weather after that. We would wait and paint the other flat on location, along with the rest of Main Street, at the last possible moment.

A few days after the hail spared us, Miss Spivey looked up from sewing gold stars on a piece of blue muslin that covered her desk at school and said, "Where is everybody?"

I stopped coloring the flyer Mr. Greene, publisher of the *Piedmont County Weekly*, had printed up to advertise the Baghdad Bazaar and looked around myself. Bolts of muslin dyed green, tan, blue, and red were piled up on every available surface, giving the schoolroom the look of a dry goods store and to some extent obscuring the fact that all but eight of the students' desks were empty. It was no mystery where the rest of them were. Like most able-bodied country people in Piedmont County, they were out in the fields with canvas gloves on their hands and big floppy hats on their heads, chopping at the first crop of weeds that wanted to compete with the little cotton plants.

Beating me to it, Florence Hodges said, "They're choppin' cotton, Miss Spivey."

Miss Spivey dragged her muslin, gold star, needle, and thread to the window. From there, if you squinted, you could see the hoes rising and falling in the corner of a nearby cotton field. It looked like somebody was throwing matchsticks in the air. "And why aren't you out there?" she asked us.

I said, "Momma won't let nobody chop cotton till they're thirteen."

"It'll crook your back," Ralphord put in.

"What about Force?" Miss Spivey asked, turning back to the window.

"She won't let him skip school to do it. They go till June in Milledgeville."

Most country schools like ours were closed already—with Miss Chandler, we never went past the first week of May—but Miss Spivey had wisely surmised that the best way to get ready for the Baghdad Bazaar was to keep as many of us as possible coming to school every day. Most of us were happy to come. It sure beat chores like chopping cotton.

Miss Spivey remained at the window, watching the matchsticks rise and fall, for a long time. Then she turned around and dismissed us, just like that, for the rest of the day. When Ralphord and I started collecting erasers and all, she said, "We'll do that later!" and hurried us out the door. She walked us halfway to our place, dropping Ralphord at the O'Quinns' on the way, before she revealed to me her plan to borrow Daddy's T-Model Ford, if she could, and go on up to Macon. "To see a man about some camels," she told Momma, and with her next breath, Miss Spivey asked for *me* to go along with her. I could scarcely believe my good fortune when Momma said yes.

The winter grounds of the Browning Brothers Circus were in Central City Park, at the end of Walnut Street, along the Ocmulgee River. Miss Spivey drove up Spring Street to Walnut and through the park entrance, and then past baseball fields and picnic areas to the circus grounds, which consisted of fenced-in fields, wooden sheds, and a row of larger buildings shaped like barns, all laid out in the shade along the river. Except for two men who appeared to be repairing the seams of

a big tent advertising sideshow attractions—LYDIA THE WORLD'S FAT-
TEST LADY and ALBERT THE ALLIGATOR BOY were on the panels I could
see—the whole place seemed deserted. One of the two men pointed us
toward a building with a fading pair of elephants painted trunk-to-trunk
on the double wooden doors. We did not expect any kind of good news
from the wizened man who sat, small and brown and sipping tea, at a
desk in the corner of the cavernously empty elephant barn, but good
news was what we got. Setting his china cup with a delicate *clink* on
a saucer edged in gold and painted flowers, he told us that two camels
on tour with the circus this spring had been "relieved of duty, I reckon
you'd say." A female who was in a family way had gotten so ornery, biting folks and making a mess everywhere, that the Browning Brothers
decided to send her on home with a gelding to keep her company.

"Are they *here*?" Miss Spivey asked him.

The news was not *that* good. The circus had been halfway down
the Georgia coast at the time the decision was made, which meant they
weren't too far from the camel trainer's hometown, on one of the coastal
islands. The camel man had convinced the Browning Brothers that it
made every kind of sense to leave those two camels at home with him,
until such time as the she-camel was ready to travel. The rest of the circus
moved on, but the camels stayed back on the island.

"Which one?" Miss Spivey asked excitedly.

The wizened old man looked at her from under half-lowered eyelids. He reached for his teacup. She had to ask again—"*Which* island, do
you know?"—before he recalled that the camel man was from Sapelo.

"So that's where they are?" Miss Spivey asked. "Two camels? On
Sapelo Island?"

That was where they were. Two camels. Soon to be three. "It's a dark
place," the old man said.

We stepped from the dim barn into the sunshine, blinking and
nearly blinded. When our eyes adjusted, we were astonished to see in
front of us, painted on the half-assembled sideshow tent, a larger-than-
life-sized picture of none other than the wizened man. He appeared to
be sitting cross-legged in midair above a banner that said OLDEST LIV-
ING MAN, a teacup and saucer in his hands. Floating over his head, four

beautifully printed words entwined with roses advised us to DRINK LIFE
EVERLASTING TEA.

"My Lord, Miss Spivey," Mrs. Boykin said when we got back to Threestep.
"Sapelo Island? That's where my grandmomma came from! Do you
reckon I'm related to that camel man?"

Miss Spivey thought that would be quite a coincidence, but Mrs.
Boykin said pretty near everybody on Sapelo Island was related somehow, most of them being descended from the slaves who used to work
the big plantation there. "And there's a lot of their relations in these
parts, too," she said, by "these parts" meaning Piedmont and Baldwin
counties and thereabouts, on account the owners of that plantation sent
their "property" inland during the war. "For *safekeeping*," Mrs. Boykin
said. "They were afraid the Yankees would come off their ships and steal
the slaves and set 'em free." Her own grandmomma remembered getting
on a boat with her momma to leave the island and then walking and
walking for days.

"You don't say," said Miss Spivey.

"Gran was just a little girl then," Mrs. Boykin said. "She didn't know
it was Milledgeville they were going to, but that's where they ended up,
right outside of town, around Hopewell. They moved the whole plantation up there, except for the very, very old folks. When the Yankees took
the islands, old folks was all they found. After the war was over, some of
those people stayed around here and some went back to the island. That's
why I still have kin out that way."

"Your sister lives out that way, don't she, Miz Boykin?" I was thinking about the seashells and sand dollars Theo and Eugene used to bring
back from their visits to the coast. Miss Spivey looked at me, astonished.
I quickly corrected myself: "*Doesn't* she?"

"Yes, she does," Mrs. Boykin said. "My sister lives on the mainland
now, but she works on Sapelo. Goes back and forth on a boat they got
that carries people out there across the water."

Miss Spivey, who seemed very excited, asked Mrs. Boykin if she knew why the Oldest Living Man would say that Sapelo Island was a dark place.

"Can't say as I know, Miss Spivey. It's mostly Negroes live there—them, and a few rich folks that come and go."

"My grandmother used to have a place on Skidaway Island," Miss Spivey admitted. "Is that near Sapelo?"

"Skidaway's closer to Savannah," said Mrs. Boykin. "You just got to cross a river to get from the mainland to Skidaway Island. Sapelo is down south maybe thirty or forty miles from there. And farther out in the water."

For a person raised around Milledgeville, she surely knew her islands.

Mrs. Boykin also knew that her sister worked in a house—"More like a palace," May said later—which was built on the foundations of the old plantation home on Sapelo from years ago. Now the house belonged to R. (for Richard) J. Reynolds, Jr., the tobacco man. Mrs. Boykin said he'd bought almost the whole island four or five years ago from a down-and-out auto industry millionaire. Her sister used to work for that fellow, before. It looked like people didn't buy a lot of automobiles when times got hard, but they sure enough didn't give up smoking, so Mr. Reynolds did all right.

Miss Spivey made some telephone calls from Bibbens' store, and she sent and received two telegrams. Before you knew it, Miss Spivey had a visit to the Reynoldses' island home all arranged. "My folks know everybody," she explained. The lord of the manor was not on the island at present, Miss Spivey was told, but she was welcome to come anyway. "So much the better," Miss Spivey said. "We're not looking for him."

I noticed right away that she said "we."

From the first, she wanted my sister May to come along. That was a surprise—to me, anyway. A bigger surprise was that May wanted to go. It was unheard-of for May to go anywhere without her children, but here she was, willing to leave them at Momma's for two whole days while she went on an excursion with Miss Spivey, and so excited about it she could hardly talk straight. "I don't got anything to wear!" she said when we went to get her in McIntyre, but Miss Spivey said she had a dress or two that would do May just fine. May was so skinny to begin with that she could fit in a regular-sized dress if the style was loose. Miss Spivey also insisted that Mrs. Boykin should come along. At first Mrs. Boykin said she was way too busy, but Theo said, "How long's it been since you've seen your sister, Momma?" and Eugene offered to pack her bag and carry her bodily to the train, if need be.

"Lord, what kind of boys have I raised?" Mrs. Boykin asked my momma. Her voice was thick with happiness.

Meanwhile, I kept waiting for Miss Spivey to invite *me* to come along. I was one hundred percent available—I couldn't chop cotton, I didn't have school—so what was stopping her? I did not for a minute entertain the possibility that she *wasn't* going to ask me. I kept on waiting, right up until the moment when May took both my hands in hers and asked me if I would help her girls keep watch on little Ed and little May while she was gone. "Ed's away and Momma will be out in the fields. Somebody's got to watch those little ones, Gladys, somebody I can put my faith in—or else I can't go."

They left the next day. Momma wouldn't let Force skip school to drive them, so they called on the train to stop at Threestep and carry them up to Macon. From there they took the Central of Georgia all the way to Savannah, where Miss Spivey planned to "hire a car," which she herself would drive the rest of the way down the coast. Mrs. Boykin would stay at her sister's while Miss Spivey and May got on the boat the Reynolds people had promised to send for them. Momma and May were both worried how May would take a boat ride, but Miss Spivey said that May spent the whole forty minutes or so standing forward at the railing with her hair and her clothes all flying back in the wind. They saw two dolphins on the way.

On Sapelo, a big fancy car was waiting for them. When May heard that the house was only half a mile from the dock, she told Miss Spivey that it might be better for her to walk than to ride on a bumpy dirt road, even in such a nice car. They could tell the driver was worried that he'd get in trouble for letting them walk, so they both got in the car right before they reached the house. The house, May said, the *house* plain took your breath away. May said the first thing you saw as you walked toward the house—before the white columns and the colored tiles and the gardens and all—was a big pool of water shaped like a cross with a statue rising up from the middle.

"It was a swimmin' pool, Gladys! And there was another one *inside* the house—a whole room with birds painted on the walls, and a beautiful tile floor with a hole in the middle, full of water! Can you believe it?" May said. "Miss Spivey and I sat at the edge and put our feet in that pool, just like we were down at the Rocky Creek, only we were *inside* the house."

May said they ate supper at a table big enough for twenty people, the three of them clustered at one end. It was just May, Miss Spivey, and the lady of the house, who looked to be about their same age and whose name was Elizabeth, but everyone called her "Blitz," she said. The only other people May saw were dressed in maids' and cooks' uniforms, and not a one of them called the lady "Blitz." That supper was the only time May and Miss Spivey saw her anyway. They stayed in a different building that was for guests, May said. She couldn't eat the food, which included a fish with the head still on it. While the soup was served—"It had toadstools in it," May said—Miss Spivey told their hostess that she was looking for a camel man.

"Oh, the *camel* man!" said Mrs. Reynolds, and May said Miss Spivey's spoon stopped halfway between the soup and her mouth.

"You *know* him?" Miss Spivey said.

"I know *of* him," Mrs. Reynolds said. She put her spoon down. "Well, you know, Dick mentioned one day that if you turn your back to the water, then Nanny Goat Beach looks like the desert, and someone said wouldn't it be clever to take some photos of a camel standing on the beach. It was about the *cigarettes*, you understand. Well, one of Dick's stable boys said he had a friend who owned a camel. And so Dick offered him a sum of money—my husband is generous to a fault. A few days later, they bring the camel and it's white! A white camel! Had they never seen a package of the cigarettes? Well, it seems they had a brown camel, too, but the brown one was ill or something. They couldn't bring the brown one. So they expected Dick to take photographs of a white camel—and *pay* them for it."

The lady of the house stopped there. May and Miss Spivey waited, but Mrs. Reynolds just went back to her soup, so Miss Spivey asked, "What happened to the camel? Is it still on the island?"

"I hope not. I believe Dick sent that camel man on his way. Haven't heard another word about it. Ah, here's the fish. Thank you, Lily."

May spent the rest of the meal trying to avoid the eye of her "trout almondine." She noticed Miss Spivey had no trouble at all getting acquainted with her fish.

The next day, after sleeping all alone in a bed big enough for six people—"I don't believe that bed would even *fit* in Momma's whole bedroom, Gladys!"—May came back across the water with Miss Spivey and they drove the hired automobile to fetch Mrs. Boykin and find out what, if anything, she had learned about the camels by asking around. "Fingers crossed, May," Miss Spivey said, crossing all of hers on top of the steering wheel as they approached the dock where they'd arranged to meet. There, standing right next to Mrs. Boykin, was a tall and lanky fellow who introduced himself to Miss Spivey as Andrew Mack McComb. "Uncle Mack, folks call me," he said. Two camels were tied to a sweet-gum tree right behind him: an enormous brown one with a kind of harness around her head to keep her from biting and a smaller one that May would have called light gray rather than white. "Done found the camels," Mrs. Boykin said.

13

No Such Place

ONE WEEK TO THE DAY after Miss Spivey and May and Mrs. Boykin returned from their trip, Uncle Mack the camel man rode into town. He and his camels had gone by truck from the coast to the circus grounds in Macon—it was a beautiful circus truck, which I saw later, with a picture of George Washington crossing the Delaware painted on the side—and after a couple of days' rest, the camels walked on down from Macon to Threestep.

Uncle Mack looked like a camel man to me. He wasn't dressed like a Bedouin or anything, but his pants were tucked into tall boots that were black and shiny, and his shirt was white with long full sleeves and buttoned cuffs, and he was wearing a round hat made of thick red felt—just like the one in Miss Spivey's costume trunk. He was riding the grayish white camel, the smaller one, whose name, according to the letters embroidered on the cushion under his saddle, was IVAN V. (I knew from studying Roman numerals what "V" meant.) The pile of cargo heaped up on the hump behind Ivan the Fifth's saddle made it look like Uncle Mack was sitting in an oversized easy chair up there. The big brown camel's name was Sabrina. Her halter was tied to the back of Ivan's saddle, so that she could mosey along to the side and behind him, her hump and huge belly rocking back and forth with each step. They were both decked out with camel bells, which was why people heard them coming in time for kids to run outside and chase after them and folks to line up along the street and watch them jingle down toward Bibbens' place. This was on a Saturday, late in the afternoon. Ralphord and I happened to be in front of Mr. Gordon's law office when the camels passed by. Behind us, we heard Mrs. Gordon say to her husband, "Do you all mean to tell me those creatures walked here all the way from Macon? That's fifty miles if it's a mile!"—whereupon Ralphord turned around and delivered point-blank to Mr. and Mrs. Gordon a camel fact he'd been saving up since last fall:

"Fifty miles ain't nothing to a camel," Ralphord said.

Luckily, there was room for Uncle Mack and the camels in Bibbens' barn, even with our minaret and onion dome and arches inside. It's not like we had much choice about where to put them. Everybody else with a barn that wasn't falling down had some kind of livestock in it that the camels—or at least Sabrina—wouldn't tolerate. Camels are even more prejudiced than people when it comes to getting along with their fellow creatures. In Bibbens' barn, there was a row of empty stalls and a little room in the corner where a hired hand had slept at one time. Mrs. Bibben called the little room "the creamery." It may have been a creamery once—Momma said the Bibbens' place used to be part of a great big farm years ago—but it hadn't been used for anything for a very long time, if the layers of old hay and broken chairs and rusty buckets and the like were any indication. Some of us were relieved from rehearsals and painting during the week before Uncle Mack arrived so we could help Mrs. Bibben clean out the stalls and the creamery and turn them into the "*caravanserai*," which is a place where people and their camels live together, Miss Spivey said. (Actually, she said "where camels and their people live.") Between them, my sister Ildred and Mrs. Bibben made that little room pretty cozy, although we never could get the smell of old hay and kerosene out of it entirely. Miss Spivey sniffed once or twice when she came to inspect, but she decided in the end that it would do. The camel man wouldn't mind, she thought, as long as he could be near Ivan and Sabrina. "He'll probably keep the camels outside anyway," she said.

"Who knows? Mr. McComb may sleep out there, too." That's what a man of the desert would do.

Miss Spivey always referred to Uncle Mack as "Mr. McComb," which was, she pointed out, his name. This led to some confusion. Mrs. Bibben had planned on the camel man taking at least some of his meals in the house, which was where Miss Spivey took hers during the week, until the Bibbens found, upon his arrival, that Mr. McComb was a Negro.

"Looks like you could have mentioned that fact," Mrs. Bibben said to Miss Spivey while about a dozen kids from Threestep School plus the Boykins helped Uncle Mack unload cargo from the camels and put it away in the barn.

"I'm sorry, Mrs. Bibben," Miss Spivey said. "I guess it slipped my mind."

You could tell they both felt snippy about it.

Uncle Mack never said a word about the kerosene smell, which was, in fact, growing ever fainter. Upon getting the camels settled in the paddock and following Eugene and Theo and a pile of other kids through the creamery room into the barn proper, Uncle Mack's first words were, "Whoa! What's all this you got here?"

He already knew about the Baghdad Bazaar—Miss Spivey had it all arranged for him to make some money giving camel rides while adding to the Baghdad atmosphere—but this was his first look at the minaret and arches and all. At Ralphord's invitation, Uncle Mack climbed up the little steps in the back of the minaret, which was stored underneath the empty hayloft. The ceiling was low there. He had to duck his head when he reached the top.

"That's where I go!" Ralphord yelled. "I'm the moo-ez-zeen!"

Uncle Mack climbed down again and delicately touched the white surface of the minaret, no doubt admiring its appearance of antiquity.

"We painted that with about five coats of kaolin," Theo said.

"*What'd* you paint it with?"

"White dirt. Ildred Cailiff came up with the formula." Theo looked around. "Is Ildred here?"

"You *made* all this?" Uncle Mack turned from the minaret to one half of what we were calling the Great Gate. He put his hands on his hips. "How'd'y'all know how to make a thing like this?"

Our Chief Engineer was modestly silent on that point, so Ralphord said, "Theo made the plans. We just followed the plans."

Theo was standing there with his notebook under his arm.

Uncle Mack pointed to the writing on the panels of the Great Gate. "You write that up there?"

"Yes, sir," Theo said. He had copied a line of Arabian-type letters from the beginning of one of Sir Richard Burton's volumes, repeating it over and over, to make a kind of border along the top of the gate. Miss Spivey guessed the line was a dedication. "It probably means, 'To my loving wife,'" she'd said, but it looked very authentic.

Uncle Mack said, "When you wrote it, did you start over to here, on the right, and go backwards to the left?"

"No," Theo said. "Why would I do that?"

"Y'all don't know what it says, do you?"

Theo didn't exactly look Uncle Mack up and down then, but you could tell what he was thinking. He was considering the odds that a circus man from Georgia would know how to read this writing from Baghdad. We were all considering that. "I copied it out of a book," Theo said. "Do *you* know what it says?"

Uncle Mack squinted at the writing for a second or two. Then he shrugged. "It looks good on there, that's all. Seems like you copied it just right."

Uncle Mack took his meals with several different families during his stay, but most of his suppers were with the Boykins. This arrangement suited us Cailiffs just fine because it meant Uncle Mack would come down the lane past our place almost every day. Often as not, he was riding Ivan the camel! If we were outside standing on the porch, Ivan would turn his head and look straight at the bunch of us. He'd give us that superior gaze camels do, the knowing smile. One time, Uncle Mack and Ivan V going up the lane came face-to-face with Mr. Gordon's automobile coming down it. Mr. Gordon, no doubt exasperated as usual from talking to the Boykins about leasing their land, came around too fast from behind the Boykins' place and nearly clipped old Ivan before he swerved (Mr. Gordon, that is), sending up a cloud of pink dust that did not faze that camel in the least, what with his sand-resistant nostrils and double-lidded eyes. Daddy was just about to send Force outside to offer Mr. Gordon a push when his automobile gave a lurch and he was rolling again.

One day, over at the Boykins', Uncle Mack told Etta and me that his full name was Andrew Browning McComb. "My momma was a Browning," he said.

Later, I asked Etta George, "If his momma was a Browning, don't that mean the Browning Brothers, the ones that own the circus, are colored, too?"

"Not *necessarily*," Etta said, and her tone of voice made me drop that topic and let it lie.

Another time Ralphord asked him where he got his round red felt hat, and he said he got it from Miss Spivey. Ralphord whistled. "From her trunk, you mean? You best give it back, Uncle Mack. That hat is for somebody in particular!" Uncle Mack just looked at Ralphord, who realized about the same time I did that Uncle Mack must *be* that somebody in particular, if Miss Spivey gave him the hat.

Miss Spivey wanted in the worst way for Uncle Mack to come and deliver us a lecture and camel demonstration at Threestep School. Among other things, she thought it would lure the older children back into the classroom now that "the first round," as she called it, of chopping cotton appeared to be winding down. My brother Force did not think this was a good idea. Force said Miss Spivey knew very well what the Superintendent would say about bringing Uncle Mack into our school. It might even be against the law. Force wasn't sure. Miss Spivey said the real crime would be to deprive the students of a resource like Mr. McComb, and besides, the Superintendent wouldn't have a lick of trouble with the idea of bringing Uncle Mack into our school if he was coming to paint something or wipe the floors, now, would he? "I'll just keep a mop handy in case the Superintendent drops by," she said to Force, who shook his head and said, "Y'all like getting in trouble, don't you?"

This struck me as mighty disrespectful of him, but she looked Force straight in the eye and never said a word about it.

In the end, though, Miss Spivey did not bring Uncle Mack *into* our school. She had us all sitting outside on chairs and logs and such in the schoolyard, waiting for him to show up with the camels. There was quite a crowd of folks from around town who joined us. Eugene and Mrs. Boykin were there, too, and Etta George, and some children from the colored school. Those children all sat a little farther off on the cushiony pine needles at the edge of the woods around the schoolyard, some of them with their baby brothers and sisters and their mommas and grand-mommas and even granddaddies along with them. When Ivan V came jingling around the last curve in the road—Uncle Mack up on top in the saddle that looked like a chair with no legs—all the colored folks stood up and clapped and cheered. That kind of surprised me, to tell the truth. Uncle Mack bowed to them from up there on the camel, and he did something with the reins that made Ivan dip his long neck like he was bowing, too.

When everybody settled down again, Uncle Mack tapped Ivan's shoulder with a long wooden stick while at the same time saying some-thing that sounded like, "Oosh," the result of which was that Ivan low-ered himself, front end first, then hindquarters, and then a final bending of his front legs that put him in a Sphinx-like position, which allowed Uncle Mack to slide off with ease. Using the long stick, Uncle Mack pointed out features that made the one-humped camel, or dromedary, particularly well suited to the desert that was his natural home. Some of these we'd already learned about during the week we spent studying *camelids*, but that only made it all the more exciting to encounter them in the flesh: the flat feet and long curvy neck, the droopy double eyelids—one pair that moved up and down, the other side to side!—and thick curly lashes, the flaring nostrils with extra folds that could close like tiny awnings in a sandstorm, and, of course, his hump. The hump was the reason a camel could go without food for eight to ten days, Uncle Mack said. Sometimes even longer. He had that built-in storage. I had been picturing a giant canteen of water up inside there, but Uncle Mack said it didn't work quite that way. He said that camels stored water in their *cells.* He said a thirsty camel could drink a quart of water in four gulps. Somebody filled a bucket from the pump so Ivan V could demonstrate.

While Ivan's lips slurped and burbled, making short work of the two-gallon bucket, Uncle Mack set us straight on what he called dangerous myths about camels' feats of endurance. (Miss Spivey wrote down *myths* and *feat*—the spelling of which surprised me, as did *cells.*) "A camel's like a human being some ways," Uncle Mack said. "They'll work hard for you, then they got to rest. They got to stock up on food and water. That's where the French and the English and all made their big mistakes. They'd drive their camels day after day, hundreds of pounds piled up on their backs, and expect them to get by on one watering a week. Drove their camels to death half the time just because they didn't know any better." There were heartbreaking stories, too sad to tell, of whole herds perishing in military campaigns in Egypt and the Afghan wars and Algeria and the like, eighty thousand camels in this war, twenty thousand in that. It was terrible to imagine the path of a retreating army strewn with the corpses of camels. Later, Miss Spivey showed us on the map the places to which Uncle Mack had referred.

Everybody wanted to know why he left the other camel in Bibbens' barn instead of bringing her along. Uncle Mack said Sabrina flat-out refused to come, due, no doubt, to the temperamental nature of her condition. "If y'all ever seen a mule plant its feet, then you have some idea of her mood," Uncle Mack said. Even Ivan couldn't get her to come, "and she's prone to follow him like puppy." Sabrina was due to give birth in July or August after expecting, in the manner of camels, for *thirteen* months, which fact instantly won her the sympathy of every woman in the audience, you could tell by the murmur that went up. Uncle Mack said the foal would weigh about eighty pounds when it was born— "No wonder it takes thirteen months!" Momma exclaimed—and would stand four feet tall, once it was able to stand. He also told us that a camel foal can almost always find its way back to the place where its mother used to drink before the foal was born. "In the desert, that's likely to be a camel well, but y'all just might find a young camel moseyin' up to your friend Mr. Bibben's watering tank someday on down the road."

"You mean he could find his way back here all the way from

Macon?" Florence Hodges asked. This was a bold move on her part, asking a question of the camel man. Mavis Davis, who was standing at the edge of the schoolyard, as far from Miss Spivey & Company as she could get, scowled at Florence long-distance for taking an interest.

Uncle Mack said, "Miss, if the stories I've heard are half true, I reckon he could find his way back here from Jerusalem."

"Or Baghdad!" said Ralphord.

Uncle Mack asked if there were any other questions, and to every-one's surprise, Arnie Lumpkin's hand went up. "What's that camel smilin' about?" he wanted to know.

We all looked at Ivan V.

"I believe he finds the world to be a funny place," said Uncle Mack.

When the informational part of Uncle Mack's visit was over, he invited everybody who wanted a camel ride to line up over by the front stoop of the schoolhouse, on which he had placed a desk for added elevation and a wooden chair to step up onto the desk. He led Ivan V over to this arrangement and parked him there. Everybody just sat and stared at Uncle Mack for a moment when he first said "camel ride," as if they could not quite believe their ears. Thinking that folks might be scared by the prospect of mounting such a tall and shaggy beast, Uncle Mack explained, "The easiest way to get on up there is while he's in a standing position. If y'all want to climb up from the steps to the chair, and then—"

That was as far as he got before there was a general stampede to get in line.

On the day after Uncle Mack's visit to the schoolyard, more desks were filled at Threestep School than had been for a while, so Miss Spivey put her question to a sizable group: Why, she asked us, couldn't we invite the children from Miss Templeton's school, many of whom had joined us for the camel lesson, to come to our school now that their teacher was gone? Most of us didn't know what to say. Mavis Davis wasn't part of that tongue-tied group.

"They can't come here!" she said.

"Why not? We do have room for them," Miss Spivey said reasonably.

"They are *colored.*" Mavis said this slowly, as if Miss Spivey needed time to take it in. "And they're ignorant."

"And they stink." That was Arnie.

"You stink!" That was me. I could hardly believe my ears. Arnie looked like he couldn't believe his, either. In fact, pretty much everyone in the room turned to see what might have come over me.

Except for Miss Spivey. She paid no attention to Arnie and me. "Well, now. Let's see," she said in that same reasonable tone. "The children can't come to school because they're ignorant. Is that what you said, Mavis?"

"Everybody heard what I said."

Miss Spivey looked around the room like this was a spelling lesson. "Who knows what *ignorant* means?" she asked.

Mavis didn't bother to raise her hand. "It means they don't know nothing," she said.

"Ah," said Miss Spivey. "I see. '*They don't know nothing,*' but they can't come to school to learn." She looked around. "Does that make sense?"

"No," I said. Mavis glared at me.

"What about the rest of you?" Miss Spivey said. "Does it make sense to keep children out of school because they are *ignorant*, which is to say, they don't *know* and need to learn? Does that make sense to you? Yes or no?"

About half the room responded, although without enthusiasm, "No, Miss Spivey." Cyrus Wood mumbled that all the country schools were closed by now anyway "except this here," but only those closest to him heard him say it. The rest were silent. They kept their eyes on the floor, or else on Mavis, who looked fit to explode.

Miss Spivey leaned back against the blackboard, half sitting on the ledge that held the chalk. I worried about her standing up with a white stripe across her backside. She seemed unconcerned about that. She folded her arms and looked up at the ceiling, buying time, I thought, trying to think of a way to win this one for the cause, although I couldn't tell you if the cause was something noble or just Miss Spivey's determination not to let Mavis win a round. She stirred on the blackboard ledge, as if she'd settled on something to say. "Some years ago," Miss Spivey began, "when I was in Baghdad—"

"My momma says there's no such place!" Mavis cried.

A stunned silence fell over the classroom. Even Miss Spivey was speechless at first. No such place as Baghdad? *No such place?* Miss Spivey stood up, blinking at Mavis for so long that Mavis took to pulling nervously at the skirt of her dress. It was the same white-and-yellow-striped dress her mother had worn to old Miss Chandler's funeral, which fact I remembered because I'd heard Mrs. Reverend Stokes whispering to somebody in church that day that this here was a funeral, not a ladies' tea.

Miss Spivey went to her teacher's desk and sat in the chair and folded her hands in front of her. "Mavis," she said, "I'd like you to come up here, please."

I believe Mavis was expecting to hear that. She left off picking at her skirt and marched up front, her shoes slapping her heels and her long chin sticking out, as if Miss Spivey had dared her to do something.

This was a moment of significance for all of us: the first and only time all year that Miss Spivey had ever called anybody to the front of the room for anything other than reciting or auditioning or writing on the blackboard (which we all loved to do). Our old teacher, Miss Chandler, would have been busy selecting a paddle from the ones that used to hang on the wall behind the teacher's desk. All of us were wondering what Miss Spivey was going to do, although we knew for a fact that she wasn't going to be hitting Mavis with any paddle. She had thrown them all away the first week of school.

When Mavis reached the front of the room, Miss Spivey said, "If you would, Mavis, pull the map down for us, please."

Mavis took ahold of the button on the end of the cord that hung from the map, and as she pulled down on it, slowly and carefully, the world unfolded as usual.

We all knew that the real city of Baghdad, the one to which Miss Spivey traveled with Dr. Janet Miller, was located in Iraq, and that Iraq, more widely known in bygone days by the ancient name of Mesopotamia, was, in its present shape, one of the "newer" countries whose borders Miss Spivey had added to the map in thick red lines. Baghdad was tucked in the Cradle of Civilization, near the ruins of ancient Babylon, Miss Spivey had told us—oh, so long ago, it seemed—between two rivers whose names she guaranteed we would remember for the rest of our natural days.

Now, the ancient city of Babylon may have been the place where both the alphabet and the rule of law got their start, as Miss Spivey said, but in our minds, *Babylon* was pretty well stuck to the word *whores*— the same way *handmaidens* was stuck to *Satan*—thanks to Reverend Stokes's frequent preaching on the loose morals and half-naked actresses in Hollywood movies, those temptations to which we all succumbed as often as we could scare up a nickel for admission. (When *Gone with the Wind* came to Claytonville, Reverend Stokes, who saw it twice, lost half his congregation by remarking, at the sight of all those bare-shouldered belles, that it was no wonder the South had lost the War.) We were all a little startled, then, when Miss Spivey told Mavis Davis to point to Babylon on the map at the front of the room.

"Babylon?" Mavis said. She sounded not only surprised but indignant, as if Miss Spivey had called her a bad name.

"Baghdad," Miss Spivey corrected herself. "Point to the city of Baghdad, please."

It was easy to find. Miss Spivey had lettered two triangular flags to say *Baghdad* in fancy letters and put one of them between the Tigris and the Euphrates and the other about midway between Milledgeville and Claytonville, Georgia, although we hadn't changed the name of our town officially as of yet.

"What if I do?" said Mavis. "It don't mean a thing. You wrote it on there your own self."

The whole room gasped. But Mavis wasn't finished.

"Just like you wrote all these here names. Eye-rack!" she jeered, and looking for all the world like one of Satan's handmaidens, she poked hard with her finger right through that fragile territory. Then instead of pulling it out in unspeakable horror, such as the rest of us were feeling, she left her finger in the hole and pulled down hard until she hit the stick across the bottom of the map, having just torn the world in two.

When the ripping sound ended, all you could hear in that school-room was the button on the pull-down string tapping on the blackboard while the torn map flapped back and forth, back and forth. Mavis stood there hunched like a person at the starting line of a race, with her hands clenching and unclenching down at her sides, and her eyes shooting bolts of defiance and hatred at Miss Spivey.

Normally, a hush like that lasts only so long. A chair scrapes, the floor creaks, a dog barks, a magpie or a mockingbird complains outside the window, and the quiet breaks up, it lets people breathe again. Not this hush. Instead of breaking up in sniffles or coughs or throats clearing, it deepened into a silence so intense and suspenseful you could almost see it, like the air going yellow before a thunderstorm. It didn't seem like there was anything Miss Spivey could do to Mavis to top what Mavis had done to the map. It didn't seem like anybody in that schoolroom was ever going to be able to draw another breath again.

That whole time, Miss Spivey didn't look at Mavis or the map. Miss Spivey stared straight over the tops of our heads at the back of the schoolroom, where Theo's Baghdad pictures covered the wall. She waited until the button stopped tapping on the blackboard. She must have been watching it, too, out the corner of her eye. When the pull-down string hung perfectly still again, Miss Spivey took a deep breath. She said, "Mavis, you are excused."

Mavis hung there for a moment, fists clenched.

Then Miss Spivey said, "You are all excused." Her eyes had shifted down from the pictures to look at the sorry lot of us. From the look on her face, I was afraid she might start to cry, in which case, I didn't know what would happen to us, but all she did was say, "Class dismissed," and then, when we went on sitting there, staring at her, she snapped, "Go on home!"

Mavis Davis took off like a bat out of hell, leaving her lunch bucket behind in the half-room and her shoes on the floor where she'd stepped right out of them in her dash for the door.

14

Brave New World

THE DAY AFTER MAVIS tore the map, I came to school scared to death
that Miss Spivey might have taken down all the pictures in the back of
the room and canceled the Baghdad Bazaar—which, thank God, she did
not. At least, she hadn't so far. You could tell she was still carrying the
weight of what Mavis had done. All day long, while we colored flyers
and sewed stars and strung camel bells, Miss Spivey kept her face empty
of expression in a deliberate, determined way. She made no attempt to
fix the map and she wouldn't let any of us fix it, either, although Ralphord and I had a plan for how we could glue strips of paper to the back
of it that would hold the torn edges together without covering up any
territory on the other side.

When we proposed this to Miss Spivey, she said, "No. Leave it. Let
it be a reminder." She didn't say of what.

Mavis Davis stayed away that next day, which just goes to show that
she knew what was good for her.

After school, I took it upon myself to invite Miss Spivey to come
on home to supper with me and Force and Ralphord. As soon as we
turned down our lane, we could hear pinging and tapping coming from
the Boykins' place. Force said, "Theo must have got home early."

"I hope he's working on that generator," said Miss Spivey.

He'd been hammering away on something for two or three evenings now in his momma's kitchen. Whatever it was, he hadn't let anyone watch while he worked on it, which irked my sister Ildred considerably.

The hammering stopped while we were still at the table, and about the time Momma brought corn fritters and syrup out to the porch for dessert, here came Theo Boykin across the yard, holding some kind of boxy metal object in front of him like the Ten Commandments or the Holy Grail and grinning like a fox amongst the chickens. He reached up and set it on the railing next to Miss Spivey, without coming up on the porch. It looked like a store-sized tobacco tin that somebody might have used for a game of kick-the-can before soldering a handle and spout on it. Prince Albert looked out serenely from down near the base of the spout.

Nobody had a word to say at first except Force, who said, "Well, now, look at that. That's quite a thing you got there."

Miss Spivey said, "Do you suppose it's a lamp?" She'd been worried lately about lighting. If Theo and Cecil Wicker didn't come through with at least a quarter mile of electrical wire and a whole lot of light bulbs (Miss Spivey was hoping, unrealistically, for a thousand and one), it was going to be a pretty dark Arabian Night, the night of the Baghdad Bazaar. Momma asked Theo if he was hungry.

"Thank you, ma'am, I've already had my supper," Theo said to Momma. He added cheerfully, "It's not a lamp, Miss Spivey. It's a magic pitcher."

Ildred asked, sounding a trifle sullen, "What's magic about it?"

"Allow me to demonstrate," he said. Holding the pitcher at the ready, he asked Miss Spivey if she would care for tea or water with her dessert.

Miss Spivey frowned. "I'm not in the mood for games right now, Theo."

Theo remained poised for pouring.

She sighed. "Tea, then. Please."

He tipped the pitcher and half filled the drinking glass on the table in front of her with what appeared to be water. Miss Spivey looked at the glass and then up at him. "Pretty weak tea," she said finally.

"Oh, my goodness!" Theo cried, making a great show of embarrassment. "I do apologize, Miss Spivey. I thought I heard you say you wanted *water*! Please allow me." In one motion, he flung the water out of the glass, set the glass back on the table, and without refilling the pitcher or tapping it or turning around and clicking his heels or anything like that, he tipped the pitcher and filled the glass again.

With tea.

Miss Spivey looked up at him.

"I *am* sorry, Miss Spivey. Have you changed your mind?" Theo said as he dumped the contents of the glass again and filled it from the same pitcher. With water. After which, he filled the glass in front of Force with tea, and then he held the pitcher over the ground and poured a stream that switched from water to tea to water before the pitcher ran dry.

Miss Spivey couldn't get over it. She took Theo's magic pitcher and shook it and turned it upside down and lifted the lid and closed one eye to look down the spout into the darkness inside. When Theo ran to get his notebook and showed us the picture and said that he had copied it from a book that was passed down through generations of Uncle Mack's family, beginning way back in the days when they were slaves, Miss Spivey was more dumbfounded than ever. Only a few pages of the book were left, Theo said. Uncle Mack kept them in a wooden box. The drawing—of a kind of jug—that Theo had copied into his own notebook did not look much like the object he'd made, not on the outside, anyway, but he said it was the inside that counted—the pipes and siphons and many chambers—that, and certain little holes in the handle to be covered and uncovered by the thumb. He showed us how it worked. "You can make it so it won't pour anything at all, if you cover both holes at once," he said.

"You made this," Miss Spivey said, "just by looking at the drawing?"

"I had to, Miss Spivey." Theo fairly simmered with glee. "The writing in the book—is in Arabian!" Even Theo said *Arabian* back then.

"You don't say," Miss Spivey said slowly, as she turned the pitcher around and around in her hands.

Later, when Uncle Mack showed her his pages from the *Book of Clever Objects*, as he called it, Miss Spivey shuffled carefully through the wooden box in which he kept them. She studied the drawings with amazement. "You don't say," she said again.

Most mornings Force and Ralphord and I were the first to arrive at Threestep School, so we were surprised to come around the bend a few days later and find the flag already flying at the top of the flagpole out in front. As we got closer, we saw that the shutters were open—a job that usually took me and Ralphord two long wooden poles and a good fifteen minutes to accomplish. The padlocks were off the outhouses, too. Standing at the foot of the three wooden stairs that led up to the door, we heard the bubble and hum of voices, quiet voices, inside. We all looked at each other. Force said, "I'll go first." As soon as he put his foot on the first creaky step to peer through the space between the double doors that never closed just right, the hum of voices stopped. Force straightened up sharply. "Goddamn!" he whispered. "She went and done it."

"What's the matter with you, Force Cailiff?" I whispered.

Force stood rooted to the spot where he'd straightened up, so I went around him and pulled the door open, making it squeal.

I don't know if I've mentioned that the desks in our schoolroom were wide enough to seat two students, although enrollment was such that each of us had a double-wide desk to ourselves, except when we were sharing books or working together on something, which Miss Spivey called cooperative learning. (Mavis Davis called it cheating.) What stopped me in the doorway was the fact that one-half of each bench in the first row, as well as one-half of additional benches here and there throughout the room, was occupied this morning by a student from Miss Templeton's school. A Negro child. They had all turned on the bench seats to look at us there in the doorway. I counted eleven of them. Not a one was smiling, and there were some—like the Baldwin girls, even though they were sharing a bench—who looked downright scared. Etta George was the biggest surprise—just the fact that she was there, I mean. She was sitting in my desk with a look beyond scared on her face. Theo's brother Eugene, who was sitting on the long bench in the back of the room, being too big and tall for a school desk, shrugged at us as if to say this wasn't *his* idea.

There were definite signs, however, that Theo might have had a hand in it. On the blackboard, across the top, above the camel facts, was a Shakespeare-type line in our Chief Engineer's handwriting that said: *O brave new world that has such people in it!* (I could tell it was Shakespeare by the way he wrote *Act* and *scene* underneath, right after *The Tempest*, although they didn't read one by that name out at May's.) There was also a drawing of the magic pitcher, insides and all, with arrows connecting its parts to a list of words that included *siphon* and *valve*, and so forth, as if Theo might be fixing to explain to us how it worked. Theo himself was not in the room.

"Gladys, Ralphord, come in!" said Miss Spivey, as cheerily as ever. She was standing up front by her desk. "Good morning, Force."

"Good morning, Miss Spivey," we all said. Ralphord looked at Force, and then at me, and then I walked across the creaky wooden floor and sat down next to Etta George. We hardly turned our heads, Etta and I, but our eyes met briefly before we folded our hands on the desk in front of us. Hers were clenched tight. In the meantime, Ralphord clumped over to his desk and sat down next to the Baldwin girls' brother Hugh.

Then Force said, "Can I talk to you for a minute, Miss Spivey?"

"Of course," she said.

"Outside, I mean."

We couldn't hear everything they said in their hushed voices outside the door, but the word *fired* came through more than once—that was Force. I didn't catch Miss Spivey's answer, if any, because that's when I heard the low but rising tide of other voices approaching. I recognized Mavis's high-pitched, humorless laughter. Of all the days for her to come on back to school. Miss Spivey came in through the front door, her face flushed but looking determined, and then Mavis and Florence Hodges were standing in the doorway in the back of the room, their mouths agape. Mavis took one look, turned around, and thundered down the three wooden steps outside. The other girl seemed just about to follow when Miss Spivey said, "Good morning, Florence. Come in, please."

Florence froze. Without turning her head of curly golden locks, she glanced around the room. A little girl whose name I didn't know was taking up the smallest possible space on the end of the bench where Florence Hodges normally sat.

"Come in and take your seat," Miss Spivey said. "I'm sure you recall that Mr. McComb will be back this morning to give us the camel-riding lesson he promised."

Florence looked over her shoulder, out the door, as if to see if Uncle Mack might be coming up the road already, and then, in what appeared to be an agony of indecision, she stepped into the schoolroom.

This same drama occurred a dozen times or more. Except for Mavis and one third-grader, everybody made the decision to stay. When somebody hesitated too long at sitting down next to their new neighbor, Miss Spivey would ask the child to take another desk, so in the end there were some desks with one white or two Negro children and some desks mixed. I saw my brother Force's face in a side window at one point when the room was almost full and then he was gone—late for school himself by then, but that was nothing new.

At a quarter after eight by the clock on the wall, Miss Spivey told all of us above second grade to open our notebooks and start copying today's vocabulary off the blackboard. The childen from Miss Templeton's school sat empty-handed beside us. Miss Spivey turned her attention to the first- and second-grade rows, draping across each of their desks some lengths of ribbon we had torn in strips from a bolt of blue muslin. She had a box of camel bells for them to string. Soon, jingling filled the room.

Etta sat beside me, her hands still clenched together, shivering like she was cold. "Don't you have no paper?" I whispered.

She shook her head.

"No pencil neither?"

She pressed her lips together.

Working very slowly and carefully, I tore a page out of my notebook and slid it over the table to her, followed by my spare pencil. She took them with trembling fingers. What was she doing here, I thought, Etta of all people? (She told me later that Theo had talked her into it, invoking Shakespeare, W. E. B. Du Bois, and—most important to Etta— Miss Leona Templeton, in support of the cause. "He reminded me Miss Templeton said we were the ones going to change the world," Etta said. I said, "What—you and Theo?" Etta shrugged. She was only telling me what Miss Templeton said.) We had both started copying words off the board when I heard the jagged start and stop of pages being torn from multiple notebooks. After that, there was only the tapping and shushing of pencils moving across paper and the jingling of camel bells. It was almost time to go outside for recess—at which point Uncle Mack and Ivan V were scheduled to appear—when we heard a car pull up noisily and stop outside the door.

The Superintendent of Schools stood for a moment in the door-way, just as each of us had. I had never seen him in person before, but I recognized his shiny scalp, red face, bow tie, and baggy suit from Miss Spivey's expert descriptions. The only surprise was the size of the man. Never in my life would I have pictured the Superintendent of Schools who gave Miss Spivey so much trouble to be a good four inches shorter than she was. She was in the back of the room when he came in, so there they were, his eyes at about the level of her chin, and her in those ballet slippers with no heels on them at all.

The camel bells—which had been getting louder as the kids got more of them strung—petered out into silence when the Superinten-dent stepped through the door. He instructed all of the Negro children to stand up—which they did at once—and file out of the school.

"If you please, sir," Miss Spivey said, "the children have their lunch buckets back in the—"

"I do *not* please, Miss Spivey," the Superintendent interrupted. He glared in a thundering way at the children standing next to the desks, said, "Git on out!" and they bolted as one for the door. Through the windows I could see them running off in different directions.

"As for the rest of you children," the Superintendent said, "I want you to tell your parents that they have the apologies of the Piedmont County Board of Education for what you have endured this morning.

School is dismissed." We all looked at him. "You may collect your lunch buckets and go," he said.

Outside, folks were waiting in the schoolyard to hear about what we had endured. Some kids walked off with their mothers' arms around them, describing their proximity to the Negro who had shared a desk or sat right behind them. My brother Ralphord and I stayed around and tried to make out what the Superintendent was saying to Miss Spivey inside. We heard him whenever his voice climbed: ". . . thought you knew better than that . . . not some fool Yankee . . . don't tell me that's how they do in Nashville, because we both know better than that!" Miss Spivey's voice was a murmur in between "against the law" and "escape prosecution." He hoped she realized the seriousness of what she had done. It would not be possible, we heard him say, for her to find another job teaching in the state of Georgia.

Miss Spivey said something to that, but we couldn't hear what.

When the Superintendent came out of the school, wiping his red forehead with his handkerchief, Ralphord and I ran off and hid in the bushes alongside the road, risking snakebite and poison ivy until the Superintendent's big black car rolled on past us. The dust hadn't settled on the road before we ran back to the schoolhouse, but Miss Spivey was nowhere to be seen, so we lit out for Bibbens' place, thinking to head off Uncle Mack and the camel. We sure didn't want the Superintendent to get ahold of them. As we came around the last bend before Bibbens' store, we ran smack into our brother Force and Theo Boykin, the two of them, standing in the middle of the dirt road *yelling* at each other. Ralphord and I stopped in our tracks. I don't believe I'd ever seen either of them *yell* at anybody, much less at each other. Here was something else new in the world.

Force was furious. We could see his eyes flashing from ten, fifteen yards away. "She'll get herself fired!" Force said. "Y'all ruined everything!"

Theo appeared unmoved. "Why shouldn't a person try and change such things as ought to be changed?" he said.

"Change what things?" said Force. "Ain't nothing gonna change. 'Cept she gets fired for breakin' the law. You know it's against—"

"So what if she gets fired?" said Theo.

Force looked shocked.

Theo seemed more than a little surprised himself at what had come out of his mouth, but he kept on. "They'll get another teacher in here."

Force said, "But what about Miss Spivey?"

"What *about* Miss Spivey?" said Theo. There was a hard edge in his voice. "She'll be all right. She'll go back to her rich daddy in Nashville is all. Or maybe take another trip around the world. That's what she's likely to do before long no matter what happens. I hope you don't think she's fixing to spend the rest of her life here."

Why not? I almost said it out loud. I had never given a thought to Miss Spivey *leaving*. Why shouldn't she stay? What about the Baghdad Bazaar? Just yesterday Mr. Hall brought two signs over to school to show Miss Spivey. The signs said WELCOME TO BAGHDAD, GEORGIA, POP. 1001. (We were really more like three hundred.) Mr. Hall had them both expertly painted by his sign-painter cousin in Milledgeville, and he was on his way to nail them up over the THREESTEP signs at either end of Main Street. I wished Theo could have seen how excited Miss Spivey was about those signs.

"How do you know what she's fixin' to do?" Force said, but before Theo could reply in his new hard-edged voice, we all heard somebody jingling up through the woods to the right of us. Force and Theo looked at me and Ralphord as if they'd only just noticed us standing there in the road. We heard more jingling, and then a camel snort, and here was Uncle Mack and Ivan V with Etta George and Eugene Boykin, all step-ping out from the edge of the woods into the sunlight. Theo and Force ran off in opposite directions, Force pounding past me down the road back toward the schoolhouse, and Theo bounding into the woods that were a shortcut back to the Boykins' with his brother chasing after him, hollering, "Theo! Wait for me!" I was still standing in the road with Ralphord, both of us pretty near dumbfounded, when Uncle Mack, Etta George, and the camel caught up with us.

For no good reason, I was thinking, *O brave new world*.

Uncle Mack looked toward the trees. "Where're those boys headed?" he asked me and Ralphord.

We said we didn't know. Then Ralphord had to add, "Force and Theo had a fight."

"A fight?" Etta George said. "Theo?"

"Not a fight," I said, and gave Ralphord my most potent like-to-cut-your-tongue-out look. "They were arguing, that's all."

"About colored children in school," Ralphord said. He dodged around, putting Uncle Mack and Ivan between us. "And about Miss Spivey gettin' fired, most likely."

My cheeks flamed up. "Ralphord, you are a jackass," I said, right in front of Uncle Mack and the camel. "They can't fire Miss Spivey one week before the Baghdad Bazaar!"

Of course, the mere act of saying those words, putting them out in the air where we could all of us hear and almost see them, made it immediately clear that the worst could in fact happen. Or possibly already had happened. I guess we all looked stricken then, because Uncle Mack said, "Y'all better come on down here with me, all three of you. Keep yourselves out of trouble."

We followed him and Ivan back to Bibbens' barn and set ourselves down dejectedly on upturned buckets in the passage outside the stalls, the smell of hay and camels filling our noses, along with just a whiff of kerosene. Uncle Mack slid the saddle sideways off Ivan's back—it was a *terik* saddle, we knew from our camel lesson—and he swung it around to the sawhorses behind him. Then he pulled the harness tied with camel bells over Ivan's head, and in the midst of the jingling—an inappropriately cheerful sound under the circumstances—Uncle Mack said, "I have to tell you, all this here Baghdad business reminds me of something that happened a long time ago, back when Browning Brothers Circus used to be in Savannah."

This sounded like the beginning of a story Uncle Mack meant to distract us with, but Ralphord and Etta and myself were so deep in our own worries that we met Uncle Mack's offer with silence. Finally, out of politeness, I said, "The circus in Macon used to be in Savannah?"

"Yes, ma'am," said Uncle Mack. "Back when I was a boy. Long before that, too."

Instead of getting on with his story, he fell to brushing old Ivan's flanks, not saying another word, just brushing and brushing that same spot for so long that it took a bellow from Ivan to break the silence this time. From back deeper in the barn, Sabrina responded with a sound like a leaky trumpet. She had been so jittery the past few days that Uncle Mack only let her out in the very early morning, when passersby were less likely to set her knocking against the fence around Bibbens' paddock to get at them.

"It was somebody I met," Uncle Mack said. He reached up and dug his fingers into Ivan's beard, scratched and tickled the camel's chin until Ivan grunted in delight. "When I was young—a little bit older than y'all but not much—I used to ride Ivan's daddy down the beach outside Savannah. That's where the winter grounds was at in those days. We'd ride on them salt marshes across the river from Skidaway Island. They were about as dry and bare as a desert, so I reckon our camels felt pretty much at home. One time I come out of the woods onto the salt marsh and there she was, on the other side of the water, settin' on a sweetgum log where the marsh ended and the dry sand began."

He stopped there and set to cleaning out the camel brush by tugging an iron comb through it. The task took all of his concentration, until Ralphord asked, "There *who* was?"

Uncle Mack looked up. He seemed to consider each one of us in turn, as if he were asking himself if we were worthy, if we deserved to hear this story.

"A young girl," he said finally. "A young girl settin' all by herself. She appeared like she mighta been cryin' before I got there, but one look at that camel of mine and she stood straight up with her eyes wide open. She had a sweet face—which I mention because that was the last I ever saw it."

"She ran off?" I said.

"I reckon she was scared of the camel." That was Etta George. She was a little scared of the camels.

"Or of meetin' a colored man—a stranger, I mean—out in the middle of nowhere," Ralphord said. Uncle Mack had his back to us just then, so I don't know if he had any particular reaction to this comment, but

Etta George gave Ralphord enough of a look that he kept going, as if to justify himself: "You don't reckon she'd be scared? A white girl, all by herself, and here comes a man she don't know—"

"Who said she was white?" Etta said, surprising all of us with her audacity. "Was she a white girl, Uncle Mack? Is that why she'd run off?"

Uncle Mack looked over his shoulder at us. "Who said she'd run off?" he asked.

"You did."

"I didn't."

"You said you never saw her again."

Uncle Mack turned around and leaned his back against the camel. He folded his arms and looked down at the three of us, sitting on our overturned buckets. "What I said was I never saw her face again. When she saw me—and it took her a minute to notice I was there, she was so busy with being surprised by the camel I was riding—the minute she saw me, she covered up her face real quick."

"You mean like this?" Etta hid her face in her hands.

"No, ma'am," said Uncle Mack. "She had her a veil. Every time I saw that girl after that, she had her face covered up with one of them veils. Even when she come riding up on a camel. They had camels, too, her people did, right there on Skidaway Island. Sometimes she wore a veil covered her whole head, like a hood. Most times she wore a smaller one, let a person see her eyes." He was quiet for a moment, remembering, and we were quiet, too. Then he sort of picked up, and as if he'd just remembered Etta George's previous question, he said, "She wasn't a white girl, and she wasn't a Negro, either. She was an Arab girl. Knew everything there was to know about camels. She taught me a thing or two." Uncle Mack laughed a little and Ivan turned his head around, his camel face looking amused and smug, as if he were in on the joke, too.

"Like the name of this saddle," Uncle Mack said. He patted the saddle he'd set on the sawhorses. "This here *terik* came from her folks. We were down to three camels at the circus back then, Ivan's daddy, who was getting on in years, and a gelding that was even older, and a mare name of Susie, so when we heard about this Arab fella come to Skidaway, we set out to make arrangements. The only one of the Arabs spoke English so a body could understand it was Miss Reesha. I thought she just picked it up talkin' to folks—she was that quick—but she told me she'd had lessons back home."

I said, "Miss Reesha? Is that the Arab girl, you mean?" I was getting a funny feeling about this story that took place right outside of Savannah.

"I do," said Uncle Mack. "Time I met her, her people'd been on that island for a few years already. They had a big barn and a couple of cabins, but some of them slept in tents, just like they would at home. She said the fiddler crabs got into everything. That was one thing they couldn't get used to, fiddler crabs skittering around."

"But what were they doing on Skidaway Island?" I asked.

"They'd run away from some enemies during a war over there, something like that. They were fixin' to leave soon, she told me, and go on back, but they were waiting on one of the women who was expecting to have a baby. She was having trouble, more than women usually do, and they were afraid she wouldn't make it if her time came while they were on that ship crossing the ocean, so they were waiting on her. She got so bad they took her to the hospital in Savannah. Miss Reesha was torn up by it all. It wasn't her mother, but they were all real close to each other, the women and the children. The whole bunch went to the hospital. They filled up a whole room, I heard tell, all those women in their veils, praying.

"Hospital didn't do her much good, though, because they wouldn't let no man touch her, not even a doctor. I reckon she would've died if somebody hadn't thought of a lady doctor they could call on. I saw that lady doctor with my own eyes one time. Y'all wouldn't believe if you'd seen her that she could be a doctor at all. She was so tiny she put everybody in mind of a sparrow—that's what they called her, some of them, the Sparrow."

By now, listening to Uncle Mack talk about Arabs on Skidaway Island and one of them having a baby, I had more than just a funny feeling. It was one thing to believe, or not believe, something Miss Spivey told me. It was quite another thing to have somebody else come along—

like Uncle Mack—and tell me the same pretty near unbelievable story about Arabs having babies in Georgia.

Etta George started to raise her hand like she was in school, then caught herself, and asked, "Did the Arab lady have a baby girl? Or a boy?"

"Baby boy," Uncle Mack said. "I remember they made such a fuss over him bein' a boy, as if a girl like Miss Reesha couldn't run any camel business that came her way." He turned his back on that and gave Ivan V a few more brisk strokes with the cleaned brush.

Trying my best to sound casual, I asked Uncle Mack the question that might just plunge that Arab lady into tragedy and her baby boy into our very midst: "D'y'all know where they went, Uncle Mack? After they left the Savannah area?"

"They went on home, like I said. Across the ocean."

"You're sure about that? They didn't go to Ohio?"

Etta and Ralphord each gave me a look. Uncle Mack turned around, too. He lifted the cap off his head—it was an ordinary cap, not the red one he got from Miss Spivey—and scratched his scalp. "Now, why would they go to Ohio?" he said.

It was a good question. I couldn't say, *to get massacred*, so I just shrugged.

He settled the cap on again and said the ship sailed downriver from the Port of Savannah and aimed straight out to sea. "It was a sight," he said. "All them at the rail holding down their veil things to keep the wind from whipping 'em off their heads, waving their free hands at us, those that could." He sounded a little bit wistful. "Month of September it was, hotter than blazes, nineteen hundred and twenty-one."

I probably don't even need to remind you that 1921 was the year my brother Force was born. In a hospital. In Savannah.

It was about this time, maybe just a day or two before Miss Spivey "went and done it," as my brother said about her bringing those children to Threestep School, that I had this dream. It was so orderly and clear that to recollect it even now gives me pause. Etta George was in it—we were in the Boykins' pecan grove—but mostly it was taken up by my brother Force and Miss Spivey.

I don't know what Etta George and I were doing up a giant pine tree in the middle of the pecan grove. It looks like we'd have needed us a ladder or a magic carpet to get up that high in a tree like that. Pine needles poked at us, our hands were sticky with sap. Everything felt as real as washing dishes. Still, I knew it had to be a dream, because if it wasn't, then why didn't I make myself known as soon as I saw who it was down there on the ground below us?

At first, we thought maybe they came to rehearse a scene. Playing a handsome youth like Alaeddin, my brother looked the part, but he wasn't much of an actor. Oh, he was happy to swoop across the stage and carry off Louise Blount, or climb down a rope from the balcony on the big flat they rolled into place in front of Dot's former Café, and with practice he got very good at dismounting Ivan the camel without catching his robes in the reins and bells and all. But when it came to kissing Louise, which he had to do twice (once while she was asleep and then again at the end of the show when Alaeddin marries the Princess), Force couldn't seem to keep from acting like she was his grandmother, the little peck he gave her, and what was supposed to be an embrace looked more like he was trying to keep her at arm's length if he could. (Watching a rehearsal one time, Daddy muttered, "You'd think that boy wouldn't have no trouble doing what's always come so natural to him.") Force said it was because everybody was watching him do it. So it would have made some kind of sense for Miss Spivey to take him somewhere—like the heart of a pecan grove—away from prying eyes, and try to get him to relax a little. She had worked for hours with my sister May, hadn't she, the two of them holed up in Bibbens' springhouse or May's own kitchen, so May could learn to read her part "with feeling"?

The trouble was, if Force and Miss Spivey were here to rehearse, then how come they weren't talking?

Well, by the time I thought all that through, I reckon it was too late for me and Etta George to make our presence known. We looked down.

Miss Spivey stood directly under the tree we were in. She was wearing the blue blouse with the square neckline and matching blue skirt, and a plain straw sun hat that covered her hair completely, at least from our aerial point of view. We couldn't see her face. She had her hands folded in front of her like she made us do when we recited a poem or a multiplication table. Force was crouched down at the base of the tree, busy picking up fallen branches and pine cones and pecans and such, tossing them left and right and over his shoulder to leave a nice, clear blanket of pine needles under the tree. That whole time, neither of them said a word. Neither did we, up in the tree.

When he was satisfied with the pine needles, Force stood up and brushed his hands on his pants, leaving long dusty streaks. By this time, Miss Spivey had taken off her straw hat. He went around behind her, to where her blouse buttoned up the back, and started unbuttoning it. Right about then, Etta George gave my arm a squeeze. I was afraid to move even enough to turn my head and look at her. Force undid the last of the buttons. Miss Spivey put her arms straight down in front. He caught her blouse before it slipped over her wrists to the ground.

She was wearing a kind of fancy brassiere that I had never seen before. Force slid the straps off her shoulders, which he kissed, first one, then the other, and then he turned his attention to the hooks in the back, which took him about two seconds to unfasten. She tilted her head back against his chest. Force took her straw hat out of her hand and skimmed it through the air. We didn't see where it landed, not with the view we now had of Miss Spivey. She was naked to the waist. Her breasts were like two globes of ivory, only whiter. Force held them, one in each hand, delicately, as if they might break.

At least he didn't take *his* clothes off. Up in the tree, I was grateful for that. He folded up Miss Spivey's blouse and then her skirt and her slip and her garter belt and her stockings—she folded up her own white panties—and made a neat little pile of them under the pine tree. When she was stark-naked in broad daylight—it *had* to be a dream—they laid themselves down together in such a way that he was stretched out on his side, his head resting on his arm, and she was leaning back against the front of him, using the crook of his neck and shoulder for a pillow. Looking down between the branches, we could see her little smile, and her throat, and all the rest of her, all the way down to her toes.

Etta breathed in my ear, "She's so white," which all but knocked me clean out of the tree, although you only had to look down to know there was no chance that Force or Miss Spivey would hear Etta or me, or the leaves whispering, or the crickets singing, or the pine needles rustling under them. And it was sure enough true, what Etta said. Miss Spivey was very, very white, not a freckle or a birthmark that we could see from above, just white, white skin, miles of it, and her red hair—lush and coppery, exactly the same color on her head as down below—with the sun shining it into little licks of flame.

Force had only one free hand, the way they were situated. One hand was all he needed. It roamed freely over the globes and hills and columns of pearl that were Miss Spivey until it reached what seemed to be its final destination. At the top of her long white legs, his hand stopped, but his fingers kept moving. They might have been playing a handful of notes on the piano or strumming a guitar. Up in the tree, Etta George gripped my arm tighter. Down below, Miss Spivey kept very white and still. When she did begin to move, we could hardly tell at first, such a gentle rolling of her hips. The little smile she was smiling faded. When she groaned, we thought maybe she was pushing him away, but he held firm until she gave a little cry—I say a cry but there ought to be another word for the low, sweet sound she made—and they both settled down, Force flat on his back now, and Miss Spivey like snow melting on top of him. If they had opened their eyes even once, either of them, they would have seen me and Etta George holding on to each other, trying hard to stay up in that tree.

But they didn't open their eyes, not until Force sat up to watch Miss Spivey put her clothes back on. He helped her with her garters in the back. She stuffed her underpants into the pocket of her skirt. Miss Spivey refused to wear any garment that didn't have pockets, sewing them herself into skirts and dresses that did not come so equipped. She said there was no use giving men the advantage when it came to carrying coins and a clean handkerchief. She never said a word about carrying underpants.

We waited until we couldn't see them anymore through the trees and then we waited a little longer. When her feet touched solid ground again, Etta George whispered a breathless, "Sweet Jesus," and I realized that my head—really, my whole self—was buzzing inside. Both of us had pine needles in our hair. Our fingers smelled like Christmas. We stole back through the grove in silence, Etta George in the lead, which didn't even strike me as unusual, although I did wish I could see her face for a clue as to what she was feeling. Parts of my body were tingling that I couldn't ever remember tingling before. I wanted to ask Etta if she had watched the whole time, or if she had closed her eyes the way I kept telling myself I ought to have done. I was plenty old enough to know that what I had seen—what they had done—was wrong. But it wasn't the wrongness I was thinking about. What I was thinking was that my brother Force and Miss Spivey were like peas in a pod back there, just like in the book, and so beautiful, the two of them, as to be a seduction to the pious. (Not that I ever was particularly pious.) As if she could tell what I was thinking, Etta George stopped on the path suddenly and turned around. She had such a look—stern almost to the point of meanness. I thought she was going to make me swear not to tell—as if she needed to—but she didn't. She said, "They didn't do the whole thing."

I looked at her.

"That wasn't the whole . . . act . . . what they done."

Now I knew that Etta hadn't closed her eyes, either.

She shook my wrist—which was something, for Etta—and whispered urgently, "D'y'all know what I'm talking about?"

"Course I do," I said, although I didn't know, at least not exactly. But I sure enough knew what *touzle* meant.

Oh, I know what you all are thinking. You're thinking that it wasn't a dream I had about me and Etta George up in a pine tree in the Boykins' pecan grove. You're thinking that it really happened, right before my eyes. That's what you all are thinking.

All right, then. It wasn't a dream.

15

Baghdad, Georgia

THE SUPERINTENDENT COULD indeed fire Miss Spivey a week before the Baghdad Bazaar—or at least he could make a formal recommendation to the Piedmont County Board of Education that they do so, which was exactly what he did. In the meantime, as many folks as could cram themselves into the deputy sheriff's office held an emergency meeting to decide what to do about Miss Spivey's latest act of impropriety, this one amounting to illegal, if not criminal, behavior, namely, letting the colored children come to school. Could the citizens of Threestep—and, it must be said, their children—continue to associate with such a woman? If not, did they have so much as a prayer of putting on an event like the Baghdad Bazaar without her? Who would be in charge? Who would wrap the turbans? Why, oh, *why* did she insist on doing like she did?

"It was all that travel and going to school with foreigners that made her strange," Mrs. Reverend Stokes said, though not unkindly.

Other folks had stronger words to say about Miss Spivey—words like "plumb crazy" and "dangerous" and "She oughta be *arrested*." That came from the elder Mavis Davis. She also objected to the heathen nature of all this Baghdad business, but those objections pretty much fell on deaf ears.

In the end, the bottom line was the bottom line.

"We got so much invested in it already," Mr. Hall the lumberman said. By *it*, he meant the Baghdad Bazaar. "All them balconies and arches built."

"And the camels, come all the way from Macon," our daddy said. He and Uncle Mack had drawn up the route for an advertising campaign via camel, which would cover three counties in six days. It was set to commence the next day.

"I went and got the painting crew ready to go," said Linwood Perkins, and he glanced at Mr. Gordon, who was sitting in the corner on a stool from Dot's Café. The deputy sheriff sounded a trifle nervous whenever he mentioned the painting crew. There had been some controversy regarding whether or not it was wise to borrow the chain gang working on the Old Macon Road (both the guards being Linwood's cousins) and have them join forces with the good people of our town in order to paint the entire block of Main Street, plus one of the flats we'd built, in a single day, namely, the Thursday before the Friday of the Baghdad Bazaar. The idea was to minimize the chance of a really good thunderstorm washing our white dirt right down the drain. When somebody asked Miss Spivey what if it rained on Thursday night, she had said firmly, "It won't."

How could we quit now? That was the question. Prizes of all kinds had been collected or contrived, game booths had been constructed and hung with colored flags. Theo Boykin and Cecil Wicker had strung *One Thousand and One Lights* along one-half mile of electrical wire connected to Theo's generator.

"Well, all right, then," said Mavis Davis, Sr., who rarely attended social events in Threestep but wouldn't have missed this meeting for the world. "If y'all wish to be seen as a town that would stand by a teacher who believes that white children and colored should attend school together—*and* who taught their children to sing and do like *heathens*, well, then—all right."

That threw a pall over the meeting. There wasn't a person in the room who didn't wish Miss Spivey had refrained from bringing colored children into Threestep School.

"She *was* careful not to set any boys next to any girls," Mrs. Hodges offered tentatively. "My Florence told me that."

Mrs. Reverend Stokes stood up then. She had a deep and abiding dislike for Mavis Davis the elder, due in part to the number of times the Reverend Stokes had found it necessary to visit the poor widow after B. Bob Davis hung himself in his barn, even though Mrs. Mavis Davis had already half defected to United Methodist in Claytonville, preferring those stained-glass windows to the plain white church in Threestep at least two Sundays out of four.

"They weren't *attending school* with white children," Mrs. Reverend Stokes said. "School let out for the year in Claytonville over a week ago. I believe that's official for Piedmont County." It was a hair she split down the middle, but the mood lightened. Folks were ready to grasp any straw in order to save the Baghdad Bazaar.

Mrs. Mavis Davis said, "I'd like to know what Mr. Gordon has to say about the legality of Miss Spivey's actions and her continuance in the position—as such."

Everybody turned to Mr. Gordon's corner. He appeared at first to be asleep and perhaps in danger of toppling off the freestanding counter stool, as if the fate of the Baghdad Bazaar and/or Miss Spivey were not of much interest to him, but when he heard Mrs. Davis say his name, he straightened up. "Ma'am," he said, "given the technicality regarding the status of the school session, to which the Reverend's wife has directed our attention, I doubt very highly whether pursuance of the school attendance issue via legal channels is likely to be efficacious at this time."

The room was quiet.

Mr. Gordon added, "There *are* other remedies."

This remark caused some fidgeting here and there. Looks were exchanged. Mrs. Reverend Stokes—who didn't like Mr. Gordon, either, for reasons that had to do with a gardening shed behind the church that burned to the ground a few years earlier, shortly after her husband declined membership in the Klan—stood up again and rephrased her point for emphasis and clarity: "I say, colored children were in the building, but they were not attending *school*. As such." She sat down.

"Well," Mr. Gordon drawled, settling back on his stool, "that sounds like 'case closed' to me, Mrs. Stokes."

Linwood Perkins was dispatched, as usual, to report the results of the meeting officially to Miss Spivey.

"You mean they're not going to make the Board of Education tar and feather me and run me out of town on a rail?" Miss Spivey reportedly said.

"No, ma'am," Linwood told her happily, although he'd meant to call her Grace. They were standing in the Bibbens' parlor. The windows faced west, and late afternoon sunlight was cutting stripes of bright color in the somber floral pattern of Mrs. Bibben's rug.

Miss Spivey raised one eyebrow and said, "I guess miracles never cease," but as Linwood Perkins said later, anyone could see how pleased she was.

Less than a week remained before the Baghdad Bazaar when the first of our camel publicity tours (these were Uncle Mack's idea) set out from town with Pinkie Lou Griffith and Florence Hodges in full Arab lady regalia up on top of Ivan V, and Uncle Mack and Mr. Hall, both in long black Bedouin robes and checkered headscarves, walking alongside. They went all the way to Milledgeville like that, handing out flyers and jangling camel bells. It took most of a day. Daddy followed them later in the truck so everybody could ride back, including the camel.

I got to ride to McIntyre on Wednesday with Ralphord and my sister Ildred, me and Ildred as harem girls with long veils overall and Ralphord decked out as *muezzin*. Ildred claimed afterward that riding that camel through the Georgia countryside was the most fun she ever had without a fishing pole. Folks came out of their houses when they heard the camel bells coming and ran down to the road to watch us pass. Out in the country they would be wide-eyed and slack-jawed in astonishment, but then some kid would dash off up the road ahead of us and by the time we'd get to the square or the general store, people would be lining the street, waving feed sacks like flags and scrambling to catch the flyers that we launched like paper gliders from our swaying seat on Ivan V. What I remember best was the farmer outside of Coopersville who very kindly offered us lemonade along with a cool drink for Ivan, failing to mention that the watering trough in his yard was adjacent to his hog pen. It turns out that camels are more afraid of hogs than of any other animal, and let me tell you, when you find yourself on the back of a runaway camel, you are more than just grateful for the overgrown saddle horn that sticks up from the front of a *terik* saddle so a person can hold on in an emergency. It took Uncle Mack and the farmer, both on horseback, a good fifteen minutes to run old Ivan down. We left a trail of scarves and veils and camel bells from the hog pen halfway back to Coopersville.

The Eskew sisters, Mamie and Harriet, wound up the last full day of the camel campaign in a swing through Claytonville on the eve of the Baghdad Bazaar. Most everybody else was either rehearsing *Alaeddin* in the schoolhouse that Thursday, or painting the town white—Main Street, anyway—all in a single day. The first thing we did was to paint the second "flat" so we could leave it lay in the sun all day to dry, and the last thing, as evening fell, was to lift that flat with blocks and tackles and roll it, upright, into place against the front of Mr. Tuttle's hardware store. Instantly the storefront turned into a white "stone" wall with arched windows and a balcony that stood up off the sidewalk at about the height of a man's head. With that last piece in place and the ropes they'd used to haul it coiled like big snakes just under the sidewalk, folks finally left off painting and took to wandering up and down the street instead, some with brushes still in hand, dazed in amazement at what had been wrought in one day's time with the help of the chain gang. Not one convict escaped in the process, which was good, at least from our point of view.

Newly painted and shimmering white, Main Street really did look like a place where none of us had ever been before. Harriet Eskew never tired of telling folks that she and her sister rode out of Threestep, Georgia, on Ivan V at seven o'clock on Thursday morning, but they came back, twelve hours later, to a place called "Baghdad."

16

The Baghdad Bazaar

PEOPLE STARTED ARRIVING before sunset on Friday in wagons, in automobiles and trucks, on horseback and on mules and on foot, some pushing wheelbarrows or pulling coaster wagons with lunch and their kids curled up in them. They came from every town the camel route had passed through and then some: from Brennan and Oconee and Claytonville and Toomsboro and McIntyre and Milledgeville and Ivey and Eatonton and Haddock and Gray—some even all the way from Macon. Donkeys and mules and old farm horses were everywhere, tethered to axles and fence posts and the telephone pole in front of Bibbens' store. People walked up and down the street looking at the arches and the onion dome and the balconies and all with their mouths hanging open, saying things like, "I drove through this town last week and there was nothin' here, just like always. Now look at it!"

With the arrival of the crowds, it seemed like everybody forgot all about whatever controversy and trouble Miss Spivey had stirred up, at least for the time being. All folks could think of was how if everybody here spent just ten cents, or fifteen cents, or twenty, or a dollar—I tell you, multiplication facts were flying. We seemed to be teetering on the brink of untold wealth. Reverend Stokes attributed the size of the crowd to God's blessing on our humble enterprise. "If I said it once," he kept saying, "I have said it a hundred times. God helps those who help themselves."

He said it a hundred times.

Shortly after sunset, Miss Spivey sent Ralphord up into the minaret and told him to wait for her signal. It was almost time for what we referred to on the flyers as the Moment of Illumination. Originally, Miss Spivey had been disappointed by Theo's insistence that, owing to the significant quantity of kerosene we had painted on our boards and mixed into our white dirt, the flaming torches she had imagined in holders on the buildings and all around the stage posed a significant risk of fire. Theo assured her that we had no need for flaming torches. Cecil Wicker had prevailed on Mr. Tuttle the hardware man for a half mile of wire and two hundred lightbulbs, offering him in payment five full months of free electricity, to be donated (unwittingly, I regret to say) by Cecil's father. Additional lights were obtained on loan from the winter grounds of the Browning Brothers Circus. Strung all along Main Street and in every corner of the Baghdad Bazaar were electric lights beyond counting (hence the estimate of 1,001 bulbs, a symbolic rather than dishonest figure, Miss Spivey had said as she fiddled with the wording for the flyer). From the minaret, Ralphord saw Miss Spivey's handkerchief emerge, fluttering, from her skirt pocket and he threw himself heart and soul into the little song she'd taught him. He was still holding the last long note when, from one end of Main Street to the other, the lights came on almost all at once.

A sharp and universal intake of breath marked the Moment of Illumination, followed by a murmur of appreciation that seemed to come from every quarter of the Baghdad Bazaar. The camels cut loose and bellowed, Ivan startling everybody over by the Camel Ride and Sabrina hollering her response to his call from Bibbens' barn. (As the evening went on, we came to realize that it was Ralphord's singing, not the lights, that set the camels off.) My brother Ralphord was so transported that he yelled from the tower, "Let there be light!"

Judging by the long lines of folks waiting to play, the Dunk Tank and the Turkey Shoot were the favorite attractions in the game area of the Baghdad Bazaar, with the Reverend wives' Cake Walk and the Duck Drop not far behind. Ralphord, who was released from minaret duty between songs, went around with me for a while, playing the games. He wasted ten pennies, one at a time, on the Turkey Shoot. He was the only one in full Arab dress among the men and boys lined up along the fence with rifles to their shoulders, squinting down the barrels, waiting for the next bird to come gobbling nervously into view. Even in a good mood, I never liked the Turkey Shoot. Between the gobbling and the gunfire, you couldn't hear yourself think.

While Ralphord aimed and missed, I won a cake with pink frosting in the Cake Walk, which was set up on the sidewalk across from the stage area on Main Street, with Pinkie Lou Griffith providing the stop-and-start music from a piano inside Dot's former Café. When Ralphord gave up on the Turkey Shoot, we ate cake and watched the Duck Drop, which was the only other game that required no skill, just luck, unless there was some skill involved in predicting which numbered square painted on a wooden tabletop would be the next to receive a deposit from one of the overfed ducklings waddling around on the table. "You mean I gotta guess where them ducks are gonna drop a load?" Ralphord asked Ildred, who was taking in bets on numbers 5 and 7, both of which looked previously stained.

I bet on number 2 and won a comb. Ralphord picked 5 and came up empty-handed. I followed him to the Dunk Tank, combing my hair.

At least a dozen boys were lined up to pay a penny for two chances at throwing a baseball to hit a metal circle that would cause the shelf on which the deputy sheriff was sitting to fall away beneath him and dunk him in the water. So far, he was still dry and looking bored back there, nothing to do but flinch every once in a while when a stray pitch hit the chicken wire that protected him from stray pitches. Of all the fellows in line, Theo Boykin was the big surprise. Everybody knew that when the CME minister in Brennan put together a colored boys' baseball team a few summers ago, he'd kept Theo out of the lineup by making him the official scorekeeper. Theo was much better at calculating batting averages (in his head, no paper required) than he was at hitting, catching, or throwing. Everybody knew that. So what was he doing in line for the Dunk Tank?

"What's Theo think he's doing?" I whispered to Ralphord.

"Waitin' in line," Ralphord said.

At this point, I was still piqued at Theo for helping Miss Spivey get herself fired. I can't deny that. We knew by now that he went with Miss Spivey while she drove Mr. Bibben's delivery truck all around the back roads between here and Brennan, picking up as many colored children as they could coax into coming to our school, promising them camel rides if they came along. Theo (and Etta!) rode in the back to make sure nobody fell off or jumped ship. I couldn't help thinking that the world wasn't going to seem so new or brave come next school year, with Miss Spivey gone.

While he waited, Theo was talking in a very lively way to some-body's cousin who was visiting from up North someplace, Cleveland, I think. A pretty girl named Lucille. She was one of maybe a dozen colored people standing around watching the Dunk Tank—some that I knew and some that I didn't—but like I said, Theo was the only one in line for the game. A crowd made up mostly of strangers had gathered to watch Theo hand a coin to Arnie Lumpkin's father, who, it was said, hadn't touched a drop since the Martians landed. He took the coin but hesitated and looked around, like he was trying to get a signal from the crowd, before he gave Theo a baseball in return.

You could tell that Lucille was a girl who had spent her formative years someplace other than Piedmont County, Georgia. She looked at the baseball in Theo's hand and asked Mr. Lumpkin boldly, "How come he don't have two balls like everybody else?"

The men in the crowd erupted in laughter, and for the first time, Theo looked around. Mr. Lumpkin might have turned over a new leaf in some respects, but he couldn't resist an opportunity like this one. He said, "Well, honey, I reckon you'd have to ask *him* about that!" The crowd hooted again, louder than before—as I am sure Mr. Lumpkin expected they would—and Lucille's face crumpled a little, like she was all of a sudden trying not to cry. Theo said something to her and reached

for her hand, but she jerked it away and ran off. "Lucille!" Theo called
after her. The crowd hooted again and whistled, some of them yelling,
"Lucille! Hey, Lucille!" and "Come on back here 'fore you break this
boy's heart!" Theo still had the baseball in his hand. He wound himself
up furiously and threw it as hard as he could, with hardly a glance at
where it was supposed to go. He said later that he didn't even see the
ball hit—he had already turned to run after Lucille—but he heard it:
thunk, clunk, and *splash!*

The crowd went wild. People came running from the pie booth
and the Cake Walk to see the deputy sheriff struggle to his feet in the
Dunk Tank, dripping and wringing out his hat. I spotted Mr. Greene,
the newspaperman from Claytonville, and Mr. Tuttle the hardware man
sort of holding each other up, they were laughing so hard. I think they
might have been drinking more than iced tea while they were waiting
for night to fall. Even Reverend Stokes was showing a lot of teeth, and
my brother Ralphord was hysterical. We looked around for Theo, thinking to congratulate him, and that's when I noticed that all the pointing
and laughing and slapping of thighs was being done by the white folks
in the audience. The few Negroes who were left appeared to be trapped
by the press of the crowd. Theo, suddenly, was nowhere in sight.

At ten o'clock sharp, everybody in *Alaeddin: Or, the Wonderful Lamp* was
supposed to report to Miss Spivey and Mrs. Lulu Blount in the hardware
store, where Miss Spivey had set up her backstage wardrobe and makeup
area. There was a flurry of veils and robes and long strips of turban waiting to be wound around various heads. Shahrazad and the Princess and
all of us harem girls were crammed into the back office with my sister
May in charge, leaving the front part of the store to the male slaves, the
eunuchs, the nabobs and viziers, and so forth. At a half-past ten, Eugene
Boykin hadn't checked in yet. Miss Spivey was in a state.

"I risk arrest by giving him this part, and then he declines to show
up?" she said.

"There wasn't nobody ever going to arrest you," the deputy sheriff pointed out calmly. Having come straight from the Dunk Tank, still dripping, to change into his Sultan robes, he had been lounging around the hardware store ever since. "Not on account of Eugene, anyway," he added.

Miss Spivey made no reply, except to send Ralphord and a couple of O'Quinns in search of the Jinn of the Lamp, while she turned her attention to the two dozen slave boys who had to get painted up white.

When the Superintendent of Schools stood fast in his refusal to allow a colored boy to take part in her production, Miss Spivey had hit upon a truly ingenious method to get around the obstacle to Eugene's debut, a method that combined camouflage with what she called "delicious irony." We had discovered the skin-covering capabilities of Ildred's kaolin formula while painting the props and scenery, thanks mostly to my brother Ralphord's tendency to drop his brush into the bucket and plunge his whole arm in after it, which arm would come out white as bone to the elbow. Now, you would expect that watching Ralphord walk around with his kaolin-covered arms looking like long white gloves might very well give Miss Spivey the idea to paint Eugene white, but she didn't stop there. In Sir Richard Burton's translation of *The Thousand Nights and a Night*, all the *jinni* and most of the male slaves and eunuchs were blackamoors—Negroes, in other words, and "heathens to boot," Mavis said—which was precisely why Miss Spivey decided to paint *all* the slaves and eunuchs, as well as Eugene the Jinn of the Lamp, white-dirt white. They worked on each other backstage in the hardware store, painting themselves from the waist on up with a creamy coat of kaolin. They would be most impressive onstage with their arms folded across their bare chests and their eyes straight ahead—boys like Sammy Bonner and Harlan O'Quinn and Cyrus Wood—standing still as statues all along the backdrop, like they were part of the scenery. A gasp went up from the audience at the end of Act I, the first time all those slaves turned smoothly on their heels and marched off the stage, most everyone having forgotten that they were real people under their white, white skin.

All of us females were dressed and ready, and the slaves and eunuchs were standing around in the hardware store with their arms folded and their faces as stern and still as they could keep them, waiting for their paint to dry, when Theo and Eugene showed up looking terrified. I don't mean that they came in screaming or anything like that. Exactly the opposite, in fact. They slipped into the hardware store so quietly that somebody had to tell Miss Spivey they were standing there, just inside the door, Theo looking at her back like he was trying to burn a hole in it. He never said a word until she turned around and exclaimed joyfully, "Eugene! At last! Mrs. Blount, here he is! Your costume is laid out in the storeroom, Eugene. Be quick, now!"

Theo started to come forward, Eugene hovering behind him, but when he saw it was the deputy sheriff sitting in the chair behind Miss Spivey, getting his turban wrapped, Theo stopped dead. He took a step backward, bumping into his brother, and said, "Can I ask you to come outside for a minute, please, Miss Spivey?"

"Does it look like I can come outside, Theo?" She held up the end of the silvery cloth that she was winding around Linwood Perkins's head. "Why is everyone always asking me to come outside?"

"It's real important, ma'am," Theo said. Eugene continued to hover at Theo's elbow like the protective spirit that he was supposed to be. Both their faces were glistening. Miss Spivey gave them a measuring look, and then she told Mrs. Blount to take everybody *else* outside in the back so the slaves could dry in the breeze. "But make sure nobody sees them." I was about to follow them out when she handed me the loose end of the Sultan's turban. "Gladys, hold this," she said. "Don't pull it, don't drop it, just hold it." And she turned to give her full attention to Theo. "You have one minute," she told him.

He looked from Miss Spivey to me to the deputy and back to Miss Spivey, taking stock of us all, I expect, before he whispered, "Etta heard folks saying I shouldn't've dunked the deputy." His eyes flickered over to Linwood Perkins. "I didn't mean to."

"You shouldn't have done *what*?" said Miss Spivey. She must have been the only person in the county who was unaware of what Theo Boykin had done. She turned around to shoot the deputy sheriff a look. "*Theo* dunked you?" she said.

"That's all right, Theo," the deputy sheriff said. "It was just a lucky throw."

"Etta and Lucille . . ." Theo began, and then he seemed to run out of breath. He started again. "Etta George and that girl Lucille overheard them say they're gonna teach me to show some respect." Eugene looked forlorn.

"They overheard whom?" said Miss Spivey.

"I don't know," Theo groaned. "It wasn't anybody they knew." He took a deep breath, as if to calm himself, but it didn't seem to work. I could see his hands trembling.

"He's got to hide, Miss Spivey!" Eugene cried.

"Y'all take it easy, now," Linwood said. "We won't let nothin' happen to Theo."

It was clear that something had to be done to calm them down. Right then my brother Force came into the hardware store, out of breath, with a Bedouin robe thrown over his Alaeddin costume and the Jinn of the Lamp's wooden sword poised in his hand. (And where had *he* been? I wondered.) Miss Spivey took the sword and handed him a paintbrush. Theo and Eugene slipped into the storeroom to change their clothes, and then Force went to work on them. The last thing I heard Miss Spivey say to Theo a little while later, as she put him in the lineup of white slaves, was, "Don't sweat!"

I didn't find out until after the fact where my brother Force went off to in his Act I Alaeddin costume (consisting of a loose shirt and tight pants like the ones Douglas Fairbanks, Sr., wore in *The Thief of Baghdad*, for which Miss Pinkie Lou Griffith had played the organ back in 1922, you may remember). While the rest of us were in the hardware store getting ready for curtain time, Miss Spivey had sent my brother back to Bibbens' to pick up that wooden sword, which got left behind somehow in the barn.

Where Force went, and why, is not as important as who he ran into when he got there.

He was coming out of the barn, sword in hand, when he looked up at the Bibbens' house and saw the light on in Miss Spivey's room. That struck him as odd right off. Electricity was not something folks wasted in Piedmont County, Georgia, in 1939, and he sure didn't notice any light on up there on his way across the Bibbens' yard *to* the barn. While he was concluding that going up to Miss Spivey's room to turn off the light (or for any other reason) might not be the most discreet plan of action, he saw a shadow pass back and forth across the ceiling of the room. That sure enough drew him up short.

Force let himself in the back door quietly, but at the bottom of the stairs he decided, instead, to announce himself by making as much noise as possible. He had clomped about halfway up when the light from under Miss Spivey's closed door went out. He stopped to listen, heard nothing, and went up the rest of the way by moonlight coming through the window at the top of the stairs. When he paused with his hand on the doorknob and his head to the door, he heard shuffling and scrabbling inside the room. He took a deep breath, tightened his grip on Eugene's wooden sword, and pushed the door inward.

Both windows were open, dotted swiss curtains blowing around like ghosts. From where he stood in the doorway, Force could see every part of the room except for one corner, on the far side of the bed. The door on the closet was open, clothes spilling off the shelves as if someone had been looking for something, but the rest of the room looked no messier than the way Miss Spivey normally kept it, with big books lying open on the little table that she used for a desk, and scraps of fabric everywhere. Force took one step into the room.

"Well, now," he said, "either y'all went out the window or you're under the bed."

Nobody had anything to say about that. Force took three long strides past one window—giving a quick glance out, just in case somebody was hanging on a rope or crouching on the back porch roof—which landed him near the other window and gave him a moonlit view of the formerly hidden corner on the far side of the bed. It took him a moment to recognize the oddly shaped object visible where the bedspread met the wooden floor as a bare foot.

"I don't see no ladder by the window, so I'm guessin' you're under the bed. Why don't y'all come on out now?"

Three or four seconds of silence followed his question, and then there was a shriek and a great scrambling and scraping as Mavis Davis did her best to propel herself out from under the bed and through the door and down the stairs and into the night. She didn't get far, though, as Force had already bounded back to the door, pushed it shut, and leaned himself up against it, arms folded across his chest.

"Force Cailiff, you let me on out of here right this minute!" Mavis cried. She had her hair braided and put up on her head and she was wearing a denim shirt and dungarees, no doubt to look like somebody other than Mavis Davis.

"I sure enough will do that," Force said amiably, "as soon as you tell me what you're doing here, hiding under Miss Spivey's bed."

"I ain't telling you *nothin'*," Mavis shot back, "and you cain't make me." Her eyes betrayed her, though, with a quick glance toward the floor. In her scramble out from under the bed, she had dropped something. It lay on the wooden floor behind her, whiter than white, practically glowing, in fact, in a patch of moonlight. A folded square of paper.

Force dove for it, but she was closer and quicker. He caught her wrist, she elbowed his chest, he lost his balance and fell back on the floor, she scooted toward the window that faced the barn. Force got to his feet. "Mavis," he said, "I want you to give me that paper." He said it kindly, but she backed away.

"I won't!" she said.

"Now, Mavis," he said, "don't make me take it from you."

"Your goose is cooked, Force Cailiff!" she cried, and she tried to fling the paper out the window behind her. Force caught her hand in his and squeezed it tight, crushing the paper in her fist. They were face-to-face, or more like her face to his chest. Mavis kept her fingers tight around the paper, Force's fingers tight around hers. Someone looking up at them from the yard outside the window might have thought they were dancing together. Mavis had to lean her head far enough back to look him in the eye.

"D'y'all think I'm stupid, like she does?" she asked him, her voice strained by the awkwardness of her position. "D'y'all reckon sometimes I don't think at all?"

"No, Mavis, I do not think that," he said in the same calm, kindly tone.

This, Mavis told me later, may have been the moment when *she* fell in love with him. In her defense, nobody standing face-to-face with my brother Force like she was, only inches away, looking into the blue of his eyes, could help but fall in love with him, at least temporarily. It was, in any case, the moment when she started to cry.

"Aw, come on, Mavis, don't cry. Just give me—"

"You want this piece of paper—well, take it!" she said.

Mavis opened her hand inside of his and he let her go, left her sobbing by the window. He stepped back and unfolded the sheet that was now crumpled into a ball. There was no expression whatsoever on his handsome face as he looked over the list of dates, times, and places where Mavis had spied on him and Miss Spivey. When he was finished, he folded it up and tucked it into the little pocket Mrs. Blount had sewn inside his Alaeddin vest. Then he turned to go.

"I got me another copy," Mavis said to his back.

Force looked at her, sadly, over his shoulder. "Mavis," he said, "I don't doubt you do."

She stayed by the window while he ran down the stairs and out the Bibbens' back door. She watched him for as long as she could see him—a figure out of a storybook running in a moonlit cloud of milky-looking dust through the yard—and then she slid down to the floor under the window and cried her eyes out.

Upset though she was, Mavis did not forget to retrieve the other piece of paper she had hidden on top of a sweater in the closet before Force showed up. It was too bad, in a way. This copy of the list, which she'd intended to leave for Miss Spivey, was the neater of the two—she'd worked harder on the penmanship—but Mavis had an appointment to keep and she couldn't show up empty-handed.

The line for the Camel Ride was still so long at a quarter-past eleven that Miss Spivey expressed her concern about curtain time getting delayed until after midnight on account of it, Ivan V being an essential part of Act I. She sent me and another harem girl, minus our veils, to communicate this to Uncle Mack.

The Camel Ride was set up at the far end of Main Street, so it was the last thing you came to while strolling through the Baghdad Bazaar. Ivan V carried two to four riders at a time, depending on their size, around a course laid out in a temporary paddock that had electric lights strung all along the fence. From a distance it looked like somebody had drawn a dotted line to make a great big oval. In the middle of the course Ivan could cut loose a little and pace instead of walking, with Uncle Mack in Bedouin robes almost running alongside to keep hold of the rope. Leaning against the fence was a sign that Uncle Mack had brought with him from the circus, which said CAMEL RIDES in big red letters. The number 5 was lettered in black next to a big red cent sign in a spot that had obviously been painted over as prices rose and fell from year to year. In the lower corner of the sign, the head of a camel looked out at the viewer with the usual superior smile and a cartoon-type balloon coming out of his mouth. *Ride the Ship of the Desert*, the camel said.

Miss Spivey need not have worried. By a quarter-past eleven, Uncle Mack had already led a total of seventy-four customers up the wooden steps of the camel-mounting platform, and he knew exactly when to close off the line. "Y'all come back after the show!" he was telling the unlucky ones left in line when Harriet Eskew and I arrived on the scene. I waved to my daddy, who was waiting with two of May's girls. They looked disappointed but didn't protest when Daddy took them each by the hand and started leading them our way. Up front of the line, some folks were taking the news a little harder.

"Whoa, now, whoa," said a skinny man in overalls with a matching skinny little boy at the end of his arm. "You cain't be sayin' that we been waiting here and now we don't get a ride."

Uncle Mack had a majestic look about him in his Bedouin outfit. The man in overalls looked small and kind of colorless by comparison.

"No, sir," Uncle Mack said to the man. "I don't mean that at all. Come on back directly after the show, and you'll get your ride, sure enough." Uncle Mack looked at the little boy—a child with sticks for arms and legs and huge pale eyes and a mouth that was always working on something, probably the inside of his cheek. It was in regard to that hungry-looking child (who would most likely have preferred a trip to Mrs. Veal's fried chicken booth over a ride on the camel) that Uncle Mack made his mistake, which was to smile at the little boy and say, "Maybe you'd like a extra turn around the track."

The fellow in overalls gave his son's stick of an arm a tug that almost knocked the little boy off his feet and said, "Who you talkin' to? To my boy? You talkin' to my boy? Did I give you leave to talk to my boy?"

"No, sir," said Uncle Mack. He had started undoing Ivan's harness but he stopped now to give the skinny man in overalls his full attention instead. My daddy kept on coming toward us, but he was moving slower now, cutting a wider berth, like he was assessing the situation. Then I heard laughter and saw over my shoulder a bunch of big rowdy boys, five or six of them, high school age or a little older, moseying down Main Street toward the Camel Ride. Ralphord tugged on my harem girl sleeve and whispered, "Gladys! Gladys! Them're the ones."

"What ones?"

"The ones at the Dunk Tank, watchin' Theo."

Arnie Lumpkin was the only one I recognized. He was in his Chief Eunuch costume: billowing pants tied at the ankle, a red scarf a foot wide wrapped round and round his belly at the waist, a smaller scarf wound like a bandanna around his head, and a wooden sword at his side. He had been bragging, no doubt, to the other boys about watching over the harem in Act II. They didn't look like the kind of boys who would know what a eunuch was, so he was probably safe there. The boys reached the paddock just in time to hear the skinny man in overalls saying to Uncle Mack, "Who d'you think you are, boy?"

"Andrew Browning McComb is my name, sir."

"Boy, your name don't make no never mind to me. We been waitin' and it's our turn to ride that critter of your'n, so bring it right here 'fore I got to do something about it."

As if that settled the matter, the skinny man in overalls took to dragging his little boy up the steps of the camel-mounting platform. When the little boy tripped on the second step, his father just lifted him by the one arm and carried him, dangling, up the rest of the way. The two of them stood at the top, waiting. There was nothing but air in front of them at the edge of the platform, and the way the man swayed back and forth on his feet was making me feel pretty nervous for his little boy. If he fell off there, it looked like he'd break something for sure. Uncle Mack must have felt the same. He led old Ivan over to the platform. It took the skinny man three tries to climb up into the saddle.

Uncle Mack gave the skinny man and his child not one, not two, but three turns at varying speeds around the oval paddock, throwing in a couple of figure eights through the middle. We could hear the little boy shrieking with pleasure every time the camel picked up his pace. At first, Arnie Lumpkin and his friends, if that's what they were, hung around the steps to the platform in a swaggering way, as if they'd had something to do with Uncle Mack knuckling under, but they soon lost interest. By the time Ivan V brought the little boy and his father around to the steps to dismount, the little boy looked tickled and lively in a way he hadn't earlier. His father was clinging to the red-wrapped saddle horn with a look of fierce determination, his lips pressed together and his face pale in the electric light. Uncle Mack swung the little boy to the platform and gave him a camel bell for a souvenir, along with a hunk of peanut brittle taken in payment earlier from somebody who didn't have a nickel, and then he waited still as a statue while the little boy's father slid off the camel, both feet first, then his backside and the rest of him following after. Watching them walk away down Main Street, the man taking one careful step at a time while his little boy hopped and bit and chewed and jingled, Uncle Mack remarked to my daddy that a swiftly pacing camel does swing his rider some from side to side. Daddy laughed, quietly but pretty hard.

After that, Ivan stood patiently while Harriet Eskew and May's two girls and I scrambled up into his saddle. We made a little procession down Main Street toward Miss Spivey's staging area, Uncle Mack leading the camel and my daddy walking alongside. Approaching the Turkey Shoot, from my position high on the camel I saw two of Arnie Lumpkin's "friends" talking to the skinny man, all three with their heads together. They looked up as Ivan passed them by. The little boy waved his camel bell at us. The father turned his head to spit. A fourth man stood near them with a rifle in his hands, as if he had been waiting for his turn at the Turkey Shoot and listening to them at the same time. When the fourth man turned around to see us pass by on the camel, I saw that it was Mr. Gordon. My first thought was that I hadn't expected to see Mr. Gordon at the Baghdad Bazaar—although I guess he had as much right to be there as anybody else. My second thought was that I wished I hadn't seen him at all.

Alaeddin began at the stroke of midnight. Reverend Stokes rang the bell at Threestep Methodist, Ralphord started singing, the camels started baying (Ivan onstage, Sabrina a distant echo from the barn), and the audience filled the street. Within minutes, all the benches and chairs and overturned tubs were taken, another twice as many were hauled in, and we still ended up with standing room only. A dozen girls in bloomery pants and face veils—me included—stood along the edges of the sidewalk, yards and yards of light brown muslin hanging from the eaves behind us, hiding the stage. At Miss Spivey's signal, each of us grabbed ahold and gave the cloth a well-placed tug. The muslin billowed down into sand dunes surrounding the tent of the Sultan, who sat majestically, stage left, in his silvery turban, the beautiful Shahrazad on a heap of colorful cushions at the his feet. White, white slaves stood like statues along the back of the stage behind them.

A genuinely cool breeze had come up after nightfall. Later, the wind would stiffen and pile up thunderclouds, but for now the breeze played the role Miss Spivey assigned to it, blowing away mosquitoes and stirring the string of bulbs, their light flickering on the faces of the actors, making them look dramatic even when they messed up their lines. It seemed like the moon itself had risen on cue. By midnight it was high enough to cast Eugene's huge shadow in the street. When Force rubbed Mrs. Blount's silver gravy boat, causing the Jinn of the Lamp to pop up out of the hole we'd dug for him at the edge of the stage while Miss

Spivey punched a sack full of flour to release a smokey white *poof*, the whole audience gasped.

Meanwhile, stage right, my sister May was nothing short of magnificent, draped in midnight-blue muslin studded with golden moons and stars. She hardly had to look at the pages that were hidden, like her belly, among the folds of fabric in her lap. In her script, Miss Spivey had combined the poor tailor's son with various comely youths from other tales, sometimes sacrificing plot to poetry. May delivered all her lines like strings of gleaming pearls: "Now, this boy," she said, "Alaeddin hight, had been from babyhood a scapegrace and a ne'er-do-well, wont to play at all times, and yet was he so cast in beauty's mould, that idleness became him."

Idleness was my brother's cue, and when he made his entrance in the big white shirt and tight pants, a group of girls from the college fairly swooned in the front-row seats.

During the first Intermission, word came around that people in the audience were asking who the actors were and where they came from. "Never underestimate the power of moonlight," Miss Spivey said to us. To Theo—who was sweating dark brown stripes down his back and arms—she whispered, "Relax. Nobody can tell it's you up there." And to Eugene, who got hit in the fez by a gob of spit while he cast a spell on the Princess, Miss Spivey counseled patience as she cleaned off his hat.

"Can't let one bumpkin spoil the show," she said.

After the second intermission, the wind picked up and clouds began to gather, but the electric lights held steady, so even with the moonlight cutting in and out amongst the clouds, things continued to go pretty smoothly until we got near the end of Act III, where the *jinn* sneaks the Princess out of her father's palace in the dead of night. I wish you could have seen the slaves pick up the sleeping Princess in her bed and carry her off. They were wearing dark robes and gloves to hide their white-painted selves, and she was wearing a white nightgown kind of thing, and the mattress was covered in black, so it looked for all the world like she was floating through the darkness by magic. The almost-invisible slaves were about to whisk the Princess around the back of the buildings and out of sight when we heard somebody shouting, faintly at first and then louder and louder, "It's coming! It's coming!"

Folks started looking around to see where the shouts were coming from. The slaves wavered and bumped into one another, letting the Princess down none too gently (we heard Louise yell, "Ow!"), and the Sultan stood up so quickly that his turban slid forward over his eyes, causing him to knock it back out of the way and almost clean off his head. In the midst of the ruckus I heard a man in the audience say, "Well, damned if that Sultan ain't Linwood Perkins!"

Everybody was standing up by now, knocking over benches and kicking buckets out of the way, trying to get a look over everybody else's shoulders at none other than Mavis Davis, running toward us up the middle of Main Street, waving her arms and shrieking, "It's coming! It's coming *out!*"

The first person to enter Bibbens' barn and come around the side of Sabrina's stall was a long-legged boy from Irwinton who outran us all, and the first words out of his mouth when he laid eyes on Sabrina were, "My Lord, they got them a two-headed camel!"

It did look that way for a while.

Uncle Mack was right behind the boy, and behind him was my brother Force and then Eugene Boykin, holding on to his fez with one hand and the hilt of his wooden sword with the other, and behind *him* was a whole row of peeling and flaking white-painted slaves.

This part of the night, when Sabrina gave birth to Ahmed, was like no other night in our lives. I can close my eyes right now and see everybody lined up against the fence along the whole length of Bibbens' paddock and into the barn—about half of us in bloomers and veils and spangly vests painted with gold stars and moons that caught up the light of the real moon peeking through clouds. When Uncle Mack came out of the barn and saw how many people were lined up outside, he pulled Ralphord, who pulled me, who pulled Harriet Eskew out of the line. Then Etta George appeared out of nowhere, and Uncle Mack hauled the four of us into the barn, where he had us hold hands—Etta on the end next to me so mine was the only hand she had to hold—to form a living gate across the front of Sabrina's stall. Ralphord and Harriet and Etta faced into the stall and watched the whole thing, but I kept my back to the action except for taking a peek over my shoulder whenever a passing viewer whispered something like, "What's that? Is that his head?" or "Sweet Jesus!"

The scene was almost biblical. You had the straw, and the camels, and halos of yellow light around everybody from the lanterns hanging on hooks near the stall. Uncle Mack looked like a Nativity scene shepherd in his Bedouin robe and headdress, and he was soon joined in the stall by horse doctor Billy Bonner, who, in the fancy pants and turban of the Vizier, was a dead ringer for one of the Three Kings. Then my sister May came along in her midnight-blue robe and veil. All she would have needed to complete the picture was a baby in her arms.

It was amazing how quiet everybody was. I believe folks did feel like they were in church at Christmastime. Although Sabrina had been restless earlier in the evening, she stood hushed and still now, as if she were concentrating. Uncle Mack said that was the way with camels. As for the baby, he came out front legs first, with his head between them, and kind of hung there for quite a while, almost touching the ground with his front feet and thus creating the two-headed camel effect—I did get a peek at that. The whole time, he was making a *humming* noise. Uncle Mack said that wasn't too unusual. He had heard it before from baby camels. He thought maybe it helped them clear out their nose and throat and all. The humming had two different notes to it. Uncle Mack said the higher pitch meant that Sabrina was working on pushing that baby out and squeezing him in the process. Once she finally succeeded and he sort of tumbled out feet first and slid the rest of the way to the straw, then the humming stopped, at least from the camel. My brother Ralphord hummed those two notes on and off for days without even knowing he was doing it. You'd have to nudge him to make him stop.

It took pretty near an hour to walk the entire population of the Baghdad Bazaar single-file down the center aisle to the stall where Sabrina was calmly giving birth. Some folks hurried on past. But most people paused for as long as they could before the press of folks behind them forced them to move on. Only a few actually witnessed the miracle of birth, but the rest got to see the baby camel chewing and sucking and yawning and pissing on its tail and then slapping the tail up on its back, splashing almost all the way over to Ralphord and Harriet and Etta and me. Uncle Mack, who got a shower of it, announced at that point, "It's a boy." Mother camels don't lick their babies clean, we found out, but if that was the point of the shower, it didn't work very well. Ahmed the baby camel remained matted and sticky-looking and prickly with straw. More like a big old skinny wet dog than anything else. When he couldn't have been but a few minutes old, he tried to stand up already. He kept trying—crouching and wiggling, lifting his backside as high as he could—but for a long while he couldn't get his front legs up to match the hind ones. The very last people were filing through when he finally hoisted his hind end up and put out first one miniature clown foot and then the other, and he was standing. A cheer went up and he fell down.

When people came out of the barn, we were amazed to find them returning to their seats in the street, looking for Act IV of *Alaeddin*.

Harriet Eskew went off in search of her sister Mamie, and Ralphord said he'd catch up with me in a minute, which meant, I knew, that he needed to answer nature's call. I went straight to the backstage area in the hardware store and found nobody there at first except for Miss Spivey, who was peeking through a curtained window at the crowd reassembling out in the street. "Oh, dear," she said. "The show must go on, apparently." When she turned around, I was shocked to see that she had been crying a good one. She was done now, but her face told the story.

I didn't know a thing about the list that Force had gotten away from Mavis, which was now balled up in one of Miss Spivey's skirt pockets, so all I could think to say was, "Miss Spivey, what's wrong?" to which she responded by tapping first one shaky finger to her lips and then two. She said, "Hold the fort, will you, Gladys?" and she slipped out the back door of the hardware store. She only had to go a few steps before she disappeared into the darkness the electric lights couldn't reach. I waited to see the match flare up, but she must have turned her back to me.

I'm going to tell you something about Miss Spivey now that you will find hard to believe. I could not have believed it myself at the time. But it's the truth.

I never saw her face again.

So what do you think Mavis Davis did with her list of times and dates and places where Miss Spivey and my brother Force touzled or tumbled or just sat and talked? I mean, with the remaining copy, the one that she was going to leave for Miss Spivey until Force came along.

Did she herself deliver that list triumphantly to the Superintendent of Schools? No, she did not. Did she give it to her mother to pass along? No. Did she give it to the Reverends Stokes or Whitlock? No and no. Their wives? No. My mother? No.

Did she nail it up to the schoolhouse door?

No.

What she did with it was this: she sold it, for cash money, to Mr. Gordon. I believe he gave her ten dollars for it.

Miss Spivey hadn't been gone for more than a few minutes when Mrs. Lulu Blount came into the hardware store through the same back door and announced to me and Ralphord, the Eskew girls, and a few other members of the cast who'd arrived in the meantime, that Miss Spivey had put her, Mrs. Lulu Blount, in charge of Act IV.

"Where's Miss Spivey?" Ralphord asked.

There was no time for questions, Mrs. Blount said. We had a show to put on.

We gathered a ragtag cast of patched and peeling white slaves. Theo, I noticed, was not among them. Then Linwood Perkins showed up, and while Mrs. Blount tucked in the ends of the Sultan's turban and deflected questions about Miss Spivey's whereabouts, I helped the Eskew girls pick the straw out of Shahrazad's veil and gown. Alaeddin and the Princess were located in the meantime, as was the Slave of the Lamp. Finally, Ralphord was dispatched to the minaret to announce, "*Alaeddin: Or, the Wonderful Lamp,* Act Four and Conclusion," and with a skeleton crew of harem girls and no Chief Eunuch in sight since nobody could find Arnie Lumpkin, the show went on.

We harem girls were supposed to spend most of Act IV lolling around on the westernmost part of the sidewalk-slash-stage. This gave us ample time to talk quietly amongst ourselves—remaining "in character," Miss Spivey said—as you would probably expect real harem girls to do. My sister Ildred was the first to look west up Main Street and ask the rest of us, quietly enough so the audience wouldn't hear, "What is that yonder, comin' up the road?" Harriet Eskew said, "Looks like it's afire." Her sister Mamie said, "Well, it hadn't oughta be. Theo Boykin said no flames, no torches."

All this talking was in whispers, while the audience listened to Shahrazad catching them up on Alaeddin and the Princess, who were about to be reunited for the final, triumphant time, after which they would live happily ever after until the Destroyer of delights and the Garnerer of graveyards came their way. My brother Force was hunkered down and hiding in the balcony right overhead of the harem, waiting to make his entrance. Ildred went, "Hssst!" up to him, pointing unobtrusively up the street, and from his slightly better vantage point, he peeked over the edge of the balcony and whispered, "Goddamn!"

One of the younger harem girls covered her ears.

"Force Cailiff!" Ildred hissed.

"It's the Ku Klucks!"

Ildred stood straight up out of the harem like a sore thumb. "How can you tell?" she said, looking up the road. I looked that way, too, but there were trees in the way—or maybe it was the corner of Bibbens' store obstructing the view. All I could see was a yellow flickering between patches of black.

By now the audience was whispering. At first, you could tell, they thought it was part of the show. Even when we could clearly see the white robes and hoods on either side of the wagon with a giant torch-like thing flaming up from the wagon bed, folks in the audience—white folks, anyway—still seemed to think it was part of the show. Ildred said, "Gladys, git!" I ducked down and scurried for the center stage door, which opened while I was still on the way. Mrs. Blount stuck her head out and cried, apparently to the audience, which had got to its feet again, "This is it! If you all leave again, we are *not* going to finish—where are they going—what is it *now*?"

"Something's coming, Mrs. Blount," my sister Ildred said. Like the audience, all the harem girls were standing now and looking up the road. Ildred pointed.

The wagon bearing the burning cross was coming straight up Main Street toward the stage area. Most folks in the remaining audience were busy getting out of the way. Many retreated to the covered sidewalk on the other side of the street, while others stepped right up onto the stage. You got the impression they planned to watch, rather than flee, what-ever was going to happen next. I ended up standing in the street next to Linwood Perkins, still in his Sultan gear, watching the wagon move toward us. I thought the flames coming off the cross looked like arms waving, reaching toward whichever side the wind blew or the wagon wheels dipped.

"Kind of makes me wish we didn't mix any kerosene into the paint," I said.

The deputy sheriff looked at me.

"So it wouldn't crack when it dried," I explained. He kept staring. "We soaked the boards to kill the termites, too."

Standing in the middle of the street, Linwood Perkins looked left and right at the "flats" pressed up against the buildings of Main Street.

"Ralphord!" he yelled. Ralphord was behind us by about half a block. "Git up there and tell everybody, git off the sidewalks! Git the heck away!"

I looked around, up and down the street, amazed at how easy it was to picture everything aflame.

Ralphord ran to the minaret. He scrambled up into the crow's nest part and hollered, in a kind of ecstasy, "Clear the decks! All hands! Clear the decks!"

I climbed halfway up the ladder and tugged on his robe. "Ralphord! Say *sidewalk*, not decks! Sidewalk, Ralphord! Folks don't know what you're talkin' about."

"All right," he said, and sang out, "Git off the sidewalk! Di-rectly!"

The flaming cross was a lot closer now. The wagon had drawn almost even with Bibbens' store. A team of white-robed and -hooded men lined up like horses were pulling the wagon from up in front, with more of the white robes pushing it from the rear.

"Who the heck are they all?" asked Reverend Stokes, who was right next to Linwood Perkins.

"I don't know, Reverend—looks like the whole town was here to begin with."

The wagon and its burden of flames had passed Bibbens' store. It was only fifteen or twenty yards from the end of our white-painted block.

Without warning, the deputy sheriff took off down the middle of Main Street, running *toward* the cross, his Sultan's robe whipping open—luckily, he was fully dressed underneath. For a terrible moment, I thought he was joining them, but then I saw him waving his arms at them and probably yelling, although there was too much noise around me to hear what he was saying. They stopped while he hopped up and down in front of them, his robe flapping, their robes flapping. The wind had picked up suddenly. It was one silvery turban vs. I don't know how many pointed hoods. Then the Klansmen shouldered their ropes and came forward. The deputy sheriff turned and ran back up the the street toward us, hollering, "Back off! Clear the area!" From the minaret, Ralphord yelled, "Abandon ship!"

As the wagon and its fiery load drew even with the end of Main Street, the whole population of "Baghdad," Georgia—times ten, I expect, with all the visitors—moved slowly backward, away from it, step by step. I found I was squeezing Ildred's hand on one side and Florence Hodges's on the other. I remember thanking the Lord that the cross went by Bibbens' place without setting the barn on fire and praying that Uncle Mack and Eugene got the camels out back through the woods and far away, just in case. I wondered if Ahmed rode on his mother's back as they made their escape. (He didn't; Eugene carried him.) I tried to believe that only moments ago, only *moments*—it couldn't have been an hour— I was in the barn watching that baby camel trying to get to his feet. I saw the first bits of glowing ash and charcoal flying in the air above the burning pole. It was a *pole* now, not a cross, the horizontal part must have fallen or slipped down, and it was right in front of the flat to the left of the stage now, right where we harem girls used to be.

To this day, I do not believe the Ku Klucks wanted to burn our whole town down to the ground, even if Eugene Boykin *had* cast a spell on the white Princess, and even if he *did* walk on the same stage, and even if he *might* have touched her, almost. They *couldn't* want to burn down our whole town because eleven black children had spent an hour or two sitting next to white children at Threestep School, or because Theo was smarter than everybody else, or just because he had written on the board, O *brave new world!* Those Ku Klucks must have thought the deputy sheriff was making up a story about the kerosene. Or they must have thought he was smelling their own burning creosote and tar. I tell you, it was downright fascinating to watch the sparks and ash roiling around in the troubled air above the flames, fiery bits flying up and circling down closer and closer to the lovely arch painted in white dirt and kerosene above the very balcony where Force had crouched, waiting for his cue. It was only a matter of time, seconds most likely, before a spark landed and we'd find out just how quickly the flames would spread: In a sheet down the front of that painted flat? In a whoosh along Main Street? It occurred to me, moving backwards with the crowd and watching a flaming ash—the biggest yet—fly up into the air, that at least my brother Force would never have to give the Princess that dreaded wake-up kiss.

The flaming ash I was watching dropped into our beautiful white balcony like a coin into the collection box. Right then, as if in response to that contribution, the sky lit up with the longest, brightest branching fork of lightning I had ever seen. The fork went out in a blue-bright flash, taking all the electric lights with it.

The image of the flaming pine trunk and the Ku Klucks in their pointed hoods was still etched against the lightning flash on the inside of our eyes when a clap of thunder punched everybody in the eardrums, announcing the arrival of the rain that had been threatening since first intermission. The whole sky spilled over like a bucket. Everybody ran for cover. I didn't count, so I can't say how many seconds of downpour it took before the burning pine went out just like that—black and wet and hissing steam like the devil.

17

Going Under

PEOPLE TOOK SHELTER FROM the downpour that night in all the
buildings up and down Main Street, except for Mr. Gordon's law office,
which was locked. They holed up in the hardware store and Dot's former Café and the deputy sheriff's office (happy to sleep in a jail cell just
as long as it was dry), and in both churches and in the schoolhouse, and
in barns and sheds and automobiles and anywhere else they could find.
Rain pelted steadily on roofs over people's heads, and in spite of all the
excitement, most folks, being unaccustomed to all-night festivities, soon
fell asleep where they lay.

By morning, it looked like Baghdad, Georgia, had fallen under a
different kind of spell. Never in the history of our town had the hour of
seven o'clock come around, and then half-past, and then eight o'clock
on a sunny Saturday morning in June, with nary a person up and stirring.
Cows were moaning, hungry chickens clucking, hogs complaining, and
still folks slept on. The sun would be high in the sky before citizens and
visitors began to free themselves from that spell, waking up one by one,
stiff-necked and sore of back and wondering if they had really seen or
only dreamed a *jinn* jumping out of a cloud of white smoke, or a boy in

a tower singing like an angel, or a princess floating in the darkness, or a camel being born, or a wagon full of flames rolling toward them in the street. It must have seemed more likely, when they awoke to the muddy slough of Main Street, that they had dreamed it all.

I myself woke up in Bibbens' barn, having fallen asleep there with my sister May and her three older girls. Our intention had been to check on the camels, but when we came dashing into the barn out of the rain as best we could, Mrs. Bibben appeared with a lantern and told us Uncle Mack had taken the camels away. She raised her voice over the sound of the rain pounding the roof of the barn. "I tried to tell him they all would be safe here," she said, and shrugged. She didn't say where they went—I had the feeling she didn't know—but they couldn't have gone far in this weather. We peeled off layers of sopping wet muslin, which we had pulled from the "sand dunes" on stage. Under the muslin, our clothes were mostly dry, although Mrs. Bibben insisted on providing warm socks for all of our feet. We curled up together like kittens on a quilt she threw down over the straw in a clean stall, May still in her midnight-blue gown studded with gold stars, and me in my harem outfit, and the girls in Sunday dresses topped by three of Mrs. Bibben's old sweaters, which fit them more like coats. At some point, while we were sleeping, Momma must have come into the barn, looking to see where we were. She'd thrown her big white bedspread over us like a tent.

I sat up under it now, puzzling over where I was, and what was making that tap-tapping sound, and had I really just heard a train whistle? Who would be calling for the train to stop in Threestep on the morning after the Baghdad Bazaar?

Bits of straw were stuck to my arms and the bare skin around my middle. When I crawled out from under the bedspread, May and the girls sighed and snuggled together to fill up the space. I struggled to my feet. The left one felt numb and tingly, not yet ready to follow orders. I was giving it a minute, aiming to limp toward the sunlight down at the end of the barn, when I saw the eye. It was looking straight at me through a gap in the boards between stalls: a big brown heavy-lidded eye with long, thick curly lashes.

"Sabrina?" I whispered so as not to wake May and the girls. "Is that you?"

The eye disappeared. Almost immediately it was replaced by lips. They curled back in a grin full of teeth that looked white and new. I limped to the end of the stall and peeked around, and there was Sabrina's baby, standing up straight on his own four clown feet. The top of his hump looked to be about even with my chin. It looked like he'd expanded a couple of sizes as he dried.

"Ahmed!" I said. "You have *grown*! What are you doin' here?"

His color was another surprise. Last night, the lantern light and shadows—plus the straw and the sac all sticking to him—had made it hard to tell what color he was, but now I could see that this baby camel was as pure white as a clean boll of cotton. He came right on up to me and started poking at my armpit, as if he were looking for something. I had to take a step backwards to keep my footing, he was pushing so hard. "Little camel," I said, "I don't have a thing you want. Where's your momma?" He was wearing a rope around his neck with the end dragging on the ground. I picked it up and shook it under his nose. "Are you causing her trouble already, sneakin' off? Hey—listen!"

The tapping I heard earlier had started up again.

"It's Miss Spivey!" I told Ahmed. She was up there now, in her room, typing with one hand tied behind her back, it sounded like. "I bet she knows where your momma is. You wait here," I said. I closed the door of the stall and rolled a wheelbarrow up against it sideways to keep it shut.

On their back porch, the Bibbens had a half dozen wooden barrels lined up against the railing. The back door was open inward, so I could see the wooden staircase rising murkily to the second floor through the screen. When I stepped right up and cupped my hands around my eyes, I could just make out Miss Spivey's door at the top of the stairs. It was closed. Behind it, the stop-and-start typing—so unlike the usual tap dance of Miss Spivey's fingers on the keys—continued. I pulled my harem costume away from my sweaty back and armpits, and then I knocked politely on the wooden frame of the screen door. Upstairs, the typewriter fell silent. I listened for approaching footsteps, but all I heard now were doves cooing in the barn behind me and one cricket, tricked by the darkness under the porch into thinking it was evening. I knocked again.

I climbed the stairs toward Miss Spivey's room with some *trepidation*, a vocabulary word from late fall that I was finding more and more useful all the time. Instead of knocking on the door, I waited. The only sound inside was a bit of a chair scrape, as if she'd started to stand up but maybe thought better of it. "Miss Spivey?" I said. There was nothing but silence in response to that, and I think I would have gone back down the stairs without opening the door at all if I hadn't been so suddenly, utterly convinced that there was nobody in Threestep who would have called for the train on the morning after the Baghdad Bazaar *except* Miss Spivey. I turned the knob and pushed. I could see before the door was even halfway open that the drawers were pulled out and the closet was empty, the shelves—except for the one that held ten green volumes of *The Thousand Nights and a Night*—were bare.

If you have not guessed who was sitting at Miss Spivey's desk, banging away at her typewriter, don't feel bad. If I hadn't seen for myself who was punching the keys one at a time with two fingers, I never would have guessed it, either. I was so surprised that I cried, "Mavis! What are you doing here? Where's Miss Spivey?"

"What does it look like I'm doing?" Mavis said.

She didn't even try to hide that she was crying. Her face was wet, her eyes were red, her nose was running. I hadn't seen Mavis cry since her daddy died, and that was so long ago I couldn't picture it. She gave out with a loud and defiant sniffle, all the while looking me straight in the eye. "Where is Miss Spivey?" I asked again.

"I did a terrible thing," Mavis said.

She had done something to Miss Spivey. I should have known. I could hardly get my breath to come. "What did you *do*?" I croaked.

"This." Mavis sobbed. She picked up a piece of paper, obviously smoothed out after somebody had crunched it into a ball. Written in Mavis's neat and tiny hand—I'd sat right in front of her in school long enough to recognize it anywhere—it seemed to be a list of dates and times and places. *Pecan grove* jumped out at me, written next to at least three different dates and times. All of a sudden, I got it. I gasped. "*How?*" I said.

"I was there," she said, and she sniffled again, long and noisily.

"Every time?"

"Every time that's written on that paper."

"You *spied* on them?" I said, and immediately wished to take it back. I more than half expected her to ask me what *I* was doing up in the pine tree that time with Etta George. All she did was go on crying, which gave me leave to say, "Mavis, that is disgusting."

"I know it," she sobbed. "But that's not the bad part, Gladys, not the *really* bad part." And then she told me that she'd sold the list of places and times to Mr. Gordon.

"You *sold* it to him? What do you mean, you sold it?"

For a second, through her tears, she gave me the kind of look I'd come to expect from Mavis Davis over the years. "I mean I gave him the paper and he gave me money for it. That's what I mean by *I sold it.*"

I wanted to ask for how much, but I didn't, not then. I said, "What would Mr. Gordon want with it?"

"I don't know!" She went back to sobbing.

"D'you reckon he wants to get her fired?"

"Oh, Gladys. Miss Spivey is already fired, for heaven's sake."

"Why would he give you money for this, then? What's it good for?"

"I'll tell you what it's good for. It's good for holding over her head, it's good for making her do like Mr. Gordon wants. It's blackmail, Gladys. Ain't you ever heard of blackmail?"

"What would Mr. Gordon want to make her do?"

"How should I know?"

"But why are you *here*, in Miss Spivey's room?"

"I am *trying*," she said dramatically, "to finish what Miss Spivey started. See this here?" She held up a pile of envelopes. The top one had *Supt of Schools* typed on it. "Miss Spivey aimed to show Mr. Gordon she didn't care what he did. He couldn't hold it over her head because she was goin' to spread it around herself! That's how you stamp out blackmail."

I reminded myself that this was Miss Spivey we were talking about. I said, "Why didn't she do it, then? Why didn't *she* type up the copies and hand 'em out?"

"She ran out of time. She said I had to do it."

Suddenly I remembered the train whistle. My heart sank even lower than it already was. "What do you mean, she ran out of time?"

Mavis sat back then and told me how she'd been hiding among the barrels on the Bibbens' back porch earlier this morning when Miss Spivey emerged from the stand of blooming crape myrtle next to the springhouse with my brother Force right behind her. I've come to believe that Mavis knew all along which side she really wanted to be on and she just couldn't figure, as sometimes happens, how she'd wound up on the wrong one. She didn't like Mr. Gordon any more than I did, after all. One way or another, when Force and Miss Spivey stopped to catch their breath together on the stoop, an arm's length away from where the barrels were lined up, Mavis had popped up like one of Ali Baba's forty thieves, and she had thrown herself on the mercy of them both.

Force was set to take pity on Mavis right away, moved by her weeping and beseeching and all. Miss Spivey was not at first so inclined. She was mad enough that she might have cast poor Mavis aside to stew in her own remorse if Mavis had not offered them what she believed to be an important piece of new information, namely, that she had sold the list of dates and times and places where she'd seen them touzling and the like to Mr. Gordon, who wanted it for what precise purpose Mavis did not know.

"Sold it? For how much?" said Force.

Mr. Gordon had paid Mavis two five-dollar bills for her detective work, as he called it—an amount that stunned Mavis when he offered it—but she did not say so to my brother Force. She didn't say anything at first. She hung her head and hoped that Force and Miss Spivey—but especially Force—could see that she was truly sorry, that she was not and never had been on Mr. Gordon's side, not really, that she was lost, she was wounded, she was stricken with grief, and that sometimes she just didn't think things through, in fact, perhaps, it was possible that sometimes she didn't think at all.

"Y'all can have the money!" she told them, tearfully digging into her overalls' front pocket for a five-dollar bill, like she was ready to cast it, Judas Iscariot–style, at their feet.

Force was set to take her up on that, too, but Miss Spivey held her hand up in the stop position—Mavis showed me just how she did it—and said, "I don't want your money, Mavis. I'll tell you what I want from you."

That's when she gave Mavis her mission, along with the crumpled list and the pile of envelopes she needed to complete it. Having done so, Miss Spivey turned her attention to helping Force get her trunk and two suitcases down the stairs. She left the typewriter behind, of course, and as soon as they were gone, Mavis set to work.

"This one here," Mavis told me, ticking the typewriter carriage up and down, "is only the second copy I made. It takes a long time to find the letters on this thing."

I said, "You ought to've tried to stop her, Mavis!"

"Oh, Gladys, you don't know how it was. She was *so* mad at me for what I done, I thought she was fixing to slap my face."

"You know Miss Spivey wouldn't do that," I said cruelly. "She never even hit you for tearing the map."

The look on Mavis's face was like *I'd* hit her then. She started crying so hard that she made the ink run on the list that was currently in the typewriter. We had to pull it on out and start over. I said I'd take a turn so she could clean up her face. I hadn't typed but *Schoolhouse* and *December 26*, when I thought of something that made my face turn hot and my blood run cold.

"You don't think Force went with her, do you?" He did try to follow that girl to Toledo, back when he was only fifteen.

"I don't think so," Mavis said from the washstand in the corner. She looked at me, her bangs dripping, over the top of an embroidered towel. "I believe she sent Force to see about the camels."

At the mention of camels, I jumped to my feet. I had forgotten all about the baby camel in the barn.

As we thundered down the stairs toward the back door, Mavis and I could hear little girls' voices, and then here they were, May's little girls running from the barn, Bitsy and Mimi and Dolly, their best dresses all rumpled and their hair stuck with straw, hollering, "Gladys! Hey, Gladys!" "Did you see the baby camel? Did you see him? He can walk!" "He pushed me, Gladys!" "He's drinking like a calf!" "Like a kitten!" "Like a baby lamb!" They pulled me and Mavis toward the barn. "Jest wait till you see!" "Gladys!" "He's so white!"

May was kneeling in the straw inside, about nose to nose with that baby camel. She was holding a bottle up to his mouth, the kind you'd use to feed a calf, and he was nuzzling and sucking on the nipple, at least until he noticed me and Mavis, and then he had to break away to see if either of us was the one he was looking for.

May raised the bottle. It was empty now. "Mrs. Bibben brought it for him," she said. "She and Mr. Bibben are looking for the camel man right now. She can't wait to tell him they found his baby camel in their barn."

"I wonder why he came here," I said. "The baby camel, I mean."

Mavis Davis frowned. "Didn't that camel man say they can always find their way back to where their momma drank water before they was born?"

I was surprised that Mavis had taken note of such a thing. "But that's if the baby's lost and looking for his momma," I pointed out. "How would he get lost?"

"He's done eatin' now," May's girls were saying. "Can we touch him, Momma?" "You said we could!"

May leaned back against the side of the stall and let the girls crowd in. Bitsy patted Ahmed's neck while Mimi tried to interest him in a handful of straw and Dolly crouched down for a look at his flat feet, leaning closer and closer until she just had to touch the impossibly thin and bony part of his leg, below the ankle. Ahmed danced a step away from her, and May said, "Dolly! I don't believe he likes that. Watch you don't get kicked."

"He's all dirty, Momma," Dolly said, and she twisted around to show us her hand.

That was the first we noticed the white dirt caked on his white, white camel hair.

Looking back, you can piece together a lot of things you didn't know were happening at the time.

While I climbed the stairs to Miss Spivey's room—and even before that, in the early morning hours, when it looked to the casual eye like no one was stirring anywhere in town—events were already occurring that would change all our lives to come. Long before I woke up in the barn, for example, Mr. John Gordon was already pacing back and forth in his law office on Main Street, smelling like fire and brimstone, which is to say, like smoke and creosote from the night before.

Mr. Gordon was one of the first to wake up on the morning after the Baghdad Bazaar, having hardly slept a wink since the downpour sent him scooting for cover. He had every reason to be feeling embarrassed and put out, if not downright nervous. Not only had the Ku Klucks of Piedmont County let him down by showing up in such pathetically unimpressive numbers last night that he might have had to cancel the event altogether if it hadn't been for some hooligans the Lumpkin boy brought along from who knows where—oh, and weren't they happy to avail themselves of Mr. Gordon's stock of surplus hoods and robes, not a one of which could be sold as anything but sadly used now. And not only had his usually intelligent and reliable yardman misjudged the staying power of copper wire when it came to holding two trunks of pine together in perpendicular fashion, the result being what looked more like a burning clothes pole than a fiery cross lighting up the night, and not only had the deputy sheriff come running—in his ridiculous outfit and with that thing on his head—to warn them against burning down the whole town, which they had no intention of doing, their sole purpose being to show that teacher she had gone too far, and not only had the sky opened up to douse their flames before they got to the schoolhouse—not only all that, but the downpour had left Mr. Gordon no choice but to unlock his office and let the sodden hooligans just about run him over to get inside, where they spread mud and soot on every surface until he woke them up to kick them out at daybreak. Mrs. Gordon would not be speaking to him this morning or at any time in the foreseeable future, once she got down here to see the mess.

With all that on his mind, the last thing Mr. Gordon needed was the Lumpkin boy appearing at the back door minutes ago, *still* wearing a white robe, now filthy, over *his* ridiculous outfit, and blubbering about camels and White Sue, whoever that was. It seemed clear that something had happened, but Arnie ran off before Mr. Gordon could figure out what, and now Mr. Gordon had to decide if he should try to get to the bottom of Arnie's babble, or if it would be wiser—and he was leaning this way—to maintain his ignorance, particularly if whatever happened involved any hooligans still wearing Mr. Gordon's robes.

When Mr. Gordon's pacing took him to the front window of the law office, he pushed the curtain aside and peered out. Main Street looked about as disenchanted at this point as a golden coach turned back into a pumpkin—a rotten, sagging pumpkin, at that. The street was a muddy slough of white dirt mixed with red and brown, the minaret and balconies exposed as nothing but mismatched lumber, the storefronts streaked white and gray. Every window was striped with dried white dirt—including the one Mr. Gordon was looking through—and lengths of dirty cloth appeared to have gotten themselves wound around every post and stuck in every crack and cranny in town. They flapped around the charred remains of the two pine trunks, one of which still stood while the other jutted out the back of the wagon, making it look like a burned-out boat with a long crazy prow. A bright June sun was shining without mercy over all of it.

Only the signs at either end of Main Street still said WELCOME TO BAGHDAD in letters that were sharp and clear. Mr. Gordon could see one of those signs from his window. The neat lettering—in real white paint which hadn't run in the rain like all the white dirt did—made him think of the roadside signs the county had required him to post out by his kaolin pit north of town. By the look and style of the letters, he wouldn't be surprised if the same fellow had painted them all. Those signs had cost him plenty. DANGER! and DEEP SLOUGH the county wanted, even though nobody used that old logging road anymore except for kaolin trucks, and their drivers knew to look out for drop-offs and white sloughs and quicksand and the like. Besides, it wasn't all that deep near the road. It was remembering those signs, Mr. Gordon told the sheriff later, that made him suddenly suspect that he *might* know what Arnie Lumpkin meant when he said what sounded like "White *Sue*." And that, in turn, made Mr. Gordon reach for a pair of rubber boots to pull over his leather shoes. He expected to catch up with the Lumpkin boy, who would have to leave his filthy white robe by the roadside if he wanted to get into Mr. Gordon's car.

All of the above came out later, when the county sheriff from over in Claytonville—a man named Butts—was asking everybody: Where were *you* between the hours of six o'clock and half-past seven on the morning after the Baghdad Bazaar?

It was long before six o'clock that morning when Mrs. Faith Boykin fired up her black iron stove. She was trying to be as quiet as she could, so as not to wake up Uncle Mack the camel man, who was snoring softly on the bed she'd made up for him in the corner of the kitchen. They were all sleeping like babies, the boys on the porch and Etta George in the bedroom, plenty of room for her long legs last night since Mrs. Faith Boykin never went to bed at all. How could she, when she had let Miss Spivey and Uncle Mack McComb talk her into sending Theo off to Macon not in September, when school started, but *today,* this very morning, at daybreak, with himself, his best clothes, and his most prized possessions (one notebook, five pencils, and the books that Miss Templeton had given him) all packed on the top of a camel? Mrs. Boykin had Theo's clothes to sort and mend and iron and fold and roll up in blankets, she had breakfast to make and a good lunch and supper to pack because who knew what he would get to eat in Macon. *Is this the right thing?* she asked her dead husband. *Is this the right thing, letting him go?*

Theo had told her, "It's for the best, Momma," not just because the Ku Klucks were riled up, but on account of the job that Uncle Mack could arrange for Theo on the circus grounds this summer.

Was any of that reason enough to let him go?

Oh, she could be as quiet as she wanted, but the sky would start getting light anyway, and Uncle Mack would get up to fetch the camels, and the boys would wake up as soon as bacon and biscuits got into their dreams by way of their noses. They were going to go, no matter how many one-more-things she found to do or pack, like this pair of pants that needed laundering. Was he just going to leave them behind? His best pants!

"Put 'em in a sack, Momma, and I'll wash 'em when I get there," Theo said as he set himself down across from his brother, plates of biscuits and bacon and gravy and grits on the table between them. When she bent over the table with another bowl of something, he stretched up and gave her a kiss on the cheek.

No matter how much breakfast she made or how careful she was for all of his seventeen years, they had gotten to this moment here, where they were right now. Uncle Mack had his humpbacked creatures standing quietly next to her porch, waiting to take her boy away. They looked like somebody had cut them out of a picture and pasted them there, big old pines instead of palm trees in the background. Ahmed the snow-white baby camel was up there on Ivan, nicely settled on the load of Uncle Mack's and Theo's belongings, looking like a prince on his throne. Uncle Mack told her that baby camels who were born in midjourney across the desert got to ride for one day only, after which they were expected to make their way like everybody else. Mrs. Boykin could tell there was supposed to be a little lesson for her in that fact. She reminded Eugene that he was coming home from Macon *this evening* with Force Cailiff in the truck. "Before dark," she said.

"Yes, ma'am," said Eugene.

She remembered a blanket they'd forgotten.

"Momma, I just have to *go*," Theo said.

Then a door slammed and they all looked over to see Ildred Cailiff running toward them, her nightgown stuffed down into and flowing over the top of a pair of overalls that belonged to someone a substantial size or two larger than she would ever be. In her good left hand, she was waving and swinging a metal bucket—no, it was Theo's magic pitcher.

"They left it on the stage last night," she said, out of breath, and offered it up on tiptoe. Theo leaned down from the saddle high on Sabrina's hump. He had to slide sideways, holding on to the tall saddle horn, to take it from her. "I'm not sure I got anyplace to put it," he said.

"All you need is this here," said Ildred, handing up a ribbon of blue cloth.

Theo looked at the ribbon in his hand as if he were trying to think of something to say other than, *I have to go.*

She said, "Use that to tie it to the saddle, Theo."

He said, "Thank you, Ildred, I will." And he did.

Later, Ildred could recite word for word the little conversation she had with Theo Boykin while he sat up on top of the camel, about to set out for Macon. She would repeat it for anyone who cared to listen, line by line.

One person who was very busy between six and half-past seven on the morning after the Baghdad Bazaar was my brother Force. After carrying Miss Spivey's baggage from her room above Bibbens' to the whistle-stop to wait for the train, Force hightailed it home. He had to get Daddy's truck so he could meet up with Theo and Uncle Mack and the camels, at the place where the old logging road came out on the highway. Now he wished more than ever that he had availed himself of the five dollars Mavis Davis offered on Bibbens' porch. Five dollars would be nice to have in his pocket when he got to Macon. He found Ildred in the kitchen leaning her backside against the dry sink with her arms folded across her chest. (With Ildred that meant one arm folded and holding the elbow end of the other.) She was wearing overalls with her nightgown stuffed into them and a red-eyed expression on her face. He said, "Is something wrong?" to which she replied, scowling, "Not a thing in the world."

Force opened the iron door of the warming oven above the stove and took out a plate of biscuits. "Theo left yet?"

"Of course they left. Daddy's wondering if maybe you forgot you're supposed to meet up with them. I think he's fixin' to go himself."

Force, who was bent over the biscuits, straightened up. "He don't need to do that."

"Force Cailiff, don't put them right in your pockets. You'll get a stain. Let me wrap some and you go tell Daddy you're ready to go."

It didn't take Force ten or fifteen minutes to get to the meeting place, a shady spot on the roadside where he'd be able to see the first of the camels coming out of the woods, a sight he was looking forward to. Force reckoned it might take them almost an hour to get to the highway. The logging road was only about three miles long, but it was overgrown in places, and they'd have to be more careful on the first stretch by the old chalk pit. "I say it's good they left later than they meant to," he'd told Ildred, "so they can see where the heck they're going." He couldn't blame Uncle Mack for wanting to make a quick and quiet getaway, after last night. Force pulled a biscuit from the cloth Ildred had tied them up in. He wasn't angry at Theo anymore or at Miss Spivey, either, but he still believed that they had been foolish and reckless in their behavior: Miss Spivey using those children to make a point, it looked like, and Theo collecting kids from fields and yards and off the side of the road without so much as asking their parents' leave. They had been asking for trouble, and trouble had certainly arrived. Maybe if the world was changed, like Theo said, they could bring whoever they wanted into Threestep School, but the world wasn't changed. Last night sure enough proved that.

Force had been waiting in the truck long enough to eat all four biscuits Ildred had wrapped for him when he heard the train whistle—which meant that it was 8:05 and that Miss Spivey, whom he'd been picturing sitting on her steamer trunk alongside the tracks, was standing up now, holding her tam onto her head and probably taking a few steps back, away from the approaching train. Force pictured the conductor reaching down to give her a hand, while the same porter who set her baggage down on the burnt grass back in August was taking it up again. And then she was making the tall step up onto the metal stairs at the end of the car, placing her hiking boot firmly on the metal tread, ignoring the glance of the conductor. She was boosting herself up, and Force could see the muscle of her calf flexing above the ankle-high boot, the shape of her knee under the hem of her skirt.

He might have fallen asleep, he thought later. When he opened his eyes, the sun seemed significantly higher. It was hot. He lifted his shoulder to wipe his face on his shirt. There were no camels in sight. They couldn't have followed the logging road and come out of the woods without seeing him here. So where were they?

In Bibbens' barn, we got the bad news from Ildred, but you could also say that she got the bad news from us. It went in both directions at the same time. She had been at the Boykins' place, having gone back to keep Etta George and Mrs. Boykin company, when Mr. and Mrs. Bibben showed up, all set to tell Uncle Mack that his baby camel was safe at their place. Mrs. Faith Boykin told them that Uncle Mack and her boys had set out on that logging road over an hour ago—going on two hours now, in fact. She expected they were halfway to Macon by now, she said, exaggerating a little. Mrs. Bibben asked, "Well, then, what is that baby camel doing at our place?" Ildred had stood between the two women as they tried to make sense of the matter. She was the one who saw straight through the fog of confusion to the significance of baby Ahmed's return, saw it like an arrow piercing straight through a heart. As Momma said later, a person didn't want to jump to the worst possible conclusions at a time like this—unless that person was Ildred, who had a sixth sense. Ildred had commenced to bouncing nervously on her toes, muttering to herself, and when Mrs. Faith Boykin looked at her, she looked back and said, "Something's happened!"

Then she took off on foot. She covered the mile and then some from Boykins' place to Bibbens' barn in record time, I'm sure, judging by the way she couldn't do anything but hold on to the wooden side of Ahmed's stall with her one hand while she gasped and writhed and coughed, trying to catch her breath, her short arm in plain view instead of tucked inside her overalls, the way she usually kept it. When she was finally able to whisper, "Something terrible has happened to them," not a one of us could doubt that she was right.

The Bibbens' truck showed up not long after Ildred did, its tires and fenders spattered with white dirt. The truck pulled around the back to where we were, half of us in and half out of the barn. Mr. Bibben dropped out the driver's side to the ground and tore around to open the back of the truck, saying, "Git in, git in! They pulled him out of the slough. He's still alive. Git in!"

It seemed like a long time that nobody moved, but it was likely no more than the second between breaths before May said, "*Who?* Who's still alive?"

Mr. Bibben straightened up from pulling crates out of the truck to make room for us. He wanted to say that he just told us who, but he could tell from our waiting faces that he had not.

At home, a crowd was already waiting. Nobody had far to go, after all. It looked like every Negro family in the county was milling around the Boykins' house, and where their front yard blended into our back yard, there was a blend of colored folks and white, the proportion of which got whiter, sure enough, as they got nearer to our house. Many of them were people I knew—the Reverends, the Wickers, the Hodges, the Veals—but at least as many were strangers left over from the Baghdad Bazaar, people who had spent the night in odd places and woke up to the news that trouble had struck at the edge of town in the early morning hours. Our front yard appeared to be the parking lot—T-Model Fords and wagons, mostly, and Ed's old truck—but also Mrs. Lulu Blount's Hudson and Mr. Gordon's beautiful Cadillac LaSalle, the shiny maroon doors and fenders streaked and spattered white. Mr. Bibben could hardly get his truck down the lane for the crowd.

It was another few minutes—time enough for us to tumble out of Mr. Bibben's truck and scramble up to Momma on the back porch—before Linwood Perkins's Model A, the SHERIFF hand-painted on the doors half covered in white, made the turn into the lane. Linwood and Mr. Gordon were inside. They were followed by Daddy's truck, with Daddy at the wheel and Ralphord—that was a surprise—in the passenger seat. Not until they went past us, oh so slowly, could I see Eugene Boykin kneeling in the bed of the truck. All I saw of Theo, past Eugene's wide back, was that he was white with clay—his bare chest and arms and feet coated whiter than they were onstage last night at the Baghdad Bazaar, and his pants dusted and streaked with white. Eugene was holding his hand.

"Jesus Lord," my mother said. "Have mercy."

It was the deputy sheriff who hopped out of his car and announced to the crowd, "He's still breathing." This sent a ripple of relief you could hear traveling in all directions from where he stood.

As soon as Daddy's truck stopped alongside the Boykins' house, one of the men jumped up into the back of it and helped Eugene hand Theo down to another two men waiting on the ground to take him. Daddy helped the four of them carry Theo to a wooden table set up in the Boykins' yard, with a sheet thrown over it and a straw-filled pillow for his head. Mrs. Boykin had no running water or full-sized bathtub in the house—nobody out here at the end of town did—so she had a mind to clean him up before they carried him inside, where she would finish bathing him, and change his clothes, and put him to bed. Eugene and Daddy and the other three men laid Theo gently down on the table, which was situated to keep his face and shoulders in the shade while the rest of him was warmed by the sun, and then the men stepped back to give Mrs. Boykin room. Smears and streaks of white were left on their brown arms from where they had cradled Theo's head or feet or white dirt-covered pants, as though they all suffered from the same ailment that had brought him low. Standing among them, only my daddy appeared to be afflicted with whiteness from head to toe. Eugene Boykin wore his face—which was battered and bloody, streaked pink and white with fear and anger—like a mask.

Mrs. Boykin was quiet as she bent to the task of washing Theo clean. Other colored ladies were standing by, helping her. They'd warmed up water from the pump by mixing it in a washtub with kettlefuls heated on the stove. One of the women handed Mrs. Boykin a pitcher filled from the tub. She took it, leaned over to kiss Theo's forehead, and, wiping the white dirt from her mouth with the back of her hand, she tipped the pitcher and poured a stream of water over his forehead that ran down over his hair, just like she was baptizing him. Somebody handed her another pitcher, and this time, as she poured it, she smoothed her palm around his head. The white dirt ran in streams away from him, and his hair was dark again. The pitchers refilled again and again, she poured the cleansing water over his arms and chest and shoulders. She let it run over his face and neck, into his ears. From the porch, we could see his skin begin to shine through the white in dark streaks and patches. Then she took the cloth towel they handed her and carefully wiped his face and behind his ears and under his chin the way she would have washed him when he was a baby.

"He's breathing," I reminded my momma in a whisper. "He'll be all right, won't he?" She put one arm each around me and Ralphord. I hoped she wasn't thinking about old Mrs. Brazel's nephew, who fell out of a boat on O'Quinn's pond when he was young. I'd heard the story many times. He was still breathing when they pulled him out, and he went on breathing for three days after that. Then he stopped.

Theo had been carried into the house when two little boys came running up the lane to report that the camel man was coming along the road. He was riding the white camel, they said. They had no other camels to report, but there was a sheriff's car—Piedmont County—driving along behind the white camel, slow, slow, slow, with two white boys in the backseat.

We waited, but only Uncle Mack and Ivan arrived, coming up the lane at a weary pace, Ivan smiling sadly and Uncle Mack with his head bowed over the tall horn of the *terik* saddle. The Piedmont County sheriff had gone straight past the lane and carried the two boys in the backseat directly to jail in Claytonville. The boys were Arnie Lumpkin and my brother Force.

They made Uncle Mack tell his story over and over again. We saw him through the window of the deputy sheriff's office, sitting in the same chair Miss Spivey sat in that time but looking weary, drawing his hand over his eyes sometimes, dropping his head into his hands. Listening to Uncle Mack, Linwood Perkins walked back and forth across the room. When the sheriff came back from Claytonville to hear the story, he perched himself on the edge of Linwood's desk. The Piedmont County sheriff wanted to take Uncle Mack to jail in Claytonville, too, for his own safety, the sheriff said. Linwood Perkins wouldn't stand for it, we heard. When the sheriff, unaccustomed to being argued with, raised his eyebrows, Linwood Perkins said, "The man needs to look after his animals."

He still had two.

Uncle Mack said the truck that came along and surprised them on the logging road had to be someone who knew they were setting out this morning, and from where. The truck was a Model A Ford, like most every other truck in these parts, and Uncle Mack didn't get much of a look at the boys in it, but whoever it was knew about camels and pigs.

"What *about* camels and pigs?" the Piedmont County sheriff asked.

Ivan V and Sabrina were circus camels, Uncle Mack explained wearily. They were accustomed to noise and surprises. It was Uncle Mack's opinion that the camels would have stepped to the side of the old logging road and waited serenely, even disdainfully, for this thing to pass, in spite of the boys banging on the rickety wooden sides of the truck, if two or three of them hadn't started up squealing and snorting and doing their best hog calls. That's what sent Sabrina off down the slope toward the kaolin pit. Ivan did his share of dancing and trying to bolt, and it was all that Uncle Mack could do, snatching up the lead rope with both hands, to stop that camel before he got to where the soft white dirt would have swallowed his feet, too. From his bed of cargo on Ivan's back, Ahmed gave a cry of alarm.

Eugene Boykin leaped to the other side of the logging road, away from the slough, and when the truck passed in a cacophony of squealing gears and hog calls and cussing and laughter, Eugene came scrambling back up to the roadbed.

"Be still!" Uncle Mack said, his voice at once so quiet and so urgent that both boys froze, Theo on Sabrina with his knees clenched and his weight forward, his hands wrapped around the saddle horn and his feet dangling above the white slough she was already mired in, and Eugene standing on the road, holding his arms out a little from his sides, almost like a tightrope walker, as if he were trying to disturb as little of the air as he could. There was some careful breathing and shifting of weight—even Ahmed kept still—and then Uncle Mack said, in a low voice, "Eugene, I got to send you back for help. Sabrina may get herself out of this, but if she can't, we'll need us something to pull her out."

Eugene whispered, "A truck?"

"Could be," Uncle Mack said softly.

The woods had already swallowed up the noise of the truck and its rowdy passengers, leaving only the shady rustling of leaves and the frustrated grunts of Sabrina, as she tested the depth of her troubles, accompanied by Uncle Mack's calm and melodious voice.

"Could be a tractor or a wagon," he told Eugene, "or mules. Whatever you can get here quick—but don't forget to ask permission. Walk away, now—don't run!—*walk* till you get far enough away that you can't hear me at all, and then wait a little longer, count to ten, because camels hear better than people, and then run as fast as you can. All right? Go on, now."

While Eugene hurried off, Uncle Mack kept talking, sometimes to Theo—"Y'all did a nice job arranging this cargo for Ahmed, he's sitting like a prince up here"—but mostly to the camels. He gave a gentle tug downward on the lead rope that hung from Ivan's bridle. Ivan folded his front legs to kneel, then lowered his hindquarters, and finally settled all the way down. Uncle Mack took hold of Ahmed as soon as he could reach him and lifted him to the ground. He tied a rope like a collar around the baby camel's neck and looped the other end over a log too big for him to pull. He did all this in a minute, ninety seconds at the most, and kept talking the whole time, using some of the Arabic words that he believed all camels understood although he himself did not know what they meant. It wasn't the meaning that mattered but the feeling they contained, and that was a feeling of home, of calm, of well-being and safety. He tried not to think about what might happen if the truck came back this way again.

Up on Sabrina, which put him three or four feet above the surface of the white slough, Theo sat as silent as a stone. He looked alarmed, nervous, but not terrified, not yet. He didn't know about camels the size of Sabrina and what happened when their flat camel feet, so useful on the desert sands, got buried in mud or clay, or whatever this was that they had been forced into. Sabrina was in well up over her hind ankles and close to her knees in front, so the slough was a good two feet deep where she stood. How much of it was muck and how much was milky water, Uncle Mack couldn't tell. If what held her feet down was thick enough, and if she kept on trying to lift the weight, he thought she might have only minutes before she broke a leg. On the road above them, Ahmed took a few restless steps, snorting and blowing, making his lips buzz, and Sabrina struggled again to get free.

"Uncle Mack!" Theo said.

Sabrina tossed her head back and made a noise like a deep roar. Uncle Mack tried singing a trill of notes to her. Her ears turned, yearning, and she stood still, but she had sunk a little deeper. Now he wished that he hadn't sent Eugene away. The first thing—it was suddenly so clear—was to get Theo onto solid ground.

"Theo," Uncle Mack said, "I'm thinking it might be easier for her to get out with you off her back. I'll just put this rope around Ivan's neck and we'll move in a little closer to you. When I reach my arm out, you grab hold."

"But Ivan will sink, too!"

"Shh, no, take a look. It's solid here." Uncle Mack shuffled forward and tapped his foot on the white ground at the edge of the slough. "All you got to do—" he began calmly, but then there was a sound like a strong wet branch breaking. It was a sickening sound, and it made Sabrina shudder and pitch like a boat, sideways, dropping Theo in the white soup. He landed on his feet, sank immediately to his knees.

"Uncle Mack!" Theo threw his arms around whatever he could reach of the camel. She was making an indescribable sound now, like a person with no breath to scream, screaming. Up on the road, Ahmed gave a real cry and then another and another, his mouth open wide, cries like a horn blasting.

"Now, you hold still right there, Theo!" Uncle Mack said. He had already pulled Ivan back. "Oosh!" he said, keeping his eye on the boy while he looped the rope around his own waist. Uncle Mack glanced down for an instant, to secure the knot, and when he looked up again, the scene before him was transformed. There was only, terribly, a camel struggling to hold her head out of the white slough, her body half submerged and heaving—only that and nothing else. Theo was gone.

For a moment Uncle Mack was paralyzed, stunned into stillness by this new configuration, unable to take it in, and then, after how many precious seconds lost, he slid heedlessly down the slope and threw himself over Sabrina. She screamed again, and up on the road Ahmed's cries reached a new pitch of alarm. Begging her forgiveness, Uncle Mack slid over the bulk of her to the other side. His feet sank completely, over the ankles, in the muck. Opaque water reached his knees. He plunged his hands under the white surface and groped and found something he could close his fingers on and pull. He pulled, pulled, and nearly flew backwards when his right hand came up with a white-soaked piece of plaid shirt. He flung it away and plunged again. His hands filled with thicker stuff—the bib of Theo's overalls—and this time when he pulled, the dark crown of Theo's head appeared, murkily, right underneath and then breaking the white surface, but no farther. "Jesus Jesus Jesus Jesus God!" He understood. She had rolled into the boy. She had knocked him down and now she held him under. Uncle Mack tried to throw his body against the bulk of her without letting go of Theo's overalls. Then he staggered up and pulled again—again, the dark crown, a finger's-width of forehead above the surface—no more? No more? He pulled and sobbed and pulled until his shoulders seemed to leave their sockets, his elbows stretched apart, and in the instant his fingers seemed to lose their grip, there was the new sound of splashing. Sabrina's body moved. It was a tiny movement, like a sharp intake of breath, but as Uncle Mack pulled again, Theo rose suddenly, white and limp, into his arms.

Eugene was halfway back to town when he saw a truck parked off the side of the logging road, nobody at the wheel. He made straight for it, and he knew in an instant, as the swarm of dirty white robes rose like maggots from the back, that he had made a mistake, that this was as far as he was going to get. Although he was such a tall and broad and muscular boy, a boy bigger than most men, he could not prevail against so many. Long minutes later, blindfolded and tied to a tree, he felt a cold splash on his neck and chest, and the sharp smell of alcohol burned his nostrils. An argument erupted about wasting good whiskey—and lumber, too, if the trees caught on. Eugene thought he recognized the voice that talked the others out of setting fire to him.

On solid ground, Uncle Mack wiped Theo's mouth and nose. He listened. He pounded on Theo's chest and listened. He opened Theo's mouth and blew a breath into him. He rolled him over and pounded his back, rolled him back and blew another breath into him, listened, blew, pounded, listened. Somebody said, "He's dead, ain't he?"

"Who? Who said it?"

Perched on Linwood Perkins's desk in the deputy sheriff's office, the Piedmont County sheriff wanted to know: Who said it?

Uncle Mack couldn't say. He didn't know. He reckoned it was Eugene at the time.

"How could that be?" the sheriff asked. "Those boys had him tied to a tree, up the road a piece. It was somebody else come and helped you save that boy. Who?"

Uncle Mack didn't know. He'd passed out himself, it looked like. Next thing he knew, he was lying on the solid ground. It took a minute for him to recognize the whitened hump at his feet—"Aw, my girl," he breathed—and another to realize that the sound that woke him, very near at hand, was Theo, coughing.

18

The Cup of Death

THE BIBBENS' PHONE kept ringing on and off all day after they carried Theo home. Twice it was Miss Spivey calling and once she asked for me, but I declined the opportunity to speak to her. It was well past supper, which May and Ildred had prepared, Momma being busy with Mrs. Boykin and Theo, when a long black motorcar turned down our lane and slipped past our house on its way to the Boykins' place. I was so sure it was Miss Spivey coming back to us, abashed and desperate to make amends, that I went inside the house to watch her from the kitchen window where I myself could not be seen. The car was a Cadillac LaSalle, my brother Ebenezer said, looking over my shoulder out the window. Like Mr. Gordon's, only black. There are no words to express my surprise when the driver came around and opened the door of that Cadillac LaSalle for a very small woman in a plain brown coat—which she definitely did not need on this June evening—and a brown felt hat. The driver reached into the backseat and pulled out a black satchel and carried it for her to the Boykins' door.

"Who the heck is that?" asked Ebenezer.

Momma came home and told us, "Dr. Janet Miller's come to look after Theo."

If Miss Spivey had sent Shahrazad or Alaeddin, I couldn't have been more amazed.

Etta George was right there in the room when Dr. Janet Miller examined Theo. She had placed her thin white hand on Theo's forehead. She had opened his eyes, first one, then the other, with her fingertips, and leaned over him to peer into each. She had taken his hand from under the coverlet, Etta said, and laid it flat on hers, first palm to palm, then turning it over and peering at it like a fortune-teller. She took a watch from her pocket and, putting her fingers on his wrist, she frowned at the hands of the watch for a long minute. When next she folded back the coverlet, baring his chest, Etta almost turned away, but the instrument—part rubber, part shining silver—that Dr. Miller pulled out from under her coat caught Etta's eye and held it. "It was a stetho-scope," she said. "She put the two ends in her ears, like this"— Etta showed us, using her index fingers—"and the other end—it was a little silver bell. She put that little bell on his chest, here and here— and there."

Ralphord asked, "What for?"

"To listen to his insides." Etta George looked at me and Ralphord and Ildred one by one. She whispered, "She let me listen, too."

"With the stethoscope?" Ildred asked sharply. She said the word as if she'd always known it. Etta nodded and touched her ears, one hand to each. Ildred asked, "What did you hear?"

Etta thought. "A drum," she said. "And the wind."

We sat for a minute, all of us, listening to leaves rustle.

"What else?" Ildred asked. "Did she do anything else to him?"

"She felt of his ribs and his arms and legs. She said he didn't have anything broken. And then she tucked the quilt around him and asked Miz Boykin what he liked to eat."

"What's your son's favorite dish?" was what Dr. Miller had asked.

Mrs. Boykin only looked at her, trying to extract the sense of what the lady doctor said from the morass of sadness into which they had all so suddenly fallen.

"If he could have anything he wanted, what would he choose? What does he like best?"

"To eat?" Mrs. Faith Boykin looked at her boy, lying so still there in the bed, and her eyes filled up, but she took a deep breath and composed herself. "If I had to say his very, very most favorite thing, that's got to be pan-fried bream, fresh out the pond."

"Anything else?"

Etta George, who could still feel the cool metal of the stethoscope in her ears, said, "What about pecan pie, Miz Boykin?"

Mrs. Boykin considered. "Theo does love pecan pie. With whip cream on it, that might be his second-best favorite."

"Do you have the ingredients?" Dr. Miller asked. "Any pecans on hand?"

"Ma'am, I got nineteen acres' worth of pecans put by. Almost."

"Make him a pecan pie," Dr. Miller said as she put the stethoscope back in her bag and snapped it shut. "Leave this door open so he can smell it. We want to let him know there's something waiting for him over here. Something worth waking up for."

Mrs. Boykin's hands went straight to her heart. She said, "You think he's fit to wake up—I mean to say, you think it'll be soon?"

Dr. Miller stood beside the bed with her doctor bag. She looked at Theo. She said, "Well, we don't know how long he was without oxygen, but his vitals are good. I think we can expect something. May I leave this here, Mrs. Boykin?" She made to set her bag on the dresser. "I believe I'll take a tour of Baghdad, Georgia." She turned to Etta. "You'll come and find me at once if anything changes," she said.

"Yes, ma'am, I will."

Etta told us she helped Dr. Miller put on her coat. "She's got a little rheumatism in her left arm makes it hard to bend her elbow," Etta said.

Ildred asked, "What do you think she meant when she said we could 'expect something'? Did she mean, expect him to be all right?"

"Sounds like it," Etta George said, but we caught something in her tone.

"What else?" Ildred asked.

"Before she left, she told Miz Boykin, if he didn't wake up when that pie was finished, she ought to start making another one."

"It don't take that long to make a pie," Ralphord pointed out.

"Miz Boykin said she could make a lot of pies before she ran out of pecans, and Dr. Miller said, 'That's the spirit.' "

Ildred stood up.

"Where you off to?" Ralphord asked her.

"I'm going fishing. I can catch some bream."

Dr. Janet Miller's tour of Baghdad began and ended at the schoolhouse, where she picked up a blue ribbon strung with camel bells and put it in her pocket, jingling it from time to time the rest of the night, both on purpose and by accident. She stood looking at the rear wall of the schoolroom for a long time, tilting her head back to see the pictures that were higher up and bending over to see the very lowest ones. She didn't look like Miss Spivey at all—more like our old teacher Miss Chandler, if anything, being so short and plain and maybe a little frail, her hair done up in an old-lady way, although I wouldn't have called her an old lady quite yet—but she talked like Miss Spivey. Not in her pronunciation, in which Dr. Miller sounded more southern than Miss Spivey did, but in the things they said and the way they said them. Now, for instance, looking at the pictures, Dr. Miller asked, "Our friend Theo drew these?"

I was following her around. I didn't think she noticed. Her question startled me enough so I didn't answer right away, which caused her to turn around. "Gladys?" she said.

If I was startled by her question, I was stunned by her knowing my name. "Ma'am?" I said, and then, "Yes. Yes, he did, leastwise the ones that are made, not from the book."

"This is one we can't afford to lose," she said.

For a minute, I thought she meant the picture. I said, "Did Miss Spivey tell you my name?"

"Oh, yes," she said. "I've heard about all the Cailiffs."

"Force, too?"

She sighed. "Yes."

My eye fell on the picture of the Prince about to kiss the sleeping Princess. Before I could change my mind, I asked, "Is Force really an Arabian prince?"

"No," said Dr. Miller. "He's your brother."

"I knew that."

"I'm sure you did."

To change that subject, I seized the opportunity to ask, "Did you hear—did Miss Spivey ever talk about my sister May? Did y'all meet May?"

"I did. May brought over plates of chicken for supper, she and Mildred."

"Ildred," I corrected her without thinking.

"I beg your pardon?"

"There's no *M*. Momma dropped the *M*."

She said, "And all the while I thought Grace was saying 'Mildred.' "

I said, as if she might not have noticed, "May's the one who's expecting."

"We listened to the baby's heartbeat," Dr. Miller said. "Your sister has a good strong baby on the way." She jingled the camel bells in her pocket. "She could stand to be a little stronger herself, though. It would help if she gained a few pounds. You have to encourage her."

"Did you listen with your—what kind of scope?"

She said it for me, and then she spelled it so I could write it on the blackboard right under *terik saddle*, which was still up there with a picture of one drawn in chalk. "Theo drew that saddle, too," I said.

"Oh? Is this school—is it the Negro students' school?"

I said, "No, but sometimes they came in here—for things. Usually just Theo."

"I see." Dr. Miller picked up a piece of chalk and drew a fat letter Y that I knew from Etta George's description was supposed to be a stethoscope. She stepped back and squinted at it.

I asked her, "Is Theo going to be all right?"

She said, "It's too soon to tell."

"When can we tell?"

"When he wakes up. Well, here comes someone."

It was my sister May at the door, still in her Shahrazad costume, but with some of the moons and stars flaking off and the long veil draped over one shoulder like a towel. She said, "There was a lot of folks coming to the Boykins' to see how Theo was doing, so Momma thought maybe I should bring them on over here, where there's some room to sit down."

Not until she stepped inside did we see that she had a large crowd behind her, mostly white people in the front—Mrs. Reverend Stokes, Louise Blount, Ildred, and a tear-stained Ralphord were right behind May—and colored people toward the back of the crowd: fifty-some people marching into the schoolhouse to sit for a spell and wait for news about Theo. There were more people coming all the time, one here, two there, this or that one leaving and coming back with another fresh-baked pie in hand, women carrying in pots of coffee and pitchers of tea and cups and plates and forks for the pies, mostly pecan, of which there were no fewer than a dozen lined up on Miss Spivey's desk before the night was over. The whole room smelled just heavenly, and although I kept counting heads all evening, I couldn't keep track. Some people paused in the doorway before they came in, but they did come in. After all the fuss about eleven colored children spending one morning in the schoolhouse, I wondered what the Superintendent of Schools would say about *this*. My momma said later that everybody's mind was so crowded with worrying about Theo that there wasn't any room for them to worry about what color the person worrying about Theo in the row behind them happened to be. Momma said it was too bad everybody couldn't keep themselves that busy worrying about each other *all* the time.

When Mrs. Reverend Stokes arrived, she announced on behalf of the local clergy that a prayer service for Theo Boykin was going on right now over at White Springs Baptist Church. "All denominations are welcome," she said, looking around at the faces, light and dark, that were looking back at her. Most folks were pleased, I think, to hear there was a prayer service going on, but nobody got up and left in order to attend. Some of the ladies got started on handing out slivers of pie to people sitting on every available surface—desks, chairs, shelves, boxes, floor, and so forth. Dr. Miller went off to check on Theo, and when she came back with no change to report, she looked around at all those people and proposed that we keep a *vigil* in the schoolhouse.

"Should we pray?" somebody asked.

"They're already praying over to the church," Mrs. Reverend Stokes said.

Dr. Miller said she thought someone might tell a story.

"Like Shahrazad," said Mavis Davis from where she sat on the floor, her back to the wall, right under the rolled-up map. She was still in her overalls.

Dr. Miller looked at her. So did I. For that matter, so did everybody.

"Shahrazad held off the Garnerer of graveyards," Mavis pointed out. Not everybody there knew what she was talking about. I couldn't help but think again how wrong Miss Spivey was if she thought Mavis Davis didn't think at all.

Dr. Miller said, "Well, then, who has a story to get us started?"

Almost to a person, we turned to May. She was our Shahrazad, after all. She was sitting at the teacher's desk, up on the platform at the front of the room, with all the pie plates arrayed before her. She turned pink. "Y'all want *me* to make up a story?"

"You don't have to make it up," said Dr. Miller, looking more like a sparrow than ever perched on top of a desk with her feet not even close to touching the floor. "You can tell a story that someone told you. Or one that you've read."

"Does it have to be true?" asked Mrs. Lulu Blount from the bench against the back wall, where all the Baghdad pictures hung.

"As true as she can make it," Mrs. Reverend Stokes said.

May searched the ceiling and also our faces—lingering for a moment on mine, I don't know why—as if she were looking for a way to begin. Now, it's true enough that Miss Spivey told May more about everything than she ever told anyone else. They came to confide in each other beyond the ordinary, as I believe I have already mentioned. It's also true that if a story is any good, it won't take long before you're picturing it in your head in a lot more detail than you're actually being told—imagining what folks look like, for example, or what they must be feeling inside. A storyteller like Shahrazad or my sister May can leave a story in your memory as if it happened before your very eyes. All of that might account for *some* of what we heard in the schoolhouse that night, but it doesn't change the fact that the story May commenced to tell us was bigger than any story she could have known to tell, and yet—another fact—she told it.

"It hath reached my ears," is how she began, but then she let that go, and with a faint, sly smile and a glance at Dr. Miller, she said: "I heard tell one time of

A Redheaded Woman Who Hid in a Harem

"The redheaded woman was our own Miss Spivey," May pointed out at the start.

(At least, she *used* to be our Miss Spivey, was what I thought right then.)

When Miss Grace Spivey came home from college in May of 1930, May said, she thought she might just go insane.

It was spring, of course, and Nashville was so thick and sweet with wisteria and honeysuckle that the very air could make a body choke. The effects of October 29, 1929, had not yet dimmed the bright round of country club dances and the like that marked the coming of spring to Nashville society, so Grace Spivey had come home to a closet full of new gowns and a tight schedule of fittings noted on her personal calendar in her mother's graceful hand. She stayed in her room a lot of the time, deliberately missing appointments with her mother's seamstress and avoiding the friends of her youth.

It seemed to Grace that those young women—Amanda Mae and Sally Ann and Abigail and Dorothy Sue and all the rest—had left their brains behind with their blue stockings at this or that women's college or ladies' seminary, their heads stuffed now with fabric swatches and bust measurements and a variety of wedding-related crises and details. Most of the graduates among them were getting married in September or October, when the weather would be perfect. Grace Spivey was firmly committed to finding a reason to be many miles from Nashville before the fall wedding season began. There was, however, one young woman whose wedding date had been moved up to sweltering June for the usual unmentionable reason, and this wedding Grace Spivey was doomed to attend. She did succeed in mortifying her mother by wearing one of last year's gowns (while all those new ones hung unhemmed in her closet!) and by ditching her boring young escort (the son of one of her father's colleagues in the family's "lumber" business) as early as she could.

Grace was surveying the crystal-chandeliered ballroom (which overlooked the ninth green at the Smoky Mountain Country Club) in search of a table with a single seat available—bride's side or groom's, she didn't care—when she felt a hand on her elbow. Beside her stood a little brown-haired sparrow of a woman, at least a head shorter than Grace and inappropriately dressed in a dark linen suit and sturdy-looking brown shoes.

"You look as lost as I feel," the woman said. "Would you care to join me at the social outcasts' table in the corner?" She might have been fifty years old, Grace guessed, but her size and subversive smile made her seem younger. The woman held out her hand. "I'm Janet Miller," she said. "How do you do?"

Grace took the bare hand in her gloved one. "Grace Spivey. Much better than a moment ago, ma'am, thank you."

Grace Spivey was the youngest person at the table by at least a decade or two, or three or four. She noticed that while the men were all in dinner jackets, not one pair of gloves lay limp beside the ladies' plates.

(Grace pulled hers off self-consciously and dropped them on the floor between her feet.) There was a round of introductions—"Oh, you're Walter Spivey's daughter—I knew your grandmother, child. A lovely woman!" Grace shook hands with the powdery woman on her left and the well-creased gentleman on her right. After that, she might as well have turned invisible for all the notice anyone took of her. The talk went on as before—such talk as Grace had never heard in Tennessee: stories of building hospitals in India, battling typhoid in China, establishing a network of women's clinics in Japan. Janet Miller—who was Dr. Miller to the members of the Women's World Relief Society of Nashville and their husbands at the table—was a central character in all of these stories, although she herself had little to say, compared to the others. By the time someone mentioned the doctor's part in rescuing an Arab spy after the Great War, Grace had given up trying not to stare at the little woman across from her. The conversation had shifted into French, but Grace didn't even notice. It diminished to whispers when the toasts and speeches began at the head table. The groom stood and toasted his bride, and finally people were free to get up and drift around the room. Grace, however, remained in her chair, her head full of snowy mountain passes and blistering desert trails and structures she imagined Japanese temples to be like, until Dr. Miller came around and settled on the edge of the empty chair beside her. They were the only two left at the table.

In the schoolhouse, the story stopped. Everybody looked at May. She said, "Next thing, Dr. Miller says something in French. I don't recollect how to say it." Everybody looked at Dr. Miller.

"Well, let's see," she said from where she sat on her desktop by the window. She swung her legs back and forth, thinking. "I suppose I asked Grace what she thought of us—or even if she understood what we were talking about."

"You asked her in French," May said.

"But of course."

"*Vous avez compris tout?*" Dr. Miller said, waving her hand at the empty table.

"Oh, yes—*oui,*" Grace said. "I boarded at school in France. I understand much more than I can say."

"Well," said Dr. Miller, "it's lovely to encounter a young woman of the world. I hope you're not getting married next week."

"Oh, no!" said Grace. "I don't even know any men."

"What about the young gentleman who is looking for you, I think, by the fountain? The one talking to your mother?"

"You know my mother?"

"She's one of our biggest donors, since your grandmother passed on."

"You're kidding." Grace looked at her mother across the room at exactly the wrong moment. Her mother's face lit up and she pointed the young man toward Grace with a nod of her head.

Dr. Miller leaned closer. "I believe it was a stipulation in your grandmother's will."

The red-faced young man came lurching in their direction. At the other end of the ballroom, a small orchestra was tuning up.

"Oh, dear," said Grace, but she needn't have worried. Dr. Miller slipped an arm in hers and turned her around toward the French doors that led to the veranda overlooking the ninth hole—and the round humps of the Smoky Mountains beyond.

"We have business to discuss," Dr. Miller said, and by the time they walked back into the clubhouse, Grace Spivey had accepted a position as Janet Miller's traveling secretary—a six-month tour of duty that would cross three continents and expand to fill most of a year. Grace had also learned a thing or two about her grandmother Spivey, whom she had met only once, that summer in Toomsboro, and who was not, as Grace's father once described his mother, a dotty Baptist widow lady who spent her life "sitting on a dry spot." Before the Great War (Janet Miller told Grace), her grandmother Spivey had owned fifty percent of an estate on

Skidaway Island. Her son wished to sell the estate to his father-in-law, a whiskey man from Tennessee. Now, the Baptist widow lady knew very well what the whiskey man wanted her remote stretch of island for— her home state of Georgia had been dry for years before the rest of the country followed suit—but she agreed to the transaction, keeping for herself only one small corner of the property, where her late husband had restored an old plantation home. Beatrice Spivey had bestowed the entire proceeds of the sale on the Women's Relief Society of Nashville, and as if that weren't enough, she had spent even more of what her son considered his money as the years went by, traveling with Dr. Janet Miller, accompanying the good doctor to many distant corners of the world until at last the Canceller of all itineraries put an end to Grand-mother Spivey's travels.

"And now I'll step into her shoes!" Grace said happily.

"Your grandmother preferred hiking boots," said Dr. Miller.

As they shook hands, Grace towering over her new employer, she was already picturing herself traversing jungle and savanna on the back of an elephant. Then Dr. Miller said, "But first, if you don't mind a little detour, I have a date to keep in Baghdad."

There were times, on the train from Basrah to Baghdad, when Grace Spivey thought she would suffocate from the heat. Or melt into a pud-dle. Or burst into flames. The train set out well after dark, all six windows of their compartment open, for although the hot wind smote them— *smote* being Dr. Miller's word—it was preferable to the smothering heat of unmoving air. It didn't take long, though, for sand to fill their nostrils and scour the backs of their throats raw, right through the silk scarves they'd tied around their faces. For the remainder of their twenty-hour journey, they opened a window only for a moment now and again, whenever the still heat that pressed them on all sides (as if they were packed in cotton like the artifacts Dr. Miller bought at Hillah) fooled one of them into seeking relief. During one of those moments, shortly after dawn, when the train was creeping along, as it sometimes did, no faster, Grace thought, than she herself might walk, she squinted through the scarf she had pulled over her head like a sack and saw through the mist of sand and silk a caravan of camels, hundreds of them! stretching their long necks disdainfully and lifting their knees. On every fourth or fifth beast a rider sat serenely, robes and scarves fluttering in a way that clearly suggested a breeze. Grace Spivey was enchanted. She forgot for a moment how gritty and miserable she felt.

"*Arabian Nights!*" she said.

Dr. Miller did not open her eyes, but she asked, "What do you see?"

"Camels!" said Grace. "At least a hundred of them." She was counting under her breath. "Have you ever ridden one?"

"Once or twice," Dr. Miller said faintly. "Just wait."

When they finally arrived in Baghdad, they were installed in a hotel-pension adjacent to the home of their host, a former camel merchant for whom Dr. Miller had done a good turn once and who was now in service to His Majesty King Faisal of Iraq. From the outside, both buildings were plain yellowing stone and stucco, but inside, Grace had her own tiled room scattered with thick Persian carpets and brightly colored cushions, and equipped, like Dr. Miller's suite of rooms, with its own gleaming bath. Droves of hotel personnel and freelance servants vied discreetly to make her wishes their command, as guests were few in the scorching summer months. The former camel merchant's son-in-law still owned a *caravanserai* at the city's edge, where Grace Spivey learned that sitting a camel, on any kind of saddle, had little to do with what she knew of riding horses. It was more like bobbing downriver on a log. She went out every day at dawn, when it was cool enough to ride, sometimes with Dr. Miller, sometimes with a guide provided by the son-in-law, and by the end of her stay, Grace had almost gotten used to the rolling gait of a pacing camel, the challenge of staying aboard while it rose to its feet, the oddness of riding with her legs dangling or tucked up under her skirt.

After each dusty dawn ride, Grace returned to the hotel and lowered herself into cool scented water drawn by unseen hands. From the bath she could see through arched windows that onion spires and gleaming tiled palaces, narrow stone streets and graceful balconies forever shaded from the sun were to be found not only in the pages of books. They were here—in Baghdad—a real place that existed in the world, a place where a Bedouin horseman might gallop by at any time, robes flying, in the street beneath her window. She slept in a bed on the rooftop and awoke every morning to a syncopated harmony of calls to prayer from all the minarets within hearing. Every morning she looked down at a labyrinth of twisting streets through which boys in ragged trousers led donkeys laden with baskets and water jars.

They were quite handsome, these boys.

To be sure, she knew there was suffering in this paradise as well. Accompanying Dr. Miller on her calls, Grace had seen goiters and tumors that distended necks and faces, she had seen malnutrition and its opposites (gout, ulcers, yellow-skinned sufferers from liver disease, a pasha—Dr. Miller's word for him—so enormously fat that his weight had crushed his feet into blackened nubs). Grace Spivey held the bandages while Dr. Miller dressed the striped back of a boy flogged for letting his donkey run amok in the market, and while she tried and failed to stem the bleeding of an old man who paid more than the price of his hand for stealing a string of dates. She had heard Dr. Miller hold forth against the plight of women like the wives and daughters of the camel merchant, hidden from the sight of visitors behind elaborately carved wooden screens. "Prisoners in their own homes," she said. "Hostages."

Regarding the hidden lives of these women, Grace withheld judgment. She thought she would have liked to see what life was like behind the screen. She wondered what such women wore under the loose layers of fabric—the long cotton dress and even longer veil—that enveloped them. She wished there were a way to ask these questions. If only she spoke the language, she could ask the "little married ladies"—as Dr. Miller called the women in the household of their host next door.

"A harem?" Grace asked about them, more eagerly than she meant to.

"I can tell you they're not all his wives. He's not *that* wealthy."

Dr. Miller guessed that the group was a mix of two or three wives plus sisters, in-laws, grown-up daughters, visiting cousins, and the like. Grace had regular roof-to-roof commerce with some of them. This was a matter of smiling and waving and holding up objects—mostly items of clothing—for comparison. The little married ladies were very interested in Grace's underclothing. She had stood on a stool to give them glimpses of her stockings and garters and petticoats—she had even held up a brassiere, which left some of her friends collapsed in giggles on their rooftop—but aside from leaving their faces unveiled for her, they had not reciprocated with any disclosures of their own.

One morning in Baghdad, standing in the street in front of the hotel, Grace found her path blocked by a donkey laden with a pair of huge water jars and led by a slender boy whose dark eyes were full of amusement, a dirty scarf tied haphazardly over his hair. It was not the first time she'd encountered a water boy and his donkey in the narrow street—one side of the hotel overlooked a water gate that opened to the Tigris—nor was it the first time one of the handsome boys smiled at her, but it was the first time that anyone in Baghdad ever handed her a folded piece of paper. "For me?" she said, and looked around. The boy grinned but had nothing to say. She unfolded the thick linen paper. In Roman letters—neatly printed if slightly odd, the inky black tail of each letter linking it to its neighbor—the note said only, *Look up.* She did. Arrayed along the wall at the edge of their roof next door to the hotel, the little married ladies were looking down at her. One of them was leaning over, beckoning to Grace, her hand sweeping like a broom toward the back of the building: *Go around to the garden door.*

Grace saw and obeyed. A gate in the stone wall swung open before her, and in she went.

It was lovely inside: a tile-lined pool, roses, plane trees near the water, mulberries along the walls. There was nobody in sight. She could see what must be the garden door just beyond the roses. It, too, swung open and the instant she stepped inside, darkness fell over her. She was caught in what appeared to be a great black sack! Many hands grabbed at her through the cloth, pushing and pulling her, half dragging her up the stairs. She would have been more than momentarily frightened but for this: she recognized the whispers and giggling of the little married ladies all around her.

Most of them, Grace learned, were not married at all. Of the eighteen women she encountered behind the carved wooden screens in the former camel merchant's house, five were married, but only two to the camel merchant. The "harem" included eleven of his fourteen daughters, who were grown or nearly grown, his widowed sister, her daughters, and the widowed sister of one of his wives. In addition, visiting for a time from another city was the eldest daughter of the camel merchant, now married, born of his first and older wife. This married daughter—a still-lovely woman approaching the end of her youth— had written the note the water boy delivered. Grace didn't think to ask where the former camel merchant's daughter had learned to write and speak English, so pleased and excited was she by her sudden admission to this forbidden world of which Dr. Miller disapproved. That it seemed a surprisingly ordinary world—unveiled, the "married ladies" looked like ordinary women, some very young, some older, some pretty, others plain—disappointed Grace just a little. She allowed herself to be seated on a fat cushion, surrounded by girls and the younger women, most of whom wore what looked like silk pajamas. A few wore long muslin gowns. One of the youngest, a girl of ten or twelve in bright yellow silk, brought her a flavored ice on a silver tray. Everyone watched her have a taste—it was sweetened lemon—and they all sat back as one, smiling, when she lifted the spoon with approval and delicately licked her upper lip.

"It is to your liking," the English-speaking daughter of the camel merchant announced. "You are from the South United States, you and your mistress, is it not?"

"My what?"

"Your mistress. The medical lady. The Doctor Miller." She paused, considering. "The one we call Sparrow."

"Do you? That's perfect! She *is* like a sparrow," Grace said. "Your English is excellent. We're from Tennessee."

"Ten-of-sea."

"That's very close. Tennessee." She spelled it.

The other woman—Aresah, she said, was her name—traced the letters in her palm as Grace pronounced them. Aresah wore a ring on every finger and bracelets thick with stones. "Tennessee," she said. "Tennessee." She looked up briskly, her long earrings swinging. "I know a story from the Southern of United States. It is an island, this Ten of Sea?"

"No, but we have mountains. Tennessee is a mountainous state."

"The story of mine takes place on an island in the ocean beyond the desert, beyond Sinai, beyond Egypt and all the lands of Africa, far, far to the west of the setting sun."

"It's not in Tennessee, then," said Grace. "Not if it's an island, I mean. It could be an island off the coast, though. There's a whole string of them off South Carolina and Georgia—"

"That one! If you excuse me. Georgia."

"You know a story that takes place in Georgia?" Grace said. "How did—Have you been there?"

And to Grace Spivey's everlasting astonishment, the lovely Aresah leaned closer—Grace could smell sandalwood and cinnamon—and whispered, "Yes!"

She had a gift for someone who lived there, the camel merchant's daughter said, producing from a pocket in her long gown a red cap made of thick felt, as round and plain as a flat-bottomed bowl. The cap was for a young man—a tall, dark, handsome young man, she said. "He tends camels in the Circasus. Do you know a person such as this?

"No, I don't," Grace admitted.

The other woman looked disappointed. She turned the red cap around and around in her bejeweled hands. "It was to be a parting gift," she said with a sigh. "But we did not meet again in time."

Grace, who wanted very much to hear the story, said, "I've been to the coastal islands. People build fancy houses on those islands. We used to visit them when I was a child. People my mother knows. My mother knows everybody."

Aresah brushed the flat top of the red cap, smiling. Her rings caught the light. "This man—who tended camels?—he was not fancy. Not rich."

"But maybe, if you tell me more, I'll get an idea about who it might be."

Aresah raised her chin in a signal to the pair of young ladies who were sitting very close to a wooden door inlaid with ivory birds and brass foliage. From the way they leaned toward the door and then straightened to nod at Aresah, Grace suddenly realized that they were keeping watch. She would have liked to ask what they were watching for and what would happen if it appeared, but she didn't get a chance. The former camel merchant's daughter had already begun to tell her

The Camel Merchant's Tale

In the Arabian desert east of Mecca, there dwelt at one time a camel merchant who cared nothing for warriors and battles but loved only his two wives, his fourteen daughters, his widowed sister, her four sons, and, above all, his many camels, so many that the ground around his tents was known to tremble with their footsteps. His name was Abu Bakr ibn Saad. With his wives and sister and nephews and daughters, he had driven one thousand camels from the desert east of Mecca to the wells west of Basrah, where they now rested, having traveled over five hundred miles in only three days' time. How, you ask, could such a feat be accomplished? The answer dwelt in the throat of the boy Ghanim, youngest of the camel man's nephews, a boy whose singing put any camel who heard it into a trance, a headlong galloping trance that made the poor beast race heedless over the sand, no matter how heavy its burden, never stopping to rest or graze or drink. The boy Ghanim could drive camels to their deaths with his singing—indeed this had happened once—but Abu Bakr had learned through such misfortune to use his nephew's voice judiciously. Now, at Basrah, his camels would rest and graze a full week before they moved on to Baghdad, giving the camel man, his wives, his widowed sister, and his nephews and daughters a chance to catch up on news and gossip with friends and kin.

It was here by the wells west of Basrah that the camel merchant first learned of the outbreak of war between the Ottomans and the English. Son of a Badawi of the Aniza tribe, a man who carried all his wealth on the feet of his camels, Abu Bakr ibn Saad dwelt far enough from any town or village to be ignorant of the latest quarrel between the Turks and the English. As for the secret society of Al'Ahd, a group bent on winning freedom from the Turkish yoke for all Arab peoples (which peoples included himself), Abu Bakr ibn Saad was utterly innocent of its existence. How could he know—why would he even suspect?— that throughout Mesopotamia, the ranks of the Turkish army were led by Arab officers who wore Turkish uniforms but whose secret aim, as members of Al'Ahd, was to overthrow the Ottoman Turks? Thus did these Arab officers in Turkish clothing secretly rejoice when the British captured Basrah, and thus were they dismayed when the same British Mesopotamian Expeditionary Force made a headlong rush toward Baghdad that ended in disaster at Kut, some fifty miles short of their objective. Many and unrecorded were the attempts of the secret society of Al'Ahd, consorting with their secret British friends and allies, to rescue the British forces besieged at Kut.

One such attempt, doomed like the others, was set in motion by four Arab officers in Turkish uniforms who galloped up to the tent of Abu Bakr ibn Saad near the camel wells west of Basrah and offered him their congratulations. He had been chosen to honor his Arab people once again by rescuing the brave but foolish Englishmen who had outrun their supply lines at Kut and now were besieged by the Turks.

Hiding his confusion, Abu Bakr invited the four to enter his tent and refresh themselves. Chosen *once again*? he thought.

"Saving the *English*?" he said cautiously. "But are they not infidels and enemies of the sultan?" At this, all four Arab officers leaped to their feet. Having no time for explanations or persuasion, three drew their pistols and one a substantial bag of coins from inside the coat of his uniform.

"You have but two paths from which to choose, old man," one of the officers told Abu Bakr, holding up the bag of gold. "You can take this in payment for your camels and flee with your family on the ship that awaits you in the harbor. Or you can stay here and perish with all you hold dear."

What could Abu Bakr do? Either way, his camels were forfeit. These officers might indeed be Arabs, as they claimed, but they were city people, he could tell, ignorant about camels. He feared for his exhausted herd in their hands. Both he *and* they were ignorant of another and perhaps even more important circumstance, namely, that the Abu Bakr whom *they* sought—long a supplier of camels and information to the British, the one who had often borne messages from Mecca sewn into the soles of his sandals or hidden in the horn of a saddle or the hilt of a sword, the Abu Bakr whose camels were well rested and fed and ready to march to Kut—*that* Abu Bakr had been captured some days previous by Ottoman soldiers (*real* Turks in Turkish uniforms) together with all of his herds. These Arab officers, with their pistols and their bag of coins, had forced the hand of the wrong camel man. When the nephew Ghanim, he of the dangerously effective camel-driving voice, offered himself in a burst of patriotic fervor to the Arab cause, the heart of *our* Abu Bakr (a man named, like so many others, for the father-in-law of the Prophet) sank even lower.

As soon as the secret members of Al'Ahd rode off with their young compatriot into the desert, a thousand camels plodding in long lines behind them, and the boy Ghanim's mother weeping vociferously in Abu Bakr's ear, the camel merchant gathered his two wives and fourteen daughters, his weeping sister and her three less adventurous sons, and, loading what they could on the two prize camels that remained to him, he led his little entourage—all that was his in the world—into the city and through winding back streets to the shining sea. With half the bag of English gold, he bought passage for them all, as he was told to do, on a steamship whose flag he did not recognize but whose destination, learned from the ship's first officer with the help of a noisy group of Arab sailors on the docks, was an ancient and familiar one.

While a thousand camels stumbled in the desert, the ship that bore Abu Bakr and his wives and sister and nephews and daughters steamed down the dark blue waters of the Persian Gulf and entered the Arabian Sea. Soon the ship would be sailing up the Red Sea toward Suez, after which it would turn left into the Mediterranean and proceed to Gibraltar and the great ocean beyond, its hold full of bundled dates and little palm trees. When the Arab sailors said "Georgia," Abu Bakr understood them to mean the ancient home of the Mamluk pashas and birthplace of his second wife, the blue-eyed Dunyizad. Much too late would he discover that the ship that dipped and rose beneath his feet was an American one, neutral in the present war and bound for home. And he would never know (though it would have come as no surprise to learn) that the body of one Abu Bakr Ibn Saïd—the unlucky camel-driving spy for whom this passage had been carefully arranged—was already headless beneath the waters of the Shatt al-Arab, already tumbling with the current toward the blue, blue Gulf.

A chain of barrier islands protects the coast of Georgia from the scouring waves of the gray Atlantic. From the port of Savannah, the islands extend in a dotted line south to Florida. They have names like Tybee, Skidaway, Wassaw, Ossabaw, Sapelo, Blackbeard, and Jekyll. Some are no bigger than a single hummock of black needlegrass. Others were big enough in days gone by for plantations of sugarcane, indigo, cotton, and rice. Later, they were big enough for palatial homes and hunting grounds owned by captains of industry and their heirs; big enough for rice plots and vegetable gardens tended by descendants of African slaves; big enough, too, for bootleggers' hideouts and for Arab "spies"—after all, why not?—in need of refuge. After an uneventful ocean crossing and a stop in the Bahamas to load sugarcane, the American ship that rose and dipped beneath the feet of Abu Bakr ibn Saad set a course for Savannah, but before the pilot boats guided it into port, it steamed around Wassaw to Skidaway, there to unload a few pallets of cargo, two prize camels, and a huddled group in long robes and veils and desert headdress.

Stepping ashore, they were gawked at—"Lord have mercy! Look what come with the dates!"—until two great canvas-covered wagons pulled by oxen arrived to carry them away. With the wagons came a motorcar freshly spattered with mud. (Already they could see that they had come to a strange and damp place.) Unintelligible men in military uniforms emerged from the motorcar and saluted Abu Bakr ibn Saad. They urged him to enter the vehicle—and he was inclined, after all the saluting, to comply—until he saw that the white-haired gentleman who already occupied half of the backseat was in fact a hatless woman dressed, to his amazement, in something like knickers and hiking boots. Abu Bakr rode instead in the wagon with his camels, standing, as they did, his face pressed into the shoulder of first one and then the other of his two old friends. That night, in a cool damp building fragrant with hay, surrounded by his soundly sleeping family, Abu Bakr dreamt as he would dream for many nights to come, of a desert strewn with camel bones.

Often, during their first months on the island, Abu Bakr was summoned to "a dwelling as big as a palace," he told his wives, to meet with various men, some in uniforms, others not. At first these men refused to believe that he could not understand their English words. (The other Abu Bakr, unhappy fellow, had been schooled in London as well as Istanbul.) Finally—though reluctant to draw the attention of these men to his daughters and wives—Abu Bakr brought with him to one such meeting his oldest daughter, a girl of fifteen who had spent two years in service to a British lady in Qurnah and there learned to speak the language of the infidels. With her help and many long pauses, Abu Bakr could at last be questioned and his answers understood. It soon became evident to all that numerous mistakes had been made. Clearly, this Abu Bakr ibn Saad was not the camel agent with whom the British had previously done business. For his part, Abu Bakr learned just how needlessly his herd had perished. Far from being rescued, the British forces besieged at Kut had been starved and sickened (the heat, the sand flies) into surrender. Just a few months after the Arab agents seized the wrong Abu Bakr, Kut fell to the Turks, securing its dark place in British military history as the most spectacularly bungled episode of the war in Mesopotamia.

For Abu Bakr ibn Saad, it was a great relief to stop pretending that he knew who he was supposed to be and what was going on in the minds of the infidels. He was also happy to hear that when the Turks had been defeated and the Arabs installed as rightful rulers of the region, he and his large family would be returned to their home. He might have been less happy had he known it would take years for these things to come to pass.

In the meantime, while they waited (and waited), there was a great deal for people of the desert to get used to on a steamy coastal island. They were astonished, first of all, by the abundance of sweet water—streams and ponds and puddles everywhere, the rain, the moss, the marsh, the green. And the island was a noisy place, the sea itself drowned out by the roar of frogs and insects every evening. ("What is that? Abu? Abu!") They marveled at the trills and cries of the birds—woodpeckers tapping and gulls screaming during the day, owls hooting in their spooky way at night—the chattering of squirrels, the almost ceaseless whisper of leaves overhead, the faint clicking and clattering of fiddler crabs scooting in great numbers across a salt marsh or a tent floor, the shriek of the wife or daughter whose bare foot encountered them there. They lived in tents they had brought with them until the first hurricane season swept half their tents into the sea. Praise God the Merciful and All-Forgiving, no one perished, neither human nor camel. They moved then to the two-story barn and sturdy cabins their host (a rich American, they were told, who owned this island) had roofed and repaired for them. The barn was enough like the *caravanserai* they knew from Basrah—the two camels stabled downstairs and people dwelling above—that the wives of Abu Bakr ibn Saad now felt as though they had moved up in the world. When the rains came and the winds blew, they felt much safer—drier, too—sheltered by walls that were two feet thick.

From the fishermen on the island—whom the little girls called *sudani*, meaning blacks—the nephews and daughters of Abu Bakr learned how to catch bluegills and bass in the lagoons and the river, flounder and perch in the sea. The girls, who knew how to wait, became quite skillful at spying mussels in the mud and oysters in the tidal pools. (The trouble was, as they soon learned, they were expected to eat them afterward.) As months went by, the wives and daughters and sister and nephews of Abu Bakr ibn Saad learned to survive encounters with alligators (best seen from a distance, they'd learned); with a dozen different kinds of snakes, all of which they avoided, whether venomous or not; with turtles, which made them laugh, carrying their houses on their backs, "Like camels do for Badawi!" the little girls said; and with the small green lizards that sunned themselves on every wall, to which the girls gave names like "Yellow Eyes" and "Lost His Tail."

Abu Bakr continued to meet from time to time with various men— some in uniform, others not—and once with the white-haired lady (dressed more decently this time), who smiled sweetly while she spoke with Aresah. (The lady owned the island, his daughter told him after- ward). Over time, the summons to the dwelling like a palace came less and less frequently. Abu Bakr was beginning to think that he and his family and his camels might have been forgotten on the island they thought of as *Georgia-across-the-sea*, when, almost four years after their exile began, men came with word that they could soon return home, not to a wandering life in the desert but to a position of honor and salary as camel driver for the new king in Baghdad.

"If only we could get there!" his first wife Fatima was heard to moan.

For, as luck would have it, Abu Bakr's second wife, blue-eyed Duny- izad of the Caucasus, was found to be with child. Remembering her previous confinement—a pregnancy as difficult and harrowing as any siege or battle—they could not think of setting out across the ocean with her, and although his first wife Fatima wrung her hands in anxious disappointment, the truth was that not every member of Abu Bakr ibn Saad's large family was as eager as she to leave the island behind.

Most certainly his eldest daughter Aresah—*Reesha* to her friends, of whom she had exactly one—did not want to go.

The young man had simply appeared one morning, riding toward her across the salt flats on a camel—a camel!—boy and beast shimmering before her astonished eyes like a mirage. He had heard about them only recently, he said: Arabs with camels on Skidaway Island. He came to learn a thing or two.

"You don't understand a word I'm saying," he apologetically assumed.

Hastily covering her face, she did not contradict him.

She took him to her father, who sat on a bench with his back to the sun-warmed wall of the two-story barn, their *caravanserai*. When Abu Bakr ibn Saad pointed to himself and said his name, the young man repeated the name, perhaps to be sure he had heard it right, and bowed a little. He was at least a head taller than her father, somewhat darker in complexion, with curly hair and eyes that were a surprising honey-brown. (Later he would tell her that color was called "hazel.") He pointed to himself and said, "Andrew McComb. But my daddy's name is Andrew, so folks call me Andrew Mack." (She repeated silently: *An-Drew-Mack.*) Using gestures, they offered him a meal—they were Badawi, after all—and he accepted, pleased to sit down with Abu Bakr ibn Saad and his nephews. He ate the rice and trout with obvious enjoyment. After the meal, the men took him down to the pasture—a sandy expanse of cordgrass—to meet their camels. Omar, the bull, stood and blew his *dulaa* at them like a child sticking out his tongue. The nephews cheered and smirked at each other. The young man was impressed. His gelding did not engage in such displays.

When he was ready to leave, Aresah and a retinue of her veiled sisters walked with him to the sunny spot where his camel, a knobby creature of considerable age, was resting. They all watched as he attempted to convince his knobby-kneed camel to lie down so he could hoist himself up onto the folded rug that served him for a saddle. When he gave up and led the camel to the fence to climb aboard, Aresah stood on tiptoe to say, "Oosh!" in the camel's ear. The camel dropped down at once on the joints of his forelegs, like a person dropping to his knees, after which he bent his hind legs to bring his hindquarters down, and finally—step three—he lowered his forequarters the rest of the way, settling himself on the ground.

"Look at that!" said Andrew Mack. "How'd you do that?"

She said, "All camels speak Arabic."

It took him a second or two to realize that she had uttered a sentence that he understood. "You can talk!" he said. She squinted at him. "English, I mean. But—how'd you do that with the camel? What did you say?"

"Oosh," she said. The camel's ears twitched. "How do you call your camel"?

"Just by his name," said Andrew Mack.

"What *is* his name?" she asked him.

"Abraham Lincoln."

"Ibrahim," she said. "I know this name. I am Aresah."

"Reesha?" was what he heard, and like that, she had a new name to go by. Andrew Mack threw his leg over the neck of his reclining camel and settled himself on the folded rug. Then he lifted his cap and said, "Pleased to meet you, Reesha. And all the rest of you girls."

She said, "Please to meet you, Andrew-Mack!" Her sisters echoed this with varying degrees of success.

"Is there a word to make him git up?"

"Yek!" she said, and Abraham Lincoln rocked himself up to stand, tossing Andrew Mack backwards and forwards and back in the process.

The look on his face apparently called for another chorus of giggles.

A few days later, Andrew Mack McComb returned to the island on a she-camel named Susie (with Abraham Lincoln in tow for the ride home), having made it clear, he hoped, to Abu Bakr ibn Saad that the Browning Brothers Circus would be happy to pay a price to breed Susie with the Arabs' bull. It was a very delicate business to discuss, and thus, Reesha had disappeared after their exchange of greetings. He worried that he might not get to speak to her at all, but when business was concluded, Abu Bakr and the cousins vanished in their turn, and it was Reesha who reappeared to show Andrew Mack how to saddle and mount and pack and feed and groom a camel in the Badawi way.

Lessons over, they set out for a ride, he on Susie and she on Gamala, the Arabs' she-camel, with two younger sisters piled on behind her and another in front holding the tall saddle horn. She let him lead the way, giving Gamala a gentle tug on the lead rope whenever she stretched out her neck to nip the flank of his little she-camel. The younger sisters giggled every time this occurred. They rode on the beach first, taking the camels so close to the surf that they all felt spray and tasted salt on their tongues. Then Andrew Mack showed them the floating bridge he rode across the narrows to get to the island. "It's not always in the same spot, though," he warned. "Bootleggers move it."

"Boot leggers?"

"That's not a word to be repeating," he said.

For his part, he was surprised at how easily she sat on the camel, in her long dress and veil that, together, covered her head to toe. They returned by way of Big Ferry Road. After the beach, the road was as cool and shady as a tunnel, their camels' wide feet padding silently on the sandy surface. Live oaks held draperies of moss over their heads. Later, when they were at the barn, pulling sea oats from the camels' tails and checking between their toes for shells or burrs, she asked him, "Where are you when you are not here, An-drew-Mack?"

She said his name in three even parts, like three pebbles, tapping one against the other. He noticed that the little sisters had disappeared.

"I just come on over from the circus grounds. We're right near the old Wormsloe plantation. How long have y'all been here on the island?"

Reesha crouched down to get a closer look at Gamala's front feet. "What is the . . . Circasus?"

"The *circus*," he repeated. "Most of the show's on the road this time of year, but I could take you all over to see what's there—you and your sisters, I mean. Cousins, too, if they want. It's not far. Just a few miles, on the mainland."

"What of the camels?" She looked up, brushed her hands on the front of her long dress. "They, too, come from the Circasus? Is it a desert place?"

He considered her eyes, above the face veil, to see if she was teasing him. He could tell, usually, if she was biting her lip or hiding a smile. "No," he said, "it's not a desert. How long've you been out here anyhow?"

Instead of answering, she turned from Gamala to hobble Susie's front legs. "Reesha," he said, but she didn't look his way. He had been warned by old Mr. Browning at the circus not to ask the Arabs what they were

doing here. To change the subject, he went to his saddlebag, which was
hanging over the fence, and drew out a wooden box about the size of a
family Bible. "I've got something to show you," he said.

Leaving the camels loosely hobbled and nibbling on cordgrass near
the barn, they walked past sweet gum and palmettos to the ruins of the
old plantation kitchen, and after poking in the grass to make sure there
were no snakes, he brushed a few loose shells off the top of the tabby
wall and they sat down, side by side, with a clear space between them,
the box resting on Andrew Mack's knees. It was made of heart pine,
smoothed and darkened to gold by handling. Boxy letters spelling MAL-
COLM MCCOMB were neatly carved into the lid. "That's my granddaddy's
name," he said, running his fingers over the letters. He opened the box
and lifted out a tattered cloth purse so old and worn you couldn't say
what color it once was. Its long braided handle was knotted together
in a dozen places. Inside the purse was a large leather wallet, the size of
a book, which he drew out. He pulled on a ribbon that held the flap
shut and a flattened roll of yellowing paper welled up inside the wallet,
several pages it appeared to be, soft as cloth. "There's ten of these papers
in here," he said, sliding them out and offering them to her. Reesha,
who had a sprinkling of sweat drops that sparkled across the bridge of
her nose, opened her hands, palms up, and accepted them. Carefully, she
unrolled the pages. Discovering that she had to turn them sideways, she
did so. She peered at the page on top.

"It is Arabic!" she said.

"That's what you all speak, ain't it?"

"Where do you get this?" she asked. A very distinct little V had
appeared between her eyebrows.

"It belonged to my great-great-grandmother. She got it from her
daddy. He's the one knew your language. It was on account of his religion.
They had to read their holy book. My granddaddy Malcolm told me."

Andrew Mack watched Reesha as she carefully lifted the first page
to see the next one, her eyes still frowning. "This is not Qur'an." She
glanced at him. "Not Holy Book."

He craned his neck toward the page she had on top, the one with
the stain over most of the drawing. A long tear up the bottom of the

page had been fixed with little strips of paper pasted between the lines, like stitches. "Can you read it?"

She sighed and shook her head. "Badawi girls do not learn this. I can read some of English now, thanks being to lessons. No Arabic. My father, he knows, but only to read Qur'an." She lifted the page and studied the next drawing. "In Qur'an, there is no picture."

"I believe the writing is directions for making the things in the pictures."

"Yes! I think is right. See this?" she said, giving him permission to lean closer, which he did. "It is a thing for . . . these." She pretended to pour.

"A pitcher?" He tilted his head. "What's all that inside it, I wonder?"

"Tricks!" she said, pleased with herself for having found that word so handily. She gently flipped the pages to other drawings—a pot, an urn, a fountain filled with pipes and chambers, valves and holes. "Arabs like clever things," she said, "tricks to fool the eyes. Wait! Wait. I have heard of such a book. My father knows some story about these book, it may be. A book of clever things."

That's when they heard the faint sound of Fatima, her mother, calling her name.

"I ask him," Reesha said. She folded the pages gently and gave them back to Andrew. "Next time you tell me about . . . who? Who the book belongs to?"

"My great-great-grandmother. Her name was Margaret." He picked up the purse by its many-knotted handle. "My granddaddy says she wore this around her neck with the pages inside day and night, underneath her clothes so no one could see." He slipped the handle over his head to show her.

Reesha stood up and discreetly brushed bits of sand and shell from the back of her long dress. Her mother called again, more urgently. "I must go," Reesha said. She turned to go back to the barn.

Andrew Mack added, "And she also wore a veil, Margaret did."

She stopped and looked over her shoulder at him. "She wore a veil? Like this?" She put her hand to her face, touching her chin through the cloth. He could tell it was her chin. He could see the outline of her nose and cheeks. He hadn't told a soul that he had seen her face that time on the salt marsh, when they first met. She hadn't said a word to him about it, either.

"I reckon so," he said. "My granddaddy says she wore it all the time, too."

Another cry came from the upper story of the barn.

"Next time you will tell me about Margaret," Reesha said. She turned and ran toward the cool darkness of the tabby barn.

"She met General Sherman!" Andrew Mack called after her.

From inside the barn, she called, "Next time!"

They were all waiting for him the next time, sitting on the low tabby wall: the fourteen daughters of Abu Bakr ibn Saad, his mournful sister, and both of his wives. Dressed in their *abayas* and veils, they looked to him like a school of brown ghosts in graduated sizes, only the little ones with their faces bare. Reesha jumped up and motioned him closer until he and she stood perhaps a camel-length apart. She spoke to the group in Arabic, then turned to Andrew Mack.

"I say we will hear of Margaret who wears a veil. What you tell in English, I tell again!"

There was so much eagerness in her eyes and voice that he said, "I reckon that might could work." He glanced at Dunyizad, who was huge and bell-like in her long veil. She looked like a woman with no time to waste. "But it's likely to take a while."

"Noon prayers are past," Reesha said. "We have many hours."

Everyone looked expectantly at Andrew Mack.

"Well," he said, "the story I know about Margaret—that's my great-great-grandmomma . . ." He took a deep breath, during which Reesha rattled at top speed and then looked at him again. "It starts when General Sherman was marching through Georgia." He paused while Reesha said whatever she said. "That was during the War"—he considered what to call it—"between the States."

Reesha looked at him and frowned. "War between states? What is *states*?"

He lifted his cap and set it back down again. "The *United* States," he said. "North"—he pointed in the direction he thought was north, and they all turned their heads or twisted around to look—"and South." He pointed at the ground beneath their feet. They all looked down. Reesha uttered some words that sounded like rain pattering hard on a roof.

Andrew Mack continued. "Now, the War between the States," he said, "that's when the North said to the South, you can't have slavery no more. So the South said, we'll just have us our own country, then. But the North said you can't do that neither. So the South said, we'll just see about that, and they had them a war, which the South"—he pointed at the ground again—"lost."

"Your people lost, An-drew-Mack?" Reesha said, surprised.

"No," he said. "My people used to be the slaves, so they won."

Reesha looked at her mother and said something that her mother repeated, turning it into a question. To Andrew Mack, it sounded like, "Momlook?"

Reesha turned back to him. "You?" she said. "You were slave?"

"No!" he said, and found his ears were burning. "And not my daddy, either."

Reesha's mother spoke again. Andrew Mack could tell that she had asked another question. He heard, "Sue Donny." She said it again, looking at him: "Sue Donny?"

"What is she saying?" he asked Reesha.

"She asks if you are black."

Andrew Mack looked at Reesha and then at the rest of them. From what he could see, he would have said they were brown, if he'd had to pick a color. It had not occurred to him that they might be white people. It looked as though it had not occurred to them that he was black, either. He turned to Reesha and said, "In these parts folks say 'colored' or 'Negro,' but 'black' is the same. You can tell her I am Sue-donny."

She rattled some words at her mother and at the same time pushed up her sleeve and tapped the brownest part of her forearm. Her mother raised an eyebrow and folded her arms across her chest. Reesha looked at Andrew Mack.

He cleared his throat. "All right," he said. "My granddaddy Malcolm and his grandmother, they belonged to a plantation on another island south of here—this was during slavery times—but early on in the war they all got carried over in boats and marched inland. They were up in Milledgeville when General Sherman's army came through, so like a lot of folks, they just followed him right out of town. They were hoping to get back down to the coast. They'd left a lot of old folks behind, including some of Margaret's sisters and all, on the island." He let Reesha work that out somehow. Then he added, "My granddaddy Malcolm was nine years old when he and Margaret marched along through Georgia to the sea. He's the one told me the story of how she always wore a veil, and how her daddy, who knew y'all's language, gave her those pages from a book he had, and how she passed them on to my granddaddy Malcolm before she died, which was not long after she talked General Sherman into giving her all those circus animals—the elephant and lions and camels and all—so the Yankee soldiers wouldn't—"

"An-drew-Mack!" Reesha cried. "What is it you speak of? What animals are these?"

"Well, that's the story I'm fixing to tell you. About where my camels came from."

"Not about Margaret who wears a veil?"

"She's the one gets the camels."

Reesha sighed. She knew that everyone was waiting to hear the title of the tale she had promised them. There was a proper order to all things, and in the telling of tales, the title came first. Knowing what she already knew, Reesha had been weaving together in her head—and looking for an opportunity to interject—a title that went something like

The Tale of the Veiled Lady, with Reference to a Book Written in the
Language of the Prophet from Which She Carried Pages
in a Bag Around Her Neck

Now, however, she threw her hands in the air and announced that Andrew-Mack McComb would beguile the long hours of the summer afternoon by telling them

The Tale of Where His Camels Came From

It was late in the year 1864. Even without the lengthy train of tattered but jubilant people walking and riding across Georgia in the wake of the army that set them free, the Federal troops led by William T. Sherman and his fellow generals made a procession so long that it took close to a full gray December day for them to pass by. The front of the line was two days' march from Savannah when word came down the road about a rice plantation up ahead with a collection of unusual animals—the sort that most of the Yankee soldiers had only heard about but never seen. The talk was of lions and monkeys and elephants—really, there was only one elephant—and also of camels.

"Camels?" said Margaret when her grandson came to tell her what he'd heard. She was rolling along in a wooden cart not much bigger than a wheelbarrow, towed by the mule-drawn wagon in front of her. One of the Yankee soldiers had arranged the cart for Margaret, in deference to her age and solemn attire. Lately, she wasn't feeling like herself. Her old bones couldn't get warm, and she knew why. Until the commencement of the current hostilities, Margaret had consumed two cups of Life Everlasting tea every day of her adult life. Her sorry state right now, on one cup every other day, was proof, if anyone needed it, of the herb's sustaining power. She was down to a single branch of dried leaves in her once-full sack, and although she sent Malcolm on foraging expeditions and kept a sharp eye on the roadside herself, no bushy plants with just the right silvery leaves could be found. Unless this army parade could carry her home in a week or less, she was sure to run out before she got there.

Her grandson Malcolm held on to the top rail of the cart's perimeter, his bare toes clinging to the smallest of ledges over a wheel. It was some kind of shame, Margaret thought, how dirty his shirt was, how little was left of his pants. She was going to wash him for a week when they got back home.

"Lions, too!" he said. "You seen lions once."

Had Margaret ever seen a lion? She must have told him a story borrowed from another lifetime, maybe from her mother's. She said, "Camels saved my father's life. They carried him across the sands to Baghdad. Malcolm, watch your foot by that wheel."

The boy leaped sideways and waved to her from the grass along the road.

Having seen what the Yankees did to livestock, she half hoped that the rumored lions and camels were rumors only. Not that she blamed the hungry soldiers for helping themselves to as much beef and pork on the hoof as they could eat—and she could see why they didn't want the enemy to avail themselves of animals left behind. It was the same reason some of the white farmers and planters shot their own livestock before the Yankees got there. That was the very worst, in Margaret's opinion: coming up on a farm where all the livestock were already dead for days and stinking like a pestilence. It smelled so bad, even in December, it made the babies cry.

William T. Browning, the rice planter who was until very recently the owner of the much-discussed menagerie up ahead, used to claim that he had captured the creatures on safari in Africa and other exotic locales. The forty-six human beings of whom he had also been until very recently the owner knew better. William T. Browning's animals had been purchased from a circus in England more than a decade before. Browning had fetched the animals across the Atlantic himself, feeling like Noah on the Ark, much to the dismay of Mrs. Browning, who expected the ship to be filled only with fine furnishings and fabrics worthy of their new home. She never fully forgave him for two hundred yards of silk on bolts that somehow ended up among the bales of straw lining the elephant's stall.

The Brownings had already fled, leaving behind the menagerie along with their more conventional livestock and their human property—the forty-six soon-to-be ex-slaves. Mr. Browning had been urged by a neighbor to sacrifice the livestock, but he refused to do it, thanks to the persuasive powers of his animal overseer, a slender black man named Benjamin. Benjamin was remarkable not only for his skills in persuasion and animal husbandry, but for the pointed beard he kept groomed to perfection with nothing but a razor-sharp cane knife, and for his immaculately white turban. (Rafters in the barn were always festooned with lengths of white cloth hung up to dry. There were other men in the coastal areas who wrapped their heads thus, but no one wore a turban so snowy white.) Under Benjamin's supervision, the people who were slaves on William T. Browning's plantation had been taking excellent care of his menagerie, as well as his conventional livestock, for many years. When General Sherman arrived at the plantation one warm day in December 1864, his troops were welcomed with a sort of circus parade, the elephant and camels and their riders decked out with rags and streamers, each of the monkeys leashed and chattering on somebody's shoulder, the two lions and one tiger pacing sluggishly in separate wheeled cages pulled along by teams of ponies.

But Margaret was right to worry. Upon seeing that collection of unusual creatures, the first thing the Yankee soldiers did was ask their superiors for permission to let the animals loose in the fields and hunt them down for sport. Their superiors wisely withheld this permission, and yet one of the lions had already been shot by a Yankee soldier pretending to be a lion tamer such as he'd seen one time at a circus in Chicago. Using a long stick and then a whip handle, he kept poking at the old beast, who was either too tired or too bored to roar, until the soldier, on a dare, got right up close and stuck his face in the sleepy lion's face in a way that must have made the lion think that this was the part of the show where he was meant to open up wide so the human could put its head into the lion's deadly jaws. The lion opened wide and scared the soldier so badly that he soiled his drawers and raised his pistol and closed his eyes and stuck his arm out straight and shot that lion right in the mouth, causing the poor beast to clamp his jaws shut in surprise.

You can bet that Yankee soldier told a different story, when he got home, about how he lost his arm in the war.

Malcolm came and told Margaret about it, his eyes brimming.

"Oh, baby," she said, and he let himself be drawn into the folds of her dress, a long loose dress of the same undyed homespun as her veil. She held him close and asked, "Is he shot dead?"

Malcolm tilted his head back and looked up at his grandmother, suddenly hopeful. It hadn't occurred to him that the lion might be shot but not dead.

"You fetch me a cup of hot water," she said, handing him her tin mug, "and we'll go have a look."

By the time Malcolm returned from the cook's wagon, walking as fast as he could with his eye on the cup, Margaret had replaced her brown homespun veil with a pale blue one that fell past her shoulders and was fixed so she could pull it across her face and keep it there. Margaret wore the blue veil as a sign of who she was, the daughter of Bilali Mahomet, faithful like her father to the Prophet, in her heart slave to no one but God. Malcolm saw it as a sign that she had hopes for the fallen lion. He held the steaming metal cup and watched her pluck leaves of Life Everlasting from a dried branch and crumble them into the water, which immediately released a pungent and familiar smell. Malcolm breathed it in, and so did his grandmother, their two heads—one round and brown, the other draped in blue—bent over the rising wisps. She stirred it with their knife, took the cup from him, and loudly sipped three times before she gave it back. He took his sip without complaining, although he didn't like the mossy taste, only the comforting smell. The metal cup was perhaps a quarter full and his nose was still crinkled when, to his surprise, Margaret crumbled the last leaves from her branch into the cup. Tamping the mixture into a paste, she said, "Thought we'd see if our lion friend needs a little Life Everlasting."

She pulled the veil across her cheekbones and took Malcolm's hand. They passed wagons and horses and staring faces of every shade until they reached the fallen lion's cage. There, the crowd parted. Voices fell silent. Not one of them—not even Benjamin the overseer in his snowy white turban—had ever seen anyone quite like this solemn woman, so straight and tall that no one would ever guess her age at well past eighty, her dark brown face half hidden by the pale blue veil.

Margaret and Malcolm stopped at the end of the wagon-cage, where four wooden steps led up to a door made of iron bars. Tall, black Benjamin came forward with a big iron key. He bowed and said, "*Allahu akbar.*"

Margaret's hand went to her heart—or so it appeared. Malcolm knew what she was really reaching for. Under her dress, inside a homespun bag that she wore on a cord around her neck, were the pages her father had given to her before he died, pages from an ancient book written in the language of the Prophet. "*Allahu akbar,*" Margaret agreed, and she added, significantly, that God was also merciful. Then she lifted her skirts ankle-high and her bare feet climbed the steps into the cage.

Most of the dried blood was near the door, where the Yankee soldier had stood with his foolish face growing paler and paler. The crowd that watched Margaret step neatly around the bloodstains on the floor had witnessed the incident. They had all heard the shot. They had seen the lion fall. They held their breath as Margaret laid her hand on the lion's head, and buried her fingers in his mane, and leaned to put her veiled face next to his ear. Only those closest to the iron bars heard her say softly, "Old lion, my mother knew your mother. How long have I waited to meet you?" When she told them, as she crouched beside the beast, that the lion was not dead, they did not believe her. They watched her scoop the paste from the tin cup and apply it to the lion's cheek, in a fleshy pad of muscle just below the temple, a spot almost hidden by his mane. She straightened up slowly, and even as she told them that the lion would soon awaken, though he would not be in the best of moods, the crowd began to murmur.

Everyone had seen the right ear twitch. (Well, some saw the left.)

Margaret exited the wagon-cage with dignity but no dawdling.

Word came around later that General Sherman wished to meet the lady with the veil.

Margaret and her grandson were welcomed by the general's orderly to the daintily decorated parlor of William T. Browning's home and offered refreshment in the form of chicory tea (they each took a polite sip) and cookies (cookies!), which the orderly had discovered in a tin in the pantry and tested on a dog, a monkey, and himself before passing the rest of them on to the general. In turn, Margaret presented for General Sherman's inspection the tin cup containing the leftover paste of Life Everlasting she had prepared for the lion. He sniffed it and said jovially, "So this is the potion that brought the beast back from the dead?"

"The lion weren't dead, sir."

The general lifted the tin cup. "And if I partake, will *I* have Life Everlasting?"

"Not in this world."

"In the next?" the general persisted.

"Might could be. Add water first."

That made him laugh. Then he leaned, just slightly, toward her. "I am told that you and Benjamin spoke to each other in a foreign tongue."

They had exchanged only greetings and prayers—such was the extent of Margaret's knowledge of Arabic—but it pleased her to say, "We speak the language of the Prophet."

"Which prophet would that be? Of which religion, which god?"

"There is only one God," she said. "Mohammed is His Prophet."

"You are Mohammedans!" the general said with more satisfaction than surprise. "I've heard there are those among you, here along the coast and on the islands, who profess that faith. Benjamin—the overseer here—has a holy book. Did you know? I came upon him praying at midday and he showed it to me. He wrote it down from memory!" the general said. "In an empty ledger book. Can you imagine that? He's kept it hidden all these years. He said Browning's wife would have burned it."

Margaret's hand went to her own treasure on the cord around her neck.

"But Cook tells me that you have come with us from Milledgeville—are there Mohammedans there as well?"

"We come from the island called Sapelo." She glanced at Malcolm. "My father was Bilali Mahomet."

"Bilali Mahomet," the general repeated. "It sounds like the name of a prince."

That made Margaret smile.

General William T. Sherman ended his brief interview with the daughter of Bilali Mahomet by conferring upon her august person (those were his words in the order that made it so) the entire menagerie formerly owned by one William T. Browning. Margaret sought the help of the general's adjutant, a young man graduated from West Point and also apprenticed in the law, to draw up an official transfer of property that recorded her sale of said menagerie—including the wounded lion, who appeared to be healing nicely—to Benjamin "Browning." The price of purchase was one brief *sura* that Benjamin copied out onto an empty page removed from the back of his ledger book. Everyone watched the quill pen move slowly across the paper from right to left, leaving a trail of lovely Arabic letters that spelled out the words Margaret had requested: *I seek refuge in the Lord of Daniel, Master of the lion's den.*

A few days after Margaret healed the lion, General Sherman's army set out on the final leg of his already famous march to the sea. (Down the road, the white citizens of Savannah awaited him with bated breath and spiked punch.) Margaret's cart was drawn by a pair of beribboned Shetland ponies now and followed by a camel on which Malcolm sat grinning triumphantly, a snow-white turban just like Benjamin's on his head.

"They're coming with us, Gran," Malcolm had announced earlier, "lions and all!"

Margaret was pleased but not surprised. Neither Benjamin Browning nor General Sherman was likely to leave the animals where returning enemy soldiers and hungry country folk could find them.

By the second day of the final leg of the ever-more-populous march
to the sea, Margaret wasn't feeling well at all. The helpful adjutant found
a space for her in a covered wagon, and, while she dozed fitfully in a
makeshift bed, Malcolm held her hand, startled by its coolness. Earlier,
she had felt hot to his touch. "Gran?" he said softly. "Are you cold?"

She turned her head on the straw pillow. "Malcolm, I need your
help," she said, and tugged at the colorful braid of cloth around her
neck.

"What you doing, Gran?" he asked in alarm.

"I am removing this that I wear."

"Why?"

"I do not wish to wear it any longer."

"Why not?" Malcolm cried.

"It makes me itch right here." She touched a spot where the braid
went around her neck.

"Oh," he said. "Here, lift your head, just right like that. There."

When he had slipped the bag off her neck, he asked her where he
should put it.

"Why, around your own neck, Malcolm."

"I got to wear it now?"

"For the time being, you do."

"What if it makes *me* itch?"

"It will." Relieved of her burden, Margaret closed her eyes, and
within seconds she was lightly snoring.

Malcolm did not slip the cord over his neck, not yet. Instead, he
scooted closer to the end of the wagon, where an opening in the canvas
cover admitted a patch of sunlight. He gently pulled the bag open along
its drawstring and, turning it upside down, he let the leather wallet inside
the bag slide out into his lap. Malcolm knew that his great-grandfather
Bilali Mahomet—he whose name had sounded to the general like the
name of a prince—had made one such wallet for each of his daughters.
Each wallet contained a different set of soft linen pages like the ones that
Malcolm laid out flat over his sunlit knees, pages full of funny drawings
of pitchers and lamps and strange creatures with water spouting from
their mouths. Malcolm also knew, having many times heard the story,

that his great-grandfather, Bilali Mahomet, had copied these pages from an ancient book and then risked everything to carry them across deserts and oceans from his old life as a free Mohammedan, a life cut short in his youth.

Even as a slave—first in the Bahamas and later on the island off the coast of Georgia—Malcolm's great-grandfather had been a figure of legend. What other slave overseer had ever been given arms to defend his master's land, as Bilali was when English warships threatened the coast in 1812? And what other island plantation weathered the great hurricane of 1824 without the loss of a single life, Bilali having gathered people and cattle safely within the thick tabby walls? His cleverness was legendary, too. People came to Sapelo from near and far to see the fountains whose water jets changed shape—from "lance" to "shield" to "lily"—by means of ingenious mechanisms Bilali had installed, and to learn the methods he perfected for growing bumper crops of Sea Island cotton and sugarcane. An exacting taskmaster, aloof from and not alto-gether popular with his fellows, Bilali Mahomet practiced his religion and wrote in Arabic script and died a very old man in 1859, when his great-grandson Malcolm was four years old.

Now, at nine, Malcolm was already long of limb, like Bilali, and his face was delicate and narrow, as dark and sweet as chocolate (which he had tasted once). He was said to resemble his mother, Esme, who waited for him in Paradise. His grandmother told him long ago that a woman who died giving birth was like a soldier who gave his life in a holy war. Margaret did not add, though she believed it to be true, that her daughter's gift was the greater, as she had brought a new believer *into* the world.

Malcolm couldn't picture his mother, no matter how hard he tried, but if he closed his eyes, he seemed to remember the long cloth coat that his great-grandfather famously wore, and a round felt hat on the old man's head. In Malcolm's only memory of Bilali, the old man was talking with someone who looked like a pale wisp of smoke, in a place that smelled of wood shavings and bristled with pipes. That was Rev-erend Goulding's carriage house in Darien, Margaret told Malcolm. She was surprised that he remembered it. "They were always building something," she said. "He was thick as molasses with that old preacher." Malcolm was right there, in his grandmother's arms, when Bilali gave the preacher "that little book of his. I didn't want him to do it," Margaret said. It was a thin, hand-sewn notebook in which advice for growing long staple cotton shared the pages with lines that Bilali recalled from his student days so long ago, all of it written in ink concocted from the juice of pokeweed berries. The minister had accepted the little book graciously, although Margaret suspected that he believed the Arabic letters weren't letters at all, but only an imitation of words. Later, she asked her father why he had given his notebook to a man prevented by ignorance from reading a single word. Margaret had to smile when she told Malcolm her father's answer: "I give it, my daughter, to show pig-eating Nazarenes that we are a people of learning."

About the other book, the one Bilali had copied in his youth, the one whose remaining pages fluttered now on Malcolm's knees in the back of a covered wagon belonging to the victorious Federal army of the United States of America, of that one, Bilali had said to his daughter: "*This* book of ancient learning is ours alone."

After a while, the weight of family history made Malcolm's eyelids heavy. He had just leaned back, almost dozing, against the foot of his grandmother's makeshift bed, when the opening in the back of the canvas-covered wagon was suddenly filled by the head and long neck of a camel! Malcolm barely had time to sit up straight in surprise before the camel withdrew its head so abruptly that one of the pages on Malcolm's lap fluttered up and flew right out the wagon after it. Less than a moment later, there in the opening formerly filled by the camel, was Benjamin Browning, his turban as snowy as ever and a look of dismay on his face, the wayward page pinched delicately between his thumbs and forefingers. A wet stain made at least a third of the paper translucent, so the outlines of a drawing—a pitcher or teapot, it appeared to be—showed through the back. Malcolm scrambled to fold the pages still in his lap and then reached for the one that hung in the air from Benjamin's fingers like a shirt on a clothesline, but instead of relinquishing it, Benjamin studied the drawing, frowning at it, until a snort and a cough brought him and Malcolm both up short.

"Who is it?" Margaret wheezed. "Who's there?"

"It's Benjamin, Gran."

"How do, Miz Margaret? How're you feeling?"

"Fine," Margaret said. She struggled to sit up, then decided against it. "No worse," she amended. "What is that there?"

Benjamin handed the page to Malcolm as he answered. "Unless my eyes deceive me, it looks like a page from the *Kitab al-Hiyal!*"

"Ah," said Margaret. "I reckon my grandbaby's showed you his birthright."

Benjamin asked, "Wherever did you get it?"

"Well, now," Margaret said, "I believe Malcolm could tell us that story."

Malcolm was immediately seized by shyness. It was one thing to tell a story to his grandmother, pausing at the parts that were tricky to remember, waiting for her to fill in forgotten details. It was quite another to have her listening while he told the story to someone else. And what did she mean by *his birthright*? Her bright eyes were on him, though, and so he said, reluctantly, "I reckon I could tell it."

"You *reckon*?"

"Yes, ma'am, I surely could."

"That's better. Help me with this pillow first," she said, "and then begin." He fluffed up her flour-sack pillow for as long as he could. Then he closed his eyes to think.

Margaret and Benjamin waited.

Malcolm gave up. "What was the year?"

"In the 1,187th year of Hijra," Margaret said.

"In the 1,187th year of the Hedge Rah—that's about the same as 1775, give or take—the father of Bilali Mahomet made up his mind to visit the holy places before the world came to an end." Malcolm leaned closer to Benjamin and added softly, "They thought that was about to happen back then, but it didn't."

"Not yet it hasn't," Margaret said without opening her eyes.

"God alone knows the time," said Benjamin.

Malcolm sat up straight and proceeded to tell, as best he could, the following

Tale of Bilali and the Book of Ingenious Devices, Which Is Also a Tale of Escapes and Near-Escapes

You hear of kings and sultans who undertake the *hajj*, as the Prophet has instructed, setting out for Mecca from the ends of the earth, with their scribes and viziers, their slaves and their followers, with camels numbering a hundred or more, all bearing goods and gold through the desert. The father of Bilali had no slaves, no followers, and certainly no camels, not even one, and yet he, too, resolved to make his pilgrimage. Although he was named Ahmad Baba—in honor of the famous scholar who owned a thousand books—the father of Bilali owned only one book, the Qur'an he himself had copied line by line, *sura* by *sura*, in his student days in Timbo. Those were the days when, as a youth, Ahmad Baba disappointed his own father, a modestly prosperous merchant who'd hoped to see his fortunes increased by a son with a head for business. Those days were long ago. Ahmad Baba had no talent for the art of buying and selling. His magic was in his hands, his instincts in his fingers (particularly when they held tin snips or a metalworking hammer); his mind was in thrall to the making of things. To look at Ahmad Baba now—a middle-aged man coaxing a sheet of copper into the shape of a pitcher or bowl, or sharpening the iron curve of a scythe, or even using the scythe to harvest a grassy field—you would never guess from his dirty tunic and sweat-stained turban that his mind was in perpetual ferment. Every stone and stick and water jar spoke to Ahmad Baba of things he had never seen, things for which he had no name: things like concentric siphons and conical valves, crankshafts and feedback controllers, floats and fail-safe systems, even self-trimming oil lamps.

Ahmad Baba's firstborn son Bilali—named by his mother for the Prophet's first *muezzin*—was cut, it seemed, of the same cloth as his father. But with this difference: Where Ahmad Baba *sensed* potential in stick and stone and jar, it was his son Bilali who could see the way to bring potentiality into actuality. Already, by the age of twelve, the boy had contrived—and his father had subsequently fashioned—a metal aqueduct that began at a bubbling spring in a nearby jungle canyon and ended just outside their little house in a tank that filled itself as it was emptied, never overflowing nor wasting a single drop. The boy had saved his mother many hours of grinding labor with mortar and pestle by inventing a simple device—a crank to turn and a funnel made of brass—to husk the tiny grains of fonio from which the people of the region made their couscous, porridge, and beer. The boy was ingenious, the father skilled with his hands. Together, they could make themselves invaluable to pilgrims and merchants, even to caliphs and kings. At the very least, Ahmad Baba thought, he and his son could earn their way to Mecca, God willing, before the world came to an end, and possibly back again, if there was time.

In so doing, they might become famous like the Banu Musa, three brothers who lived in Baghdad in the Golden Age of Learning. This, too, Bilali's father Ahmad Baba dared to dream. He had seen a copy of the *Kitab al-Hiyal*—the brothers' famous *Book of Ingenious Devices*—during his student days in Timbo, when a visitor from Baghdad came to work with scholars on deciphering the ancient script. He had never seen a picture in a book before. These were line drawings of *things* like containers and lamps—fountains, too, with animal heads called "idols" by the scholars who studied the text. The pictures themselves suggested secret, ingenious, and perhaps forbidden powers hidden inside each device: sinuous tubes, curved handles, pitchers and pots with round bellies and narrow necks and all manner of chambers and passages inside. The objects floated on the lines of script around them like vessels riding waves in the sea. When the visitor who brought the book from Baghdad spoke of the House of Wisdom, where the Banu Musa had worked and studied, Ahmad Baba didn't know if it was a place that still existed or one that had closed its doors in ages past. He knew only that he wished to go there, to stand where the sons of Musa had stood and hold in his hands the *Kitab al-Hiyal*. How often he had done this in his dreams!

This, his heart's desire, grew stronger as he watched his son Bilali grow, watched him put to use the powers of liquid and balance and timing and air, which Ahmad Baba could sense all around them. When the boy's grandfather, still the prosperous merchant, offered to finance a trial year of study for Bilali—pinning fresh hopes on his grandson— Ahmad Baba had thanked the old man without restraint. If Bilali just once laid eyes on the *Book of Ingenious Devices*—well, Ahmad Baba was uncertain exactly what would happen, but he was almost sure that God willed greatness for his son, and that the key to that greatness could be found in the *Kitab al-Hiyal*. Not even the wife of Ahmad Baba suspected that when the time came for him to add *al-Hajj* to his name by making pilgrimage to the holy places, he would carry with him his dream of setting foot in the House of Wisdom with his talented son. That Baghdad lay perhaps another thousand miles beyond the holy places seemed a problem Ahmad Baba and his boy could solve when the time came. There was little they could not do, if they put their minds and hands to it, together.

Two years, he thought, should suffice for the journey, both *hajj* and House of Wisdom included. Three at the most. God willing.

Bilali, now a serious fellow of fourteen years, greeted the news of a pilgrimage with guarded enthusiasm. His father had come to Timbo in an oxcart (to be exchanged later for a pair of camels) that was obviously loaded for a long journey. Bilali suspected that neither his mother nor his grandfather approved of Ahmad Baba's plan—if they knew of it at all. To show his father that he was neither a cowering child nor entirely ignorant of the world, he asked bravely, "Will we go to Shinqiti and join the caravan to Cairo?"

"Yes and no," said Ahmad Baba.

"Yes *and* no?"

"We will go to Shinqiti," his father said.

Bilali waited.

"But we will not go to Cairo with the caravan. Only to Rabat. From there"—his father paused dramatically—"we will go by sea."

"In a *boat*?" Bilali said.

His father laughed. "Unless you've learned to swim."

From Timbo to Shinqiti, as the grassland gave way to rocky sahel and finally to the desert, they made themselves invaluable, according to plan. Ahmad Baba repaired countless pots, knives, chain links, pitchers, and stakes with his metalworking hammers and the portable forge that his son had contrived for him. Bilali designed and his father constructed a trough like the one at home whose water supply—from any nearby stream or camel well—was cut off and reopened automatically when animals drank from it. Working together, father and son made fasteners and containers, they repaired and modified, they suggested and improved and improvised. Their little tent was frequented by merchants and pilgrims from one end of the caravan to the other, most of whom offered them a coin or two in return for their trouble. Others merely reminded them of the holy *baraka* they were certainly piling up in heaven by their service to God's faithful pilgrims.

"You would think they might be more concerned with piling up blessings for themselves," Ahmad Baba grumbled.

When they reached Shinqiti, perhaps twenty days into their journey, the caravan tripled in size, adding pilgrims and merchants in about equal numbers. Now many dozens of camels carried great baskets of rice, and others giant scabbards stuffed with tusks of ivory, or leather bags of various sizes that might have anything from gold to cola nuts inside. One whole group of camels appeared to suffer from a malady that caused thickening and irregularity of their hides, until you looked closer and saw that they were heaped with goat- and sheepskins. At least a hundred camels carried pilgrims or merchants of substance, both men and women (not on the same camel, of course), who looked out from under veiled canopies at bobbing heads and churning sand below.

At the end of the caravan, accounting for perhaps a quarter of its length, was the human cargo. Some walked without encumbrances. Others were chained. All were dark-skinned like Bilali and his father. The men covered their heads and upper bodies as best they could with lengths of cloth and tattered robes or tunics. The women were veiled, like Muslim women, from head to toe. Once, when Bilali was hurrying (as he had been told to hurry) past the contingent of slaves, he heard two women talking, speaking Pulaar, the language of his people. One of them was weeping, he could hear, and it was all he could do to keep from running up to them, although his father had forbidden him most strictly to speak or mingle with the unfortunate ones. The women Bilali overheard could not be anyone they knew, his father said. "Muslim women are not taken for these purposes."

"But they wear the veil."

That was to protect the trader's investment, his father said grimly, but Bilali's heart was not eased, not even when the dealer in ancient books—another newcomer at Shinqiti—said the slaves had come from Niger, which was no place near their village, and that, besides, Muslim women were not taken for these purposes.

"Why does the book trader know where the slaves are from?" Bilali asked his father later.

"He is a merchant among merchants. They talk. You see how he knows everyone already. Why do you ask such a question, Bilali?"

The boy hestitated. "Do you think he trades only in books?"

His father smiled. "I have heard no cries for help from inside the boxes his camels carry."

Bilali wanted to like the book dealer. Sidi Masrur's well-creased skin was medium brown, his beard was thin, his body so slight that his long robes seemed to be animated by the air. The sleeves all but covered his fingers. With him came six camels, each one carrying four great boxes, two balanced one atop the other on each side of the hump. If you walked close to one of the boxes and sniffed, Bilali discovered, you could smell old parchment, paper, leather covers, and dust. Whenever Sidi Masrur opened one of the boxes, the scent of ancient learning rose from it like steam from a cooking pot. Bilali would have liked to trust the man who dealt in such tantalizing merchandise.

"We *are* in his debt," Bilali's father reminded his son.

Ahmad Baba referred to the incident of the saddle, wherein they had learned that not everyone welcomed young Bilali's ideas for improving the world. Somewhere between Shinqiti and Fez, perhaps eight or ten days into that leg of the journey, the Tuareg saddle used by all the camel drivers seized the boy's attention. A wooden frame gave the saddle a tentlike shape to protect the camel's hump from the crushing effects of rider and cargo. The design was more than a thousand years old.

Bilali considered the height and curvature of the saddle's wooden frame, the triangle it formed when regarded from either end. With his eye, he measured the angle of the inverted V at the top of the triangle. He watched as camels were loaded, observed how the "tent" did or didn't flatten out a bit, how the wooden legs of the frame pressed into a thick cushion placed underneath the saddle, padding the camel's shoulders and hips. He made drawings with a stick in the dirt. When, in halting Arabic, he proposed to one Moroccan camel driver a small adjustment to the angle of the V, the camel driver scowled as if he might be thinking about it. Then, without warning, he spat hard into the dirt, scattering Bilali's drawing into rolling beads of dust and saliva. He growled some incomprehensible words and lost himself in his herd. Bilali was still brushing off his sleeves when Sidi Masrur, the book trader, who had heard and seen all, told the boy that the driver had cursed him in classical Arabic for presuming to improve on God's own design. His eyes twinkling under a greasy turban, Sidi Masrur said, "It would seem that not only the camel but the Tuareg saddle was delivered to his tribe directly from the hand of God."

After the briefest silence, Bilali asked, "Do you believe it?"

Sidi Masrur said quietly, "I do not, but I would not say as much to my camel driver."

Suddenly it struck Bilali that the book trader was speaking to him at this moment not in Arabic, but in Pulaar. Reading the surprise on his face, Sidi Masrur explained, "It behooves the merchant to converse with his clients in a manner that makes them feel at home. In this way, trust is built between them." He spoke Yoruba and Hausa as well as Pulaar and several dialects of Arabic, he said.

In the interest of science and the spirit of knowledge, Sidi Masrur encouraged Bilali to go ahead and make his small adjustment to one of the saddles that bore his coffers of books. Bilali had his father make two V-shaped copper tubes, into which he fit the dowels that were formerly tied together to give the saddle its tent shape. When that one small adjustment allowed the camel to double its load without so much as blinking a double-lidded eye, every camel driver in the caravan—with the exception of the one who had cursed Bilali—got in line for their V-shaped tubes, fashioned in the portable forge of Bilali's father from whatever copper pot or brass pitcher the camel driver could provide. In one language after another, Sidi Masrur proclaimed that the boy—sometimes he said the "*sudani*," although the book trader's skin was not much lighter than Bilali's—was worth far more than his not-very-considerable weight in gold. Enthusiastic caravaneers and camel drivers agreed. At the time, neither Bilali nor his father was as alarmed as they should have been by these flattering pronouncements, only some of which they understood. They were too busy counting their dirhams. They now had sufficient resources to pay their way by land and sea to Mecca and back again. Ahmad Baba had not yet mentioned to his son Bilali the side trip he had in mind. Having traveled north for weeks now, and with the breadth of Africa yet to cross from west to east, Ahmad Baba had come to regard the journey to Baghdad—perhaps nine hundred miles each way—as a mere detour. He would present it thus to his son, when the time was right.

As for Sidi Masrur, trader of books and other commodities, he became their closest associate and advisor. "Regard me as your *rafiq*," he said, using the word as medieval traders did, to mean companion, partner, comrade, friend. One night the three of them were sipping thick, sweet mint tea on cushions placed on the ground around his campfire of camel chips, when Sidi Masrur confided his intention to leave the Shinqiti caravan at Marrakech or Fez and proceed to the coast from there.

"We shall do the same!" said Ahmad Baba. "Do you know a boat? Perhaps we can continue our journey together, if God wills it."

Bilali sipped his tea and tried to remember if he or his father had previously mentioned to Sidi Masrur their plans to travel by boat to Alexandria, instead of taking the overland route through the desert.

"That would be truly a pleasure," the book trader said. He told them that once they reached Suez, he would help them find a boat bound for Jeddah, the port that was only one day's journey from the holy places. He himself would be going on. He had been hired to procure a certain book in Baghdad, if he could, for subsequent delivery to a scholar in Tripoli who was willing to pay a big price for the ancient volume.

"You will travel to *Baghdad?*" Ahmad Baba said.

"Of course," said Sidi Masrur. "Baghdad is always on the book trader's route, especially if he seeks, as I do, the work of the Banu Musa."

Ahmad nearly dropped his glass of tea. "*The Book of Ingenious Devices?*"

Bilali looked up sharply at the name of a book he had been hearing about for as long as he could remember. He felt a flush of shame at the meagerness of his efforts to find a copy of it for his father during his own year in Timbo.

"You know it?" Sidi Masrur sounded pleased. "I suppose I shouldn't be surprised. Not when your own boy could himself be a son of Musa bin Shakir, for all his cleverness!" The book trader's pale and suddenly unreadable eyes slid over to Bilali and rested on him. "Not that the father is anything but worthy of such a son."

Bilali knew what was coming next. He tried to signal his father to keep quiet, but Ahmad Baba could not resist saying, in a whisper, "I have seen the *Kitab!*"

Sidi Masrur's whole face darkened for an instant. "Where?" he asked.

"Truly, sir, it was in Timbo," said Ahmad Baba. "In my student days."

When he turned to Bilali, Sidi Masrur's face had regained its even expression. "You've only just come from learned Timbo, have you not? Did you, too, lay eyes on the *Kitab* of the Banu Musa there?"

"I inquired," Bilali said, and this was true, he had, "but no one knew of it."

"Perhaps your father saw it in a dream," the book trader said. He threw back his head and drained his glass.

"I saw it," Ahmad Baba said firmly. "It was a large book, in size like a shield."

"Like a shield?" Sidi Masrur sounded doubtful.

"A small shield." Ahmad Baba continued, switching for some reason from Pulaar to his slow and deliberate Arabic. "It has a cover of leather that once was red. Some pages are torn. Some ink is faint." He paused the width of a breath. "Inside the book, there are *pictures*. One hundred pictures," he said, "of one hundred devices."

Sidi Masrur nodded slowly, like a man convinced. "You have seen it," he said.

As it happened, the book trader knew a great deal about the *Book of Ingenious Devices* and even more about the Banu Musa who had written it. "Their father, Musa—or Moses, as the Christians say—began his career as a highwayman, making the roads unsafe in Khurasan."

"No!" said Ahmad Baba in dramatic disbelief, although Bilali had heard this same story from his father many times.

Later, when father and son were rolled up in their blankets for the night, Bilali asked his father if he had ever mentioned the *Book of Ingenious Devices* to Sidi Masrur—"before tonight, I mean."

After a long silence, Ahmad Baba said, "Perhaps I did."

Over their heads, the sky was milky with stars, and although cold air touched their faces, the sand beneath them was still warm. Bilali waited a moment before he asked, "Baba, do you think the book trader is really looking for the *Kitab al-Hiyal*? Do you think he really has a customer who wishes to buy it?"

"Of course. Why would he say so if he did not?"

"To win our trust?"

"Bilali, I will tell you what I believe about Sidi Masrur. I believe he is our *rafiq*. I believe that God has sent him to us. If we hadn't met Sidi Masrur, I would not even know that it is possible to go almost the *whole way* by boat."

"But that was always our plan," Bilali said. "To go by boat." How many times had he rehearsed the route in his mind? In Rabat they would find passage on the sea to Egypt—a voyage of many weeks. In Egypt there would be a three-day journey overland from Cairo to Suez, and then another boat to the Red Sea port of Jeddah, and after that just one day's camel ride to Mecca. Most of the time they would be on the water, or so Bilali hoped fervently. After walking alongside their laden camel from Timbo to Shinqiti, and from there almost to Fez, he was looking forward with his whole being to pressing the tired soles of his feet to the deck of the long-promised boat.

"Oh, yes, surely, to Jeddah and the holy places one can go by boat," his father said. "But did you hear Sidi Masrur say that he would go on all the way to Baghdad? To Baghdad, Bilali!" Ahmad Baba shook his head in wonder. "Now, *that* is a place I never thought I would live to see."

Twenty-two days after its departure from Shinqiti, the caravan reached Fez. Most of the merchants and pilgrims stopped there to prepare for the task of continuing their journey along the northern edge of the Sahara, taking the desert route to Cairo, but a third of them formed a different group, bound for Rabat and the sea. Bilali and his father followed Sidi Masrur to the vicinity of the carpenters' guildhall in Fez, where by tradition the caravan bound for Rabat assembled. There they joined leather merchants and others from Fez who wished to carry their goods eastward by sea. The carpenters' guildhall was located at one end of a great bazaar teeming with people and merchandise. Bilali had never seen such an assemblage, not even in Timbo. What he would remember best about Fez was the smell of cedar chips mingling with the fragrant wares of perfume sellers and druggists. For the rest of his life, the sweet smell of cedar would make him glimpse his father's face as it was in the market at Fez, alive with hope and excitement.

Less than two days' journey beyond Fez brought their smaller caravan to Rabat. They skirted the old city and snaked down narrow streets until the sea opened up before them like the sunlit pages of a book. As he had promised, Sidi Masrur helped Ahmad Baba find passage on one of the sailing ships that bobbed in the harbor. When Bilali admired a caravel with a dashing air and two sails—one square-rigged and one triangular lateen—the book trader shook his head. "See the flag? French. And there is no way to tell if they have paid their tribute or not. You don't want to board a Christian ship unless you wish for personal acquaintance with pirates."

"Pirates?" Ahmad Baba said.

"Bandits of the sea," said Sidi Masrur. "Arab pirates. They'll board a Christian ship, empty all purses and pockets, and gather up the passengers to sell for slaves."

"But they won't attack a Muslim ship?"

Sidi Masrur smiled. "Not if they care for their souls as well as their purses."

The boat he found for them—and then boarded himself— appeared to be waiting for something on the wharf. Bilali stood at the stern rail while his father went to settle their account with the captain. The cool breeze made him want to remove the turban his father had ceremoniously wound around his head this auspicious morning, the day they set sail for the holy places. Bilali watched a dozen or so of the people his father called the unfortunate ones looking anxious and restless on the wharf—the women veiled, the men wrapped in what- ever they could make of their tattered piece of cloth. He wondered if they, too, would come aboard, and if so, where were they going—not to the holy places, he felt sure. A worldly friend in Timbo had told him that most of the male slaves sent north and east would be sol- diers, and most of the women concubines. A familiar voice, suddenly at his elbow, said, "In years gone by, they would have been traded for Barbary horses."

Bilali turned quickly. He took one step back from the stern rail as Sidi Masrur leaned forward over it, resting his elbows, the better to con- sider the milling group on the wharf. "The usual rate was fifteen slaves for one horse, although the trader might take fewer in exchange if some had special knowledge or ability. Someone like you, Bilali, with your talents, you might stand for five mere laborers. Perhaps ten."

"But I am not a slave!" The boy meant to say this calmly, but his heart was pounding. Then he heard the rattle of the anchor chain and the deep collective voice of the oarsmen as they pulled together, turning the bow of the white-sailed lateener toward open water. From where he stood, Bilali could see most of the deck. The captain was just below them, calling up to someone about the position of the rudder. Ahmad Baba was nowhere in sight. He had been gone a long time now. "Where is my father?" Bilali said, and when Sidi Masrur only looked out at the wharf as if he hadn't heard, a sudden weakness in Bilali's knees made him grip the rail. The second time he asked, he could hear the tremor in his voice. "Where is he? What have you done to him?"

But Sidi Masrur said only, "Look! We are under way."

From Rabat, the lateener sailed up the short Atlantic coast of Morocco, through the straits at the foot of Tariq's Mountain, which the English called Gibraltar, and into the Mediterranean Sea. After the first day, Bilali stopped begging the book trader to tell him, at least, what had happened to his father. Had they killed him and thrown his body into the sea? Or had they merely put him off the boat and left without him? Sidi Masrur couldn't say, nor could the captain, and the rest were not certain who this Ahmad Baba was. As they sailed from port to port across the northern coast of Africa, Bilali stopped speaking to any of them. He spent the hours watching the sailors at work. Sidi Masrur expected attempts at escape—not at sea, of course, but when they landed in Algiers and Tunis and Tripoli, and again in Alexandria, where Bilali spent their twenty days of quarantine chained to a timber in the private quarters of Sidi Masrur, just out of reach of the book trader's throat. Sidi Masrur was especially watchful of his charge on the three-day journey by camel from Cairo to the Gulf of Suez and the Red Sea. Only then did Sidi Masrur breathe more easily. When, a few hours out, the captain of their Red Sea ship called, "Ahoy!" to an Arab pirates' dhow, all the crew and the handful of passengers came running to the sides to see, including Bilali and his captor. Sidi Masrur did *not* expect the boy to do what he did then, just at the very moment when the pirates made their surprising musket shot "across the bow," whether of greeting or warning, no one could say for sure. Everyone on board the lateener hit the deck, except for Bilali, who took the opportunity to vault himself over the rail. He barely missed the great wooden rudder as he somersaulted into the sea.

The brisk shock of hitting the water drove everything from the boy's mind, including the fact that he couldn't swim.

The pirates fished him, half drowned, out of the sea, and when the boy kept sobbing, "My father is dead," the pirates thought *they* must have killed him. (It would not be the first time their musket shot across the bow found an unintended mark.) They wanted only for the other vessel to identify herself. Why did the captain fly no flag? (This was, in fact, never explained.) Why did he run the risk of being taken for a Christian ship? The boy sniffed and shivered and hardly understood a word as the pirate captain, thumping his chest with both pride and contrition, explained that he, Süleyman Reis, commanded a crew of Mohammedans. Their *jihad* against the infidels who sailed the Red Sea was meant not just to fill their purses (and the ship's hold) with treasure, but to win them entrance to Paradise. Only God knew how much hard-earned *baraka* they had canceled out by killing one of the faithful—worse yet, one who was *on his way* to the holy places, who had not yet completed the *hajj*. Would that they had struck the poor man down on his way home instead—not that they meant to do it either way! Süleyman Reis assured Bilali. In reparation, they dried the boy off and warmed him up and fed him. They would have returned him to his people if they could have, the captain of the pirates said, but a brisk wind from the south—the last vestige of monsoons that had conveyed them from the Indian Ocean and through the Gate of Sorrows into the Red Sea—filled their triangular sail and swept them away from the other vessel. They promised to carry him wherever he willed to go, but when the boy said Baghdad, they were taken aback.

"It can be done," Süleyman Reis said, "if God wills it." He tucked his thumbs into his sash and considered. The pirate captain wore a pointed turban and a pair of tunics over loose pants and soft leather shoes like slippers, good for pacing the deck. The wide sash around his slightly bulging middle accommodated three long knives and a sword. More than once Bilali wondered how he managed not to stick himself when he sat down.

"If the wind was right," Süleyman Reis continued, "we could carry you to Basrah, and there hire a small craft to go upriver." He was standing amidships with the boy and looked up at his gently billowing lateen. "The wind will not be right for a few months yet."

"Months!" said Bilali. He, too, looked up at the great triangular sail over his head. On this side of the mast, opposite the sail, at least two dozen lines of rope ran down from the spar like a lopsided spider's web, crisscrossing here and there, with wooden blocks or pulleys in different spots on each line, as if they'd chosen where to perch themselves. The lateen on the other ship, the one he'd boarded with his father, was much more elegantly rigged than this one. Ahmad Baba had pointed out the beauty of it right before he went off in search of the captain, leaving his son at the rail to gaze down and ponder the mysteries of displacement as the two-hundred-ton lateener rolled gently on the waves in the harbor. Without warning, Bilali's eyes filled with tears and his nose started running. He addressed both problems with his sleeve before he remarked, still looking up, "You don't need so many ropes."

"What do you mean?" asked Süleyman, cocking one eye upward again.

The boy paused, as if considering, and then he asked, "Have you ever heard of a knot called Toes of the Camel?"

Süleyman Reis had not.

They tested the new rigging by setting sail for Jeddah, where the pirate captain left four men to guard the ship with muskets. (In the harbor, as they rowed in to shore, Bilali kept a sharp eye out for the lateener.) Süleyman Reis hired camels for the rest of the crew to accompany the boy to Mecca.

It was near the end of the twelfth month of a year near the end of the twelfth century of Hijra. Almost twelve hundred years had passed since the Prophet fled across the desert. Many believed the end of time was at hand. Outside Mecca, where Bilali and the pirate crew camped in rented tents, pilgrim caravans filled the whole horizon. Bilali and the pirates purified themselves, casting aside their ordinary clothes (and knives and swords) and wrapping their bodies in the garb of *ihram*. They completed the *hajj* twice: once for his father and once for themselves. Two times seven times they circled the Ka'bah, where Abraham once stood. Seven times two times they hurried back and forth between the rock and the hard place, as Süleyman put it, remembering how poor

Hagar searched for water in the desert. On the ninth day they rose *very* early, with a minimum of grumbling, and climbed Mount Arafat (twice). They cast stones at the devil and in the valley of Mina they sacrificed two sheep.

They returned by camel to Jeddah, where their ship lay at anchor, feeling exhausted and exonerated and so pure and light and generous of spirit that Süleyman Reis did not so much as draw his sword when Bilali spotted the evil Sidi Masrur pacing up and down the dock, as if waiting for a customer, a book tucked under his arm. Süleyman Reis was feeling so generous, in fact, that he took Bilali by the upper arm and handed him over to Sidi Masrur, saying, "Go with your uncle."

"My *what*?"

"It's time you returned to your studies in the House of Wisdom, nephew," said the suddenly avuncular Sidi Masrur, taking Bilali's other arm.

"He did ask that we deliver him to Baghdad in the end," Süleyman Reis pointed out, as if in defense of a boy's desire for a little adventure before settling down to the books. He let go of Bilali, now that the book trader had a good grip on him, and held out his hand. A little awkwardly, still holding the book under his arm, Sidi Masrur dropped a small, lumpy leather purse into the pirate's palm. "You are a very clever boy," Süley-man said to Bilali, tossing the purse into the air and catching it again with a most satisfying clink of coins. "If anyone should be studying the ways of science and the Banu Musa, it is you."

"It was his father's greatest wish," Sidi Masrur said.

Bilali had planted his feet, prepared for a struggle to the death, if need be—what better time, after all, having just completed the *hajj*?— but when he saw what book was tucked under the book trader's arm, all the fight emptied out of him, replaced by a surge of pure grief.

The book was the Qur'an, his father's handwritten copy.

Aboard the lateener once again, Sidi Masrur had the boy bound hand and foot belowdecks until such time as the ship was well past the Gate of

Sorrows, riding the seas again with no other vessel in sight. When Bilali was finally permitted to emerge from the darkness below—blindfolded to save his sight—he sat unmoving against the ship's wales and practiced squinting until he found that he could open both eyes in the murky light behind the cloth without a stab of pain.

Bilali was still blindfolded when he jumped overboard a second time, Sidi Masrur shouting and cursing above him, unable to believe the boy's poor judgment and his own ill luck. This time, there was no pirate dhow to save him. Indeed, Bilali had no wish to be saved, although he couldn't help taking one more last breath every time the waves tossed him upward, until a miracle of God—the Compassionate, the Merciful—lifted him up on the highest of whitecaps and cast him upon a hidden and uncharted reef. When the boy staggered to his feet in the ankle-deep water washing over the reef, the ship's crew and passengers saw him standing on the surface of the ocean. They praised Allah vociferously as they watched Bilali walk away across the water. Sidi Masrur demanded a party of rowers to take a dinghy in pursuit of his property, but the captain of the lateener was tired of the book trader's demands, and an uncharted reef was far too treacherous to approach. After additional prayers of thanksgiving for the miracle they had witnessed, they sailed on.

As he walked, half blind, in a daze, across the Gulf of Aden, Bilali's eyes stung from seawater and sunlight, the blindfold long gone the way of his turban. When he stopped and turned and could finally look behind him, his breath caught in his throat. The lateener was a toy ship retreating brilliantly across blue water that lapped the horizon all around. When he turned back to look ahead, far ahead, he saw a brown line between water and sky, land of some kind, perhaps at the end of the reef or perhaps impossibly far beyond it. He walked toward it, the water bathing his ankles, the sun assailing him from every direction, until he could walk no more.

When he awoke, he was curled up on a sandy beach in the shade of another miracle. This time it was a camel taking her ease like the Sphinx, as if the two of them had stopped to rest together. Bilali climbed aboard and wedged himself as best he could between the hump and her long neck, delighted to find there a leather bag provisioned with dates and a fat water bottle. She stopped at every camel well between the Gulf of Aden, where Bilali had stepped ashore, and the giant *caravanserai* on the outskirts of Basrah, a journey of eight hundred miles or more. Bilali replenished his provisions when he could, sometimes joining a caravan as it wended from well to well, but keeping mostly to himself. On the outskirts of Basrah, with regret and a rumbling stomach, Bilali traded his miracle camel for food, clothing, and a small amount of money, enough to purchase passage on one of the little round boats that paddled upstream to Baghdad.

Bilali found the once-great city in a state of some decline: sprawled between and around two sluggish rivers, dusty, hot, sleepy, except when the tunnel of a street opened into a market where buyers and sellers swarmed. At a stall in a fruit and flower market, Bilali learned that the House of Wisdom where the Banu Musa lived and worked had fallen when the Mongols crushed Baghdad five hundred years before. "They say the Tigris ran black with ink from all the books cast into the water," a citrus vendor said. His neighbor, a seller of pomegranates, disagreed, claiming instead that "the river ran red with the blood of the scholars." The second merchant also pointed out that there was still a certain quarter of the city wherein many scholars dwelled. "Perhaps you will find there what you seek." With a few minutes' labor fixing an unbalanced scale, Bilali purchased two pomegranates and detailed directions to the Street of Scholars.

It was a street like many others, barely wider than a man's spread arms or the carefully balanced load on a water boy's donkey, a tunnel-like street with yellow-white buildings crowding over it, as if the arched windows and little stone balconies on one side of the street had secrets to whisper to the houses on the other. The boy walked up and down its length four times—from the mosque and minaret that closed it off at one end to the blank wall down at the other—without encountering another living soul. He knew from his days in Timbo that true scholars were a quiet bunch, spending their time bowed over books, but this street felt quiet as a tomb. He learned later that some of the narrow houses were, in fact, tombs, with their lifelong resident scholars now buried under the floors. Bilali was on his fourth trip down the street when he stopped suddenly to read the words painted in white on a blue tile next to a plain wooden door in the center of the block.

BAYT AL-HIKMA, the sign said. The House of Wisdom.

Bilali folded his arms. He knew with the utmost certainty that the little sign had *not* been there on his previous pass down the street. And yet, having traveled three thousand miles by land and sea to catch a glimpse of the work of the Banu Musa, how could he leave without seeing what was inside?

He knocked and the door opened. A kindly-looking man who wore the turban of a scholar and whose beard was white although his eyes were youthful, greeted him, saying, "God is great."

Bilali bowed respectfully.

Inside, he followed the scholar (there seemed to be only this one— Ibrahim ibn al-Kindi was his name) through one shadowy room into the next. They came to a chamber furnished with thick carpets and lined with shelves made from tightly woven palm branches on which leather-covered books were stacked, from the floor to the not-very-lofty ceiling. This was the library. The scholar al-Kindi gestured toward a book of large dimensions that lay open on a low table. "This is perhaps what you seek?"

Although he had never seen it before, Bilali recognized the book at once from his father's descriptions of it. From the doorway, he could see a drawing on the right-hand page of the open book—a container of some kind, with a handle and spout. Black script surrounded the drawing like scalloped waves around an island, the waves spilling onto the left-hand page, promising movement and mystery (which are in themselves a kind of escape, al-Kindi would argue later). It was the *Book of Ingenious Devices*, the *Kitab al-Hiyal*. Young Bilali knew when he saw it that the world might come to an end for him here, in the so-called

House of Wisdom, but he couldn't keep his heart from beating faster—
Here it is, Father, I am touching it, the book is in my hands—as he knelt to
turn the page.

∾⊶⊷∾

It didn't take long for Bilali to wrest from Ibrahim ibn al-Kindi, that
impoverished and duplicitous but kindly scholar, everything he knew
about Sidi Masrur's plans for him.

"He knew I would come here," Bilali said.

"He knew you would, if you survived."

"And you are in his employ?"

Al-Kindi bowed his head. They were sitting on a low stone wall in
the unkempt garden at the center of the House of Wisdom. The old
man removed his scholar's turban, as if he were unworthy of it, and let
his white hair fall over his face. "He offered me the *Book on the Long,
Curved Figure* by al-Hasan," the old scholar admitted. "Also, he fed me
for a year."

Such an investment would demand a large return. "How much can
Sidi Masrur hope to get for me?" Bilali asked.

"He already has a buyer. You are a very valuable commodity, my
boy." Al-Kindi toyed with the folds of the turban in his lap. "In fact," he
said, "the sultan's vizier has made a substantial payment in advance."

"The *sultan's* vizier?"

It seemed Bilali's destiny lay in the service of the sultan at Topkapi,
who took great interest in the Banu Musa and their ingenious devices.
"Their fountains, especially," al-Kindi said. "The sultan loves fountains."
Although a slave, Bilali would live a life of relative luxury in the Topkapi
Palace, al-Kindi said. He would spend his days in study and invention,
figuring things out, in short, doing what he loved best to do. "Does that
sound so uninviting?" al-Kindi asked. "It is the equal of my own life,
except for the luxury, which, as you can see all around you, *I* do not
enjoy."

"But I would be a slave," Bilali said.

"You would."

If it was easy for Bilali to get Ibrahim ibn al-Kindi to reveal the plans of Sidi Masrur—including the estimated time of the book trader's return to Baghdad months hence—it was easier still to convince the old scholar of that which he most fervently wanted to believe: that Bilali had no wish to escape his "destiny." A boy whose father was dead and whose home was thousands of miles away was in a very precarious position, Bilali admitted. Such a boy could do much worse than the Topkapi Palace. That understood, it seemed sensible to save a little money for the market by letting one of the guards go, and entirely reasonable to keep the other one on only at night, more to safeguard the library than to prevent an escape. The boy appeared willing to bide his time in the House of Wisdom, eating well, and learning what he could from al-Kindi, who was a genuine scholar of the Banu Musa with many stories to tell. Bilali spent every moment he could hunched over the fragile pages of the *Kitab al-Hiyal*. (The manuscript in al-Kindi's possession was over three hundred years old. "Much newer than the original!" he said.) Bilali memorized the difficult Arabic line by line, he studied every curve and angle in each device, learning them so well that at night, by moon or even only starlight, he could reproduce the drawings and the text from memory on paper he stole from al-Kindi's hidden cache during the day. The boy was struck, in the process, by how playful the sons of Musa were, how like magicians or tricksters, so many of their devices serving no more purpose than to trick or please the eye, unless it was to demonstrate their gift for bringing into actuality the potential power of liquid and volume and air.

With the dirhams they saved by dismissing the guards, al-Kindi encouraged the boy to purchase the necessary materials and make one or two of the devices. "For the pleasure of it," al-Kindi said, hinting, "A fountain would be nice."

Bilali did not have the time for such niceties, for he was not so resigned to his fate as he pretended to be. When he had copied all one hundred ingenious devices—that is to say, when he had a complete *Kitab al-Hiyal*, its loose leaves slipped inside a leather envelope he'd fashioned—*then* he would run away from the House of Wisdom, regretting that he had to leave al-Kindi without saying good-bye. He would find a caravan to join, one moving to the west, and he would make himself indispensable to it, he would invent and repair and improvise his way home. How surprised and (he hoped) pleased his mother would be to see him. And his grandfather.

That, at any rate, was his secret plan, and he would, in fact, accomplish most of it. He would join a westward-wending caravan, and he would manage to hide his loose-leaf *Kitab al-Hiyal* from the bandits who raided the caravan as it crossed the Hijaz, and later, from the slave traders to whom the bandits sold him, utterly unaware of the price they could have asked. Bilali would keep the *Kitab* out of sight for many weeks among the unfortunate ones, clutching it awkwardly under his tunic, burying it in the sand beneath his feet at night. When it was finally discovered at the market in Alexandria, where opportunities to hide something on one's person were limited indeed, he would convince the auctioneer to convince the British planter who purchased Bilali to buy the *Kitab* as well. (After their long journey in hiding, the pages looked almost as ancient as Bilali claimed them to be.) On a vast plantation in the Bahamas, Bilali would make himself invaluable to the British planter, and years later, when he left the Bahamas with wives and daughters and a new owner, bound for an island off the unknown coast of Georgia, the *Book of Ingenious Devices* would go with them.

In the meantime, as a boy in the House of Wisdom, Bilali resolved to learn as much as he could from the old scholar, who appeared eager to teach him, even though Bilali was at times, as he himself knew, a trying student. When al-Kindi revealed one day that al-Hasan, the youngest of the Banu Musa, had been captured by the Caliph Amin during the siege of Baghdad, Bilali interrupted to protest, "I thought the Caliph was a patron of the Banu Musa."

"Not *this* Caliph," al-Kindi said. It was during the time when the sons of the most renowned and recently deceased Harun al-Rashid were at war, brother against brother, al-Kindi explained. Amin was the elder son, but everyone knew that his half-brother Ma'mun, the son of a Persian slave girl, was his father's favorite. The Banu Musa were in the camp of Ma'mun, whose troops besieged the city. "Once captured by Amin, our friend al-Hasan would have spent his life in servitude," al-Kindi said, "had he not escaped. The Caliph Amin felt a great fondness for hand-some boys, you see, and the youngest of the Banu Musa was at that time a handsome boy."

"He escaped, you say?" Bilali sat up straighter on the low wall in the garden, right next to the place where a fountain would have been nice.

"It's quite a story," said al-Kindi. "When Caliph Amin sent his vizier to make the new captive an offer he could not refuse—not if he wished to keep his head—what do you think al-Hasan did?"

"Did he run away?"

"Impossible. Armed guards on every side."

"Did he draw out a hidden sword and slay the vizier and the armed guards?"

"Obviously impossible."

"Did he accept the offer of the Caliph?"

"Of course. Now we are getting somewhere, Bilali. And then?"

"He betrayed his brothers and his father and became the consort of Amin?"

"Of course *not*." The expression on Ibrahim ibn al-Kindi's face sug-gested sudden doubts about Sidi Masrur's judgment in the matter of young Bilali's brilliance. "Think again."

But the book trader was not wrong about young Bilali, who knew very well that clever al-Hasan, youngest of the Banu Musa, would deceive the weak-minded Caliph in some way. It was almost too easy, and the deception was distasteful to Bilali. Did a person of intelligence always have to sacrifice integrity in order to make use of his gifts?

"Perhaps," said Bilali, "al-Hasan devises some clever trick or . . . object?"

"Of course!" cried al-Kindi. "An ingenious object to deceive the foolish Amin! We are talking about the Banu Musa, are we not? Al-Hasan turns to his brothers Muhammad and Ahmad for help, sending a message to Ma'mun's camp in the hollow hilt of a sword." Al-Kindi leaned forward. "Don't you want to know what kind of ingenious device they devised to save al-Hasan from the Caliph Amin?"

"Yes, sir, I do," Bilali admitted, whereupon al-Kindi told the tale, since lost to history, of

The Caliph and the Magic Pitcher

In the second century of the Hijra—the year 762, by the Christian reckoning of our time—the Abbasid Caliph Abu Ja'far al-Mansur drew with a stick on the ground beside the Tigris a great circle one mile wide, enclosing a dusty village. The line the Caliph drew on the ground was covered with bales of cotton—hundreds of bales, or perhaps thousands—all soaked in naphtha and set afire. When the flames died, a charred outline remained on the ground, marking the shape of the new capital. Caliph al-Mansur placed his Palace of the Golden Gate at the center of the Round City, surrounded by a wall of immense thickness. Three horsemen could ride abreast along the top of this wall. Four great metal gates—so massive that a company of men was required to open or close each one—permitted entrance to the inner city. Date palm trees brought from Basrah were planted everywhere, until the new city had more palms than Basrah, and they yielded plentiful fruit. Watered by canals in use since Babylonian times, gardens and orchards and fields spread out around the new city, gardens and fields that would flourish for another five hundred years, until invading Mongols destroyed the ancient canals and returned the land to the desert. Caliph al-Mansur called his new capital Madinat al-Salam. The City of Peace.

The locals called it Baghdad.

Even before al-Mansur's son Mahdi succeeded his father as commander of the faithful, Baghdad had outgrown the Round City. Al-Mansur soon built himself a pleasure palace on the Tigris outside the Khurasan Gate. He called it Khuld, or Paradise Castle, and built another for his son on the opposite bank. Mosques and houses grew around each new palace, inhabitants flocked to the riverbanks, markets filled new suburbs. Already one whole bazaar was devoted to the sale of Chinese silks, another to brass and copper wares, another to spices, aloes, and sandalwood. One market offered teak for shipbuilding, another jewels and the new porcelain from China. In others food was sold: fruits, meats, grains, and prepared delicacies for every taste. Paper, linen, cotton, and rice from Egypt, perfumes and produce from Persia, pearls and weapons from Arabia, all were bought and sold in Baghdad, bazaar par excellence of the Middle East, heart of the Islamic empire, a new kind of Eden sprung up near the site of the old.

Under the rule of Mahdi's son, the renowned Harun al-Rashid, Baghdad enjoyed a golden age of music, literature, art, and luxury—an age made famous, like Harun himself, by tales from *The Arabian Nights*. Though quick to laugh and prone to late-night adventures, Harun al-Rashid was at the same time a fearless soldier and prudent administrator, particularly when he followed the advice of Ja'far the Barmecide, the Caliph's vizier and boon companion, famous in his own right for getting Harun out of tight spots and awkward episodes. The empire expanded in size and influence under the rule of Harun al-Rashid. Visitors from East and West left Baghdad awed by the splendor of his court. (The envoy of Charlemagne returned to a Europe still blinking away the Dark Ages with gifts that included two elephants and a most ingenious water clock, in which miniature knights marked the hour by opening tiny doors.) But the Caliph Harun could be cruel and jealous as well. When his friend the vizier displeased Harun by falling in love with the Caliph's sister (and, it must be added, by building a palace across the river that rivaled the Caliph's in splendor), neither friendship nor privilege could save Ja'far the Barmecide. Dismembered and displayed on the bridge across the Tigris like any condemned man, he wore the same terrible look of disbelief on his skewered head.

The two sides of Harun al-Rashid's nature—the stern and the frivolous (as well as the jealous and fickle)—appeared to be divided between his two sons: soldierly Ma'mun, who fought beside his father in rebellious Khurasan, and pleasure-loving Amin, Harun's elder son, who succeeded his father as Caliph in Baghdad when Harun fell ill and died.

Everyone knew that Amin was a man who enjoyed games and singing more than government or war. It was said that his mother Zubaida, favorite wife and now widow of Harun al-Rashid, had to interest her son in the fairer sex by dressing young girls as page boys and sending them in to join Amin's revelers. They were likely to find the new Caliph riding a wooden hobbyhorse borne by slaves about the hall while nervous guests sang and slave girls danced around him. When his half-brother Ma'mun refused to send revenues from the provinces to support such revels, Amin dispatched an army of forty thousand men to encourage his brother's obedience to himself the Caliph. Amin's army was routed by a force one-tenth its size under the command of Ma'mun's fierce ally, Tahir the Ambidextrous, and seeing this, the surviving troops hailed Ma'mun as Caliph instead and set out to march against Baghdad in turn.

It was late in the ensuing two-year siege of Baghdad, while Amin still ruled as Caliph, that the youngest of the sons of Musa resolved to visit a friend in the city. The friend had made a discovery while distilling petroleum. Instead of the usual thick and odorous lamp oil, al-Hasan's friend al-Razi had produced a thin, clear liquid that burned without smoke. (*It is like water set afire!* said the message al-Razi sent to Ma'mun's camp concealed in the folds of a camel driver's turban.) To avoid interference from the defenders of the city and also from his brothers, who advised against a visit to Baghdad while Baghdad was under siege, al-Hasan and a most trustworthy slave named Bab Sabu had secured the use of a *kellek*—a small raft made of inflated goatskins following an ancient Babylonian design—in which they floated noiselessly downriver under cover of darkness. In hopes of escaping capture, Bab Sabu took the precaution of landing two water gates away from the home of al-Razi, lately the inventor of kerosene and long a friend of the Banu Musa.

It was a precaution taken in vain.

Al-Hasan wished most heartily that he had listened to his brothers now that the severed head of Bab Sabu stared at him in startled agony from the bottom of the boat. Had Bab Sabu been a more important, if equally unfortunate, personage—like Ja'far the Barmecide, to take an example from history, or like the Caliph himself in days yet to come— his head and perhaps the rest of him might have been displayed on a bridge over the Tigris until it shriveled and dried like a bundle of dates in the sun. Because he was merely a slave, the head of Bab Sabu soon followed his body, still twitching, into the river. Al-Hasan was stuffed into a wooden trunk along with the goatskins, which the henchmen took care to deflate, and the trunk was carried off to the palace of the Golden Gate in the heart of the Round City. What with the horror of the beheading, the press of soggy goatskins, and the lack of air in the trunk, the youngest of the Banu Musa passed out cold before he got there.

A dream of flying woke him. He felt himself lifted into the air. When he dared to open his eyes, he saw a distant white ceiling and tall narrow windows, like obelisks of pure blue sky, casting bars of sunlight on the opposite wall. So it was morning—or maybe afternoon—and he was flat on his back on a broad taut sheet of silk caught up along its edges by six tall and burly fellows. They lifted him effortlessly in the cradle of silk and then lowered him gently into a cool bath of perfumed water. He was naked, he noticed.

"My tunic!" he cried.

In the corner of the room, two unveiled girls in colorful silks looked up sharply from a smoking brazier. One of them was using a poker to push the last strips of linen from al-Hasan's tunic—stained with the blood of Bab Sabu—onto the burning coals.

Seeing them, al-Hasan recognized two unfortunate facts in the same instant: First, it was far too late to retrieve the folded paper from the pocket sewn inside his tunic by the hand of Bab Sabu. (He could only pray to God, the Merciful, the Compassionate, that his brother Ahmad had made another copy of its contents.) Second, the presence of these lovely unveiled girls—and there were more, he saw now, perhaps a dozen of them, arranging fruit on a large platter laid out on a spread of Persian carpets, pouring water into the tiled pool, standing by with thick towels and a gold-trimmed robe—could mean only one of two things. Either the Caliph was planning to give all these women to al-Hasan—which did not seem likely, he had to admit—or he was about to forfeit his own (largely untried) manhood and join the ranks of these eunuchs, the only males outside the Caliph's family who were permitted to look upon the harem unveiled. (Impending death was a third possibility, but why would they go to all this trouble to prepare him thus for that?) There were guards ouside the room, flanking the arched doorway. He could see the left shoulder of one and the right of the other. He could not help but glance downward. Under the water, he was all there.

It did not bode well, he thought, when an opulently dressed young woman, bejeweled in every possible way and draped in strings of pearls, entered the room and clapped her hands. Everyone sprang into action. The brazier was snuffed out, he was helped from the fragrant bath, two girls commenced to dry him with thick cotton towels (this activity started to have its effect, even as frightened as he was), and another (not quite hiding her smile) presented him with a gold-trimmed robe of honor. Anxious to be covered, he held out his arms and she slipped it over his head. The golden hem brushed the bare tops of his feet, as if he had been measured for it. Then the well-dressed young woman clapped her hands again and everyone else disappeared except for one of the eunuchs, a black giant of a man.

"You must be hungry," the girl said. It was her voice, more than her unveiled face, that told him she was no older than he was, despite the splendor of her dress. She gestured to the platter on the carpet at his feet, which contained a selection of Shami apples and quinces and pears, as well as an orange, two limes, and a pomegranate. He was suddenly famished. "Please sit," she said, and when he did, she sat facing him, crossed-legged, the platter between them. "The pears are especially delicious." She smiled. "Like drinking from a pear-shaped cup."

As he took the first bite, he glanced over his shoulder at the brazier that held the smoking ruins of his tunic.

"Is this what you are looking for?" the girl said, holding up the folded piece of paper.

Pear juice ran unheeded down al-Hasan's chin. He swallowed. A chunk of pear he had neglected to chew slid painfully down his throat.

The girl handed the paper to him. He unfolded it with his less sticky hand, comforted to see his brother's drawing, every pipe and plate and inconspicuous hole so neatly labeled in accordance with the instructions Ahmad had written out on the other side. There was nothing incriminating about the diagram, he thought, or even—he turned it over—the directions.

"Abdul Dalama has examined this paper"—she nodded toward the eunuch and he nodded back—"and he tells me it says the object pictured has the power to distinguish infidels from believers. Is this correct?"

"No," said al-Hasan. His voice was rusty. The last time he had spoken, it was to Bab Sabu. ("Hurry up!" he might have said, or, "Watch where you put that paddle.") From the corner of his eye, he saw Abdul Dalama's huge shoulders bristle. He hastened to clear his throat. "It only *appears* that the pitcher has this power."

They both looked at him with exactly the same degree of menace and doubt, the beautiful reclining girl and the towering slave.

"It's a trick," he said. "An ingenious device to fool the eye."

"Why did you bring it to Baghdad hidden in your tunic?"

"I wanted to show it to my friend." He almost said al-Razi's name but stopped in time. To calm himself, he breathed in long draughts of musk and ambergris still rising from the bath and from his own skin.

"But why did you *hide* it, this"—she lifted the paper—"'magic pitcher'?"

"Because it is a *trick*," he said. "If everyone knew how it worked, then it would be good for nothing."

The girl and the eunuch continued to give him their steady, opaque look.

"If I had one to show you, then you would see."

That sent a glance darting between them.

"How long would it take you to make such a thing?" the girl asked him.

"That depends," he said. "If I had the proper tools and the materials—"

"How long?"

"Two days?" It was only a guess. His brother Ahmad was the maker of ingenious devices. Al-Hasan was the mathematician, the geometry man, the great deducer, mostly to be found with his nose in the latest translation of Euclid. "Perhaps three days."

"Perhaps," the girl said. She leaned forward and selected a grape from the platter of fruit. "*Perhaps* you would like to know what the Caliph has in mind for you, al-Hasan bin Musa bin Shakir," she said. "Or perhaps"—she glanced at the imposing Abdul Dalama—"you already know."

Al-Hasan avoided glancing at the imposing Abdul. "I have heard that the Caliph takes pleasure in . . . boys . . . I mean, youths who are not—"

"The Caliph takes his pleasures with whomsoever he pleases." She popped the grape into her mouth. "The only distinction he makes is in what happens when those pleasures are denied him. If *I* refused him, for example, or displeased him in some way, he would have me roundly beaten. Only if he felt *particularly* bored or frustrated would he take more serious measures, perhaps calling upon Mustafa al-Janna for a demonstration of swordsmanship. Wait—you've never heard of Mustafa? He is famous! A swordsman so strong and so swift he can whisk off a prisoner's four limbs and the head, all before the body hits the ground. I've only seen it twice. It is very impressive—messy, of course, but impressive. Incredible, really. Is it not, Abdul?"

"It takes practice, my lady," the eunuch said impassively.

"Of course it does—Oh! But you grow pale needlessly, al-Hasan. The Caliph Amin would never have Mustafa practice on a handsome boy like yourself. What have you? Fourteen years? Fifteen?"

"Seventeen," whispered al-Hasan. It was a lie.

"In truth? You look younger. I advise you to be younger. Now, if *you* refuse the Caliph, he will merely remove your testicles. Well, he will *have* them removed—perhaps by Mustafa! What do you think, Abdul?"

"There is virtue in the swiftness of the blade, my lady."

Al-Hasan struggled to his feet. The room reeled as he staggered to a window and looked down. The drop to the ground was just far enough to mean certain death. The girl's voice seemed to come from afar.

"If you feel you might vomit," she was saying, "may I recommend the brazier rather than the window?"

He turned around. "What can be done?" he cried. "Is there no escape?"

She said, reaching for another grape, "That depends."

"On what?"

"On you."

❦

The plan of action he devised required that messages be sent to his brothers Ahmad and Muhammad, the elder two of the Banu Musa, and to their friend al-Razi, inventor of kerosene. (To al-Hasan's surprise, Abdul the eunuch hid these messages in the split soles of his sandals. It seemed that the well-dressed girl and her servant had secrets of their own to keep from the Caliph.) Al-Razi dwelled in the Street of Scholars in the newest quarter of Baghdad. Al-Hasan's two brothers were camped with their lord Ma'mun's allies in the palace on the opposite bank from that of the Caliph Amin. All three of the Banu Musa had been summoned by Ma'mun a few weeks earlier to take careful measurements and verify predictions regarding the Tigris at flood stage. Ma'mun did not wish to see his troops inundated by spring floods before he seized the city.

"Do not mention my name," the girl told al-Hasan as he wrote out his messages on bits of parchment in the tiniest possible script.

"How can I mention it when you have never told me what it is?"

"How wise of me," she said, but when she and the eunuch Abdul Dalama returned the next day, she told him she was called Gamal'Abayad.

"White She-Camel?"

"A person as clever as yourself surely knows that *gamal* also means 'beautiful woman.'"

"To whom? A camel driver?"

The towering Abdul Dalama placed a large wooden trunk on the floor. "Take care," he whispered. "Her father was a camel driver." He drew his finger across his throat.

They had come to deliver the materials Al-Hasan needed to make the magic pitcher. (A return message from his brothers had arrived in a water jar before dawn.) Al-Hasan thought the trunk at his feet looked

a lot like the one into which he had been stuffed upon his capture at
the river. It smelled of fish and goats. His heart sank as he rummaged
through the box. It would be difficult enough to construct the device
from sheets of newly pounded metal. The assortment of brass pots and
ewers and other metal containers in the box meant additional hours of
cutting and disassembly before the real work could begin. And what
had he told her? Two days? Three? "Where is the tool for soldering? I
must have one! Every seam must be so tightly sealed that air cannot—"

She stooped to pull something from the box. "Is this what you
seek?"

He took what she offered, hiding his surprise. She lifted a squat
metal pitcher from the box, turned it appraisingly, replaced it, and chose
another. "A woman may know more than you think, al-Hasan," she said.
"Your lord Ma'mun's Persian mother was very young when she gave
birth to him. You already know, perhaps, that she was not the Caliph's
first wife? And that the first wife cast her out immediately after Ma'mun's
birth, even before the child was weaned? Think of it! The mother of
Ma'mun—he who will soon, very soon, be Caliph and Commander of
the Faithful on earth—was sold to a camel driver! And the camel driver
sold her years later to a metalsmith in Isfahan, shortly after she gave
birth to me. The camel driver was hoping for a male child, you see. The
metalsmith cared more about the length and strength of my fingers than
what was between my legs."

The youngest of the Banu Musa was not accustomed to women
speaking to him so frankly. He cleared his throat. "Then you are Ma'mun's
half-sister! Does he know of this?"

"Ma'mun has many, many half-sisters." She examined a battered
brass ewer the size of a donkey's head—the very one they would soon
transform, adding a long spout, a hollow handle, and numerous compart-
ments and passageways within. "But only one of them is a *metalsmith*."

The work on the pitcher had barely begun when the Caliph Amin sent
word, commanding al-Hasan's presence at the evening's revelry under the

dome in the Palace of the Golden Gate. Appropriate clothing, oils, perfumes, and a persuasive escort of eunuchs would be delivered to him.

The White She-Camel (as he could not but think of her) scowled
when he shared the distressing news. "We knew it was coming," she
said.

"How can I get out of it?" al-Hasan asked her.

"You cannot, I'm afraid."

"But . . . if he desires—"

"What other choice is there, al-Hasan? We have to bide our time
until the pitcher is ready." Taking up the soldering iron, she added, "I
know the prospect does not please you, but from my own experience, I
can tell you this: it is not a fate *worse* than death."

It was a fate that al-Hasan was determined to avoid.

Whether alone or with the surreptitious help of Gamal 'Abayad,
he labored without cease in the day, and at night he attended such
revels as were expected of him, somehow remaining out of sight until
the Caliph had consumed too much wine to remember his own name,
much less the existence of his prisoner, the youngest of the Banu Musa.
The revels grew stranger each night. The Caliph Amin came and went
at odd times, missing the meat course on the first night and delaying
the dessert of tiny layered almond cakes that looked quite delectable but
tasted like paper, which was what, in fact, they were. ("Who eats cakes
made of *paper*?" al-Hasan asked Gamal'Abayad the next day, and she said,
"Residents of a city two years besieged.") On the third night, supper was
lacking entirely, as if it had been forgotten, much to the disappointment
of al-Hasan and many of the other guests. As for the Caliph, he rode
and rode his wooden horse around the candlelit courtyard at the head
of a phalanx of his best officers, each of them mounted on the back of
a soldier outfitted with bit and bridle and broom-straw tail. There were
no horses left in Baghdad, Abdul Dalama told al-Hasan, every last one
slaughtered and eaten. "Last night's meat course?" al-Hasan whispered
as the Caliph rode past. Abdul Dalama, who was being so kind as to

shield the youngest of the Banu Musa from the Caliph's gaze, remarked over his massive shoulder that the population of cats in the city appeared to be dwindling.

But it was the following afternoon when the fate that was not *worse* than death drew closest to al-Hasan. He had finished rereading his brother Ahmad's missive regarding the relatively safe and effective operation of the magic pitcher (having long since eaten the pomegranate peel in which the message was hidden), and he was practicing the smooth and—it was to be hoped—imperceptible shifting of his thumb from one small hole on the handle to another, testing the pitcher by pouring either water or nothing at all into a pair of drinking cups placed side by side on the window's stone sill, when he heard a commotion outside the door. A slave named Yuqub who had been delivered to him just this morning as personal servant, bodyguard, and jailer all in one turned around at his post to assess the newcomers and immediately fell to the floor. Amin himself came through the door, stepped over the flattened Yuqub, and looked around the room. Strips and pieces of metal cut from various utensils curled on the stone sills of the windows and, hazardously, on the floor. The brazier smoked beside a large stone jar of cold water. Tools and bits of wood lay strewn about.

Al-Hasan's heart rose into his throat. His first thought was, *Here it comes.* Having never seen the Commander of the Faithful at quite such close range before, he discovered that the Caliph, when standing on his own two feet, was an ordinary-looking man. Tall, yes, but bald at the temples and perhaps paler than average, with a hooked nose and small eyes that were half closed at the moment, a result of tipping his head back to regard al-Hasan appraisingly, his arms folded across his muscular chest.

"You have been avoiding the Commander of the Faithful, O youngest son of Musa."

Not sure if he would get in more trouble by admitting this was true or by telling the Caliph he was wrong, al-Hasan said nothing. He noticed that the Caliph's entourage of nabobs and amirs, gathered in the doorway behind him, appeared to be signaling to al-Hasan with increasing urgency. They were pointing to the floor. Al-Hasan looked down at his bare feet on the black and white marble tiles—and then he understood.

"Oh, get up, get up," the Caliph said. "And take off your robe."

Al-Hasan reminded himself: *It is not a fate* worse *than death.* He hung his robe over the brazier.

"Now your tunic."

"To hear is to—"

"Just do it, my boy."

Al-Hasan thanked God the Merciful, the Compassionate, that he had wrapped his loins in linen this morning, something he did not do every day. In the doorway, the Caliph's entourage watched him now with expressions of perfect blankness. Yuqub had not lifted his face from the floor.

"And now, perhaps . . . the turban!"

So saying, the Caliph plucked from al-Hasan's sweaty neck the loose end of his rather meager and lopsided turban, which, together with the linen down below, was all that kept the youngest of the Banu Musa from a state of complete nakedness. Al-Hasan closed his eyes. The Caliph skimmed his finger across the boy's chest, just below the collarbone, causing him to break out in goose bumps, whereupon the Caliph laughed and said, "How we love these handsome Persians."

Al-Hasan hunched his shoulders and held his breath and waited for whatever was coming next. To his great surprise—and greater relief—the Caliph abruptly stopped tickling his chest and said, in a different tone, "Well, what have we here?"

Al-Hasan opened his eyes. The Caliph was at the window, holding the modified pitcher up to the late afternoon light. It looked sadly improvised, al-Hasan thought, every dimple and seam visible.

"It is my gift for you, Commander of the Faithful," al-Hasan said. This was a little stratagem, in case the Caliph discovered the pitcher before they could spring it on him in public. In a burst of inspiration al-Hasan added, "And it is also the reason for my seclusion. I have only just completed it."

At least the Caliph Amin didn't laugh. Al-Hasan stumbled on.

"I know you have many pitchers, Commander of the Faithful, and all are more beautiful than this one, I am sure, but *this* one . . ." He darted a look at the doorway. "This one is a magic pitcher."

"Magic?" said Amin. He tipped the pitcher, as if to pour. "In what way *magic?*"

Al-Hasan lowered his voice. "If we can be alone for a moment, sire"—he prayed this was not a mistake—"I can explain."

Amin's eyes lit up in surprise and anticipation. He waved at his entourage and they disappeared through the doorway, Yuqub following on his hands and knees. When al-Hasan intimated that the device could be used to expose unbelievers into whose cup the pitcher would permit no liquid to flow, the Caliph was beside himself at the prospect.

"Show me," he said, "show me!"

Al-Hasan dipped a carafe into the water jar and poured its contents slowly and carefully into the mouth of the pitcher. He handed the Caliph a cup—"If you will, my lord." The Caliph gripped the cup with both hands, eagerly.

Al-Hasan tipped the pitcher carefully.

No water issued forth.

Al-Hasan tipped the pitcher farther, and then a little farther, with the same result.

Amin's face darkened. Fury rushed across his features, preceded by something else. Was it fear? The pitcher wobbled in al-Hasan's hand. Although terror threatened to overcome him at any moment, he held the Caliph's eyes for another second, and another, and while they were both pinned in each other's gaze, the boy shifted his thumb imperceptibly, uncovering a small hole in the hollow handle of the pitcher. Water trickled forth.

The darkness drained from the Caliph's face, but when the cup was full, he flung the water out the window with one disdainful thrust.

"I must say that your magic pitcher doesn't work *particularly* well."

Al-Hasan apologized. "I'm afraid I need more practice." It would also help, he thought, if he could put his clothes back on, but he didn't say this, adding instead, "It is a trick, you see."

Amin's face darkened again. "I do not care for tricks."

Al-Hasan took a deep breath. "If I may be bold, my lord, I think you will enjoy this one."

He was right. As the youngest of the Banu Musa explained how the pitcher worked—how covering the little hole kept air from entering the pitcher, which, in turn, prevented the water from pouring out—the Caliph's expression changed. By the end of al-Hasan's second demonstration, using the cups on the stone sill of the window, the Caliph was bouncing on his toes.

"Oh, my dear boy," he said. "*Think* of the possibilities. How absolutely *ingenious*."

When Amin called for the door to be opened, the gleeful satisfaction in his voice and on his face left everyone in the Caliph's entourage quite certain of what had just transpired between the Commander of the Faithful and the youngest of the Banu Musa.

On the terrace of the Khuld that night, a thousand and one candles turned darkness into day.

The family and guests of the Caliph were a little more anxious than usual, being in plain sight of Ma'mun's troops on the other side of the river, but the Caliph had resolved to display his valuable (and cooperative) prisoner in the sight of his foes. The banquet laid out on platters of silver and gold included roast mutton and quail and the great fish called *biz*—each fish a platterful—together with every kind of fruit and sweet cake. Ma'mun's troops could not discern from the other side of the river that all these delicacies were made of clay and tar. Although the wine was merely water, the Caliph announced that it had been obtained by his father, the renowned Harun al-Rashid, from a band of holy *kalandars* who were themselves, as monks, forbidden to taste their own wares. It would be served from a special pitcher—here Amin raised his voice to carry across the river—by their honored guest, the youngest of the Banu Musa, Al-Hasan bin Musa bin Shakir.

The youngest of the Banu Musa rose to his feet, breathed deeply to still the shaking of his knees, and lifted the pitcher above his head for all to see. He avoided looking at Gamal'Abayad, who was seated on a Persian carpet at the feet of the Caliph, her hand resting lightly on the base of an iron lampstand that was as tall as a shepherd's crook. An oil lamp shaped like a gravy boat hung from the lampstand on a golden chain, illuminating the eager face of the Caliph as he explained the special nature of the magic pitcher. The Caliph's voice rose for emphasis on certain words, such as *unbeliever* and *exposed*.

All around the terrace, goblets trembled and faces paled. The Caliph Amin was too busy enjoying the terrified expressions of his guests to notice that Gamal'Abayad had curled her fingers around the iron pole of the lampstand. Above her veil, the girl's eyes were bright.

Then the Caliph stood and raised his golden cup. He would be served first.

On the other side of the Tigris, in the camp of Ma'mun, slaves and soldiers stood ready with long poles and little round boats by the water gate. Al-Hasan's brothers—the elder two of the Banu Musa— each gripped the other's arm, their eyes fixed on the candlelit terrace across the river. No one saw the veiled girl shift slightly on her Persian carpet. The lampstand leaned now toward the empty cup in the hands of the Caliph, as if to take a look inside, and as the brightly burning lamp swung forward on its chain, al-Hasan moved his thumb from the hole in the handle of the pitcher and poured forth not wine, not water, but a colorless serving of kerosene. Burning lamp met flammable liquid. From the other side of the river, the brothers of al-Hasan saw a flaming stream that lit the air above the Caliph's cup. And then the pitcher fell, spilling flames.

The fiery hem of al-Hasan's magnificent robe of honor made him run all the faster to the edge of the terrace, where he hurled himself into the river, the White She-Camel right behind him. In the water, the long robe gave him trouble, though, entangling his legs. He coughed and struggled and spit and coughed and floundered, but the opposite bank with its little round boats seemed no closer. He had no idea what had become of Gamal'Abayad. Al-Hasan went under. It is said that the Tigris ran deeper in those times. He struggled to the surface once again, then sank again, and then time stretched out calmly before him the way we've heard it does, giving him a chance to rue the bitterness of ending thus, if end this was, before he had read half the books of Euclid or written a single one of his own. And that's where the story *almost* ended—right *before* the rescue of Gamal'Abayad and al-Hasan—because that's when Theo Boykin woke up.

You forgot about him, didn't you? You, and the Garnerer of graveyards.

My sister May barely had time to deposit Gamal and al-Hasan, gasping and sputtering, on the banks of the Tigris, before we heard a big commotion heading our way across the schoolyard. It was Etta George come running, waving her arms over her head and pulling at her hair, my own mother right behind her, the both of them whooping and laughing, almost in hysterics, shrieking, "He's awake! He woke up! Theo woke up!"

Pretty near everybody jumped up and took off for the Boykins' house, except for me and May, who was worn out with storytelling.

"Well, praise Jesus," May said wearily. "I just about *knew* he'd come around, didn't you?" She was still sitting in Miss Spivey's chair, her arms wrapped around her big round belly as if she had to hold on to keep it from rolling off her lap. From where I sat, the window was behind May, the pale blue sky tinged with pink. She sat up straight.

"May?" I said. "Is it the baby?"

"Baby's fine," she said. "Kickin' me."

I came and sat across from her, and then I asked what everybody was going to be asking once they had time to think about what they'd heard. "May," I said, "how did you know all those things to tell?"

She shrugged. "Miss Spivey told me some."

"But there was things in that story—I don't see how—"

"Everything was laid out for me in my mind, Gladys. All I had to do was say it out loud."

"That sure enough sounds strange, May."

"It sure enough was."

We heard an automobile coming up the road, getting closer and louder. I looked out and saw Daddy had come back to get us. Leaf shadows were trembling in patches of light against the wall of the school-room. May turned around in her chair to look out the window at the first bolt of sun coming through the trees. "My goodness," she said. "We set up all night."

After the fact, all kinds of theories would be put forth to explain May's feat of storytelling in the schoolhouse that night. (It was, as my brother Force said, a situation lacking in *verisimilitude*.) Mrs. Reverend Stokes saw significance in the fact that May, like Shahrazad, was in a family way. Plenty of folks believed that babies waited in the mind of God before they came out into the world, and as Mrs. Stokes said, *He* sure enough knew the whole story. That's when I found out that Mrs. Reverend Stokes had carried and lost five babies in her life, and every time (she told my momma) the baby had warned her in a dream that it was just too sweet up there in heaven for him or her to give it up and get born. Mrs. Stokes didn't need to hear a thing about *verisimilitude*. She knew this for a fact: "The whole time May was talking, her baby was whisper-ing directly in her ear."

19

Finis

THEO BOYKIN WOKE UP, but he wasn't the same.

Dr. Janet Miller warned us that it might take some time. She said he would tire easily, but stimulation in moderate doses would be good for him. She particularly recommended reading to him. "Read things that he knew before the injury." She called his near-drowning in the white-dirt slough "the injury." (In the end, the county sheriff called it "an accident.") She said, "You never know what will open a door."

We set up a schedule. Ildred and Etta George were the most frequent readers, my brother Force and Eugene Boykin next, and after that came me and Mavis Davis and a whole host of folks from the fifth grade on up. Miss Templeton came all the way from Chicago when she heard— she brought W. E. B. Du Bois (in book form, I mean)—but she couldn't read to Theo for as much as a page before she'd be crying. Theo would open his eyes and say, "What's the matter?"

It was Ildred who discovered how much he had lost.

She told me how her heart lifted when she came to read to Theo one day and found him out in the back, looking at the electrical genera-tor. He was bent over the tractor engine, and when she hollered a joyful,

"Hey! Theo!" he straightened up and turned around, unsmiling, a deeply puzzled look on his face.

After a moment of silence, Ildred said, "Well, here you are outside walking around!" A little of the joy had leaked out of her voice. There was something wrong with Theo's eyes. When she read to him, he usually kept his eyes closed. Now he was looking at her—but that was the problem. He was looking *at* her. His gaze fell on her like a dim beam of light. It bumped into her and bounced off again. She was glad when he turned to look at the contraption behind him instead.

"I made this," he said.

"Well, I know you did," Ildred began, but then she stopped. He was telling himself, not her, a piece of news.

He remembered faces and most names and some places. He recognized everybody after a while. He remembered how to do the things he had to do. He could read, though never as flawlessly as before. That's why we never could convince any doctor that there was anything wrong with this particular colored boy. So he couldn't recite the Declaration of Independence or remember a whole scene from Shakespeare, or figure a batting average in his head? Well, now, the doctor himself couldn't do so well as that. Mrs. Boykin eventually took Theo all the way to Atlanta, but to no avail.

In desperation, Etta George wrote to Dr. Janet Miller, who was in China now, arranging for a women's clinic to get built. It was more than a month before we heard back from her. In the letter, which arrived with Etta's name and *Threestep, Georgia*, surrounded by Chinese writing on the envelope, Dr. Miller said the brain was an organ whose mysteries had yet to be plumbed.

On the morning after that night we sat up in the schoolhouse—which was the night after the Baghdad Bazaar—Momma and Ildred served the biggest breakfast you ever saw. They fed all the folks who'd waited all night for Theo to wake up. I don't know how they did it on such short notice. Like the loaves and the fishes, the food just kept coming: eggs and

pancakes and fried potatoes and grits and biscuits with jam. My brother
Ebenezer and Ed had set boards on sawhorses to make a huge long table
in the yard between the Boykins' house and ours, and they brought out
every chair in both houses as well as barrels, stepladders, wood from the
woodpile, and anything else that looked like a person could sit on it.

My job that morning was to stay inside the house with May and
make sure she didn't get out of bed until Momma called us both to
come on out and get our breakfast. It was an easy job, considering that
May was sound asleep when I first tiptoed into Momma's room and
settled myself with a pillow on the rug. I believe I had just dozed off
when I heard knocking on the front door. I scrambled up to get it as fast
as I could, thinking it was odd they didn't go right around to the yard
out back, where everybody obviously was. I opened the door, and then
I stopped short and looked up.

Standing on the porch outside was a very tall, very white man—I
mean about as white from head to foot as the painted white slaves in
the *Arabian Nights* pageant. He looked like he'd been dipped in flour.
His face and neck and bare arms were all dusted white, as were his pants
and shirt and shoes—but when he lifted his cap, the hair underneath
was black.

"I'm looking for Jefferson Cailiff," he said. "I heard something happened to my boy." As he worried his cap, a dusty shower of white dirt
sifted from his sleeves like snow.

Your boy? was what I was thinking, but I nodded toward the lane
alongside the house. "My daddy's back there with the other folks."

He glanced over that way nervously, then he looked down at me
again. He squinted, as if he were trying to think who I might be. "I'd be
in your debt," he said finally, "if you would fetch him for me, please." He
sounded like he was from up North. He slapped the cap on his thigh,
releasing a white cloud, and added, "Name's Ralph Ford."

I about fell to the floor. What was *Ralph Ford* doing here, right in
my real life?

As if he could read my mind, he said, "I promised I would never set
foot in Threestep again, after all the trouble I brought down on Lily and
on you all—I know I promised—but I have to know about my boy."

I must have squeaked out something in reply.

In Momma's room, May was stretched out on the bed in her slip, but she wasn't asleep. With complete disregard for her delicate condition, I said, "May! Ralph Ford is on our front porch. *Ralph. Ford.* He sent me to fetch Daddy! May, it's Ralph Ford! On our porch."

"Oh, my," she said. She was not as excited as I expected her to be, which was probably good, considering. "I wondered who you were talking to. You better get Daddy." She slid on over to the edge of the bed to sit up.

"He says something's happened to his boy!"

Sitting up, May looked half sad, half worried, and completely worn out. "You better find Daddy right away, Gladys."

"But where did *Ralph Ford* come from all of a sudden?"

She sighed. "Dry Branch, I reckon. That's where he lives."

"In Twiggs County?" Twiggs was two counties over from Piedmont. "Ralph Ford who saved our daddy's life in France lives in Twiggs County?"

"He works in the white dirt plant."

That was a fact I could believe, given his appearance.

"Go get Daddy, Gladys, and we'll see what he has to say."

"But who's Lily? He said he brought trouble down on Lily."

"Lily was his wife. How long were you all talking, for him to tell you his life story, for heaven's sake? Hand me my dress." It was hanging on the back of Momma's chair.

I handed her the dress. "Lily is the name of Mrs. Boykin's sister," I said. "Is Ralph Ford married to Mrs. Boykin's sister?"

May gave me a steady look. She said, "He was."

I pictured the man standing in the doorway, every inch of him that I could see covered in white dirt. I said, "May, are you saying that Ralph Ford *is* a colored man?"

"Gladys, if I answer that one question, will you go get Daddy this instant?"

I said, "Yes, I will."

She said, "No, he is not."

True to my word, I turned and ran to the front door.

Ralph Ford was gone. The porch was empty. Nothing out there but Momma's neatly swept front yard. It was enough to make me wonder if he'd been there at all—until I looked down. White footprints led to one side of the porch, as if he might have stepped down there, and sure enough, when I raised my eyes, I saw him and my daddy in the lane under the pine trees, walking away from the house toward the road. Daddy had his arm around Ralph Ford's shoulders. The man was half a head taller than Daddy, which was odd to see.

Breakfast was not what you'd call a festive occasion, considering everything that happened, but pretty much everybody I cared about was there. Even May ate a bite before she went back to bed for the rest of the day, incidentally avoiding me and my questions. Eugene Boykin, whose face was still puffed up from the beating he took, came out of the house with Dr. Miller, as if she'd talked him into it. The top of her head about reached his elbow. The only ones missing were Theo, who was sitting up in his bed eating pie with a dazed look on his face, and Uncle Mack, who was out in the barn with the baby camel, and my brother Force. He was still over in Claytonville in the county jail with Arnie Lumpkin at the time.

Miss Spivey was missing, too, of course, but I wasn't so sure how much I cared about her right then, I'm sorry to say. Fooling with my brother Force was one thing, and forgivable, to my mind. Running away was not.

Ralph Ford was also there. I don't know where Daddy took him to clean up, but he wasn't dusted white anymore. Now you could tell he was a black-haired man with what they call olive skin, which is really a shade of brown. He was sitting near the other end of the big long table, next to my daddy and right across from Dr. Janet Miller and Eugene, his head and shoulders sticking up taller than anyone else. Having Ralph Ford at the table was like having FDR or Douglas Fairbanks, Sr., drop by—someone you believed existed but never expected to see in the flesh. I was still eating pancakes when Ralph Ford got up from the table.

A lot of eyes followed him as he disappeared around the front of the house, but nobody said a word about it, and neither did I.

After breakfast, we didn't know what to do with ourselves. Ralphord, who must have thought Ralph Ford was just another stranger at the table, tagged along with me until we ran into Etta George coming out of the Boykins' house with a covered plate in her hands. She said Dr. Janet Miller was in there asking Theo who people were and what year it was.

"He don't know what *year* it is?" said Ralphord.

I said, "Do *you*?" He said, "It's 1939!" but he had to think about it.

Etta George lifted the covered plate and said, "This is for Uncle Mack."

We found him in the corner stall of Bibbens' barn, sitting on his heels like a Badawi camel driver while he tended to Ahmed, a whitened ribbon's worth of camel bells wound around his hand. The wreckage of Sabrina's cargo, only one bundle of which had been saved, was spread out to dry in white heaps on the straw-covered floor. Theo's magic pitcher sat atop one of the heaps, looking like a pitcher made of clay. I took over holding the bottle for Ahmed. Before Uncle Mack took his plate from Etta, he sat down on a bale of hay and set his wooden box—the one in which he carried his pages—on his knees. When he opened the wooden box, we saw a thick white paste coating the inside, and that was all. Ralphord asked, "Where's your pages?"

Uncle Mack looked into the box.

Later that morning, Daddy didn't have to ask me twice if I wanted to go with him to Claytonville to get my brother Force out of jail.

Deputy Sheriff Linwood Perkins had already gone to Claytonville the day before to try and talk the county sheriff, a man named Butts, into letting my brother go. Sheriff Butts said no. He said that even if Force *wasn't* guilty of beating up the one colored boy (he meant Eugene) and almost drowning the other, not to mention destroying valuable property (he meant the camel)—even if Force wasn't guilty of all that, he was sure enough guilty of resisting arrest when he refused to cease and desist from pounding on the other white boy (that was Arnie Lumpkin) while the sheriff was trying to get them both into his vehicle. Sheriff Butts thought that a night in jail was the kind of thing that might do my brother Force some good. My daddy told Linwood Perkins that he had some ideas about what kind of thing might do Sheriff Butts some good, but Linwood advised Daddy to keep those ideas to himself.

Daddy had some kind of idea in his head right now, some particular reason he'd asked me to come along, I could tell by the way he sat for a minute, rubbing the steering wheel with his thumbs. Finally, he put the Ford in gear. As we bumped down the lane, he said, slowly, as if to give me time to take it in, "Ralph Ford used to be married to Mrs. Boykin's sister Lily. Did you know that, Gladys?"

I knew I wasn't supposed to know it—and for all of my life until this morning, I hadn't known it, so it was true enough for me to say, "No, sir, I *didn't*."

"Well, he was. They met each other when he came to visit me after the war, and they ran off together."

"Why'd they do that?"

Daddy glanced at me, then back out the windshield. "I reckon they fell in love."

I couldn't see much out the windshield myself. This was before my growth spurt. I waited until we'd turned onto the road before I asked Daddy the same question I'd asked May.

"Is Ralph Ford a colored man?"

"No, Gladys, he is not." Daddy paused to shift again as we picked up speed. "That's why the Ku Klucks set fire to the Boykins' peach orchard," he said. "Almost got their house burnt down with it. Our chicken coop, too."

"*That's* how our chicken coop got burnt? Ku Klucks?" I could see it like a flash: white-robed night-riders coming up our lane in the darkness, torches in the air.

Daddy continued. "When Ralph and Lily came back again the next year, they were married. Mr. Boykin told Lily it was too dangerous for them to stay with the Boykins in Threestep. For them and for us. I hope you can understand that, Gladys."

Daddy went quiet after he said that. He looked like he was trying to decide what else he could tell me at my young age. "Up North," he finally said, "Ralph Ford's people thought Lily was white. Now she was expecting, she had to worry about how her baby might give her away. That's why she came down here and went on out to that island, before her time came, where she and Mrs. Boykin had some kin."

I thought about that for a minute, and then I asked, "Did she have a boy or a girl?"

"She had a little boy," Daddy said. He knew that wasn't what I was really asking. "Color of chocolate."

I looked at my hand, braced on the seat. It was about the color of bread dough.

"Ralph found a home for colored children in Atlanta—a good one, started many years ago by a lady who worked for the railroad after she was freed. There were people on the island who would have been happy to take the child—distant cousins of Lily and Mrs. Boykin, I reckon— but life was pretty simple on that island. Ralph thought the boy would have a better chance for a good life in Atlanta. Lily appeared to agree with that plan."

We were coming into Claytonville now, going past the railroad yard, where they had big piles of white dirt on the side of the tracks, every-thing dusted white from the rails to the road we were on. It was slippery. Daddy said, "Ralph got Lily and that baby as far as the train station in Savannah."

They were ordinary words, but the way he said them, I didn't think I wanted to hear the rest of the story.

Daddy was coming back home from Savannah himself at the time, he said. He didn't say why. He was in the station, already on the train, looking out the window of the coach car, when he caught sight of a handsome couple stepping out of the depot on the other side of the tracks. They were engaged in a fierce argument, or so it seemed from the look on the man's face—the man's face! Daddy sat up straight in his seat on the train. It was Ralph Ford. And Lily. He hadn't seen Ralph Ford or Lily for months, not since Mr. Boykin turned them away. Lily was cradling a bundle of blankets. Daddy hurried back to the end of the coach car and down the little steps. "Ralph!" he called.

Lily spun toward the familiar voice. From her startled expression, Daddy thought that she was going to run away into the depot, but then something changed in her face, in her whole body, and she came running across the platform toward the trains instead, calling, "Mr. Cailiff? Is that *Mr. Cailiff*?" as if she'd been looking for him all of her life so far.

Maybe, if she'd had more time, she might have gone back inside the depot and walked across on the second floor to the other platform—or maybe she was too desperate to think that straight. Just at that moment, everybody's ears were split by the whistle coming from the Central of Georgia. That was Daddy's train. Steam billowed up from under the cars. Lily must have felt that it was now or never. She stopped dead at the edge of the platform. From the other side of the tracks, looking at her face all lit up with sudden hope and craziness, Daddy said he could tell—he was prepared to testify—that she fully expected him to catch that child. When Ralph Ford saw what she meant to do, he started to move toward her, as did two uniformed station attendants, but they were too late, all of them.

The little bundle of baby flew up in the air, sailing over one, two, three sets of tracks, so startled that it didn't make a sound, although the little hands shot out of the blanket like stars.

When Daddy pulled up in front of the red-brick family home of Sheriff Butts, we had been quiet in the car since the edge of town. A great big cottonwood tree shaded the walk leading up to the white porch that wrapped around the house. You would never guess, if you didn't already know, that inside that house was a jail. Daddy asked me if I wanted to come inside with him. Although I'd wanted to see the bookcase in the dining room that hid the iron door to the jail ever since my brother Ebenezer told me about it (not saying how he knew), I didn't have the heart for it now. I said I'd wait out on the porch. They were working on the Piedmont County Courthouse across the street from the sheriff's at the time, making it bigger. Ebenezer and May's husband Ed had stood in line for two days, hoping to get on that construction job. I was sorry it was Sunday today, all the hammering and sawing stilled. I would have welcomed a racket right then. I kept seeing the face in the portrait in Mrs. Boykin's parlor, so pretty and hopeful. I kept seeing the little hands like stars.

Force came out first, looking like a mournful shadow of his usual self, with a black eye and a swollen lip messing up his handsome face. Arnie Lumpkin must have gotten a few licks in, too, while they were busy resisting arrest.

"Hey, Gladys," was all he said to me.

Daddy offered to let Force drive us home. I knew my brother was in a really bad way when he declined.

Arnie Lumpkin was released from jail "for lack of evidence" a few days later. By then Uncle Mack had told Linwood Perkins and Sheriff Butts that he was almost a hundred percent sure it was Arnie Lumpkin, white robe and all, who helped him pull Theo out from under Sabrina in the slough. Arnie didn't have a word to say about it one way or the other. He wasn't talking much to anybody.

My sister May must have been waiting to hear Daddy's truck come back from Claytonville. When I walked past the house, I heard, "Pssst— Gladys!" from the front window. I was surprised to find her sitting in Momma's rocking chair. She was supposed to be asleep in bed. She said she couldn't get comfortable lying down. What all did Daddy tell me, she wanted to know. I told her some, the parts I could bring myself to say out loud, and then I said, "Well, I wonder what Daddy was doing in Savannah. Back then, I mean. Don't you?"

"Visiting Momma," May said promptly. "It was right after Force was born. We've got to go to Savannah sometime, Gladys, you and me, take my girls with us. It is a beautiful place. The hospital where Momma was?

It's a big old brick building, with all kind of what you call wrought-iron balconies and tall windows. And right across the street was the park with a big fountain and that Spanish moss hanging on the trees. Momma had her a view out that hospital window."

"You were there? Daddy took you to Savannah?" I said. This was a part of the story of my brother's birth I had definitely never heard. "You went right to the hospital?"

"They wouldn't let us go inside," May said. "We had to stand on the sidewalk and wave to her. Momma was on the second floor. There was a big window they wheeled her right up to, with Force in her arms. She blew us kisses down to the sidewalk. And then she unwrapped him a little and she had the nurse hold him up higher so we could see his foot sticking out of the blankets. I didn't know what it was about at the time, but that was the *foot*. She was showing Daddy the foot. Oh, my, Gladys! I remember him laughing. He was just so happy to see her. I know he was scared she would die. He would've stood on that sidewalk looking up at her all day, if Ildred hadn't started pitchin' a fit."

I said, "*Ildred* was there, too?"

May caught my tone. "She can't remember a thing about it, Gladys, she was so small. She don't even remember staying with Aunt Virginia till Momma came home. After the Ku Klucks came around that time, Daddy didn't care to have us sleeping at our house, in case they set another fire at night."

I had been living in a world I knew nothing about. That's what I was thinking. Here we were, May and I, sitting in Momma's bedroom, but it was like we were sitting in two different worlds. Tragedies and wonders had happened in hers that I'd never heard of. I had to ask her, "May, did you *see* Lily throw her baby across the tracks?"

She had. I could tell by her face. "Can you imagine how awful that was for her, Gladys? How desperate she must've been? I reckon she thought if Daddy brought her baby back here and gave him to Mrs. Boykin, at least she could see him again sometimes. Poor Lily!"

We sat in silence while I worked up the courage to say out loud the question I couldn't bring myself to ask Daddy.

"Did the baby die?"

May looked surprised I would even ask. "No," she said.

"No? He got throwed across the railroad tracks and—was he hurt bad?"

"No."

"How can that be true?" I asked her.

"On account Daddy caught him," she said.

"Daddy *caught* him?"

"He sure did. Daddy didn't tell you that part? He must have thought you knew, Gladys. Everybody on that train hooted and cheered when he did it, too. I don't know what would have happened to Lily if Daddy hadn't caught the baby. She might've gone to jail. Although anyone could see she wasn't right in her head at the time she did it."

"Are you saying that Daddy did in actual fact give the baby to Mrs. Boykin?"

"Of course he did," May said. "It's not our place to mention it, though. Maybe I ought to try the bed for a while, Gladys. I'm about to fall over, I'm so tired."

I held the rocking chair still so she could get up, my mind going a hundred miles an hour the whole time. I had more things I wanted to ask May, plenty more, but her eyes were closing already, so I only said, "If it wasn't for Daddy catching that baby, we'd have lost Theo way back then, before we ever knew him!"

May roused herself enough to say, "It wasn't Theo Daddy caught. It was Eugene." She dropped off to sleep without another word.

He'll snap out of it, people kept saying.

We wanted to believe that, and so we watched Theo's face, waiting for the flash, the cleverness, to return to his eyes, watching for the half smile, the slow tilt of his head that meant a really good idea had just popped into it. Everybody watched Theo's face—Mrs. Reverend Stokes and the Bibbens and Linwood Perkins and Mavis Davis and even Arnie Lumpkin—but Theo's face stayed blank. He didn't talk much, either. As weeks and then months went by, it got harder and harder to believe that it was Theo in there.

Then, in April, when we hadn't heard from Miss Spivey for almost a year, a package arrived at Bibbens' store that was addressed in her own handwriting to *Theophilus Boykin, Chief Engineer of the Baghdad Bazaar.* The package was about the size of a small suitcase and appeared to have come, from the writing on the wrapper, all the way from Baghdad. The one in Iraq.

Word spread. You would have thought Mr. Bibben was the Pied Piper, the way we chased his delivery truck from the store to the Boykins' kitchen. Half a dozen of us crowded in to watch Theo dig through the excelsior until he got to a book covered in reddish leather, maybe twelve inches by eighteen in its dimensions and about two inches thick. Along with the book there was a note with May's name on it. It came out that she had written to Miss Spivey shortly after the first Baghdad Bazaar, almost a year ago, strongly suggesting that Miss Spivey ought to get hold of one of those *Kitab* books of *Ingenious Devices* and send it to Theo directly. May believed it might bring him around. Miss Spivey had finally found one.

In her note, she told May that the book was worth quite a lot of money and should be handled carefully. The cover—plain red leather with Arabic letters in gold—was clearly new, but the book itself was *old*. The pages had feathery edges and a sweet smell. Theo sat down at the kitchen table with the book in front of him, the features of his face arranged into a flat look of mild interest. He learned to do that after a while, practiced with a mirror. (I believe he knew that something was wrong from the way we looked at him.) He turned the pages carefully. We stood around the table and watched, waiting for him to say something. When he had turned about a dozen pages, he sat back and said, "I can't read this anymore."

"It's in Arabian, Theo," Ildred said. "You never did know Arabian."

"Good, 'cause I can't make heads or tails."

"Keep looking awhile," Etta George suggested gently.

Theo turned another page or two. Then he sat straight up and said, "I know this one! I know all about it."

We couldn't read the words, of course, but all of us recognized the magic pitcher from Uncle Mack's lost pages. Ildred ran to get the one Theo made. Mrs. Boykin had cleaned it up and kept it on a shelf in her pantry. Theo took it up in his hands, turned it this way and that, and then he started explaining to us how it worked. He sounded like he had just discovered America. We filled it with water, and he put his thumb on the one hole in the handle and then the other, so it wouldn't pour out, and then it would. Then, all of a sudden, he stopped talking. He had thought of something. He said, "I know a story about this here."

Ildred pressed the heel of her hand into one eye, then the other, and asked, "How does it go?"

"It's got two caliphs in it," he said.

Ildred slipped her arm through mine and we leaned our heads together, grinning like Cailiffs.

Theo laughed. He *laughed*. "The other kind," he said, and he proceeded to tell us a story that we already knew. When he came to the end, I asked him where he learned that story. Did he read it somewhere? He frowned. "Gladys, I don't rightly know where I got that story from."

"Maybe Miss Spivey told you," Ildred said. "Or Uncle Mack."

He considered that possibility. "Maybe." He picked up his own magic pitcher and tipped it over the cups on the table, slipping his thumb back and forth on the handle to make the water stop and go until it ran out entirely. He shrugged. "It seems like I've known that story for a long time."

That was all he could tell us.

The next morning, Theo was missing from his bed. Eugene ran all over until he found him in Bibbens' barn, leaning over the base of the minaret, which had sustained some damage. "Theo?" Eugene said, and when Theo looked up, his face was alive again.

The second Baghdad Bazaar was therapy for Theo Boykin, pure and simple. The third and the fourth were, too. By the fifth, the proceeds from which were used to pay off Mamie Eskew Veal's mortgage when one of the Veal boys did not come home from the war, we realized that Theo's transformation from shadow of his former self to Chief Engineer again was, like that of the town, a temporary one. My momma called it "seasonal." She said Theo was like the trees budding out in spring, the way he responded to the light of lengthening days.

He would start "waking up" in April when the boys hauled the flats and things out of the barn for painting and repair, his face gradually growing more alert, his movements quicker as days passed. He'd start talking more, coming up with ideas for little improvements and clever repairs, eager to make something new for this year's bazaar from the *Kitab al-Hiyal* Miss Spivey had sent to him. It appeared to be easy as ever for him to look at those line drawings sprinkled with Arabic letters and make them pop up three-dimensional in his brain. And that was only one step (well, it was actually many complicated steps involving welding torches, tin snips, soldering irons, and the like) from making them real in the world. For a long time, Theo constructed at least one new and, of course, ingenious device every year. We put them on display in a tent we called the House of Wisdom.

During the Baghdad Bazaar, Theo would go around dressed in his Bedouin robes, doing little demonstrations with various ingenious devices, telling the story of the two caliphs while pouring or not pouring from the magic pitcher, things like that. Every year, even after we knew better, we couldn't help but hope he'd turned the corner for good, but by the time the camels left town, he'd be quiet again. We bought our first camel in 1943, hoping that would keep Theo on board year-round, but it didn't. We also turned the story of the two caliphs into a play— that was mostly Mrs. Blount's doing—and we came very close once again to burning down the town when somebody went and put actual kerosene into the magic pitcher for the climactic scene. No one was hurt, thanks to quick thinking by the White She-Camel (played by my sister Ildred), whose mighty left-handed toss of the pitcher sent it flying through the air like a meteor hauling a tail of flame. One building did catch fire, though, whereupon Cecil Wicker, then chief of the Baghdad

Volunteer Fire Department, made a strategic decision to save the buildings on either *side* of Mr. Gordon's law office, it being pretty far gone by
the time folks could get out of their costumes.

In the time between bazaars, Theo worked for May's husband Ed
and my brother Ebenezer, who added automobile repair and salvage to
their stove business, mostly so that Ed could be at home more with the
children. I mean no disrespect to automobile mechanics—my brother
Ebenezer made more money in that line than all the rest of us put
together, and Force didn't do too bad, either—but anybody who thinks
Theo Boykin being an automobile mechanic for the rest of his life is a
happy ending, well, I feel sorry for that person. Etta George came home
from her medical studies one year and said that as far as she could tell it
was a "persistent stupor" that Theo was in, and that there was always the
hope that what pulled him out of it once could do it again and maybe
for good. Much later, she admitted to me her true opinion that Theo's
"radical alteration of function and affect" every spring was more a matter of our perception of him than of reality. In other words, Theo took
an interest in the Baghdad Bazaar. Beyond that, we were seeing what we
wanted to see. To which I say: everyone is entitled to her own opinion.

He returned to us every year until 1991, when he passed away at
the age of sixty-nine. It happened in January, not long after Mavis Davis
Bonner and her church group came back from trying to be human
shields by camping out around mosques and minarets in Baghdad (the
one in Iraq). Theo was in Bibbens' barn with Ildred and her husband
Jack when he suddenly lit up as if he'd been struck with a *really* good
idea. At first it seemed as if the miracle we'd been waiting for, lo, these
fifty years had finally come to pass, because here it was still the dead of
winter and the light was back in Theo's eyes as if it were April or May.
But it wasn't a miracle. It was a stroke. I remember sitting around the
emergency waiting room with Ildred and Force and Mavis, looking at
the TV while that CNN reporter described the bombing (over and over
again) from the top of some hotel in Baghdad. It took me a while to
place it, but the excitement in the man's voice put me in mind of listening to that other "reporter" tell about the Martians coming across the
river in New York City on the radio, in 1938. It sounded like *War of the*

Worlds, only this time there was no Bedouin outside the window to tell us that it wasn't for real.

Cailiff's Stove & Auto Repair still occupies a corner building in Baghdad, Georgia, with a three-bay garage on Spring Street. There are not and never have been any stoves or auto parts in the storefront window. It's Ingenious Devices, wall to wall: our permanent collection of self-trimming oil lamps and all kinds of vessels—some sliced in half the long way so you can see the siphon pipes and chambers inside. You can hardly believe what Theo was able to do with sheet metal and scraps. But the piece of resistance, as Ildred has always called it, is the hydro-powered organ. Theo spent several years on that one. They carried it outside on a wagon bed flanked by camels for his funeral, Pinkie Lou Griffith playing away on it at the age of ninety-five with tears streaming down her ancient face.

I have put off telling you about May.

May was supposed to take comprehensive examinations at Peabody High School on the Wednesday following the first Baghdad Bazaar. If she passed, she would receive her high school diploma from the Department of Education of the state of Georgia by virtue of the power invested in Peabody High School, or vice versa, I'm not sure. Miss Spivey had arranged this in advance with a very nice teacher at Peabody by the name of Miss French (who, ironically, taught English) so that May could get her diploma before the new baby was born, but with all the worry and excitement about Theo—and the sudden departure of Miss Spivey—May's appointment with Miss French came and went.

"I'm not sure I was ready anyway," May said, trying to make the best of it.

On the last Friday in June 1939, three weeks after the first annual Baghdad Bazaar, my sister May gave birth to a baby girl that she named

Grace in spite of everything. May labored long and hard—that pain she always had in her side just about did her in—but they both came through it all right, much to everyone's relief.

In September, May was surprised to receive a letter from Miss French, offering to reschedule the examinations. "Well," May said, "I reckon I've about forgotten everything by now." Unbeknownst to any of us, she made an appointment with Miss French anyway, and she passed every one of those exams. The *Milledgeville Ledger* took a picture of May sitting in a chair on the stage at the graduation in June, wearing the beautiful long gown that Miss Spivey had given to her for this very purpose. She had a corsage of roses on her shoulder and her diploma in her lap, with five of her children standing around her and big Ed behind her, holding Grace, the new baby. The picture was grainy, given the newspaper technology of the time, and they got the names of the children in the wrong order, but we sent a copy to Miss Spivey at the Nashville address Mrs. Bibben had for her, not knowing that she was out of the country.

In February, Mrs. Blount asked May if she could play Shahrazad again at the *second* annual Baghdad Bazaar, but May said, "Let somebody else have a chance this year." She was expecting again. Ildred was all for dragging Ed off and having him fixed like a steer. By the way Momma pressed her lips together when Ildred said *that*—instead of threatening to wash her mouth out with soap, no matter if she was twenty-one years old—I could tell that evil thoughts had crossed Momma's mind, too.

May was feeling too poorly to attend the second annual Baghdad Bazaar at all. Momma missed it, too, as she was staying out in McIntyre with May by then, keeping an eye on her and little Ed and baby Grace. The girls—Bitsy and Mimi and Dolly and little May—were staying at our place and coming to school with me. (Mrs. Lulu Blount was our teacher for the year. She was no Miss Spivey.) The pain in May's side was worse than ever this time. It kept her awake at night. They had the doctor come from Claytonville, but he couldn't find anything. (Years later, May's granddaughter Bette would insist it was all the white dirt May had taken to settle her stomach over the years sitting in a lump in her intestine. Nobody will ever know for sure.) Momma and Daddy had just about decided to take her to the hospital—"In Savannah?" May said dreamily, although they had in mind someplace closer by—when she went into labor at home on June 13, 1940. The doctor was there when the baby was born. "A boy for little Ed," May said in a whisper, and called him Jefferson, after his granddaddy. As soon as the doctor left, she made Momma fix her hair and get her some lipstick to put on so the children could come and see her. Momma wanted her to just lie back and take it easy, but May insisted on seeing her children. Ildred and I helped Ed get all their hands and faces scrubbed before he marched them into the bedroom of the little house in McIntyre.

May looked like a ghost, I thought, she was so pale, but she was sitting up in bed as we came in, smiling, with pillows all around and the baby in her arms. She left lipstick kisses, one by one, on Bitsy and Mimi and Dolly and little May, and she was putting her hand out to touch little Ed's curly head when she got a look on her face. She seemed to be paying close attention to something going on inside her. Then her head fell back on the pillow, and with me and Ildred in the doorway and Ed and all her children crowded around her, just like that, barely one month past her thirty-first birthday, my sweet sister May was gone.

A baby crying for his mother is like a door that opens into every kind of grief. That's why you have to pick that child up and rock him and make him stop. It's not so much the baby you're worried about.

At the very moment my brother Force set his foot down on May's front porch, he heard a wail go up inside the house that stopped him cold. Before he took another step—before he even took another breath—the door banged open and May's children burst out onto the porch, keening and sobbing like the motherless children they now were. Ildred and myself, also sobbing, were right behind them and without a word spoken or a decision made, we helped Force herd them all into the Ford. "Take them!" Ildred cried. "Git them away from here!"

Force had to clench his teeth to keep from wailing or shouting himself, just to drown out the sound of them. They clung to each other in the backseat—no one would let go of whatever arm or neck they were clutching to ride up front with Force. They reminded him of the unweaned kittens whose mother ate rat poison in Billy Bonner's barn. They were that inarticulate and inconsolable. He drove them all the way to Milledgeville and circled around the college square, passed the Baldwin County Courthouse and the governor's mansion and the Military Academy he had finally graduated from that spring. They stayed in the car, sweating and clinging to each other, while he bought them ice-cream cones at Rosie's. They were quiet then—only sniffing and hiccupping—while they licked the ice cream flavored with tears, but when he turned down the road that led back to their house in McIntyre, they started crying and wailing again, the volume rising with every dip in the road that brought them nearer to the house, until they were crying like those kittens again. Four times Force sped up again and shot past the lane that led to the house instead of turning.

The fourth time he drove around the college square in Milledgeville, he thought about the train station. He thought about buying tickets and putting them on a train that would take them farther and farther away from what waited for them back at the house in McIntyre. He wondered if it was possible to take them to a place so far away that they would forget all about the house and the baby and May falling back on the pillow, distance doing the work of time in healing their sorrow, miles taking the place of years. If there were such a place, Force would take them there. He would take them all the way to Baghdad, the real Baghdad, if he had to. He would make them forget that they had a mother who died. They would wake up on rooftops to the cries of street hawkers or in cool-tiled rooms, a sweet voice outside the window singing real words from the top of a real minaret. They would snap their fingers or rub their rings and a great *jinn* who looked just like Eugene Boykin would arrive in a puff of colored smoke, saying, *Your wish is my command!* and he would deliver to them, as Force could not, their hearts' desire.

They were about halfway between McIntyre and Baghdad, Georgia, when the Ford ran out of gas. As soon as the engine started stuttering, Force pulled off the road onto the grassy shoulder, lumping and bumping and rolling along a few more yards and a few more until the T-Model Ford stopped at the top of a little rise that gave them a view of the white dirt canyon where Miss Spivey got her first glimpse of kaolin. Force could see her, suddenly, holding the stick as if she might lick the dipped white tip of it.

"Why're we stopped?" one of the girls asked warily from the backseat.

"Out of gas," said Force.

This news was met with silence—now he *couldn't* take them back, was that what they were thinking? Some scrabbling around behind him ended with little May popping up on the back of the front seat. She balanced there on her hips and the palms of her hands for a moment, like a seesaw, and then slowly tumbled forward. She was going on six now. She crawled into Force's lap. He hoisted her up so that her head was under his chin. In the backseat, little Ed was sleeping, stretched across his three sisters' laps. Mimi, in the middle, had her eyes closed. The other two looked out their respective windows at the sky.

"What are we gonna do?" asked Bitsy, the oldest. She was almost eleven now.

"We'll wait," Force said. "I reckon somebody'll come along."

They sat by the road for a while like that, the children quiet, exhausted by grief. Nobody came along.

Then, sounding half asleep, little May said, "Uncle Force?" She was limp and heavy in his lap. She raised a languid arm and laid her hand on his cheek.

"What, sugar?"

"Are you really king of Baghdad?" That story had gotten around.

"He's not king. He's Cailip," said Dolly, who was eight.

"Not Cailip, *Cailiff*," Bitsy corrected her. "Course he's a Cailiff. So's Grandma and Granddaddy and Gladys and all." She stopped there. Little Ed whimpered in his sleep.

"But is he Cailiff of Baghdad?" Mimi asked.

"No," Bitsy said firmly, "he ain't."

"He is, sure enough!" Dolly said. "Jest look at him."

To facilitate this, little May reached up and put both her hands to his face, one palm on each cheek, and turned his head toward the backseat.

"Well," said Force, "are y'all just gonna keep on talkin' about me like I'm not here?" It was hard to understand him, with little May squishing his cheeks together with her two hands, as hard as she could. In spite of herself, Mimi giggled.

"It ain't his face that proves it," Dolly said. "It's his arm. He's got the mark on his arm. Show us your arm, Uncle Force."

He laid his arm out long on the back of the seat, then twisted it so they could see the scar, about the size of a quarter.

"It used to be a picture of a eagle, right?" said Dolly. "You had a eagle but they burned it off."

"Oooh," little May said in the front seat. She let her hands slip down from Force's cheeks. "Did it hurt? It musta hurt."

"He was only a baby when they did it," Dolly said. As soon as *baby* came out of her mouth, she stiffened. So did Force.

Mimi didn't seem to notice. "Tell us how you got switched at—"

"Tell us about Alaeddin," Bitsy interrupted fiercely. "Tell us about the lamp."

"It was a magic lamp," Mimi said, sounding eager. "All you had to do was rub it and a jinnie came, poof! 'Yer wisht is my command!' "

"We already know that story," Dolly complained.

"Tell it, Uncle Force," Bitsy commanded. "Tell it now."

"All right, all right," said Force. "Just give me a chance. Little May, set still. All right, now." Force cleared his throat. He decided that if somebody didn't come along by the time Alaeddin met the Princess, they were all going to have to get out and walk back. "It is said," Force began, "that there lived in the city of Baghdad a young boy, the son of a tailor who was as poor as a mouse. Alaeddin was his name. Now, Alaeddin didn't mind being poor, long as he could go around with his friends and have a good time in the marketplace, but it about worried his mother half to death."

Force stopped short. He held his breath.

"Not for long!" Mimi shrieked. "'Cause pretty soon he finds his treasure!"

"It's under the ground," said little May.

"He just opens a door and walks right down and finds it," Dolly added. She had already forgotten that she didn't want to hear this tale again.

Please Don't Sue Me

Afterwords from Miss Gladys Cailiff
Written by Her on the Occasion of the
72nd Annual Baghdad Bazaar

EVERY SPRING for more than seventy years now, the people of Baghdad, Georgia, have been rolling out the minaret, nailing up the arches, and touching up the paint and plaster in preparation for our annual bazaar. All that time, I thought folks knew what it was that we were doing every spring. I thought most everybody understood what it was about. This past year, however, some folks got a notion that we ought to change the name of our town back to what it used to be. When the subject came up at the January breakfast meeting of the Baghdad GA Chamber of Commerce, my brother Force looked at the business community sitting around the tables and booths in the Arctic Circle, and he said, "Then what are we going to have, come June? The Threestep Bazaar? What do Arabian Nights got to do with a place called Threestep, Georgia?"

"Maybe the whole Arabian deal is not such a good idea anymore, Uncle Force," said our grandnephew Sam, who is currently president of the Baghdad GA Chamber of Commerce, the members of which seemed inclined to agree that it might be wise to change things up a bit. "Maybe have us a music fest instead of a bazaar," one of them actually said.

When we told former bazaar coordinator Mavis Davis Bonner all of the above, she poked her bony finger at me (heedless of the IV attached to her arm and all her monitors beeping) and she said, "You got to tell the story, Gladys. That's the only way to stop 'em. And I mean the real story, the *whole* story."

I am not a natural-born storyteller like my sister May, but I have done my best.

That said, I can tell you there are more Spiveys, Cailiffs, Gordons, Lumpkins, Peacocks, Boykins, and McCombs in the state of Georgia today than you can shake a stick at. Just to give you some idea, I have heard from five different Ms. Spiveys currently or formerly in the field of education, and the number of Gordons who happen to be lawyers—or have great-granddaddies who were lawyers—are legion. (Some of them really are descendants of General John B. Gordon of the ex-Confederate armies, the first Grand Dragon of the Ku Klux Klan in Georgia.) Not only that, pretty much everybody who lives on certain sea islands off the Georgia coast has a person by the name of Bilali—though spelled in a variety of ways—on their family tree. My great-grandnephew little Sam set me up with email, and for weeks I went around telling folks my address was GladysCailiff@yoohoo.com, but it looks like everybody found me just the same.

I am happy to report that *most* people are satisfied with sending a note or an angry email if they don't like something they read.

I am even happier to report that I have received many messages of support, the most surprising of which was an email from an engineer in Saudi Arabia who thanked me for confirming the cockamamie story his grandmother used to tell them about living on a secret island in America when she was a little girl—they all thought it was the dementia talking. Along those same lines, a fellow from the International Institute for Truth in History told me how surprised *he* was to "see in print an account, however oblique, of the intelligence debacle behind one botched attempt (of many) to rescue British troops besieged at Kut."

As for the most frequently asked question, the answer is that Theo Boykin's priceless copy of the *Kitab al-Hiyal* was donated—or *repatriated*, as my niece would say—to the historical archives of Baghdad University about a year after Theo's death, which was as soon as his mother could part with it. As near as we can tell, that *Kitab* disappeared in the widespread looting that followed the bombing of Baghdad in 2003.

Sir Richard F. Burton's ten volumes of *The Arabian Nights* I kept for myself—a fact still remembered (fondly, I hope) by former fifth-graders from Joel Chandler Harris Elementary School in Claytonville, where I started teaching in the 1950s and kept on right through the thrown eggs (and worse) of the 1960s, and for another twenty-seven years after that. Mavis still has Miss Spivey's typewriter.

Etta George was the first woman from Piedmont County ever to earn an M.D. degree. She moved to Atlanta but comes home most years for the Baghdad Bazaar.

And yes, Eugene did become an actor. Out of consideration for his privacy, I have refrained from revealing his professional name, which you might recognize.

Mrs. Faith Boykin lived well into her nineties. After Theo passed on, she sold her Piedmont County property to a kaolin conglomerate for an undisclosed sum and spent her final days sitting pretty with her sister Lily on Sapelo Island.

To those who never met Theo Boykin, and to those who remember him as a handy fellow who didn't have much to say, let me say this:

I know Theo Boykin was not the Messiah. He wasn't the Twelfth Imam or the Second Coming, either, although some of us sure enough prayed, year after year, for his return. Theo was simply a very intelligent and creative young man—the smartest person in Piedmont County— until ignorance and bigotry cut him down to size. Nobody knows how many like him have been taken from us, long before we ever got a chance to name a street or a high school after them. Even Arnie Lumpkin could see that he was in no way superior to Theo Boykin. What Arnie and plenty of other folks couldn't do was *admit* they could see that. *That*'s the secret that everybody knows: We are *not* superior. We know very well that the Almighty has no particular wish for *us*, whoever we are, to prevail. That's the secret folks will guard with their lives. The one they'll lynch and burn and bomb for.

Here in Baghdad, Georgia, I believe we have to thank both Theo Boykin and Miss Grace Spivey for bringing that secret to our attention. And May? My sister May brought more believers into the world with one night of storytelling than the Reverends Stokes and Whitlock did in a lifetime—and they were professionals in that line.

When my in-box got out of hand recently, one of my former fifth-graders—thank you, Tavonte Smith—helped me put together this auto-reply:

> Thank you for your interest in Baghdad, Georgia. A good time to come see us in Piedmont County is the second weekend in June.
>
> For the record, I do see your email even if you get this auto-reply. I try to answer your questions in the order they are received, although it is my personal philosophy that life is way too short to spend it all in front of a computer screen. Furthermore, I am now of an age where we have to face the possibility that some questions may go unanswered.
>
> For updates, "visit" our website, www.baghdadbazaarGA.com.
>
> You need that GA in there or you wind up in Iraq.

Acknowledgments

THIS NOVEL OWES its very existence to the peerless editing of Alane
Salierno Mason, the energetic efficiency of Denise Scarfi, the enthusiasm and faith of Valerie Borchardt, and the loving attention paid to every
page of nearly every draft by Liz Huett and John Stefaniak.

My greatest debt is to my primary informants: my mother, Mary
McCullough Elleseg; her sister, Frances McCullough Martin; and their
cousins, Grace Califf Stanford and Royce Califf. Their stories about
growing up in middle Georgia were my first inspiration.

As always, the Creative Girls—Eileen Bartos, Ann Zerkel, Tonja
Robins, Mary Vermillion, Kris Vervaecke, Jane Olson, Mo Jones, and
Marjorie Davis—lent a hand, but I owe special thanks to those who read
the WHOLE thing (twice): Kate Kasten, Bruce Brown, and Suzanne
Kehm.

Among the many helpful people in Georgia who gave me their
time and attention, I mention gratefully Muriel Jackson and Christo-
pher Stokes in the Genealogical & Historical Room of the Washington
Memorial Library, Macon; Jane Simpson, Library Director at Georgia
Military College, Milledgeville; and Marilyn Daniel of the Washington
County Historical Society, who gave me a tour of the Old Jail House in

Sandersville. (Any historical mistakes or liberties taken in the novel are mine, not theirs.)

I am also grateful to Kathy Hodson in Special Collections at the University of Iowa in Iowa City, and to the helpful library staff at the University of Georgia in Athens, where I was able to turn the handwritten pages of the real Bilali manuscript.

Information crucial to the writing of the novel came from many sources, including these: *A Plain and Literal Translation of . . . The Book of the Thousand Nights and a Night, with Introduction, Explanatory Notes on the Manners and Customs of Moslem Men, and a Terminal Essay upon the History of The Nights* by Sir Richard F. Burton; *The Pilgrimage Tradition in West Africa* by Umar al-Nagar; *The Pilgrimage of Ahmad, Son of the Little Bird of Paradise: An Account of a 19th-Century Pilgrimage from Mauritania to Mecca,* translated by H. T. Norris; *African Muslims in Antebellum America* by Allan D. Austin; *Drums and Shadows: Survival Studies among the Georgia Coastal Negroes* from the Georgia Writers' Project, and *Georgia: A Guide to Its Towns and Countryside* from the Federal Writers' Project; *A Baghdad Chronicle* by Reuben Levy; *The Camel-Bells of Baghdad* by Janet Miller; *The Book of Ingenious Devices* by the Banu Musa bin Shakir, translated by Donald R. Hill; *A History of Iraq* by Charles Tripp; *Sapelo's People* by William S. McFeely; *Sapelo: A History* by Buddy Sullivan; and—especially—*God, Dr. Buzzard, and the Bolito Man: A Saltwater Geechee Talks about Life on Sapelo Island, Georgia,* by Cornelia Walker Bailey, a direct descendant of the enslaved West African Muslim named Bilali.

Thanks go to Farhan al-Rwaili, Van Huett, Theodore Wheeler, Leslee Becker, and Edward Mullaney for their assistance and suppport.

An excerpt from *The Cailiffs of Baghdad, Georgia* appeared, in slightly different form, in *Epoch* magazine, edited by Michael Koch.

I am grateful for the support of Creighton University and the Nebraska Arts Council.

And finally, special thanks go to my sister Sandra for saving my life, just in time for the final revisions.